And his national bestseller
FALSE ACCUSATIONS

"A riveting story with a truly frightening villainess. This is a terrific book!"
—John Saul

"Compelling . . . rivals Crichton, Cornwell, and Turow—you won't put this one down till the end."
—Fred Wynbrandt, former assistant director of the California Department of Justice and liaison to Congress and the FBI

"Will grip you from the opening page to the . . . astonishing last paragraph. A great murder mystery."
—*Times Record News* (Wichita Falls, TX)

"A fantastic reading experience."
—*Midwest Book Review*

"A page-turner."
—*San Jose Mercury News*

"Chilling."
—*Booklist*

"A slick thriller. . . . You may think you know what's going on, but there are several surprises in store. Likely to appeal to fans of Grisham and Crichton, *False Accusations* measures up well."
—*The Mystery Reader*

ALSO BY ALAN JACOBSON
False Accusations

THE
HUNTED

ALAN JACOBSON

POCKET BOOKS

New York London Toronto Sydney Singapore

This book is a work of fiction. Names, characters, places and incidents are products of the author's imagination or are used fictitiously. Any resemblance to actual events or locales or persons, living or dead, is entirely coincidental.

POCKET BOOKS, a division of Simon & Schuster, Inc.
1230 Avenue of the Americas, New York, NY 10020

Copyright © 2001 by Alan Jacobson

Originally published in hardcover in 2001 by Pocket Books

ISBN: 0-671-02681-X

First Pocket Books paperback printing February 2002

10 9 8 7 6 5 4 3 2 1

POCKET and colophon are registered trademarks of Simon & Schuster, Inc.

For information regarding special discounts for bulk purchases, please contact Simon & Schuster Special Sales at 1-800-456-6798 or business@simonandschuster.com

Front cover design and illustration by Mee Ra Song

Printed in the U.S.A.

for Jill,
whose natural wisdom guides me,
whose tenderness touches me,
whose heart warms me . . .
I have no secrets from you

There are many truths, some valid for one, some for another. Things are not what they seem. . . . It is a lesson we must learn and relearn because we keep searching for certainty, and certainty does not exist.

—*Harrison Salisbury*

August

The United States Attorney stood on the courthouse steps, the hot August air oppressively still and heavy with humidity. Reporters were gathered around him, microphones and cassette recorders shoved toward his drawn face.

"I only have a brief statement for you. At twelve-thirty this afternoon, Judge Richard Noonan held a hearing on newly discovered evidence in the Anthony Scarponi murder conviction of six years ago. The defense has secured what Judge Noonan has determined to be a credible witness who can provide evidence of Mr. Scarponi's innocence. Collaterally, the Department of Justice has failed to locate former FBI agent Harper Payne, who was the central witness for the government in the original trial. As a result, Judge Noonan has ordered the release of Mr. Scarponi on two million dollars bail pending the scheduling of a new trial."

A flurry of questions burst forth from the press corps. Instead of answering them, the U.S. Attorney turned and walked back up the courthouse steps. A screaming headache was beginning to take shape, and the last thing he needed was two dozen journalists asking the one question he had been asking himself repeatedly the past several days: How could this have happened?

September

The apartment was a sparsely decorated studio on the outskirts of Washington, D.C., secured by contacts he had maintained while incarcerated in the maximum security prison in Petersburg, Virginia. He had hoped the day would come when he would be out on his own again, free to roam the streets like a jaguar prowling for its next quarry.

Anthony Scarponi knew that to have true freedom, the tiny device implanted in his buttock had to be removed. Some foreign physicians would perform such a procedure without asking questions, but to find one in the United States would be time-consuming and dangerous.

There was only one possible course of action.

He stood with his right leg up on the edge of the bathtub, a large magnifying makeup mirror perched on a step stool beneath his buttock. A high-intensity halogen light lay on the floor, flooding his skin with enough brightness that if he looked away, he would have a temporary blind spot. His paraphernalia was laid out across the bathroom counter, within reach of his left hand: syringes filled with lidocaine hydrochloride solution, sterilized stainless steel probes, a scalpel, forceps, clamps, gauze rolls, pads, and suture kits.

After injecting the surrounding area with anesthetic, he began by opening a long slit overlying the tiny, delicate scar line left by the surgeon's original incision. It was tedious work at first, as he had to locate the exact position of the microchip they had implanted. That it was buried toward the rear of his buttock made the probing more difficult. Though he was not supposed to know this had been done to him, he had sources. Even inside a maximum security federal prison, he had sources.

According to his informants, a couple of guards had taken him from his cell on a Monday—and didn't return him until the following Sunday. Scarponi surmised he had been drugged, then kept sedated until he could heal. It took him a few months, but he eventually learned what they had done to him.

An hour later, the lidocaine syringes lay empty, the last one having been injected forty minutes ago. He was now working on sheer determination, grit, and guts, using the skills of discipline his Chinese mentors had taught him. After much tedious probing and searching, he finally found the tiny device. Carefully, he extracted the foreign body, which was a quarter of the size of a penny, and placed it gently into a Pyrex dish filled with saline solution.

Ten minutes later, he tied off the last suture, packed away all evidence of his crude surgery, then chased down an ampicillin capsule and a Vicodin tablet with a glass of water. Scalpel in hand, he walked over to the rat that was lying still in its cage. It was fast asleep, the drugs he'd given it two hours ago having done their job in marked contrast to the largely ineffective lidocaine he had used on himself.

He suddenly realized that he should have chosen a guinea pig instead of a rat. Then it would have mirrored his own situation so closely the feds couldn't help but see the irony in what he'd done. In the end, though, it didn't matter, because he wouldn't be around to feel their shock, taste their hatred.

He removed the rodent from its tiny prison, made his incision, and did his deed. He stepped back and laughed a shrill howl, marveling at his masterpiece, intrigued by what the feds would think of his latest feat.

January

I've got her tied down to the chair. I slap her. She likes it, she smiles at me. She wants more."

Dr. Lauren Chambers swallowed hard, then leaned forward in her seat. "Who is this, Steven, who's tied down?"

"Gina. My girlfriend. The others are unconscious."

Lauren bit her bottom lip. This was one of the most extraordinary first sessions she had ever experienced with a patient. Steven Simpson, a forty-year-old state worker, had come to her because he had lost his ability to fight off his sexual urges. But they weren't just sexual fantasies, her patient was quick to point out. "They're torture fantasies," he had said. "There's a huge difference. Haven't you been listening to me?"

Normally, Lauren had no difficulty focusing on her patient. She was a professional, and when she walked into the office, she left her problems at the door. But today was different. She forced herself to look at this person, really see this man, who wore oversize, rose-tinted glasses and a bright blue polyester shirt opened at the collar. She decided that if a dictionary publisher were searching for a defining image of the word *geek*, Steven would qualify. His hair was frizzy and wild, parted and combed across his head in an apparent attempt to tame it. But the effort had failed miserably, and he looked more like a mad professor than the moderately paid state worker drone that he professed to be.

Judging by what he had just told her, she had to agree with him. These torture fantasies were not merely a benign form of sexually oriented daydreaming.

Though in a hypnotic state, Steven smiled. "She wants more."

"Steven," Lauren said, "you mentioned others. How many women are there?"

"There are four. They're all strapped into chairs. I'm more intrigued by the last one, the blonde."

"These . . . sessions you have with Gina and her, uh, friends. Are they just fantasy, Steven, or are they real?"

"There's blood. She's grinning at me so I slap her again. There's too many of them, too many women. The blood is coming from her nose, it's dripping down to her chin. I smear it all over her face with my hand. She's laughing. She loves it, she wants more. She wants me to hit her again. But there's a noise from behind me. It's Cynthia. She's naked. She's calling my name."

Lauren suddenly felt uncomfortably hot. She knew she was taking risks by placing her patient under hypnosis on his initial session. Establishing an accurate diagnosis and a trusting rapport with a patient often took the better part of two meetings. But from what she had seen in their first forty-five minutes together, Steven's case required immediate intervention.

Although therapy could sometimes get stressful—and this one certainly qualified—she never feared for her safety. Yet something about Steven made the hairs on the back of her neck stand at attention. She pulled a couple of times on her silk blouse, attempting to flap some cool air against her moist skin, then refocused on her patient. "So what happens next, Steven?"

"I take Gina, right there on the chair."

"While she's tied down?"

"Definitely."

"And how does Gina feel about this?"

"She orgasms."

Lauren paused for a second. "Does she cry out?"

Steven licked his lips. "Oh, yes. Very loudly." He threw his head back and lifted his hands. "Owww," he groaned. "Like that."

"Oww? You mean, like she's in pain? Is she in pain, Steven?"

He smiled again. "Intense pain."

Lauren looked down at her pad. *This man routinely rapes his girlfriend. But is it fantasy or reality?* She shook her head. "How does that make you feel, Steven? How does her pain make you feel?"

"It makes me come. It makes me feel special. But not as special as tying her down. I make the ropes so tight they cut into her skin. So tight that they hurt. The ropes hurt, they hurt me."

Lauren's head snapped up. *What did he just say?* "The ropes hurt *you,* or do they hurt her? Who's tied up, Steven? You or Gina?"

Her patient did not answer. A tear coursed down his cheek.

"Steven, remember, no one can hurt you here. You're completely safe. No one will judge you. You can tell me everything."

He smeared away the tear with the swipe of a hand. "Gina. Gina is tied up."

"Does Gina say anything to you afterwards?"

"She's angry. She went away for a couple of days."

Lauren sat for a moment, trying to think of the best treatment approach to use on Steven. She knew what she had heard: her patient had clearly stated that *he* was tied up, which could explain many things. Was he abused as a child? Had he been tied down and tortured by one of his parents? She shuddered at the thought.

A noise in the hallway grabbed her attention and she glanced at the large black-on-white wall clock behind her patient. She needed to bring this session to a close. But what a time to have to end it!

She sighed deeply. She knew she could not leave him in his current state. If she could curb his overwhelming desires, it might keep him in check until she had a chance to work with him further and probe deeper to reach the root cause of his psychosis. Right now, she needed an immediate, albeit temporary, measure to accomplish this. To make it work, she had to take him down deeper.

"Steven, we're going to talk more about this next week. In the meantime, I want you to close your eyes, let your head fall back against the chair, and focus on my voice." She used a calm, melodic tone to relax him. "That's it, just let everything go. I want you to picture yourself at the ocean. The waves are effortlessly rolling up the sand and tickling the tips of your toes. The soft breeze is blowing the hair off your face. Now think about all your anger, frustration, tension . . . and toss it out into the ocean. Watch it float away as it bobs up and down on the waves, moving farther and farther away from you."

Her patient's facial muscles went flaccid, causing his cheeks and mouth to droop slightly. He was now exactly where she wanted him. She had performed so many hypnotherapy sessions in graduate school that she was affectionately known as the Underlord, a nickname she did not particularly like. Still, it was a good-hearted attempt by her colleagues to honor her exceptional hypnosis skills.

"Each time you feel a sexual urge coming on, when you feel yourself losing control, you'll feel intense pain in your left temple. It will be an explosive headache that will last for five minutes and then subside. Do you understand what I'm saying, Steven?"

He continued to lie back in the chair, his head extended and cocked to one side, his mouth hanging open. He smacked his lips a couple of times, swallowed, then said, "Yes."

"Good. Now, I'm going to wake you up. You won't consciously remember anything we talked about. When I snap my fingers, you will awaken refreshed and happy."

He opened his eyes and sat up, looked around, and focused on Lauren. "What happened, Doc? We were talking, and then . . . I don't know, you're sitting there looking at me."

"Everything went fine, Steven. You just went into a very relaxed state for a few moments." She glanced again at the clock and rose from her chair. "Next week we'll talk some more, try some things that I think will help."

"I feel great."

"Good. I want you to feel great." Lauren smiled. "This was an excellent first session, Steven."

"What about those thoughts, those fantasies?"

"I don't think you'll have any problems with them. But you'd better carry a bottle of Excedrin with you."

Lauren followed her patient out into the hallway, where the shared receptionist sat behind the desk wearing a telephone headset. The other therapists had gathered in the area, as they all had completed their sessions at the top of the hour. Lauren ignored their burgeoning discussion and looked over at the receptionist.

"Did my husband call?"

"No, Doctor, he didn't. Just like the last hour, and the hour before that."

Fortunately, the bizarre case Steven presented had helped take her mind off Michael, even if only for a few minutes. Lauren looked away and headed back into her office. She stood in front of a photo on the wall, the one she had taken of Michael in their backyard a few years ago, shortly after purchasing their house.

"Michael," she whispered, "please come home."

As Lauren readied herself to leave the office for the evening, she prepared a short list of items she needed at the local Placerville Food & More. She opened her purse and popped a Xanax tablet into her mouth, maneuvering it with her tongue to the back of her throat and forcing it down with a few gulps from the water fountain. She hated having to rely on medication, but it helped her avoid the extreme anxiety she sometimes felt in open, public places. Michael understood and, as a result, always did the grocery shopping. Walking into the market and feeling totally lost only made her miss him more.

Food & More was packed with shoppers who had stopped in after work on their way home for dinner. Lauren stood in line, fidgeting, keeping her eyes low and away from those around her. She dabbed at her brow with the back of her left hand. The Xanax should be taking effect soon, she told herself. In the meantime, she had to take her mind off her escalating apprehension before it became incapacitating.

She fixed her gaze on the checkout magazine rack, where the cover of the latest issue of *Time* grabbed her attention. The large photo showed a haggard young woman, whom the caption identified as

Brittany Harding, with the bold headline "False Accusations . . . or Not?"

Lauren picked up the magazine and thumbed to the article. She recalled this case dominating the local headlines a year or two ago. A prominent surgeon had been arrested for murder, yet it turned out that a psychotic acquaintance of his had actually committed the crime and framed him for it. Lauren remembered the case well because she had once referred a patient to the surgeon, Dr. Phillip Madison. Though her patient's prior orthopedist had diagnosed psychogenic pain—commonly known as "it's all in your head"—Lauren felt her patient required a more comprehensive workup. She made the referral and Madison discovered a spinal tumor, which he deftly removed two days later. She was glad to read that Harding's appeal had been denied. Madison was a good physician.

"Damn shame about that, wasn't it?"

Lauren looked up and noticed that the elderly woman in front of her was looking at the photo spread of Brittany Harding and Phillip Madison.

"I remember when that happened," the woman continued. "It's the lawyers, they're the problem."

Lauren looked at her but did not respond. She closed the issue of *Time* and put it back on the stand. With Michael gone, she knew she would not be in the mood to do any reading.

Just then, a man in the adjacent aisle was opening a register. "I'll take the next person in line."

Lauren moved her cart over and the checker began to scan her items as a young female bagger popped open a plastic sack.

"Chilly out there tonight, isn't it?" the man asked.

Lauren forced herself to look at him, nodded, then looked away. Her heart began pounding and she could feel a drop of perspiration course down her spine.

"Cash, check, or—"

"Cash." Lauren handed him a twenty, avoiding eye contact, and pocketed the change.

"Need help with that ba—"

"I've got it," Lauren said, scooping up the sack and heading away from the mass of people.

"Have a nice day!" the man called after her.

Lauren's agoraphobia had begun four years ago when her attempt at running her own practice had come to a screeching halt. A friend of hers, another psychologist who had moved to Placerville, California, several years earlier, had suggested the two of them form a partnership and go into practice together. Wanting desperately to get out from under the rigors of institutional care, Lauren had jumped at the idea.

Two years later, with their practice growing slower than anticipated, Lauren's partner announced she had purchased a thriving practice from a retiring psychologist. She informed Lauren she was dissolving their agreement—and that, effective immediately, she was taking the staff and her patients with her. With a decimated practice, the next three months proved devastating for Lauren.

Now, as she drove her car, she thought of the day Michael had sat her down and helped her see what had to be done.

"You've given it everything you have, honey," Michael had told her. "But things are out of control. We need to make a change."

"Close the practice?" Lauren asked, fidgeting with her gold necklace, trying to maintain control.

"What's left of it, yes. The lease is coming due in five weeks. I just don't see things turning around overnight." He stroked her hair. "I know this is not what you wanted to happen, but your ex-partner abandoned you. None of this is your fault."

Lauren buried her face in her husband's chest and cried.

Over the next few weeks, Lauren fell into a deep depression. Michael bore the burden of handling the closure, selling off what few assets she had—furniture and various pieces of office equipment—and finding another psychologist in town who would assume care of Lauren's remaining patients. Had it not been for Michael's constant attention, she would never have gotten through it.

As she exited the freeway, she realized for the thousandth time today just how much she missed her husband. She made a few turns and headed deeper into the rural area of Placerville. The headlights of the car that had been behind her since she had exited the freeway were annoying and distracting. On such dark roadways, the lights stood out painfully against the background, poking at her eyes like needles.

Lauren made a left turn and the car stayed with her. She made another left and then two rights, and each time, remaining a good two blocks back, the other vehicle shadowed her moves.

Perspiration began trailing down her back again and her breathing became labored. Here it was, the day after her husband had failed to return home from a ski trip, and she already had more stress than she was equipped to handle. Now, a car was following her. Or was it? Was her propensity for anxiety making simple coincidence into something more significant?

Her heart began pounding and her mouth was so dry it felt as if her throat had closed down on her. She knew these symptoms well, and she fought them hard. Though she had given up her dependence on antidepressants a year and a half ago, the occasional Xanax remained her sole residual crutch. And although it should have reached full strength by now, she felt as if she had never taken it.

Just then, something exploded in the rear of her vehicle. The car swerved right, but she steered into the slide and quickly regained control. She had only felt this sensation once, many years ago, but it was unmistakable: she had a blowout. She accelerated hard, but the car responded sluggishly.

She glanced up at her rearview mirror. The headlights seemed to be bearing down on her. As she slowly gained speed, she started having more difficulty controlling the car as it thumped along, yawing left and right. But there was no way she was going to stop.

She knew the streets in this neighborhood of Placerville like the layout of her house, and twenty yards ahead was a one-lane dirt road that was nearly impossible to see at night if you did not know it was there.

Going forty-five miles an hour, she pulled the steering wheel hard to the right. The car's wheels left the pavement as they, too, were surprised by the sudden turn. Lauren swerved wide into a narrow ditch along the left side of the shoulderless road. She floored the accelerator, but the rear wheels spun aimlessly in the loose gravel and dirt.

Lauren cut her lights and quickly got out of the car. She glanced over her shoulder for the headlights, but didn't see them. Was she just being paranoid, like one of her patients?

Not willing to take the chance, she scampered up the slight embankment, pushing the brush aside with frantic hands. As she ran, she struggled to maintain her balance on the hard-packed underlying ground that was pocked and uneven. She caught her toe in a crevice, and before she could adjust, her other foot landed in a deep indentation and she plunged forward, face first, slamming her chin into a large rock half-buried in the ground.

Sharp pain shot through her jaw.

Lauren shook it off and got to her feet again, moving with purpose toward her house, which sat about a stone's throw up ahead on the hill that was now visible.

Before she had gone ten feet, a flash of light hit her in the back and silhouetted her form against the tall brush. She spun and saw a car turning onto the road, approaching the spot where her disabled vehicle was parked. She stumbled forward, pieces of the high, prickly thistles slicing at her lips and cheeks as she ran by.

Twenty yards to go, ten until she reached her backyard, where Tucker, her black Doberman, would be standing watch. Maybe her pursuer would see the dog and leave her alone.

Off to the left was the back of the Andersons' house, but Lauren knew they were out of town. Beyond the Andersons' property sat an older one-story ranch where an elderly couple resided. The house was dark—but even if they were home, the man was ill and the woman was nearly deaf. They probably wouldn't be able to render any substantial assistance.

As Lauren climbed the low wooden fence that lined her property, she whistled. "Tucker, come!" she said in a frantic whisper. But the dog did not appear. "Tucker!" she called again, somewhat louder, to no avail.

She reached the back door and fumbled with her keys, finding the correct one but having difficulty inserting it into the lock. She let out a whimper of frustration as she repeatedly stabbed at the metal cylinder with a nervous hand. Lauren took a breath, calmed herself, and made one more attempt. The key slid in and she turned the knob.

Lauren slammed the back door behind her and flipped the locks shut. Tears were running down her face and her lungs were burning from the run through the cold January air. She pressed her back against the door and rested for a moment as her mind cleared. Was someone really following her, or could it have been a neighbor—someone who lived on the same block or even a block or two over?

She should've made a few nonsense turns, just to be sure—but she hadn't. She took a breath to calm herself. She suddenly felt foolish. This whole situation with Michael was getting to her, putting her on edge. *Get a grip*, she told herself.

Just then, a loud thump coming from the other room startled her. She immediately froze and her heart began banging inside her chest. The adrenaline that had cleared from her bloodstream only seconds before was again surging through her body.

In the seconds that she took to decide what to do, Tucker came bounding around the corner, his stubby tail wagging.

"Jesus, you scared the crap out of me." She bent over and hugged the dog, smiling at how silly she had been. "You're supposed to be outside. Did I leave the door open? Is that how you got in here?" Lauren walked toward the garage, expecting to find the side door ajar. She flipped on the light and peered in. The door was closed.

Then, it hit her. "Michael!" she yelled. "Michael, where are you?"

Lauren moved swiftly through the house. But the doors and windows were locked. There were no notes. And Michael's Chrysler was not in the carport.

Lauren stood there for a second, then looked down at the dog. "I know I left you outside this morning." She began wandering from room to room, again hoping to find some kind of explanation.

Her mind flashed on the headlights in the darkness . . . on the car that had been following her. Or *had it* been following her?

She walked into her room, sat down on the bed, and stared at the antique bureau where her wedding picture sat. Happy times, the photo said, full of blissful promise for the future. That was only four years ago, yet it felt like an eternity. So much had happened since then, little of it good.

She curled up on the bed, hugging her knees tightly against her chest. As tears began to roll from her eyes, Tucker came over, sat down, and licked her face. He nuzzled her cheek and did not move until she touched his snout and stroked it. He loved it when she did that. The dog stayed right there by her side, the only calming influence in her life other than Michael.

And right now, Tucker was all she had.

Lauren lay there for several minutes. Unable to step out of her role as psychologist, she couldn't help but analyze her own thoughts and feelings. She concluded that, despite all that had happened this evening, the fact that Michael was away—that he hadn't returned home when he was supposed to have—was wearing on her. She glanced at her watch. He was now thirty-four hours overdue.

Suddenly, Tucker lifted his head. His eyes were wide and his ears straight up, like radar zeroing in on an errant noise.

"What is it?" Lauren asked, straining to hear what had caught Tucker's attention.

The dog looked at her, then, satisfied that the noise was not a threat, rested his head back on the bed.

Lauren chewed on her bottom lip for a moment, then pushed Tucker aside and knelt at the edge of the bed, reached underneath, and pulled out her wicker trunk. It was the same trunk she'd had as a child, the one she had lugged from dorm to apartment to its final resting place beneath their bed shortly after marrying Michael.

Lauren opened it and moved aside some personal effects: an old jewelry box with the chains, rings, and necklaces she had worn as a teenager; the dress her mom had bought for her sweet sixteen, folded neatly and sealed in a small cardboard container; and a weathered oak box that had been in the family for fifty some odd years.

She removed the box, pushed the trunk aside, and sat cross-legged on the floor. She reached around her neck for the delicate chain she had worn for the past twenty years and fingered the small metal key that hung from it. Although Michael did not know the whole story behind it, he knew it had been a gift from her father, and that it held special meaning for her. Just after Lauren's partner announced her intention to leave the practice, Michael had had the key gold-plated in an attempt to lift her spirits.

Using the key, Lauren unlatched the tiny lock that sealed the wooden box. She lifted a velvet-covered object from the container and held the heavy weight in her left hand. She sat there staring at the soft bag for a long moment before reaching inside and pulling out her father's Colt six-shooter pistol. The chrome was tarnished and dull, the handle worn . . . but the letters N.R.—her father's initials—were still visible. She held the gun in her left hand and slowly caressed it with her right. Gentle strokes, the smooth ridges of the cold metal passing beneath her fingertips. Had it been her lover, it would have enjoyed the intimate contact.

She brought the pistol over to the desk in the loft and flicked on the halogen light. As she began to clean it, she thought back to the night when she had first become acquainted with this old friend.

It was 2:46 in the morning twenty-five years ago when Lauren was awakened from her sleep by shouting from her parents' bedroom. She ran down the hall in the direction of the commotion. There, in the dark, she heard the sobs of her mother . . . then the scream "Lauren, get out!" and the gunshot, the one that sent her father hard to the floor. The dark-masked figure had then turned and pointed the gun at Lauren. She stared at the barrel, the fear welling up in her chest as her mother screamed, "No!"

And then the gunshots, the two that struck the intruder in the chest, and the one that whizzed by her head as the man fell to the floor, blood pooling out around his body in a matter of seconds as she stood there. Too scared to move—

Until her father called to her, in a weak voice.

He was flat on his back, his own blood pumping from a hole in his abdomen, the Colt lying in his open hand. Little Lauren looked at her mother, who was crumpled in a corner, her face frozen in shock.

The terrified ten-year-old grabbed the phone and dialed 911, gave the location of their house, and told the woman, "My dad's hurt, he got shot, hurry! There's blood all over, please hurry!"

Lauren inserted a small wire brush into the barrel of the gun and slowly rubbed the stiff fibers along the inside of the steel wall. As she thought about that night, she remembered the paramedics carting her father away. He survived that injury but had been paralyzed from the waist down, a condition that caused his premature death five years later. He had left her the gun in his will, along with an apology for not being able to leave something more valuable to make things easier for her. But having the gun that had saved her life was far more precious than he could ever know.

She polished it lovingly and brought the chrome to a bright, reflecting shine, just as her father had liked it. One by one, she inserted the six bullets and took aim at the wall in a phantom shooting stance. But she felt strangely repulsed by the thought of using the gun. In the years since his death, she had viewed the firearm with conflicting emotions: it may have saved her life, but one just like it had sent her father to an early grave.

With the immediate threat now behind her—if that car was even a threat to begin with—Lauren returned the Colt to its box and placed it on her night table. She lay back on the bed and Tucker spread himself out across the wood floor in a spot where he could see clear down the hallway to the staircase.

She grabbed Michael's pillow, closed her eyes, and gently rubbed her face against the soft cotton, taking in her husband's familiar scent.

"Michael, where are you?" she whispered, then fell off into a fitful sleep.

THREE

Lauren had only slept for three hours before awakening suddenly at one o'clock in the morning. She was lying on her bed and sweating profusely, still gripping Michael's pillow. Tucker was on the floor near the doorway, sleeping.

She sat up and was instantly wide-awake. Her mind was swirling with thoughts . . . questions about patients, progress notes she had forgotten to dictate, and . . . Michael. She looked back at the bed where the sheets were still tucked in.

She stood and went downstairs to the kitchen. She turned on the light in the garage, but Michael's Chrysler wasn't there. Neither was her car, for that matter—and then she remembered she had left hers on the side of Pike Road.

Lauren opened her purse and pulled out her A-1 Roadside Assistance card, dialed the number, and told the operator where her Honda was parked. She asked the dispatcher to send a truck in the morning to change the tire and tow the car up to her house.

With that out of the way but still feeling wide-awake, Lauren went to the cupboard, boiled water for a cup of tea, and added a dash of milk. She nursed the hot drink until she started to feel the slight pull of fatigue on her eyelids.

She climbed into bed and lay there awake for another half hour. She was tired but her mind was still focused on all things Michael—from dates they had had before getting married to events in their everyday life.

As the hours passed, her fears that she might never see him again became almost suffocating.

The overcast morning came upon Lauren suddenly. She awakened with a start, a noise out on the roadway below jogging her out of a dream she couldn't recall. Lauren rolled out of bed and stumbled downstairs to the kitchen, where she expected to find Tucker sitting next to his bowl.

But the dog wasn't there.

She gave a whistle, but there was still no response. "Tucker!" she yelled. "Where are you?"

She hurried through the house, moving from room to room, continuing to call out his name. As she reentered the kitchen, something slammed against the door. Lauren recoiled backward, her shaking hands finding the countertop behind her for reassurance. Something hit the door again—but this time, she caught a glimpse of Tucker's head protruding above the glass window.

Lauren stood there for a second staring at the dog, her heart banging out an angry rhythm in her chest. She pushed away from the counter and shook her head, annoyed with herself over her ridiculous behavior.

She opened the door and let him in, then walked over to the garage and scooped a cup of dog food out of the bag. As he inhaled the small chunks of food, it suddenly hit her: *When I went back to bed, he was inside.*

She racked her brain, trying to figure out how he could have been getting in and out of the house.

The ring of the doorbell interrupted her thoughts and sent Tucker barking and running toward the front door. Lauren peered out the peephole and saw a tow truck driver standing on the porch, her car hitched to the man's vehicle behind him.

"It's okay, boy," she told the dog. She grasped Tucker's collar and held him by her side as she pulled open the door. The driver introduced himself and explained that he needed the key to access the spare.

"If you don't mind, can you tow it into my carport around back?"

"No problemo," he said.

Lauren handed him the key, then hurried into the bathroom, showered, and dressed. She wanted to get to the sheriff's office by nine-thirty, as it was a full forty-eight hours since Michael had been due home, and she could now file a missing person's report.

After towel-drying her hair, she looked out and saw her Honda in the carport. She handed the man a $5 tip and headed out the door.

Her father had always said that the morning sun brought new hope, new opportunities. But there was no sun to be had . . . only low-hanging gray skies. As she drove to the sheriff's department, Lauren could see black clouds hovering over the Sierra, no doubt dumping inches of new snow on its peaks.

The El Dorado County Sheriff's Department had the distinction of being the oldest such law enforcement organization in California. Although it had already wrapped up its well-publicized sesquicentennial celebration, its anniversary had only served to underscore that its current home was vastly in need of renovation. Located in rural, picturesque Placerville, the single-story, mustard-colored building looked every bit as outdated as its thirty-two years indicated. Its only redeeming feature was that it was set up high on a hill overlooking U.S. 50, a four-lane highway carved through a mountainside thick with a blend of aging pines and redwood seedlings.

Lauren pushed through the double doors and immediately saw the receptionist, who was seated behind a bulletproof enclosure to the right of the entryway. The woman was engrossed in shuffling some papers and seemed to ignore Lauren's presence. Finally, without looking up, the receptionist spoke into the microphone that snaked up from the countertop in front of her. Her voice was tinny and muffled.

"Yes, can I help you?"

Lauren stepped closer to the glass but did not see a microphone. "I'm here because I, I can't find my husband. I mean, it's not like I can't find him, it's that he was supposed to be home a couple of days ago and he's not, and I was told I could file a missing person's report today," she said, running fingers through her shoulder-length, honey-brown hair.

The woman did not initially respond. Lauren wondered if she had heard her; maybe she needed to press a button to activate a speaker. As she glanced around the ledge in front of her, the woman finally looked up, swiveled on her stool, and walked out of the small reception booth into an anteroom that fed into administrative offices.

Lauren stood there, wondering if she should sit down or wait at the window. She took a few breaths to calm herself. With everything that had happened to her the past forty-eight hours, her stomach was rumbling and her eyes were roaming the hallways scouting out the nearest restroom.

Just then, a heavy metal door next to the reception booth opened with an electronic click. A large, smiling woman in her late fifties, her dark hair pulled back into a bun, stepped into the hallway. "I'm Carla Mae. I'm a volunteer here, helping out the community service officer. You say your husband might be the victim of foul play?"

"No, I said he's missing."

"Oh." The woman threw an annoyed glance at the receptionist. "C'mon with me." She took Lauren by the crook of her arm and started off down the corridor. "Sorry for the misunderstanding. Miss Dawson doesn't always give me accurate information."

She led Lauren down a narrow hallway lined with dark brown carpet, tan brick, and walnut paneling. Small rectangular signs protruded into the corridor from the tops of doorframes, noting RECORDS DEPARTMENT and COMMUNITY SERVICE OFFICER. Rather than windows, dark one-way glass reflected back at Lauren from all the doors lining the hall.

Finally, they arrived at a room marked AUTHORIZED PERSONNEL ONLY; Carla leaned against the door and stepped inside.

"Our community service officer, who usually handles missing persons, is out ill this week with that bad flu going around. Nasty stuff, I'm told." Carla slipped beside Lauren and motioned to one of two red vinyl chairs whose arms were worn down to the metal substructure. "Have a seat. The deputy will be by shortly."

Lauren settled into the hard chair and looked up at Carla. "Any idea how long that might be?"

"He's smack-dab in the middle of a big murder investigation. Maybe you heard about it yesterday, that rich computer guy who was shot and killed in his own home. Terrible, terrible. Anyway, Deputy Vork is trying to coordinate with the authorities in Sacramento and he's just a tad busy at the moment."

"Is there someone else I can talk with?"

"Normally there would be. But the detective who handles missing persons took leave and moved to Utah. His mother was quite ill and she needed constant attention, poor thing." Carla shook her head. "So we're a bit shorthanded." She sat down behind the desk at the PC, clicked with the mouse, struck a few keys, and looked over at the LaserJet. "I'm printing a form for you to fill out, to save time. Answer as many of the questions about your husband as you can. Normally, the community service officer would do all this, but we'll have to improvise. One of my strengths is thinking on the fly."

Carla pulled the two-page form from the printer and handed it to Lauren with a pen. "Fill out as much as you can and I'll make sure Deputy Vork comes by as soon as he gets a break in that murder case." Carla rose and moved toward the door. "Is there anything I can get you? Coffee, tea, portable heater?"

Lauren looked up, unsure if the woman had made a joke.

"You *are* tense," Carla said, a smile spreading across her cherubic face.

"I'm fine, thanks," Lauren said.

• • •

Lauren sat for thirty-five minutes alone in the interview room, the cold penetrating to the bone. A shiver rumbled through her body. She glanced over at the one-way glass in the door and wondered if she was being watched.

It took her less than five minutes to complete the form Carla had given her. It consisted primarily of questions regarding Michael's physical description, schools he had attended, date of birth, and social security number.

She put the form aside and gripped the arms of the chair. In front of her was a metal and wood-laminate desk that appeared to be from the early seventies. The room itself was finished with the same dark paneling she had seen in the hallway. Duty clipboards marked WARNINGS and NOTICES were hanging from nails haphazardly slammed into the wall. Binders expounding rules and procedures were stacked on a small desk to her right, and a baseball cap hung from the pull tag that was attached to a gray metal fuse box.

She turned her body slightly and noticed a small corkboard behind her, with bulletins and employee memos pinned to it. The familiar "DARE" bumper sticker was affixed to the side of a metal file cabinet—but after her initial glance, she realized the slogan "DARE to keep kids off drugs" was replaced by "DARE to keep cops off donuts." She wrapped her arms around her torso and closed her eyes. The room was starting to feel very small.

Just then, a tall, thick man with a full mustache and a hard brow entered the room dressed in an olive and tan uniform. A handgun, baton, flashlight, and an assortment of communications paraphernalia dangled from his utility belt. He leaned against the edge of the desk and crossed his arms. "I'm Deputy Vork. I was told you've got a problem, ma'am."

Lauren straightened up. "Yes . . . my husband was on a cross-country ski trip in Colorado and was supposed to be home day before yesterday. When he didn't show up, I called here to report it. They told me I had to wait forty-eight hours before he was considered missing."

Vork looked down at the form and scanned Lauren's answers. "Six-one, one-ninety, brown hair, and hazel eyes. Thirty-eight years old?"

"Thirty-nine in two weeks."

"Uh-huh, yup. Got that right here." He turned the form over and hiked his eyebrows. "You're a doctor?"

"Psychologist."

Vork nodded, then put the form down and looked at Lauren. "So . . . Colorado, you said?"

"An old college frat buddy of his was starting some kind of cross-country-skiing tour company somewhere near Vail. This was supposed to be their first big trip, and he invited a bunch of his buddies to help him out, kind of like the maiden voyage or something."

The deputy nodded. "Then you knew—"

"Excuse me, sir," a young man said, poking his head through the door. "We've got a Channel Ten reporter here, he wants to ask you some questions about the Ellis case."

"Tell him I'll be out as soon as I can." Vork turned back to Lauren. "It's a big case, people are all bent out of shape over that computer tycoon's murder. Sorry about the interruption, ma'am." The deputy reached over and picked up a pad and pen from the desk. "So you know where he went, then."

"Somewhere near Vail, that's all I remember. They were going to be camping in the backcountry."

Vork nodded. "Okay. Did you know these people, these frat buddies he was going with?"

"I never met them. And I don't remember Michael talking about them much."

"Do you know which fraternity it was?"

Lauren shook her head. "All I remember is that it was one I'd never heard of."

"What college did your husband go to? We can get a list of their fraternities and take it from there."

"It was some place back east. New York or New Jersey, I think."

"You don't know where your husband went to college?"

Lauren shifted in her chair. "We talked about it when we first met. It came up a couple other times when he told me how much he hated the humid summers. We've had a lot going on in our lives. The school he went to twenty years ago just wasn't that important."

"What about the names of the people he went skiing with? Maybe a phone number?"

"Michael said he was leaving me a note with everything on it. He called my office and said there was an accident on the freeway, and that he needed to leave right away so he didn't miss his flight. He said he was writing it all down—his friend's name and number, the flight number, everything. But I can't find where he left it."

"So he never actually told you where he was going?"

"He did, he gave me all the details, but when he called, I was rushing to go into an appointment with a patient who was late. I had patients scheduled back-to-back so I had to get the session started. I scribbled his information down somewhere, but I can't remember where." She looked down at her lap. "I must sound like a complete idiot."

"Not at all, Doctor. I'm sure if it was something you felt was important at the time, you'd remember where you wrote it. But he said he was leaving you all the information, right?"

Lauren nodded, then looked at Vork. "I got home late that night and was exhausted. I looked for his note, but I couldn't find it. I figured he'd be home in a few days, I never thought—" She put a hand up to her mouth and stifled a cry.

"Here," Vork said, handing her a tissue. "Take a minute to get yourself together."

Lauren wiped her eyes. "I'm fine. I'm sorry."

"That's okay, I understand." The deputy scratched at his ear for a second. "I have to be honest with you, though. A lot of these missing husband cases are just some straying from the hive, if you follow my meaning . . ."

"Straying . . . you mean another woman?"

"An affair, yes, ma'am. We get a lot of missing persons around these parts, and other than the occasional skier or backpacker in the mountains getting lost over the side of the road in a snowdrift or some such problem like that, it's a man doing something with a woman on the side."

Lauren sat there, trying to decide if she should be angry with the deputy or give serious credence to what he was saying. "Michael wouldn't do that to me."

"Is it possible he just up and left, walked away from some kind of stressful situation? 'Cause that's also a major reason—"

"No," she said tersely.

"Well, then. Let's take this from another perspective. Do you know—"

A loud buzz on his phone interrupted him. "Deputy Vork, line three, please," the voice on the intercom said.

"Excuse me a second." Vork punched the line button, then listened for a moment. "Well, tell Detective Jimenez I'll be out soon as I can. And have the people from Channel Thirteen wait with the good people from Channel Ten. I'm in the middle of an interview here." He nodded another couple of times, then sighed. "Look, LuAnne, do me a favor and set up a press conference. Do it in the break room and give me fifteen minutes, okay? I'll talk to all them reporters together. I'd rather not go through the same story five times." He slammed the phone down and looked at Lauren. "Sorry again, Dr. . . . Chambers. As I was saying . . . do you remember what it was that I was sayin'?"

"All you said was 'Do you know . . .'"

"Oh, yeah. Do you know if your husband had any enemies, anyone he'd had arguments with recently or in the past?"

"If he did, it wasn't something he told me about."

"Any business problems he complained about?"

"He was a supervisor, so he had a lot of people under him. I think he had a good relationship with them. But he never brought his work home. He never complained about anything."

"What about financial problems? Did you handle the family finances or did Michael?"

"Michael did. I was never any good at math, and after the first few bounced checks, I just let him handle it all."

Vork sighed, then stroked his mustache. "Okay. When you go home, I want you to look around and see if you can find something that might have the name of your husband's college or fraternity on it. If we get that, I can put someone on it, track down his friends. Meantime, I'll alert the sheriff's department in Vail, let them know we may have a group of people stranded somewhere. Maybe we'll get lucky. If they've got a report of another family member missing, one of your husband's buddies, we'll know we're on the right track. But again, I want to be honest with you, Dr. Chambers. If they haven't had other calls, they may not put much effort into it. We're not sure of our facts, and they don't want to be wasting their time. And sending up a whirlybird in the high country is expensive and risky business. I'm sure they wouldn't want to put anyone in danger if we didn't know for sure your husband and his buddies were even out there. I don't even know where to tell them to search."

"Then they're not going to do it, are they?"

"Honestly, I can't say they will. I wouldn't. But I will make the call, I promise you that much—"

The phone buzzed, followed by a filtered voice through the intercom speaker. "Deputy Vork, please report to the break room." Vork shook his head. "Sorry again."

"There is something else." The deputy nodded for Lauren to continue. "I got the feeling last night that I was being followed, when I was driving home."

"You sure about that?"

"I think so. I mean, I was sure of it at the time, but . . . I think so. Yes."

"What kind of car was it?"

"I didn't see it, it was dark out. All I saw were the headlights."

"How many people were in the car?"

"I—I don't know. Like I said, it was dark."

"Why do you think it was following you?"

"Because I made a lot of turns, and it turned with me, always staying about two blocks back."

Vork regarded her for a second. "Don't take this the wrong way, but have you ever had that feeling before, that someone's following you?"

"I'm not paranoid."

"If you don't mind me saying"—Vork crossed his arms over his chest—"maybe your concern over your husband has put you on edge. Being a little paranoid would be a normal reaction, wouldn't you think?"

"Look, Deputy, I'm the psychologist here. Don't try—"

"I didn't say that to make you uncomfortable. But we do get some training in psychology. Helps us to understand the criminal mind and such."

"Your point?"

"From what I remember, and correct me if I'm wrong since you're the expert, but isn't paranoia kind of a reaction to a situation that poses no real threat, or some such thing like that?"

Lauren nodded, her gaze finding the ground.

Vork let that thought hang in the air a long second. "Well, then," he finally said, "I'm no doctor, but is it possible that this feeling of being followed is just, I don't know, an offshoot of the fact that your husband's missing?"

"No, Deputy, it's not." Lauren knew that it was possible, but she didn't want to admit it out of fear that it could taint everything she had just told him about Michael's disappearance.

"Is that a professional opinion, Dr. Chambers, or did it come from the heart? Which hat are you wearing right this second?"

Lauren didn't answer.

The door swung open and the young man who had intruded earlier poked his head in again. "I don't know if you heard the page, but—"

"Thank you," Vork said. "I heard it. I'll be right there."

The door closed and Vork stood. "Sorry I couldn't be of more assistance. If you find that note he left, or the name of that college or fraternity, we can take a more aggressive approach. In the meantime, I'll get all the info out to every officer in California through our CLETS system, just in case."

Lauren, her eyes still focused on the ground, nodded. "Thanks for your help," she mumbled. A second later, the door clicked shut.

After Lauren had walked down the hallway and made her way through the front doors, she heard someone call her name. She turned slowly and saw Carla Mae hurrying after her into the parking lot. Lauren stopped, then squinted against the gray brightness and waited until Carla caught up to her.

"Was Deputy Vork helpful?"

"Not really."

"He means well, he really does, Dr. Chambers."

"I'm sure he does. Thanks for your help." Lauren turned and continued on toward her car.

"It's this murder investigation, it's got everyone all stressed out," Carla called after her. "We don't get many killings here, and being shorthanded and all, it's made it hard to deal with other important things, like your problem."

Lauren stopped and turned to face Carla. She did not feel like speaking with anyone at the moment. She wanted to go to her office, rummage through her desk again, and see if she could locate Michael's information. "Don't worry about it." Lauren forced a smile. "I'll be fine."

"I'm sure you will be, missy. But we're going to make sure of it."

"How's that?"

"I need a photo of your husband, the sooner the better." Carla held out a hand and wiggled her thick fingers.

Lauren saw the impatience in Carla's mannerisms and realized that the woman was serious. Lauren opened her purse and pulled out a wallet-size photo they had taken last year at Dean Porter studios. "Will this do?"

"That's perfect. We can crop you out. No offense, missy."

"What are you going to do with it?"

"I'm going to make up a flyer that we'll post all over town. And as soon as I get back to the office, I'm going to get our phone tree up and running."

"Phone tree?"

"Neighborhood Watch. That's how we do things here. Everyone comes together to help everyone else."

Lauren allowed a smile to spread across her face. "Thank you, Carla."

"Tonight at, say, seven o'clock, we'll all gather in the middle school gym. Don't be late."

Lauren found herself nodding. "I'll be there."

• • •

Lauren drove to her office in Cameron Park, a ten-minute ride west of Placerville. As she approached the exit off U.S. 50, she dabbed at the perspiration across her brow. Freeway driving was one of the more difficult tasks for an agoraphobic to handle. Blaring music made the ride more tolerable by minimizing all other surrounding stimuli. In this case, an Elton John love-songs CD Michael had bought her a few months ago provided the diversion. She lowered the music, slowed onto the Cameron Park exit ramp, then turned right into the small office complex.

Lauren pushed through the door to her office and sat down at her desk. Six files were piled to her left, and another was lying on her blotter with a microcassette recorder tossed across it. She realized she had never dictated the notes on her new patient, Steven Simpson, the one with the sadistic torture fantasies. She looked down at her pad of scribbled notes and shook her head. Only next week's visit would tell her if she'd had a positive effect on Steven's behavior.

Lauren opened her drawer, again trying to locate the slip of paper, pad, or message slip on which she'd written Michael's information. She had searched her office yesterday, to no avail. Now she was back, hoping that a fresh look at things would produce a different result.

She rummaged through her files, checked her wastebasket, which had since been emptied, and then cradled her head in her hands, elbows resting atop her desk. In her mind, she walked herself through Michael's phone call. It was hectic; she had just taken a call from another psychologist about a patient. As she hung up, her late appointment came running out of the elevator—and then the receptionist informed her that Michael was on the phone.

She opened her eyes and looked around the office. She remembered walking in and grabbing something to write on as Michael was rattling off his itinerary. She kept telling him to slow down, but he said he would leave a note for her and that he had to go before the traffic made him miss his plane.

Her eyes roamed the office and came to rest on an issue of *Sports Illustrated*. "That's it!" she said, rising from her chair. She lifted the magazine and looked for her handwriting. Finding it clean, she walked out of the room and into the waiting area where the other magazines were haphazardly tossed on a large coffee table in between two couches.

None of the issues had her handwriting on the back. But she remembered it all now, from Michael's phone call to scribbling her notes across the back of a magazine. After making sure no stray issues were beneath the couches or in the empty rack on the wall, she walked up to the receptionist, who was fielding a phone call.

Lauren knew that either a patient had taken the magazine home with him or her, or—

The receptionist disconnected her call and was looking at Lauren. "Yes, Doctor?"

"Do you know if there are any other magazines floating around the suite? I wrote something down on the back of one of them and I can't seem to find it."

"I did a clearing just before the patients went in, about half an hour ago. I put all of them on the table."

"Do you remember seeing one that had my writing on the back?"

"Not offhand. But you know how patients are.

Sometimes they ask to borrow one, but most of the time they just take them."

"If you find it, would you please call me immediately?" Lauren then turned toward the stairwell. "And do me a favor and reschedule tonight's and tomorrow's patients for another time. I've got some . . . personal matters to deal with."

Lauren headed back to her car, angry that she had not written Michael's itinerary down in a safe place. But, as Deputy Vork had said, at the time it did not seem to be important. Michael had said he was leaving the information for her.

So why wasn't it there when she got home that night?

Lauren returned to her car and headed down Cambridge Road toward the freeway. She was on her way to Michael's office in Folsom, where she hoped to find an enlightening morsel or two of information. Though she had spoken on the phone with his secretary at length yesterday, it was not the same as being there and examining his office herself.

After stopping at the traffic light, Lauren noticed that her fuel gauge light was lit. Her eyebrows rose in disbelief. *Empty?* She had filled the tank a couple of days ago. She tapped the dashboard plastic in front of the gauge, but the orange warning light continued to glow. Fortunately, an Arco station was a mile away. She hung a U-turn and headed back toward Cameron Park Drive.

Standing outside in the chilled wind, Lauren alternately lifted her feet, trying to generate some warmth. After another gust hit her, she took shelter inside the car and rubbed her hands together. She'd figured the tank would only take a few gallons—thus confirming her thought that the gauge was defective. But as the LCD readout approached seventeen gallons, she realized that something was definitely wrong.

And it had nothing to do with a faulty fuel gauge.

FOUR

auren walked up to the new four-story office building on East Bidwell Road and shielded her eyes
from the high gray sky that was bouncing off the
reflective glass. Inside the lobby, the directory displayed the company name, Cablecast, and listed the
three floors that it occupied. She had not been to
Michael's office since his division had moved suites
six months ago and had to ask several people before
finding the proper floor and section.

Lauren introduced herself to Amber, Michael's secretary. Dark skinned and thin, Amber was not what
Lauren had expected.

"People in his group have been in and out of his
office," the young secretary said. "After we talked yesterday, I checked around, and everyone said they'd
left things pretty much as they were."

Lauren thanked her and proceeded in. Amber was
a lot more attractive than Lauren had imagined.
Certainly, if what Deputy Vork had said was true,
then Michael didn't need to go all the way to
Colorado to have an affair. He had a sweet, young
candidate ten feet outside his office door.

Lauren shook her head and scolded herself for having such thoughts. But were such thoughts any worse
than imagining her husband buried under ten feet of

snow, the victim of a sudden snowslide in the middle of Colorado backcountry?

She stood just inside his doorway and took in the character of the office. It was dark and the air was stale, with an old, nicked and pocked wooden desk pushed over to one side of the ten-by-ten room. She reached over and turned on the bright, overhead fluorescent lights. Piles of reports were stacked on his desk, along with a dusty collection of silk flowers protruding from a nondescript vase, and a photo of Lauren, one he had taken himself in their front yard with Tucker. She walked around and sat in his creaky chair, trying to take everything in. She couldn't resist playing the psychologist. *Was this a happy office or a sad one?* she asked herself.

The hum of Michael's PC caught her attention. Like most corporations, Cablecast kept its computers running all the time. She reached over to the monitor that was squeezed in amongst the folders and turned it on. As the image appeared on the screen, she realized that Cablecast used Microsoft Office, a suite of software she was familiar with. She started Outlook and clicked on the CALENDAR icon.

Lauren searched Michael's schedule for the days before his departure, hoping to find a name or phone number that could give her more information as to where he had gone. She clicked through the prior two weeks without finding any reference to the trip other than one entry on the day he was to leave: "Skiing."

Before closing out the software, she decided to check his in-box for E-mails. She scrolled through the more recent messages that had arrived while he was away—all of which appeared to be work-related—and found one from a month ago sent by someone identified only as "targard." Frustrated that it didn't provide the person's name, she read through the short message:

Mikee, my man. Ready for the big trip next month? We're getting things squared away and should have all the t's crossed in a few days. It's a go! Can't wait to see all you guys. It'll be like old times. Gotta run. Catch you soon.

The message was unsigned. Lauren reread it, then realized there was nothing of use in there . . . other than that this was a real trip. If she had had any doubts after speaking with Deputy Vork, they were now extinguished.

She hit REPLY and composed her own message:

Hi. This is Lauren Chambers, Michael's wife. I don't have your number or I would've called. But Michael was supposed to be home two days ago and I haven't heard from him. Can you tell me if you and your party arrived home safely, and when you last saw my husband? My number is 530 555-9283, or you can reply to this e-mail if that's easier.

Thanks,
Lauren Chambers

Lauren hit SEND and waited as the message was transmitted across the cable modem hopefully to someone who could provide some answers.

She gave one final look through Michael's drawers, hoping to find a letter, a memento from his frat days, or something else that might indicate where he had gone. There was nothing. But she did find his pocket-size handheld PC. She powered it on and checked the in-box. The only message was an E-mail Lauren had sent him a couple of weeks ago. The calendar was identical to the one she had seen on Michael's desk-top computer.

She slipped the little PC into her purse, took one more look around her husband's office, and covered her eyes. As tears began to well, she realized she could no longer keep her emotions under control. She sat there and wept, praying that Michael would soon be found alive.

FIVE

Pupils round and reactive to light."

"Plantar reflexes downgoing."

"BP ninety over fifty."

"Severe blow to the head—"

"Stabilize C-spine."

"Abdomen rigid . . . possible internal bleeding—"

"Prepare to transport, get him on the spine board. Stabilize and roll on my mark. Ready, one, two—hold it, he's coming around."

The view of the gray sky rotated into view as a sudden wave of dizziness made Michael Chambers nauseous. "Where . . . ?"

"You were in an accident, sir, we're paramedics. We're taking you to the hospital."

"They shot at me, had to go off the cliff."

"Uh, look, sir, you collided with the center median, took out another car. You didn't drive off a cliff."

"Gotta go—" Chambers tried to sit up, but was held down by a couple of hands.

"Hey, hey—you're in no condition to get up. We've gotta get you to the hospital. You suffered a severe blow to the head and you might be bleeding internally . . ."

"Sir?"

The voice was distant, and fading rapidly.

"He's losing consciousness again . . ."

• • •

Michael Chambers opened his eyes and felt groggy. He blinked a few times and tried to clear his vision.

"Doctor, he's awake."

The female voice came from his right, where a nurse was preparing an injection. "This will only hurt for a second," she said as she pricked his skin with a needle.

"Well, Mr. Doe, looks like you're going to make it."

The doctor was smiling at Chambers with lots of white teeth, and the nurse's dialect indicated they were probably somewhere in the South.

"Where am I?"

"Virginia Presbyterian. You had a nasty car wreck and the paramedics extracted you from the vehicle and transported you here. I'm Dr. Farber."

The room was beginning to come into focus. Chambers rotated his head, searching for a wall clock. "How long have I been here?"

"Oh, about two hours."

"Two hours—" He started to sit up, but he felt sharp thigh pain and his headache intensified. "Oh, that's not a good idea."

"Careful there," Farber said. "We had to do a little emergency surgery. Nothing major, but you had something lodged in your thigh and we had to get it out before you developed a nice little infection."

"Not to be ungrateful, Doc, but right now, my head is spinning and hurts a whole lot more than my leg." Chambers put a hand on his forehead.

"We gave you another shot for the pain, but it probably hasn't kicked in yet. As for your head, I've got you scheduled for an MRI to make sure you don't have any internal brain swelling. You took a hell of a blow. I've called neurology for a consult, but they're a little backed up at the moment." The doctor paused to sign a chart the nurse had handed him, then turned back to Chambers. "Mind telling me what your name is?"

"My name?"

"You didn't have any identification with you, and the car you were driving in was reported stolen."

"My name. My name is . . . my name is . . . I don't know. How can I forget my own name?"

"You've suffered a concussion, probably from hitting your head on the steering wheel. Paramedics said you bent it pretty good. But it also appears as if you had another blow to the posterior portion of your head very recently. Judging by the looks of it, I'd say it's not from this accident. Do you know anything about that?"

"No, nothing."

Farber nodded. "How about where you were born, let's start with that."

Chambers stared at the doctor's white coat, his mind a blank. "I don't know."

"Can you recite the alphabet for me?"

Chambers frowned. "A, B, C, D, E, F, G—"

"Okay. I'm going to tell you a color, and I'm going to ask you in a minute what color I told you. Magenta. Got it?"

"Magenta," Chambers repeated. "Got it."

"By the way, what color is magenta?"

"Kind of a purple-red."

"Good. Okay. Tell me, do you know where you live, what your home address is?"

A long silent moment passed, then Farber clicked his pen open and jotted a note in the file. "How about what you ate for breakfast this morning?"

"Eggs."

Farber regarded his patient for a moment. "You're sure about that, eggs?"

Chambers looked away. "No, I'm not sure. I don't remember eating anything this morning. I can't even remember what I was doing before I woke up here."

"Can you count backwards by ones and threes?"

"Look, Doc, are all these questions necessary?"

Farber sighed. "Since I've called for neurology, I guess not. They'll go through everything with you in much greater detail. I was just hoping to narrow down what we're dealing with."

"How serious is this? I mean, I'm gonna get my memory back, won't I?"

Farber raised his eyebrows. "Generally, the more severe the concussion, the more substantial the neurologic deficits could be. And if you've had any concussions in the past, it could make the effects of this one that much more significant." Farber looked over to the nurse. "Can you page neurology again?"

The nurse nodded and walked over to a wall phone.

Chambers looked at Dr. Farber. The man was about thirty years old and had short, dark hair with deep rings beneath his eyes. "You look tired."

Farber smiled. "I've been on for thirty-three hours and I'm looking forward to a nice warm shower and my very comfy waterbed. Do you remember anything about what happened to you, how you got into the accident?"

Chambers shook his head.

"Do you know why you had a bullet in your thigh?"

Chambers looked hard at the doctor. "A bullet?" Something wasn't right. A stolen car, a bullet . . . *Am I a victim or a criminal?* He felt an overwhelming sense of unease, of the need to protect himself. He looked away from Farber. "No, I—I don't."

Farber pulled a penlight from his breast pocket and flicked it into Chambers's eyes. Farber shook his head, then sighed again. "Well. Until we can find out your name, we're going to call you John Doe. Like I said, you're scheduled for that brain scan and I've been told the police have some questions for you—"

"They asked me to let them know as soon as he's lucid," the nurse said.

Chambers's gaze shifted to the nurse. "The police—for what?"

"Anytime a person comes into the ER with a gunshot wound, we're required to notify them."

"Can't it wait, I'm still feeling real tired." He gave them a slow, gaping yawn and looked at the doctor with glassy eyes. "I don't think I'm up to answering a bunch of questions just yet. Besides, I can't remember anything."

Farber turned to the nurse. "Would you tell them he's still out and it may be a little while?"

The nurse frowned. "Yes, Doctor." She disappeared out the door.

"Doc, this memory thing is temporary, right?"

"I'd prefer to look at it optimistically. But to be honest with you, until I get that consult from the neurologist, I can't say how permanent, or temporary, it's going to be. Diagnosing it properly is the key. There are a number of possibilities—postconcussion syndrome, retrograde or posttraumatic amnesia, and a host of psychological or organic causes. We've drawn blood and we'll run a tox screen to make sure you haven't ingested any kind of drug that'd explain your memory problems. The MRI will help. And depending on what that shows, we may also get an EEG to rule out epileptic disorders. Until we know when and where that bullet came from, it's possible the bullet and the accident are completely unrelated. In which case, a seizure could explain why you drove off the road."

Chambers let his head fall back onto the pillow.

Farber gently patted Chambers's shoulder. "Radiology should be down for you shortly. You can rest here in the recovery room. When the X-ray techs come and wheel you out, the police may see you, so you may not have any choice but to speak to them at that point." Farber scribbled his signature on the metal chart and hooked it to the end of the bed. "I'll tell them they have to wait until after you get the brain scan, but my experience with the police is that they seldom listen to what I have to say."

"Thanks for your help, Doc. I'll remember you in my will."

"Then for my sake, I hope that concussion isn't too bad." Farber turned and headed for the hallway.

"Hey, Doc," Chambers called after him. "You forgot to ask me something. Magenta."

Farber smiled, then walked out of the room.

As soon as the door closed, Chambers eased himself off the bed, the pain from his left thigh masked somewhat by the medication. He felt a slight pulling sensation and reasoned it was stitches. As he stood upright, he felt dizzy and his head began throbbing more intensely, like a jackhammer on cement. He took a deep breath, steadied himself, and waited for a few seconds for his eyes to clear before hobbling across the floor and through a pair of double doors that led to a supply room. There were trauma capes, surgical gloves,

stethoscopes, sphygmomanometers, and an assortment of cath kits, electrode pads for ECG units, trach
tubes . . . and surgical scrubs. He pulled out a pair of
freshly folded burgundy pants, a shirt, and a surgical
cap. He quickly slipped them on, tossing his hospital
gown into a basket in the corner of the room.

A bullet? he thought. *That can't be good.*

Until Chambers could determine if he was a felon
wanted by the police or an innocent bystander, he
could not put his trust in law enforcement. But one
thing he felt he *could* trust was his instincts. And
right now, they were telling him to put as much distance between himself and the cops as possible. Self-
preservation was a powerful emotion.

He took a stethoscope off a hook on the wall and
wrapped it around his neck the way Farber had worn
his. A few footsteps later, he was at the door and
peering out. Two police officers were coming down
the hallway, pointing at the adjacent room where he
had been lying a few moments ago. He waited until
the cops were nearly at the entrance to the recovery
room, then pushed through the door.

Chambers walked out of the supply room, heading
down the corridor, trying to carry himself as naturally
as the leg wound would permit. He wondered how
long it would take the police to realize that he was the
person they were looking for. They would probably
grab a nurse or doctor and ask what had happened to
the patient known as John Doe. Then, they'd flash on
the doctor they had seen leaving the adjacent supply
room; they would do a quick search of the cabinets
and find the bloodied gown. Then they'd be heading
in his direction. All told, he probably had three minutes, unless something unexpected occurred.

Chambers quickened his pace and a second later was turning down a long corridor where the hospital laboratory was located. He slipped into the sprawling, open suite, which was well-lit from above with banks of sleek, brushed-aluminum fluorescent light fixtures. A few lab techs were busy processing samples, and a nurse was dealing with a line of patients at a long counter.

Chambers walked through the lab, limping slightly as he passed the reception station, and proceeded into the work area. He grabbed a patient chart and pretended to look inside while he thought about how he was going to get out of the hospital. He had no money, no car that he knew of—Farber had said the one Chambers had been found in was stolen—and nowhere to go.

He closed the chart and headed toward the back of the lab, where he noticed an elevator. He took it up to the second floor and glanced out into the hallway: the sign indicated patient rooms, the cardiac care unit, and ICU. None of these would do.

He needed food and a quiet place to think. But if the police started searching the hospital, it would be best if he was out of the building. Or would it? If he was lucky enough to avoid a search, he could wait a few hours and then leave. By then, they would be focusing their efforts elsewhere—why would a sane person remain in a place where the police were looking for him?

The third floor was more promising, as the directory indicated that it was where the doctors' lounge was located. As he approached, the smell of chicken and potatoes hung in the air. His stomach contracted again.

He walked into the lounge and hesitated as he glanced around. A couple of physicians were sitting on a couch reading journals. Another was half-reclining, her eyes closed, the exhaustion of a long shift etched in her face. He continued on into the adjacent café, picked up a tray, and surveyed the food. I'll take a little of everything, he felt like saying. Instead, he settled for a scoop of potato salad, a tall Coke, a ham-and-cheese sandwich on wheat, and a container of yogurt.

At the register, an elderly woman smiled at him and began ringing up his food. "That'll be six-eighteen."

"Oh," Chambers said. "I'm sorry, I forgot to tell you this is on Dr. Farber. He asked me to have you put it on his account."

The woman hesitated and crumpled her wrinkled face. "I really need verification—"

"I should've told you before you rang it up." He leaned closer to her graying hair and lowered his voice. "Dr. Farber lost a bet to me," he said as he noticed the other cashier with the Washington Wizards T-shirt on. "Took the Wizards and lost big. Kept forgetting to pay up. Told me to grab a late lunch and have you put it on his tab."

"Dr. Farber shouldn't be betting on basketball games. I didn't never think of him as the gambling type."

Chambers shushed her with a finger to his lips. "I wouldn't bring it up. He's very embarrassed about it."

The woman nodded, consulted a hospital listing, and entered a key code into the register. She placed the receipt on the tray and nodded. "He won't hear a word out of my mouth about it."

Chambers shoved the receipt into his shirt pocket. "I'll make sure he gets this so he can deduct it from what he owes me." He winked at her and carried his food over to one of the tables in the far corner of the café, where he had a clear view of the entire lounge. With one eye on the entryway, he consumed the entire meal in less than five minutes.

He pushed the tray aside and rested his face in his hands, trying to assemble what few facts he had into some sort of a cohesive scenario that might help him discover who he was: He had been shot in the thigh, stolen a car, and gotten into an accident on the highway after hitting a center median. He'd had emergency surgery, the police wanted to speak to him, he couldn't remember his name, and he had no identification on him. Despite his best efforts, it was not coming together. He fought back a yawn, gathered his energy, and pushed himself up off the chair.

Chambers left the lounge and felt the sudden heaviness of exhaustion pervading every part of his body. He made his way down the hall, checking nameplates on the walls, looking for a place where he could rest. He found the doctors' on-call room and pushed in through the door.

Three cots were set up inside the cramped room. He gingerly climbed on the one against the wall, curled into a ball on his side, and fell instantly into a deep sleep.

The Virginia state policeman checked his watch and pressed the phone receiver to his ear. "We had security posted at all stairways and elevators the minute we realized he was missing. . . . Yes, sir, we've scoured the bottom floor." The man looked at his partner. "Yeah, I guess it's possible he got through to another floor before we posted the guards. He could have left the hospital, too. If I were him, that's what I'd do. Get as far away as I could. But if he's still here, what goes up has to come down, you know what I mean?" He nodded, then looked at his partner. "Any ambulances missing?"

"I'll check," the other officer said, then walked off toward the ER intake desk.

A few moments later, the officer returned just as his partner was hanging up the phone. "Well?"

"All ambulances accounted for."

"Well, this is just fucking great. FBI's getting involved. Agents are on their way over from the Washington Field Office."

"Feds?"

"Yeah, they say he matches the description of a guy they're looking for."

"We need to find him before they get here or we'll never hear the end of it."

The cop nodded. "Then we'd better get our asses in gear. We've got maybe thirty or forty minutes. We'll start with a thorough search of all floors. Between hospital security staff and the units already on their way, we'll be able to cover the place in twenty, twenty-five minutes."

"Fucking feds," his partner said as they strode purposefully down the hall. "This is *our* manhunt."

Michael Chambers was in such a deep sleep he had hardly moved since lying down on the cot. In the past two days his body had been subjected to the type of trauma that would ordinarily take weeks to recover from. But for the time being, a few hours of uninterrupted sleep would have to suffice.

At the moment, he saw himself wading barefoot through a rose garden. There were bright reds, whites, yellows, pinks . . . colors and varieties of roses such that he had never seen before. He stopped and looked down at his feet, which were standing in the cool, moist peat moss. A sweet scent hung on the air and he sucked it in deeply, filling his lungs with the competing aromas.

He looked down again—and saw deep gashes across his feet, blood oozing everywhere, as if the thorns from the rosebushes had swarmed his bare legs and sliced the skin to shreds. He bolted upright in bed, instantly awake, and realized he was dreaming. As he struggled to see his feet in the dark, the door suddenly opened and light spilled into the small room, creating a tall, thin shadow on the wall next to the cot.

Chambers threw a hand up to his eyes to block the light. He looked around, still agitated from the nightmare, dizzy and completely disoriented. "What are you doing?" he shouted.

His visitor, dressed in a light blue uniform, closed the door slightly and the room darkened again. "Sorry, sir, hospital security. I—I didn't mean to wake you, but a patient's taken off and he's wanted for questioning by the police. We've got orders to search all rooms. Nobody's come in, I take it."

"I've been on for thirty-three hours straight," Chambers said, recalling what Dr. Farber had said to him. "I've been dead to rights ever since I fell asleep."

The man nodded, pulled out his flashlight, and swung it around the room beneath the three cots. "Okay. All clear." He apologized again for disturbing him and left.

Shit. They were searching the entire hospital. He wouldn't be able to leave, at least not for a while. But since this room had already been checked, he would hopefully not have to pass the scrutiny of a real cop, one who wouldn't be so easily dissuaded with a physician's woeful story of exhaustion.

He lay back, closed his eyes, and within seconds was drifting off again to a deep sleep.

SEVEN

The evening air had dipped below twenty degrees. Lauren hiked up the collar on her down jacket and watched as people filed into the cozy Herbert Green Middle School gymnasium. She tucked her gloved hands deeper into her pockets and closed her eyes. *You can do this,* she told herself.

Lauren caught sight of a smiling man who was bundled up in a parka, standing near the gym entrance. He was greeting people as they approached, even helping an elderly woman who was having a difficult time pulling the door open. After holding it for her, he took a moment to play with a little girl whose mother was reading a flyer she had been handed.

The man reminded her of Michael . . . outgoing, always willing to help, good with people. Qualities Lauren wished she herself had.

Lauren had gotten used to having Michael to rely on when facing an uncomfortable situation. He would be there by her side, coaxing her through it, always claiming to understand what she was going through. But having never been riddled with phobias of any sort, Michael could in no way understand the difficulties an agoraphobic faced in everyday life . . . the accommodations that had to be made. The excuses that had to be given. A fear of open spaces, of being out in public, of standing in lines, sitting in movie theaters, riding in elevators . . . as a psychologist, she understood what her problem was. She knew that in her case it had its roots in an unresolved event in her childhood, the repressed anxiety surrounding the shooting of her father and the loss caused by his eventual death. Years later, the loss of something else central to her identity—her practice—had brought it all to a head.

But being in the field didn't solve her problem, it had merely allowed her to diagnose it sooner. After four years of therapy, she had learned how to decrease its effects, how to compensate for and work through her condition. But she had not completely recovered.

A loud rapping noise on the side window startled her. She cleared the fogged interior glass with her forearm and saw Carla Mae standing beside the door.

"You coming in, or should we just hold the meeting without you?" With her round face bundled up, and with her shouting through the closed car window, it was hard for Lauren to tell if her new acquaintance was being friendly or antagonistic. But the slight squint of the eyes told her Carla was smiling.

Lauren took a deep breath, pulled the handle on the door, and popped it open. "I'm coming in, of course. I just didn't want to be the first one in, you know, having to tell the story over and over again before we even got started."

The two of them walked into the gymnasium together. Well-worn folding metal chairs had been set up across most of the wood floor. Beneath one of the basketball hoops was a long table outfitted with a black tablecloth and an embroidered, orange Neighborhood Watch emblem.

Carla took Lauren's elbow and led her over to the table. Lauren, however, kept her head down, listening to the echoing chatter of the people in the room. She could tell there was a good turnout. She felt her stomach do a somersault and rested a hand across her abdomen to steady it.

"We'll get started in a minute," Carla said into Lauren's ear. "I figure you can tell us about what happened. Include everything you know. Then tell us what you can about Michael." Carla stopped for a second. "You all right, missy? You don't look so good."

Lauren's hands were clammy and she felt nauseous. She forced a smile and lifted her head to look at Carla. "Just a little hungry. I'll be fine."

"Are you ready for me to call the meeting to order?"

Lauren shrugged. "I guess so. I'm not good about baring my soul to strangers. You'd think I would be, doing what I do for a living."

"Don't think twice about it. Everyone who's been through this can tell you it isn't fun. But we're not here for entertainment, we're here for support. Get that straight and you'll get the most out of it."

Lauren nodded. "Then I'm ready."

Carla lifted a gavel and struck it twice on a small wood block on the table. The room quieted a bit, and she pounded the block once again. "All right, all right, settle down." As the noise dropped to a tolerable level, Carla began, "Tonight we're here for Dr. Lauren Chambers, whose husband, Michael, is the subject of our meeting. You've all had a chance to read the flyers you were given on the way in. So, I might as well just have Lauren tell you the rest."

Lauren lifted her head—and lost her breath. Her eyes darted nervously around the room: nearly the entire gymnasium was full of people, all looking at her, waiting to hear what she had to say! She cleared her tight throat, and took a deep, calming breath.

"Thanks for coming," she started in a weak voice. "As you know, my husband, Michael, is missing."

"Louder," a man in the back row yelled. He had a cold stare, a bushy beard, and a black knit cap on. Something about his eyes bothered her.

"Lauren," Carla urged, "please continue, a little louder so everyone can hear you."

Lauren broke her gaze from the man in the back. "Sorry," she mumbled. "I said, my husband, Michael, is missing." The words were forced, as if the strain of the situation were making it difficult for her to speak. In reality, it was her anxiety over facing a gymnasium full of strangers.

"I don't do a lot of public speaking, so I'm sorry if I'm not any good at it." What she wanted to say is that she'd rather be in bed, hiding under the covers. "Michael went cross-country skiing in Colorado with some fraternity buddies and was supposed to be home a couple of days ago. I haven't heard from him." She looked over at Carla, who nodded for her to continue. "Michael is very responsible and I'm sure he'd have called if he was able to."

"Do you think he left Colorado?" someone asked.

"I don't know. Unfortunately, there isn't much I know about his trip, or who he went with. I wrote it all down, but . . . I can't find it."

"So he could still be in Colorado."

"I guess."

"But he may not be," Carla cut in. "He might have made it back to town, in which case we all need to be on the lookout for him. His photo is on the flyer, and a bunch of us worked into the early evening tonight to get a hundred of these notices up all around town. I've got another thousand of them, and I'll need volunteers who can take them into Sacramento, El Dorado Hills, Cameron Park, Folsom, Gold River, Rancho Cordova—the whole Highway Fifty corridor between here and the airport."

Lauren found herself staring at the floor. *Look up!* she told herself. *If I don't look interested, why would anyone else care?* She forced her head up and again felt her heart rate increase, her chest tighten. Her eyes bounced around nervously—and again landed on the stare of the man in the back. She felt repulsed by him and suddenly wondered if he was the one who had followed her last night.

"I've got plenty of flyers," Carla said, "so take as many as you think you'll need."

A number of neighbors raised their hands, and the stack of papers was passed back to them.

Carla leaned over to Lauren's ear. "I think you should thank them again for coming."

Lauren pulled her eyes away from the man and nodded to Carla. "I want to," she started in a soft voice, "I want to thank all of you for coming out tonight." She squared her shoulders and tried to make eye contact with some of the women, whose faces tended to be less threatening to her. "I love my husband a great deal, and we've been through a lot together. I'm really hoping we'll be able to find him."

"Lauren has already spoken with Deputy Vork about this, so I'm sure we'll have law enforcement's support. If you see someone who looks like Michael Chambers, or if you find out something about him, please don't try to analyze the information yourself.

What could seem unimportant to you could be very significant to the sheriff's department." Carla picked up a flyer and pointed to it. "Our chapter's phone number on the bottom of the flyer encourages anyone to call with information. I would ask all of you to do the same." She turned to Lauren to see if she wanted to add anything. Receiving a shrug in response, Carla turned back to the gathered crowd. "Of course, I've got some of my brownies here, and Sam brought coffee from his restaurant. But before we start stuffing our faces, if anyone has a question, fire away."

After a handful of questions were answered, the crowd began to disperse into neighborly groups. As Lauren made her way toward the food, she again caught a glimpse of the man in the back row. He was still seated. And still staring at her. People passed in between their gazes, but he did not move. Lauren felt a chill and turned toward Carla, who was busy motioning to someone.

"Nick, come here for a minute!" Carla said.

"Carla," Lauren said, grabbing her by the elbow, "there's a man in the back row. He's been staring at me since the beginning of the meeting."

"Probably just interested in what you had to say. Everyone was listening very closely, I assure you."

"No, it was more than that. There was something . . . creepy about him. Cold. The way he looked at me."

"Well, missy, I know practically everyone here. Point him out."

Lauren looked at the back row—and the man was gone. Her eyes quickly scanned the room, but people were milling about. Some had their backs turned or their faces were otherwise difficult to see.

"He was just there," Lauren said. "He must have gotten up."

"If you see him again, let me know."

"Howdy, Carla Mae."

Carla spun and embraced her friend. "Good to see you." They pushed apart and Carla turned to face Lauren. "I want you to meet Nick Bradley. Just about the nicest person you could hope to know."

"Now, Carla, don't go overboard," Bradley said with a toothy smile that carried a warm charm. He had a medium build and wavy, earth-toned hair, with a poise and ease of movement that made Lauren at once comfortable—and wary.

"Nick was the one who started Neighborhood Watch here, about two years ago. Without his persistence, it never would've gotten off the ground."

"You're being much too gracious."

"I saw you," Lauren said. "At the door earlier, helping that elderly lady."

"If it involves helping somebody, we're probably talking about Nick," Carla said. "Which is why I called him over. I think he's just the person you should get to know."

"Why's that?" Lauren asked.

"Well, Nick's a private investigator. I'm sure he could do a lot to help you find Michael."

"At your service," Bradley said with a slight bow.

Lauren forced a smile but could not get out of her mind the image of the stranger in the back of the gymnasium. Her eyes again began to dance around the room.

"Did I say something wrong?" Bradley asked, following her gaze.

"No-no," Lauren stammered. "I'm just . . . there

was . . ." She sighed and shook her head. "I'm just tired."

"After what you've been through, I don't doubt it," Carla said.

"I'd like to help you find your husband, Dr. Chambers."

"Call me Lauren, and I'm afraid I'm not in a financial position to pay a private investigator."

"We'll take up a collection." Carla turned toward the crowd and reached for her gavel. "We've done that before—"

"We don't need a collection," Bradley said, holding up a hand. "It's on the house."

"And why, may I ask, would you be willing to do all this for me?"

"Because I knew your husband, Lauren. I did some work for his company, and they paid me well."

"You knew Michael?"

"Like I said, I want to help. When Carla called and told me who was missing—"

"Who do you think put up most of the flyers this afternoon?" Carla asked.

"So what do you say?" Bradley asked. "Am I in?"

"I need some time to think about it, okay? I'll let you know tomorrow."

"Time is the one thing we don't have," Bradley said. "The longer Michael is missing, the harder he's going to be to find."

"Do you have a card?"

Bradley searched his pockets but came up empty. "Afraid I don't have any on me. I'll write my info down for you. Call me anytime. Day or night, okay?"

He grabbed a flyer off the table and penciled in his phone numbers. Lauren took it and thanked him.

"You don't find many folk like Nick, I'll say that much," Carla said as Bradley walked off. "I think you should take him up on his offer."

"Thanks so much for getting this together tonight. It means a lot to me."

"Maybe when this all blows over and Michael's back, you'll come out to help one of us just like your neighbors did for you."

Lauren glanced at the mass of people in the gymnasium and shuddered slightly. The truth was, she would truly like to reach out and be able to help others. "Maybe a lot of things will change in the future." Lauren turned and walked out the door, fighting off the feeling that the man in the black knit cap was behind her somewhere, following.

EIGHT

FBI director Douglas Knox sank down into his kitchen chair. The five-mile run along the Potomac had done him good. After yesterday's tense stand-off at a militia farmhouse had degenerated into a major confrontation, he had spent a sleepless night tossing in bed and replaying each of his command decisions, as if doing so could change the result. He had spent the better part of today in briefings with the media and meetings with the president and his advisers.

Although it was an important part of his job, Knox despised hostage rescue and domestic terrorism situations. Anything that left him without total control tore him apart inside. No wonder his blood pressure was higher than it should be and his list of medications was quickly becoming longer than his seventy-five-year-old mother's. From the exterior, he looked fit; only prematurely graying hair provided any indication that the job had worn terribly on him.

The burn in his lungs from the twenty-degree Washington air hurt and felt good at the same time. The run had cleared his mind—as it always did—and allowed him to focus.

He kicked off his Nikes and put his feet up on the wood chair opposite him, grabbed the unopened mail from this morning that his wife had left on the table for him, and put the coffee mug to his lips.

He started to tear open the edges of the envelopes: a couple of bills from the cable and electric companies. A postcard from his sister who had been vacationing in Hawaii—she had called him a couple of days ago, so why she'd even bothered to send the card in the first place didn't—

The next letter caught him by the throat:

HARPER PAYNE. DEAD OR ALIVE, YOUR CHOICE. FAIL TO DELIVER HIM AND YOU'LL PLACE CERTAIN PEOPLE IN YOUR LIFE AT RISK. WE KNOW WHERE SYLVIA SHOPS. WE KNOW SHE GETS HER HAIR DONE AT MARCEL'S ON THE SECOND THURSDAY OF EVERY MONTH. WE KNOW SHE BOUGHT THE PINK NIGHTGOWN SHE WEARS TO BED AT THE BOUTIQUE ON FIFTH. AND WE KNOW A LOT MORE. LOOK OUTSIDE YOUR BACK DOOR AND YOU'LL FIND AN EXAMPLE OF OUR HANDIWORK. YOU HAVE SEVEN DAYS.

NOTE: THIS WAS PRINTED ON A HEWLETT-PACKARD LASERJET 6 WITH HAMMERMILL PAPER BOUGHT AT STAPLES OFFICE SUPPLY IN THE EASTERN UNITED STATES. THOUGHT WE'D SAVE YOU THE TIME OF RUNNING IT THROUGH YOUR LAB. BUT DO WHAT YOU HAVE TO, BECAUSE WE DEFINITELY WILL. HARPER PAYNE, SEVEN DAYS.

Knox dropped the letter on the table. He walked toward the back door, not knowing what he was going to find—if anything. Were they watching to see if he went to the door? And if they were, was he inadvertently signaling them he was taking their threat seriously? He stood with his hand on the knob, then decided against opening it. He flipped on the porch light and separated the honey-colored curtain. Lying there on the stoop was Cocoa, the cat's fur parted along her stomach, her intestines splayed out beside her body.

"My God," he said under his breath. *How the hell did these people find out where I live?*

A remnant of his days as a member of the Army Special Forces—then as the chief legal counsel for the Senate Select Committee on Intelligence—paranoia was as much a part of his personality as his compulsion for neatness, with one exception: the former was learned, while the latter was an inborn psychopathology inherited from his father. The result was that he had his security-detail driver take a circuitous route home every evening, all the while carefully surveying the rearview mirror for any suspicious vehicles following them. A sensor disguised as a compass mounted beside the stereo was designed to alert them if an electronic tracking device had unknowingly been installed on his car.

He rummaged through the kitchen drawers to find a Ziploc bag. Using a tissue, he slipped the letter and envelope inside the protective plastic covering, then sealed it. He was suddenly aware of the cold perspiration lining the inside of his sweatshirt.

Just then, his eighteen-year-old daughter, dressed in an oversize FBI Academy T-shirt that extended down below her knees, walked into the kitchen. "Hey, Dad. How was your run?" She opened the refrigerator, withdrew a carton of orange juice, and poured it into a glass. She started to leave the kitchen, but apparently realizing that she had never received an answer, hesitated. "Hello . . . You okay, Dad?"

Knox was staring at the letter and thinking about Cocoa. "Fine, honey. The run was just fine."

Melissa shrugged. "Whatever," she said, and walked out.

Knox stood up from the table, ground his molars, and reached for the phone. "Fuck you, whoever you are," he said under his breath as he punched numbers into the keypad.

This was not a good day for this. Not a good day at all.

NINE

Lauren was shivering by the time she arrived back at her car. It was not that far of a walk from the gymnasium, but the temperature had dropped again and the wind had picked up. She sat down and started the engine, cranked the heater to its hottest setting, and disengaged the emergency brake.

Or tried to.

"What the hell?" She pushed in the release button and attempted to pull up on the hand brake. It was ratcheted to the highest setting—which seemed impossible since she would be physically unable to set it that hard. Clumsily maneuvering in her down jacket, Lauren turned her body around and pulled her knees onto the bucket seat, then yanked on the lever with both hands. She grunted and moaned, knowing that all she had to do was move the brake up one notch to release it.

As she held her breath and strained one last time, the handle unlatched and then dropped down into a disengaged position. "Jesus," she said, leaning against the seat for a second while she caught her breath.

A loud rumble from her stomach reminded her that she had not eaten all day. She repositioned herself in the seat, buckled her restraint, and pulled away. As she drove out of the lot, she started replaying the meeting in her head. Although she wished she had appeared more self-confident, the response had been nothing short of spectacular. To have so many people show up at a neighborhood gathering with the sole intent of helping her find Michael truly demonstrated the strength of "community" at work.

As Lauren drove down the dark, winding road toward her house, she felt the need to check her rearview mirror. There were no headlights—which brought a sense of relief, the state of mind she had been missing since Michael's disappearance.

Lauren pulled into her garage and greeted Tucker as she walked into the house. He jumped up, gently placing his front paws on her chest and licking her on the cheek. "I know, you want to eat." She filled his dog bowl with food, then headed into the kitchen. She unwrapped a frozen pizza and slipped it into the oven.

A moment later, she caught a glimpse of Tucker's untouched food bowl. "What's wrong? I thought you'd be starving."

The dog rubbed against her thigh and she patted him on the head. "Well, I'm going to eat, even if you're not." She checked on her pizza, then began setting out a couple of plates, glasses of water, and napkins. Then she stopped herself. The euphoria of the community meeting had vanished in an abrupt realization: she was setting the table for two, but only one would be eating.

After finishing dinner, Lauren pulled Michael's hand-held PC from her purse and powered it on. She touch-screened into Microsoft Outlook and plugged the tiny unit into the phone jack. She dialed in and retrieved his E-mail, then configured the device so it could also receive her E-mail.

There were no responses yet from Michael's skiing buddy, "targard." Lauren selected Amber's message that was still in Michael's in-box, and hit REPLY. She wrote Amber a short note asking if she could find out if Cablecast was satisfied with the work Nick Bradley had done for them. She then touched SEND and powered off the unit.

She stood and walked over to the cupboard, grabbed a chamomile tea bag, and filled a mug with the instant-hot faucet. She reached into the refrigerator to add some milk to the tea. But the carton was empty.

Empty?

I just bought this yesterday, she thought. *Have I used that much of it? If Michael were here, he would've bought a larger size.* But she realized that was not the point. How could she have used all the milk?

She took a sip of the hot tea and then spilled it down the drain. She had grown accustomed to drinking it with milk, the way Michael liked it. She shook her head, then folded her arms across her chest. "Michael this and Michael that. It's time for me to stop being so dependent on him for every aspect of my life." She looked down at Tucker, whose ears had puckered as if he were listening to her tirade.

She tossed the spoon into the sink, then walked upstairs to the bedroom. She fell back onto their bed and kicked her shoes off. "Where are you, Michael? It's time to come home!"

She rolled over and grabbed his pillow again, hugging it against her chest and burying her face into the down.

But she didn't pick up Michael's scent. She looked at the pillow, then jumped off the bed and backed away. "Oh, my God. Oh my God!" She lunged forward for the Colt she had left on the night table. With trembling hands she grabbed the key around her neck, undid the metal lock, then struggled to pull the weapon from its velvet bag.

"Who are you?" she yelled into the dead air of the house. "Show yourself!" Tucker came running up the steps and into her room. Lauren swung the Colt at him, startled by the approaching noise, and was immediately relieved it was the dog. But upon seeing the gun, he began to bark, which only served to elevate her stress.

She looked down at the bed again and knew something was very wrong. She shoved her hand into her pocket, found Nick Bradley's phone number, and started dialing.

He answered on the third ring.

"Mr. Bradley, this is Lauren Chambers. I'm going to take you up on your offer," she said rapidly.

"Is everything okay, Lauren? You sound—"

"No, everything's not okay. Can you come over right now?"

"Now? Are you sure—"

"I need you to come. I think someone's been in my house. He may still be here, I don't know."

"Okay, Lauren, I'll be right there. I'll call the sheriff on the way and have him meet me there. Meantime, can you get out?"

"I've got a gun," she said loudly, hoping the intruder would hear her.

"That's real good, Lauren," Bradley said slowly, "but I need you to just calm down or you're not going to do anyone any good. If you go waving that gun around, the deputy isn't going to want to help us out, do you understand what I'm saying?"

"Just come."

"I'm on my way, Lauren, just hold it together."

She gave him the address, then sat down on the floor, her back against the wall, the Colt pointed at the doorway.

It took Nick Bradley only five minutes to drive the two miles that separated their houses. The loud rapping at the back door made her jump.

Lauren pushed herself off the floor and moved slowly out of the room, her eyes darting from side to side as she approached the stairs. She cautiously made her way into the kitchen, flipped on the porch light, and parted the lace curtain. Nick Bradley was standing there, eliciting a loud bark from Tucker.

"Are you okay?" he shouted through the door.

Lauren nodded, and the dog began barking. "It's okay, boy," she said, stroking his head. "He's a friend." She told Tucker to sit, then unlatched the lock to let Bradley in.

"The sheriff should be here any minute," Bradley said, eyeing Tucker while stepping into the nook. "Tell me what's wrong."

"It's the sheets," Lauren managed to say before sitting down hard in one of the chairs. "I can't take it anymore . . ."

Bradley sat down next to her, glancing again at Tucker, whose eyes were fixed on him, the dog's weight forward, ready to pounce. Bradley gingerly removed the Colt from Lauren's hands and placed it on the table. "What sheets are you talking about?"

"There are cheap floral sheets on the bed. My mother gave them to us when we got married. We've never used them."

"And you think there were other sheets on the bed when you left."

"I'm sure of it. And that's not all. There have been other things, too. It started with the dog. First he was out, then he was in. Then the emergency brake and the milk—"

A knock at the front door sent Tucker running.

"The sheriff," Bradley said. "I think it might be a good idea to tie the dog up somewhere."

"He'll be fine," Lauren said as she made her way to the door. She told Tucker to sit, then looked through the peephole and saw a deputy standing there. She wiped her eyes with her sleeve, then opened the door.

"I'm Deputy Matthews, ma'am. Is everything all right?"

"Thanks for coming, Deputy. I'm Nick Bradley, the one who called."

"Dispatch didn't give much information."

"Dr. Chambers thinks that someone may have been in her house. I got here just before you did."

"Did you see anyone, ma'am?"

Lauren looked down at the carpet and shook her head.

"Did you hear noises or was something stolen?"

"Nothing was stolen, but I'm sure someone was—or is—here."

"Mind if I take a look around?" Matthews asked.

"I'd appreciate it," Bradley said.

Deputy Matthews pulled a flashlight from his utility belt and his Smith & Wesson from his holster. "Stay here."

After the deputy walked off, Lauren flopped down onto the couch in the living room, a cozy rectangular room in a country motif, with lace curtains, navy and white sofas, and an often-used fireplace. Bradley settled onto the edge of the couch next to Lauren.

"Your Colt is licensed, isn't it?"

"It was my daddy's. I don't know. I've had it locked away for several years."

Bradley rubbed at his forehead. "All right, we'll worry about that later. Meantime, you want to talk about what happened tonight?"

Lauren turned away.

"When the deputy comes back here, assuming he hasn't found anything, he's going to want a more complete explanation."

"I don't know where to start, it all seems so crazy."

"The beginning is always best."

Lauren's face flushed and tears began to well up in her eyes. "I can't handle this, Mr. Bradley, I'm coming apart."

"Please, Lauren, call me Nick." He placed a hand on her shoulder. "If you just tell me what you know, maybe I can help."

"Okay," Deputy Matthews said, walking down the hallway, "the place is clear. Now, what was the first indication that there was an intruder?"

Lauren looked at Matthews and pushed away the tears with her fingers. "It's the flowered sheets in my bedroom. Michael and I hate them, we never use them, but they're on the bed."

"Is Michael your husband?"

"Yes, he's missing."

"Oh, you're Lauren Chambers—I've got it," Matthews said, bobbing his head. "I saw a notice on the briefing board tonight when I started my rotation. Okay, go on. The sheets."

"They weren't there before, when I woke up this morning. There were solids on the bed, and I could smell Michael on the pillowcase. Then when I went to the refrigerator, the milk carton was empty, and I just bought it yesterday. And the parking brake in my car when I left the Neighborhood Watch meeting was set so hard I almost couldn't get it unlatched—"

"I'm a little confused, ma'am," Matthews said. "I don't mean to interrupt, but what was it that made you think someone was in your house tonight?"

Lauren sniffled and looked at the deputy with wide eyes. "Don't you see? The sheets. Someone changed the sheets on my bed!"

Matthews chuckled. "My wife always complains about the house chores. She'd be glad if someone changed the sheets—"

"You think this is funny?" Lauren said, her voice rising an octave.

"No, ma'am. I'm sorry. You're right, I shouldn't be joking at a time like this." Matthews glanced sideways at Bradley, who was focused on Lauren. "Was there anything else?"

"Isn't that enough?" Lauren said, stifling an urge to cry again, but failing.

Bradley reached over and pulled her close against his shoulder. "Deputy, how about getting Dr. Chambers a few tissues?"

Matthews frowned, then walked off, his stiff boots clunking against the wood floor as he went in search of a box of Kleenex.

"Lauren, you have to calm down. He's not going to listen to you if you yell at him."

She nodded and looked up to find Matthews approaching with a tissue box in his hands.

"Thanks," she said, pulling one out and wiping her eyes. "This has just been a tough time, with Michael gone. I didn't mean to yell at you."

"Not a problem, ma'am. I understand."

"I'll be right back," Bradley said, "I've got to go use the bathroom."

Lauren looked at Matthews. "I told Deputy Vork about a car that was following me last night, but he didn't seem to think it was important. Then my dog was in the house when I know I'd left him outside. The next morning, he was outside when I'd left him *in* the house with me the night before. With what's been going on, I'd think that person who was following me is doing these things, to drive me from my home."

"Now why would that person, assuming for a moment there is such a person, be doing that? What would he accomplish by driving you from your house?"

"Domination, power. I'm a psychologist, Deputy."

"So who is this person?"

Lauren looked down and shrugged. "I don't know."

"Why would he be trying to dominate you?"

"Some criminals get off on that. Like rape, it's all about power—"

"But we're not talking about rape here."

Lauren shrugged again, then looked up to see Bradley returning to the living room carrying a glass of water. He placed it on the coffee table in front of Lauren, who picked up the drink and took a sip. Staring into the glass, she said, "Rape could be his next step."

Matthews shook his head. "Ma'am, I don't mean to downplay—"

"Deputy," Bradley said, "can I have a word with you for a moment in the kitchen?"

Matthews nodded.

Bradley placed a hand on Lauren's shoulder. "Will you be okay here for a few moments?"

Lauren shrugged off his hand. "I'll be fine."

"I think she's gone off the deep end," Matthews said. "And you know I have to run that Colt." He looked at the kitchen table, where the gun had been lying. But it was no longer there.

"First things first," Bradley said. "I agree she's upset, emotional. Her husband's missing, so to me, her reaction is perfectly understandable given the circumstances. But I do think there's something really wrong here. There are too many coincidences—"

"What, that she thinks she put her dog in one place, but he's really in another? She can't remember that she finished a carton of milk? Or that her bedsheets are changed and she doesn't recall doing it?"

"I admit it sounds strange on the surface, but what if she's telling the truth?"

"I don't doubt she's telling the truth, Mr. Bradley. I just think she's under a lot of stress with her husband gone, and she isn't quite in touch with things. I'm sure she'd be the first one to admit it's taking a mental toll on her."

Bradley shook his head. "What if what she's telling us actually happened? Suppose whoever's responsible for her husband's disappearance is also behind what's been going on here?"

"That's a huge leap, first of all. We don't know

why her husband's not come back. Could be he's screwing around behind her back. Or he could be buried under a snowbank somewhere in Colorado."

"Those are possibilities, I agree. But if none of those scenarios are the real deal?"

"What would you like me to do, Mr. Bradley? We don't have the manpower to post a twenty-four-hour watch on her place."

"I just don't want you to wait until she disappears like her husband before you decide to do something."

Matthews regarded Bradley for a moment. "Fair enough. You got me. I'll put in a request for hourly drive-bys to make sure everything looks okay. Will that do?"

"Only your department can say if that's sufficient, Deputy. But I can tell you I'm sure Dr. Chambers will appreciate anything you can spare."

Matthews nodded, bid his good-byes to Lauren, and left.

"Hourly drive-bys aren't going to do much, are they?" Lauren asked.

Bradley, standing by the front door, leaned forward and peered out the peephole. "You never know. But if you're asking whether I think it means you can feel safe and secure, no, I wouldn't go that far."

Lauren nodded, then looked at the dog. "Tucker's my best security system."

"Except that someone's been in your house and Tucker hasn't stopped him."

Lauren was quiet.

Bradley turned away from the door and stepped into the living room. "I'm sorry."

"No, no. That's okay." She lifted her palms off her

knees and extended her hands. Tucker pushed up off the floor and bounded over to her. "It is kind of strange, though."

"Unless whoever's doing this is someone your dog knows."

"He doesn't know anyone well enough to be comfortable like that."

"For all you know, whoever's been handling Tucker could've been coming by your house every day when you weren't home, making friends with him, feeding him treats. Hell, even steak. No way that dog would turn on him. He'd be his buddy. If that's the case, this guy's a real pro."

Suddenly, Lauren's eyes widened. "That could be why he wasn't hungry tonight. I filled his bowl and he never ate."

"When the perp came over to change the sheets, he probably gave the dog a nice juicy meal."

Lauren crossed her arms in front of her chest and hugged herself. "I feel so violated. Dirty."

"I think you should consider staying somewhere else—like a motel, or a friend's place."

"I won't be driven from my home, Nick. That's what this sick bastard wants. That much I know, that much I understand."

"But I'm looking at it from a safety perspective. Maybe psychologically it appears that he's just trying to drive you from your home. But I think it's more than that. Each incident has grown bolder. It's as if he's playing with you. Almost torturing you. If he doesn't get what he's looking for, he may turn up the stakes a little bit."

"I'm not leaving my house, Nick." She said it staccato, as if each word deserved emphasis.

Bradley rubbed at the back of his neck, then sat down on the couch. "Why don't we talk about Michael for a moment. Did he have any enemies, financial problems, did he owe anyone any money—"

"None of that."

"You said at the meeting you'd written down the place where Michael had gone, but that you couldn't find it."

"I wrote it down on a magazine at my office, but a patient must've taken it. I went to Michael's company and found an E-mail on his computer from one of his buddies, the one I think who was organizing the trip. I replied to it and asked for his name and number."

"If you give me the E-mail, I can probably track him down through his Internet service provider, assuming it's not a Web-based E-mail address."

Lauren rose from the couch and walked back into the kitchen, where she found the handheld PC. She turned it on and began tapping the screen with the stylus, navigating through the software. "I went through his desk but couldn't find anything that would help."

"You don't mind if I go there myself and poke around?"

"Of course not."

She turned the PC toward Bradley, who pulled a pad from his pocket and jotted down the E-mail address. "This 'targard' could be a company name. I'll check it out."

"Don," Lauren said. "Or Dan. Maybe it was Dave."

"What?"

"One of his frat buddies. I just remembered Michael mentioning him once. I think it was Dan."

"I'll check into it. Do you know which fraternity it was?"

Lauren thought for a moment, then shook her head. "I checked through his stuff yesterday to see if I could find something, a plane reservation or a car rental confirmation number, or whatever. I didn't see anything with a fraternity logo on it, not even a pin or a shirt."

"I can do some legwork on it, but once I figure out which one he was a member of, I'll need Deputy Vork's help. Frats don't release rosters to anyone without a court order. But what about a yearbook? Maybe we can start there."

"I couldn't find one. He once told me he had a fire in his apartment just before we met. He lost most of his stuff."

Bradley clicked his pen shut. "How about your relationship with Michael?"

"What about it?"

"Were you two having problems, was it strained, that sort of thing."

She hesitated for a moment. "I've been thinking about that ever since Deputy Vork told me that most cases of missing husbands are actually men leaving their wives behind."

Bradley studied Lauren's expression for a moment. Her eyes were downcast, and she was fiddling with a small piece of paper in her hands. "Is that possible, Lauren? You've got to be honest with yourself here, and with me. No matter how painful it might seem."

"At first, no, I didn't. But now . . ." Lauren's eyes met Bradley's. "I guess it's possible."

"Do you want to talk about it?" Bradley waited for her to gather her thoughts.

"Are you playing therapist with me, Nick?"

"I've heard it helps." He smiled warmly.

"Michael had been a little down the past few months. I don't know how to describe it. And I didn't even see it that way until today. But maybe that's the whole problem. It's always about me, the focus is always on me, ever since we got married."

"Let's back up a minute. You said he seemed down. How so?"

"Restless. Bored." She shook her head. "I'm a damned psychologist and I couldn't even see the signs under my own nose."

Bradley placed a hand on hers. "How was he bored? You mean with you?"

"With everything. It all started with me. I ran into problems with my practice. Things didn't work out, and I ended up having to shut it down. I had a bad time with it, accepting it, you know? I lapsed into a nasty depression, I was prone to panic attacks ... Michael had to leave his job in San Francisco."

"That could've been a positive for him. The commute's a bear."

"It was a huge negative. He was a software engineer for an upstart Internet company that had incredible potential. He said that one day we'd hit it big and money would never be an issue for us. He was excited, passionate about his work. That's why he never cared about the commute. He would stay over some nights, when he had to work late. They had a cot in the back room where a few of them would sleep." She sat there for a moment, staring off at the wall before continuing. "He left that job because he needed to be home for me every night. I wasn't doing well and he didn't want to be that far away."

"Do you think he resented you for it?"

Lauren snorted. "Michael would grin and bear it, never let on that he was upset or disappointed. But about a year and a half after he left the company, they went public and the remaining partners took in fifty million apiece. And where was Michael? Working that dead-end job he found with Cablecast. When he left the Internet company, we needed money right away. Cablecast had an opening for a network account manager. He jumped at it and that was it. About six months later I was well enough to take a counseling job with the state. Of course, Michael arranged that one for me, too." She shook her head. "He's done everything for me. And I just let him do it."

"So he gave up an exciting, stimulating career for something that was boring with little room for advancement or personal growth. It would be only natural for him to have developed resentment, don't you think?"

"I didn't see it at the time, but now . . ." She looked down at her lap. "I'd have to say it wasn't just professional boredom. Michael was born in Los Angeles, he loved city life. When we met, I had a job that was tied to Placerville and he was just starting work with the company in San Francisco. Cost of living was much less here, and it reminded me of my home, in Wyoming. He missed the city, its excitement. I shouldn't have forced him into living such a quiet life. It just wasn't him."

"That said," Bradley softly remarked, "I think you should take a minute and consider the possibility that maybe Michael did just leave . . ."

Lauren was quiet for a moment, but then shook her head. "It just doesn't feel right. I can't explain it, but I really believe that Michael's not here because he *can't* be, Nick, not because he doesn't want to be."

Bradley nodded. "Okay. Then we need to get started on trying to find Michael instead of waiting for him to find us. I'll go to Cablecast, poke around a little, then look into his buddy's E-mail address and see what I can do to narrow down where he went in Colorado. I know you said it was near Vail, but you can cross-country ski practically anywhere there's snow, so it could be tough. But we may get lucky and catch a break. At some point, I might need to go there, but I've got a friend who can get some of the legwork done for me. I'll look into the fraternity, then check with the airlines and monitor your credit cards in case Michael or someone using his card makes a purchase. All the standard missing person stuff. You say he wants to be found. Fine, then I'll assume you're right. But if I start seeing otherwise, I'm going to tell you that, too."

Through glassy, red eyes, Lauren said, "I understand."

"I've got some herbal stuff that works for me when I have a tough time sleeping." He dug into his left pocket and pulled out a small black film canister. "I always keep some in my glove compartment. In my line of work, I find myself sleeping on a lot of crappy motel beds." He popped open the lid and handed her a couple of brown capsules. "Take these and you'll have a restful sleep. Looks like you can use it."

"What is it?"

"Valerian root extract. All natural, don't worry."

Lauren took the pills and washed them down with the glass of water. "How long till they take effect?"

"About twenty minutes." Bradley stood and stretched

his legs. "I'll be right back, I have to dig your Colt out of the dishwasher." He smiled. "Better there than in the deputy's car getting run for a license he's probably not going to find." He winked and walked out of the room.

In the kitchen, Bradley pulled the Colt from the silverware tray in the dishwasher, opened the cylinder and gave it a spin: six rounds were loaded. He snapped it closed and walked back into the living room, where Lauren was lying on the couch, her head resting against the back cushion, her arms splayed out and her eyes closed.

Bradley inserted the Colt into his front jeans pocket. He looked down at Tucker, who was lying beside Lauren's feet. "Guess she didn't need the pills, huh, boy?" The dog's ears bobbed up and down with Bradley's voice, but Tucker did not move.

Bradley bent over in front of Lauren, placed her arms over his shoulders, and lifted her swiftly and carefully off the couch. He carried her upstairs and laid her in bed, then slipped her shoes off and pulled the covers over her body. He saw the floral sheets and instantly understood why she didn't like them.

Tucker lay on the wood floor at the foot of the bed. Bradley stood there for a moment, watching the gentle rise and fall of Lauren's chest. Then he hit the light switch and bathed the room in darkness.

TEN

Michael Chambers was sitting on the cot staring off into the pitch-black of the room. *What is it with roses?* he thought as he recalled yet another dream about the fragrant flower. *Am I a florist?*

He swung his legs off the bed and found a light switch on the wall. A bank of bright fluorescents hummed to life, causing him to snap his eyes shut. He wondered how long he had been asleep, then cracked his eyes open to look for a wall clock. He had been awoken by a police officer—no, a security guard—looking for a patient. But how long ago had that been?

There was no clock in the room, but there was a phone. He lifted the handset and asked the hospital operator for the time: it was five-fifteen in the evening. He fished around in his shirt pocket and found the receipt from the doctors' lounge where he had eaten. It was time-stamped 2:02 P.M. He felt tired, but not exhausted, which was an improvement. The nap had done him some good.

He called information and a moment later was speaking with the Yellow Cabs dispatcher. He requested that a taxi meet him at the front entrance of the hospital in ten minutes.

"I need you to be on time," Chambers said. "But I

want you to wait for me in case I get delayed. If I'm not there, I'll be on my way."

After receiving assurances the driver would be given his instructions, he hung up.

Chambers quickly combed his fingers through his hair, then stepped out of the room. A couple of doctors were standing by the nurses' station, signing patient charts. Except for an elderly woman shuffling along with an IV stand, the rest of the corridor was empty.

As he made his way down the hall, he made eye contact with one of the nurses and nodded, figuring that a direct approach would be less conspicuous than avoiding her gaze and appearing shifty. Once down the corridor, he pilfered a patient chart that was hanging in a holder on a door and carried it with him into the elevator. He pretended to be absorbed in a printout of diagnostic test results as he descended the floors, the doors eventually opening at the main level.

He stepped out of the elevator with a doctor and a nurse. The physician headed left toward the emergency room, and the nurse matched him stride for stride in the direction of the front entrance. Through the clear glass doors, he saw the taxi pulling up to the curb. But he slowed his pace when he caught sight of the security guard stationed off to the right.

Chambers closed the patient chart, tucked it beneath his arm, and strode confidently toward the doors. As he passed the guard, he threw a quick half smile at the man and continued on, out into the cold night air. With only a pair of hospital scrubs covering his skin, gooseflesh immediately popped out across his arms. He calmly sat down in the warm backseat of the cab and slammed the door shut.

"Okay, Doc, where are we going?" asked the cabbie. He had a walrus mustache and a dash of silver in his wavy black hair.

Realizing he had not formulated a plan, Chambers directed his gaze downward, toward the seat. He could ask for a Laundromat and hope that someone who happened to be of similar build was doing his laundry. Or, he could try to steal a pair of pants and a shirt from a store. Either way, there were risks.

"Where's the nearest mall?" he asked.

The driver smiled. "Three blocks down. You didn't need a cab to take you three blocks."

"That's okay. My car's down and I don't have long before I have to be . . . back in surgery."

The cabbie nodded and pulled away from the curb. Chambers knew he did not have any money to pay for the ride—let alone to buy clothes with—but he did have one thing of value: appearance and presumption.

As the man pulled up in front of Macy's, Chambers leaned across the bench seat and told him he would be back in fifteen or twenty minutes. The driver nodded and shifted the car into park as Chambers left the cab and headed into the mall.

He found a directory and quickly scanned the list of potential targets. He wanted a store that was large enough that he could put the clothing on without having to check into a fitting room suite, where an employee might be counting the number of items with which he entered—and exited.

Macy's was his best bet. He strode into men's casual wear and made a quick assessment of the available sales staff. One clerk was at the register with a customer and one was straightening and refolding clothing on a display. Since he was already somewhat conspicuous in hospital scrubs, he knew he needed to be fast and be out.

Surveying the display of Badge jeans, he picked a stonewashed pair—they'd be harder to tell new from used—and grabbed a 34 waist, hoping it would fit. He yanked off the large cardboard placards that were fastened to the rear pocket with clear nylon filament and bent down behind a rack that displayed sweatshirts.

Checking again that the sales staff was busy and that no customers were in sight, he kicked his tennis shoes off and slipped the jeans on over the scrubs, not an easy feat with his thigh throbbing and the stitches pulling. Although he could have used a 33, they fit well enough so as not to attract attention. He pulled a gray sweatshirt off the table in front of him, used his teeth to break off the tag, and slipped the garment over his head.

He shoved his tennis shoes back on and faced the task of having to somehow bend over to tie the laces. He was able to knot the right by resting his foot on the display, but there was no way he could lift the left to do the same. Gingerly, he knelt down as far as he could, resting his head against the display for balance. He tied a quick knot, then pulled himself up and glanced around to see if anyone was watching.

Convinced he had remained unnoticed, he moved off into the sportswear department in search of a jacket, where he found himself staring at a full-size fashion photo in the adjacent lingerie section of a twenty-something woman smelling a red rose. *Rose*—

"Can I help you?" The voice was sweet and youthful. Chambers turned and a woman in her early thirties was standing there, her eyebrows raised. "Uh, I'm looking for the entrance to the mall."

She directed him out of the store, and a couple of minutes later he was moving past the various cart vendors who had set up shop along the center of the ground-floor walkway. The one selling fresh cut flowers caught his attention. He was greeted by a thin woman holding an arrangement of long-stemmed roses accented by a smattering of baby's breath. She smiled broadly and locked eyes with Chambers. "Would you like a bouquet for your loved one? It's only eleven ninety-nine . . ."

Chambers was staring at the roses, mesmerized by the deep crimson velvet of the petals. He shook his head, then backed away from the woman, who had turned her attention to the next customer standing at her booth. He turned and bumped into a blue kiosk with the AT&T globe logo emblazoned on the side. He stood there reading the advertisement scrolling across the computer screen: "It's all within your reach." His eyes glided down to the keyboard, where instructions were mounted: "To access the Internet via AT&T WorldNet Service®, swipe your credit card in the slot to the left . . ."

The Internet.

Chambers sat down in the seat and watched as the words scrolled by him: "Send or retrieve E-mail messages, surf the Web, make purchases . . ." He looked down at the console again. "Set up your own free Hotmail® Internet E-mail account. Just log on . . ."

Chambers glanced at the screen. *It's all within your reach.*

He shook his head. *That's what we have at the office.*

WorldNet. The office—what office? He slammed his fist down on the console and tried to concentrate.

All within your reach.

Roses.

No, just rose.

Just Rose.

Then it hit him: just_rose@hotmail. Yes, that was familiar. But what did it mean? Was it his own E-mail address? A friend's? His mother's? A girlfriend's? Who was Rose?

Chambers let his eyes roam around the mall. He needed a credit card. He headed toward the other end of the mall, then entered a Dillard's department store. He wound his way to the women's petite section, where he chose a rack that provided an adequate view of the cashier. Waiting for the right moment to approach, he watched four women come and go, only one of whom had placed her credit card on the counter in such a position that he could have safely taken it. But it was a proprietary Dillard's card, and it would not have done him any good.

Just then, the cashier placed a Citibank Master-Card on the countertop and moved to lift the phone. Chambers quickly made his way toward the register and placed his hands on the counter—his right hand covering the credit card.

As the woman hung up, he excused himself. "Which way to the parking lot?" He reasoned that when they finally realized he was the one who had taken the charge card, they would first search the place they thought he was headed: to a car, out back, in the lot.

"Behind you, just past the shoe department." He

turned to look where she was pointing, as did the woman whose card he was now palming.

"You sure it's not that way?" he asked, pointing in the opposite direction as he slipped the card into his front pocket.

The woman forced a smile, trying to mask her impatience. "I'm sure. It's back that way, behind you."

"Must've gotten turned around," Chambers said as he flashed an embarrassed smile. He turned and quickly made his way down the aisle in the direction of the parking lot. As soon as he was out of view, he circled around the store and headed back toward the mall.

As Chambers was approaching men's sportswear, he heard an announcement over the public address system. "Security to women's petite, security to women's petite." He grabbed a blue baseball cap, tore the tag off, and pulled it down over his head.

A minute later he was back in the mall, hobbling toward the AT&T kiosk. He was only hoping he could swipe the card before the bank put a hold on the number. Even if the woman—Ellen Haskins, according to the name on the card—reported the theft immediately, he figured it would take a few moments for them to take the information and freeze the account.

Only a few steps away now, he could see that the chair was occupied by a youth about eighteen years old.

"Hey, you going to be long?" Chambers asked, trying to allow some of the urgency to pervade his voice.

"A few more minutes," the youth said, keeping his face glued to the screen.

Chambers glanced around. He waited another few

seconds, then leaned over the teen's shoulder. "Look, I need to log on, get a message out. It's real important."

"Hang a second, dude, and I'll finish my surfing. Just checkin' the scores. ESPN's got this cool site, everything you need—"

"That's great. But this is urgent. I need to get on-line."

"If it's that important, why didn't you just bring a laptop," the kid said, brushing the long, stringy hair off his face.

Chambers didn't answer. As the teenager pointed and clicked with the trackball, Chambers looked around, back toward Dillard's, to make sure the search for him wasn't spilling into the mall.

"'Kay, dude, it's yours." The youth stood and shuffled off, his baggy jeans rubbing against themselves as he headed away from the kiosk.

Chambers settled into the seat, held his breath, and swiped Ellen Haskins's card. A few seconds passed. He suddenly became aware of his heart thumping as he peered around the edge of the kiosk, expecting to see security guards heading his way.

Just then, an acknowledgment popped up on the screen. The WorldNet homepage came into focus and he clicked on the Hotmail banner that advertised free E-mail. He zipped through a series of welcome and registration screens until he was confronted with the field that asked for his name and a user ID, which would become his E-mail address. He thought for a second, then chose lost_in_virginia@hotmail.com as his address. Finally, he was logged in as a registered user. He hit the COMPOSE MESSAGE link and waited for the screen to appear.

With his fingers poised over the keyboard, he took a second to glance around the mall. Two men in dark suits were a little past Dillard's, their heads rubbernecking back and forth.

Walking in his direction.

No doubt looking for him.

ELEVEN

Douglas Knox was pacing his expansive suite at FBI headquarters, one of several offices in the high-security area known as Mahogany Row, so named because of its wood paneling.

Up six steps, back six steps. Before turning, Knox would glance out his window at downtown D.C., then spin and resume his pacing. Each time, the same number of steps. A path had been worn into his carpet twice in the past two years, and it was scheduled to be replaced again by building maintenance once the current crises were resolved.

As he made his umpteenth pass in front of the window, his phone buzzed. "Agents Waller and Haviland to see you, sir."

"Send them in." He put his hands on his hips and barely waited until they had passed through the door. "Well?"

Haviland cocked his head a bit, shot a glance at Waller, and shrugged. "LaserJet 6, standard Hammer-mill copy paper, probably purchased—"

"On the fucking East Coast in a Staples office supply store. Yeah, I know that shit. Anything I don't know?"

"Aside from your prints, it was totally clean, sir," Waller said. "No saliva on the stamp or envelope. Must've used a sponge."

"Must've used a sponge. That's all you can give me? The best fucking crime lab in the world and you tell me the perp used a fucking sponge?" Knox punched the intercom button on his phone. "Liz, I want to see the Lab Section chief in my office in ten minutes. And the deputy assistant director." He slammed the handset down and turned back to Waller. "What kind of sponge, what trace elements were in the damn water they used to wet the sponge? You understand what I'm saying? I can't believe none of this was done."

"It might have been, sir. I've only got a preliminary report. The tests are all run sequentially—"

"Don't try to cover for the section chief," Knox ordered. "Just give me your report."

"Alternate Light Source has been completed," Haviland added, "without result. Questioned Documents is scouring every sixteenth of an inch of the paper for indented writing and anything else that'll tell us who sent it."

"If there's a speck of dirt embedded in the fibers, I want to know the origin of the mineral composition of the goddamned dirt." Knox paused for a moment, then started to pace again. "What about the postmark? I want the postal inspectors flown in from California. Am I making myself clear?"

Waller nodded. "Postal inspector is en route, sir."

"Anything back from Division Six?"

"The Profiling Unit just completed their threat analysis." Haviland handed Knox the hastily prepared report. Knox took it and tossed it on his desk.

"And, what's their risk assessment?"

Haviland cleared his throat. "They concluded that it's extremely valid. Based on all known information, they gave it a rating of Good credibility and a High

level of risk. The fact that they had your home
address, gained access to your yard, and had knowledge of Mrs. Knox's personal habits all indicated a
high degree of preparation and sophistication."
Haviland paused, but Knox's pacing continued without a break in stride.

"On Division Six's recommendation," Waller said,
"we've initiated a full-scale investigation. As we
speak, I'm having the phone records and list of visitors to Anthony Scarponi pulled, which should—"

"Scarponi?" Knox stopped pacing and faced the
agents.

"The Viper," Haviland said, "the international hit
man—"

"I know who he is, Agent Haviland."

"Sir," Waller said, "with all due respect, we believe
there's a strong indication Scarponi is behind this.
Word on the street is that Scarponi put a contract out
on Harper Payne six years ago. Payne's the only one
who can hurt him. He gets rid of Payne, his problem's
solved." Waller stopped, no doubt allowing his comments to fester a moment on the director's brain.

Knox turned and looked out the window at the
city. "I agree with your assessment. But keep your
eyes open. Scarponi may be the most obvious, but I
don't want to ignore other possibilities. Am I clear?"

"Yes, sir," Waller said.

"Scarponi's got to be under surveillance," Haviland
said. "I can check with the marshal, find out who's in
charge of his case, find out who he's called. That
might help us rule him in or out as a suspect."

"I'll handle it," Knox said.

"Sir, you don't need to be burdened with that. I
can—"

"I said I'll handle it, Agent Haviland," Knox said firmly.

"Yes, sir."

"I won't let them have the upper hand. Regardless who it is, I'm not giving them Payne." Even though Knox knew that was the proper response, his voice wavered slightly, as if he might actually consider trading the life of Harper Payne—a man he had never met face-to-face—for the life of a member of his family. He wondered for a second if the two agents had picked up on the slight unevenness of his voice. "Not that I have Payne to give them, even if I wanted to."

"No, sir," Haviland said.

Knox turned to face them. "Status."

"After our initial contact two days ago," Waller said, "we've not been able to locate him. There's a report of someone possibly matching his description at Virginia Presbyterian, and SAC Lindsey has sent a contingent of agents over. That's our only lead."

"Have Lindsey get four agents from my security detail over to my house, separate cars, round the clock. My wife leaves, I want two of them with her. Get another two on my daughter. She's a sophomore at Georgetown. And get every available agent on this investigation. I want answers and I want them fast. Lindsey has a problem, have him call me—no, have ADIC Maguire call me."

Waller was nodding. "Yes, sir. Do you want Metro PD alerted—"

"No, I want this handled internally." Knox was aware that it wasn't every day that two special agents were called into the director's office. They didn't have any new information of substance to offer him, and they certainly didn't have the answers he wanted.

Knox knew they were shitting in their pants. But he didn't care. He wanted information, answers, results.

Control.

He turned back to the window, sighed deeply, and bowed his head. "I'm making you two personally responsible for finding Payne."

"Yes, sir," they answered simultaneously. Waller cleared his throat. "Sir, about Scarponi—"

"If he's involved, I will personally see to it—" Knox stopped, focused his eyes on the cars crawling along Pennsylvania Avenue, seven stories below. "If he's responsible for this letter, he's declaring war, gentlemen. Witness Protection or not, Harper Payne is still one of ours."

Five minutes after Waller and Haviland had left his office, Knox turned away from the window. He reached across his desk and hit the intercom button. "Elizabeth, a moment please."

Seconds later, Knox's assistant, Liz Evanston, entered with pen and pad in hand. She was a thick woman of sixty, silver hair coifed and trimmed to perfection, just like her work. Liz had been the FBI director's personal assistant since 1968. Having started her employment under J. Edgar Hoover, she knew the ins and outs of how to find information within the Bureau, and because of that she was an invaluable resource. As each director came and went, she was one constant that maintained continuity and helped keep the director's office running smoothly.

"Find out what you can on Agents Jonathan Waller and Scott Haviland. They're out of WFO," he said, referring to the Bureau's Washington Field Office.

"SAC Lindsey should be able to tell you everything you need to know about them."

"With all due respect, sir, I disagree." It was the exact language and tone she had used with each of the prior directors, and it always seemed to work.

"Who do you think you should speak with?"

"Their squad supervisor, Sam Gardner."

"Gardner. Yeah, you're right. He'd have a better feel for these two than Lindsey would."

"And he'll tell me a lot more than SAC Lindsey."

"You're too good, Liz, you know that?"

"Yes, sir, I do. I'll have that information for you shortly." She turned and walked out, a smile hovering at the corners of her mouth.

An hour later, after having met with the Lab Section chief and deputy assistant director, Knox was still pacing by the window, running his fingers through his hair. First the left hand, then the right. When he finished one stroke, he would start again with the other hand. He had a trump card to play, and he was thinking hard about using it. Two men, Hector DeSantos and Brian Archer, members of the elite Operations Support Intelligence Group, were at his disposal should he need them. But timing was everything. And in this case the big question was when to bring them on board.

Just then, his intercom buzzed. "I have that information for you, sir."

"Bring it in, Liz."

She walked in and headed for the window, positioning herself in Knox's path, as she always did, to prevent him from pacing. "According to ASAC Gardner," Liz reported, "Agent Waller has an impeccable record.

He heads up the division's Fugitive Squad. He's dedicated, bright, committed, and very driven."

"And off the record?"

She glanced down at her notepad. "He can sometimes be a little volatile, get swept into the emotions of a case and take it personally. If it's a case he feels strongly about or gets frustrated with, he has a tendency to disregard standard protocols."

"To the point of jeopardizing the success of the mission?"

"He's never crossed the line, at least according to Gardner. No reprimands have made it into the file, so Gardner is either telling the truth or he's handled it internally."

Knox turned and again looked out his window at the cars moving along Pennsylvania Avenue. "What about Haviland?"

She consulted her notes again. "More cerebral and by the book than Waller. He takes his work seriously and doesn't take chances. Gardner likes to partner them up whenever possible because Haviland has a calming influence on Waller. My take is that Haviland keeps Waller in line when he's dangerously near the edge of crossing over it."

"So why did Lindsey send these two over?"

"Mainly because Agent Waller heads up the Fugitive Squad. His specialty is tracking down difficult-to-find people. Also, according to Gardner, they knew Agent Payne fairly well. They worked with him for a while before he went undercover."

Knox nodded, turned, and began to pace in the opposite direction. He had heard enough, and it was his way of telling Liz that he did not require her presence anymore.

"Fugitive Squad or not, Agent Waller may not be the right person for this assignment," she said.

Knox stopped and looked out over the District again. He remained there for a moment, stoic and silent. Liz took the hint and placed her notes on the director's desk.

"Nice work," Knox said to the glass.

"Yes, sir. Let me know if you need anything else." Liz closed the director's office door on her way out.

After hearing the lock click, Knox walked over to his desk and picked up Liz's notes. He made one more run through the information, then shoved the pages through the shredder.

TWELVE

"S hit."

Michael Chambers broke out into a cold sweat. If the men in suits were indeed coming for him, he didn't have much time. He turned his attention to the keyboard and began tapping out a message.

Rose—
I need your help. I was in a car accident and I can't remember who I am, where I'm supposed to be, or even who you are. For some reason your name kept popping into my head, and then I remembered what I think is your email address. Can you tell me who I am? There's not much I can tell you about me, other than what I look like. I'm about six feet tall, medium build, dark brown hair, and hazel eyes I think. My waist is a 33.

He paused, glanced back to check on the approaching men. His eyes found them, no more than twenty yards away now. But they didn't have the appearance of store security personnel, and they obviously were not the cops who had been searching for him in the hospital.

Maybe they weren't looking for him after all.

I'm in Virginia, in a mall near Virginia
Presbyterian Hospital. If you know who I am,
please write me back ASAP.
—Lost in Virginia

Chambers entered a few other variations on the
"rose" theme of the E-mail address in case his jumbled memory was incorrect. He quickly scrolled
down, hit SEND, and received the MESSAGE SENT confirmation.

He logged off and peered around the edge of the
kiosk. The men—whoever they were—were now a
few strides away. He pulled the bill of the hat lower
on his face and slid out of the seat, strolling casually
down the other side of the mall, in the opposite direction of the men.

He had walked no more than twenty paces when
he realized he had left Ellen Haskins's MasterCard at
the AT&T kiosk. He stopped and turned to look in
the direction from which he had just come and
noticed the two suits huddling over the Internet terminal.

*Okay, store security. All they want is the credit card.
Slap on the wrist probably. I'll explain the amnesia and
that'll be that.*

Chambers turned and headed off in the direction
of Dillard's, where he would leave the mall and grab
the taxi that was waiting for him. He had gone
another five yards when two other men in navy blue
suits suddenly stepped out in front of him. As one of
them held up a two-way radio to his mouth,
Chambers spun and ran off, back in the direction
from which he had just come.

Within seconds, his path was blocked by the original two men, the tall one holding Ellen Haskins's credit card in his hand. The shorter man locked eyes with Chambers and pressed the button on his two-way.

"We've got him."

THIRTEEN

Chambers could feel his heart pounding in his ears. This was not mall security. This was trouble. Big trouble. Those instincts he had had in the hospital emergency room kicked in again, and he instantly felt he had to find a way out.

To his immediate right was the flower stand he had passed earlier. It was now his only means of exit. With a store to his left and the men in front of and behind him, there was no other choice. He bolted right, jumping and grabbing on to the post of the ornate display wagon. Under all his weight and momentum, the cart started to tip over. With a huge crash, the potted plants and floral arrangements spilled across the floor behind him, blocking the entire walkway.

Chambers darted down that side of the mall, the two men who were not blocked by the downed cart in close pursuit. They were frantically shouting orders into their radios, no doubt attempting to line up coverage in and around the area in anticipation of their suspect's next move.

Chambers turned and headed into Dillard's, suddenly becoming aware of the pulling pain in his thigh. Limping slightly, he moved in an irregular, weaving manner through men's sportswear, suits, and casual wear. Angles and distance, he told himself, were the most effective ways of eluding a pursuer. But how did he know that?

He fought off a swell of dizziness, then dumped the baseball hat, grabbed a windbreaker off a hanger, and ripped off the tags. After slipping the jacket on in one motion, he moved left toward the exit—and slammed into a man in a suit. They both fell backward, Chambers landing against a display table of jeans, on his left, sutured thigh. He let out a low grunt, then realized he was in trouble as the man parted his suit coat.

Is he reaching for a gun?

Chambers leaned back on the table and fully extended his right leg in a swift uppercut, his tennis shoe connecting hard with the man's jaw. The man reeled backward, striking his head on a coatrack before crumpling to the floor. Blood oozed immediately from a gash on the left side of his face, where Chambers saw a white wire connected to an earpiece that had become dislodged.

Chambers stepped around the fallen man and continued on toward the exit. Nothing at the moment made any sense, but for now all that was protecting him were his instincts.

With his hands shoved deep into the pockets of his windbreaker, Chambers walked briskly toward the cab, which was still waiting at the curb where he had left it. As he approached from behind the first line of parked cars, he noticed that the driver was now wearing a baseball hat. The top two buttons of his pea coat were open, revealing a white dress shirt unbuttoned at the collar.

And he no longer had a mustache.

Chambers immediately turned right and headed down the next aisle, attempting to lose himself amongst the cars. He was reasonably sure that the driver had not seen him; if he had, he would have radioed his suited buddies, and another car would be waiting for Chambers as he emerged from the aisle.

He turned right again and moved through the lot. A moment later, with apparently no one following him, he reached the edge of the mall's property. He crossed a small maintenance driveway and headed toward what appeared to be a main street a block away, where a Mobil station occupied the nearest corner. But before he had gotten far, he heard the swerve of tires moving quickly on pavement. He ducked down behind a brick wall that was part of an adjacent building and watched as three dark sedans sped by.

After they had passed, Chambers moved out from the cover of the wall and continued on, crossing the street. He walked quickly, the pain in his leg stinging with each stride. He entered the station's minimart and caught sight of the very visible video surveillance cameras mounted near the ceiling in the corners of the store. They all appeared to be aimed at the cash register, which is where, he figured, most of the substantial crimes occurred. He grabbed a small bottle of Excedrin off a shelf and sauntered around the shop, pretending to browse. He glanced out the window, scanning the area. He then palmed the bottle and shoved it deep into his pocket.

Chambers headed outside and nonchalantly walked past three of the cars that were parked around the same island. He caught a glimpse of keys in two of them, so he had a choice. A burly man was standing by a Ford Escort, while a young woman was leaning against the back of a Chevrolet Tracker SUV. The decision was easy.

Chambers sauntered up to the Tracker, grabbed the door handle, and yanked it open. He turned the engine over and was shifting into drive when he heard the woman scream. In the side-view mirror, he saw the large Escort owner turn and head toward the Tracker. Chambers accelerated hard and swerved out of the station, gasoline spewing into the air as the hose twisted and writhed like a snake.

He entered the interstate and took the SUV up to sixty-five. There was about a half tank of gas, so for the moment that was not a concern. His priority was putting some distance between himself and those men at the mall, before they could zero in on him. He also knew it would only be a matter of minutes before the state troopers were alerted to the stolen Tracker. The faster he got off the main drag, the better, but only after he could first gain some distance.

He exited at the first opportunity, took the loop around, and headed back onto the interstate in the opposite direction. If anything, those witnesses who had seen him entering west would cause the police to look in that direction. If he was now headed east, it might buy him some time. Time and distance . . . and soon he would add angles.

Tooling along at fifty-five—he didn't want to violate the speed limit and get caught on a routine moving violation—Chambers reached into his pocket, pulled out the Excedrin bottle, and ripped off the protective plastic wrapping with his teeth. He popped a couple of the tablets into his mouth and swallowed them.

After driving for another fifteen minutes, he jug-handled off the interstate and found a quiet two-lane switchback that curved abruptly around a hillside. As he negotiated the turns, a hard rain began to slam against the windshield. He searched for the wiper control, a difficult task since the truck's interior, and the winding road, were both dark.

Chambers turned on the interior lights, quickly bent his head down, and found the wiper switch. When he looked up, another bout of dizziness struck and his vision faded to a hazy gray, like a television tuned to an off channel. He slammed on the brakes and felt the vehicle swerve. The front tires skipped and groaned along the slick, wet asphalt, finally grip-ping just before the wheels slid off the edge of the roadway.

He knew he would be better off pulling into the next available turnout and resting. But he wanted a little more distance, and the farther he went along this road, the narrower and less traveled it got. He continued on for another few minutes, trying hard to focus and maintain control of the vehicle. Light-headed, hungry, and tired, he breathed a sigh of relief as he finally spotted a dirt turnout along the embank-ment. He carefully edged the Tracker off the road and shut the engine. He reclined the seat and glanced at the dashboard clock: it was five minutes after seven. He could rest for an hour or so, drive back toward a populated area, dump the SUV, and hitch a ride.

As he was going over the plan in his mind, he drifted off to sleep.

FOURTEEN

Lauren awoke with a start, bolting up in bed as if a gunshot had been fired outside her window. The sun was just starting to bathe the sky in orange light, and the house was quiet. Tucker stood up and walked over to her side of the bed, placed his head on her hand, and waited for her attention.

Lauren realized she was wearing her clothing from last night. *Last night* . . . she tried to remember what had happened, where she was. She noticed the rough floral sheets, then thought of Deputy Matthews and Nick Bradley.

She swung her legs off the bed and headed downstairs, where she found Bradley lying on the couch, his shoes on the floor by the coffee table.

"Morning," he said.

Lauren noticed his tired eyes and sat down on the chair beside the sofa. "You look like you got very little sleep."

He managed a smile. "Less than that." He moved his legs onto the floor and stood, stretching his body skyward. "I wanted to make sure you were okay. Since you didn't want to leave your house, there was only one other alternative."

"I can't thank you enough. I remember Matthews leaving last night, but not much else."

"I went into the kitchen to get your gun, and you were out before I got back." He reached into the waistband of his pants. "Speaking of which, here's your Colt."

Lauren looked at it a moment and hesitated, then took it.

"Be careful with it. It's loaded."

"I'm the one who loaded it." She flipped the barrel open, spun it, then clicked it shut. "I know how to handle it."

"I can see that." He reached over and began to put his shoes on. "Just remember, if you pull it out, you're shooting to kill. Hesitate, and you're giving your target a free shot at you. And I guarantee you *he* will be shooting to kill."

Lauren nodded. "I know. My daddy used to tell me that. Actually, *tell* isn't the right word. *Ordered*, or *commanded*, might be more accurate."

"Sounds like he taught you right." Bradley finished tying his left shoe, then arose. "Well, I'd better get to my office, start making some calls. Get the wheels in motion." He regarded her haggard appearance for a second and hesitated. "Will you be okay by yourself? You can come with me to my office—"

"It's broad daylight, I'm sure I'll be fine."

"You've got my number. Call me if anything doesn't seem right to you. Anything, okay?"

She smiled. "Okay."

"I'll be back in the evening, say around six."

"Thanks. For everything."

Bradley headed toward the back door. "If I find out anything about Michael, I'll call you. Otherwise, stay alert and be aware of your surroundings."

After she heard the door close, the quiet of the

house made her feel uneasy. She held the Colt in her hand and felt the weight of the weapon. Aiming it at the door, she lined up the sight with the knob.

"Shoot to kill," she said.

Lauren spent the morning and early afternoon at the Neighborhood Watch Center, a makeshift room that had once been a sheriff's department storage closet that Carla Mae had commandeered two years ago. It provided a base of operations for the organization, complete with its own phone line and answering machine, small rolltop desk and chair.

Because of its cramped quarters, Lauren sat just outside the room. Throughout the day, she fielded calls providing leads and reported sightings of Michael that led nowhere. Finally, with her frustration building, she left the sheriff's department and drove forty-five minutes to Sacramento. Though the ride was difficult for her, she divided the trip into manageable units with brief rest stops at a couple of freeway-accessible gas stations. With Elton John blaring from the speakers, she managed to maintain control over her anxieties.

Her first stop was the Cordova Shooting Center, where she polished her rusty skills. Lauren did well by all measures, except her own, which was nothing short of perfection. The target was ripped to shreds directly over the spot representing the heart, where her father had taught her to aim. But a number of other shots had missed their mark. If she had fifteen bullets and an ample amount of time to shoot at a still target, her assailant would be dead many times over. But if he was in motion, and she only had the six rounds she expected to have in her revolver, she could not be assured of disabling her enemy. And that bothered her.

But it didn't bother her as much as having to rely on the weapon for her safety. She wished she could toss it in the river, put that part of her life behind her. But like a bad dream, it would not release its grip. The memories were too strong. She remembered the days when her father had taken her to the open field on the land they had owned in Wyoming. She was much too young to be handling a gun, but after the experience with the intruder, her father wanted to make sure she was prepared to defend herself. In an eerie way, he seemed to know that he was not going to be around in the coming years to look after her.

She recalled one day in particular when she was having difficulty hitting the beer can target. "When it counts," he had told her, "you'll get the job done, sweet thing. You'll be in control, you'll know how to handle the gun. All you've got to do is keep calm. And shoot to kill . . . because your enemy won't be showing you no mercy, that much I guarantee you. Trust your daddy on that."

Lauren realized she was sitting in her car, staring ahead at nothing in particular. The memory of her father's voice was soothing, almost cathartic for her. She started the engine and headed back to the freeway. Fifteen minutes later, she arrived at the California Department of Justice building, a sprawling, modern facility that housed a horde of agencies with more than two thousand employees. She parked in the visitors' lot in the back and pulled her raincoat tight across her body as the brisk winter wind blew hard against her face.

A moment later, the guard in the large bulletproof

security booth was regarding her driver's license. "You say you've got a three o'clock with someone in Missing Persons?"

Lauren nodded. "Ilene Mara."

The guard lifted a phone and spoke into the receiver in a muffled tone that Lauren could barely hear. He hung up and handed her a card to fill out.

"Give this back to me when you're done," he said. "I'll have someone escort you to Missing Persons."

Lauren slid the completed form back through an opening in the thick glass and waited as the man read it over, filed it in a slot, and handed her a red visitor's pass. She glanced up at the black-and-white video monitors that lined the wall behind the guard. They displayed views of the vast parking lot as well as various landmarks in the building.

Just then, a buzzer sounded and the metal door to the left of the security station snapped open with an electronic click. "Mrs. Chambers, I'll take you back to see Ms. Mara now." A young man in his late twenties with a prominently displayed identification placard clipped to his shirt was standing in the doorway.

With her escort, Lauren walked the halls of the building, noticing the photos and artifacts that were displayed in glass enclosures depicting important triumphs in law enforcement.

They took the stairs up to the third floor and entered the Missing/Unidentified Persons Department, where the escort introduced Lauren to a lady standing nearby.

"You're here for Ilene?" the woman asked.

Lauren nodded. "I'm a little early."

"Have a seat, I'll let her know you're here."

Lauren's gaze immediately took in the harried

activity of the large room. Telephones rang, intercoms buzzed, voices murmured. She dabbed at her clammy forehead, closed her eyes, and took a deep breath. Shutting out her surroundings, she gathered herself and then opened her eyes. Mazes of cubicles filled the entire suite, the kind that can be rearranged easily and quickly depending on need. Judging by the intense wear marks in the carpet lining the aisles, however, the cubicles had not been moved since the building had been built.

On the far wall was a huge white board—at least twenty feet across—filled with names, physical descriptions, and places and times the missing persons were last seen. Although she could not make out much from this distance, she hoped Michael's information was on the list.

"Hi, I'm Ilene Mara."

Lauren turned and faced the short, gaunt woman, who was smiling. Shaking hands, Lauren was surprised by the woman's firm grip. "Lauren Chambers. I really appreciate your meeting me on such short notice."

"Oh," Ilene said with a wave of a hand, "short notice is the credo around here. Time isn't just money, it's lives."

Lauren felt a little uncomfortable with that comment, as it sounded like a sales pitch used on a promotional brochure.

A few seconds later they had made their way to Ilene's cubicle. On the material-covered, five-foot-high walls were photos of different sizes and quality, some studio-produced and some family snapshots. Photos of people. Children, women, men. Smiling photos of individuals Lauren knew were missing. Many of whom were probably dead.

"Well, Mrs. Chambers—"

"Please, call me Lauren."

"All right, Lauren. I have your husband's file right here. Deputy Vork forwarded it to us yesterday." Ilene moved the file over so that Lauren could see it. Lauren scanned the report, which contained the information she had provided on the questionnaire, as well as the notes Vork had made following their meeting.

Lauren sighed. "So what do I do now?"

"Well, there's not much for you to do. It's in our hands now, ours and the law enforcement community's."

"And what are you doing about it?"

"Report of your husband's disappearance has been entered into CLETS, an electronic database information system that extends from one tip of California to the other. Anytime someone fitting your husband's description is stopped by law enforcement personnel, we get notified. Your report is also sent to the FBI's National Center for the Analysis of Violent Crime. Every night this report is compared against unidentified-deceased reports that come in from coroners across the country. If we get a hit—I mean, a match—we compare the unidentified person with the missing person information we have—by looking at scars, teeth impressions, fingerprints—"

"But that's after someone's dead," Lauren said, fighting back a knot in her throat. "What do you do while they're alive?"

"That's mostly the job of law enforcement. You should be sure to tell them everything you possibly know about your husband, who he might have had disagreements with, where he might go, that sort of thing. It's important to be thorough."

Lauren glanced at the photos hanging behind Ilene. "That doesn't seem like it's enough."

"The CLETS system, the electronic database, really does work. Very well, in fact."

"But what if he's not in California anymore? Does this electronic system work if he's found in another state? The last place he was, at least that I know of, was Colorado."

Ilene Mara paused, looked down at the ground. "No. No, it doesn't."

"Why isn't it linked up with other states' databases?"

"No other state has a method of identifying adult missing persons. There are no central repositories. In New York, for instance, if they can't ID you in one county, and you're missing in an adjacent county, your body sits in a morgue until you're lucky enough to be identified."

"My God, who set up such an inept system?"

"It's not as easy to link things as you might think. California went to some extraordinary lengths and expense in setting up CLETS. But if you consider that there are one hundred and seventy thousand missing person reports each year in California alone, you can see why."

Lauren fell silent, the magnitude of what she was up against suddenly hitting her. Just then, Ilene's phone rang.

"Excuse me for a moment."

While Ilene spoke, Lauren again looked at the photos pinned to the walls of the cubicle. She knew that for each one of the pictures, for each one of the smiling faces, there was a story. Some horrible story as to why that person was missing. Some horrible nightmare as to why he or she was never going to return home again.

"Lauren?" Ilene had hung up the phone and was facing her again.

"Huh? Yeah, I'm sorry, I was just . . . thinking."

"I realize this is hard on you. But you have to think about your husband, make sure you've told the police everything. I have an obligation to tell you that a majority of the time when a husband takes off, it's of his own free will."

Lauren looked away. "So I've been told."

Ilene leaned forward, placed a hand atop Lauren's. "It's also possible, since we're discussing all the possibilities, that he was arrested for something in another state, and he's too embarrassed to call home."

"Arrested for what?"

"We've had a number of men who get involved with a prostitute and are arrested in the sweep—"

"My husband, with a prostitute?" Lauren laughed. "If you knew Michael, you'd realize how funny that is."

Ilene's phone rang again, and she apologized, then snatched it up. She placed the caller on hold and turned back to face Lauren. "I've got to take this. But I want you to know you can call me at any time if you've thought of any new information."

Lauren nodded, then stood up. "Thanks."

"One last thing. Though the natural reaction is denial, it's important for you to at least acknowledge that there could be foul play involved here. Your husband could've had some kind of argument or problem with someone you don't even know about."

As Ilene said this, Lauren thought about the person who had been in her house.

"Point is, your safety could also become an issue."

Ilene paused for a moment, then placed a hand on Lauren's left forearm. "Are you okay?"

Lauren, who had been staring off into the distance, focused her gaze on Ilene. "Everything's fine. I'm just a little overwhelmed by all this."

"Perfectly understandable." A back-ring sounded, reminding Ilene someone was on hold. "Until we can be sure of the reason for Michael's disappearance, I'd recommend you take all reasonable safety precautions. Lock your doors and don't go out alone at night, unless absolutely necessary."

Lauren's eyes landed on the photos in the cubicle. "Michael's going to end up like one of the people in those pictures, isn't he?"

"I certainly hope so. Those are the ones we've found."

Lauren managed a half smile. It felt good to have hope. "Thanks for your help."

"That's why I'm here." Ilene turned to pick up the phone and paused. "Please be careful, Lauren."

FIFTEEN

Hector DeSantos nodded to the military guard at the front entrance and presented his identification card for scrutiny. The man waved him on and he proceeded through the metal detector, placing his Pierre Cardin attaché case on the X-ray scanner and retrieving it as it exited the machine. After crossing the lobby, DeSantos removed a key card and held it in front of the electronic reader next to the elevator, then entered a code on the adjacent touch pad. The red light flashed green, and the doors slid open.

Inside, he pressed the basement button. There was a slight pause while the computer compared his fingerprint to the digital "signatures" of all authorized personnel. Suddenly, the doors closed and the car began descending.

After exiting the elevator, DeSantos nodded to the guard who was standing at the entrance to the floor. The stiff, uniformed man returned the acknowledgment with a slight dip of his chin, and DeSantos continued on. The click of his highly polished Allen Edmonds wing tips against the tile flooring echoed as he made his way down the long corridor. The Navajo white walls were barren, save for charts delineating emergency exits and placards on doors with people's names and ranks.

DeSantos stopped at a room at the far end of the hall and placed the palm of his hand on the glass panel beside the door. An electronic beep sounded, followed by the appearance of a yellow light beneath his fingertips. It moved slowly down to his palm, then faded from view. A computer-generated female voice said, "Please wait while the database is scanned."

DeSantos, a member of the highly covert Operations Support Intelligence Group, or OPSIG, stood at the door awaiting admittance, his right foot tapping repeatedly. OPSIG, buried in the bowels of the Pentagon, was a brainchild of Douglas Knox's while he was the chief counsel for the Senate Select Committee on Intelligence. Their unwritten mission statement empowered them to gather the necessary intelligence that would ensure the security and success of covert operations. As a result, the core group of twenty agents with Special Forces training, initially handpicked by Knox, were ready to leave for anywhere in the world at a moment's notice, either on missions of their own or as support for other CIA operatives. Aside from rigorous refresher training programs that harkened back to their Special Forces roots, much of their time was spent analyzing national security threats in situation rooms such as the one DeSantos was about to enter.

After five seconds had passed, the metallic lock released and a green light flashed above the door. DeSantos walked in, ignoring the walls chock-full of computer screens, electronic charts, maps, and monitoring devices. The room lighting was muted, and a medium-size, oval conference table sat back from the two computerized "tech walls," as they were called. The deep blue industrial carpet added to the darkness, as if by design. Cool air streaming in through the ceiling panels provided a continuous white-noise background and offset the intense heat radiating from the plethora of electrical equipment that lined the room.

DeSantos sat down on one of the firm, blue ergonomic chairs and tossed his attaché case on the conference table where his partner, Brian Archer, was seated. Archer, rail thin with a military-style crew cut, was focused on one of the many television screens, where a taped news report was playing.

"This our new assignment?" DeSantos asked with a slight Latin American accent.

Archer leaned forward in his chair. "Shh."

DeSantos removed his glasses and pecked at a few pieces of dust, then replaced the spectacles on his nose. "You couldn't wait till I got here?"

Archer reached for the television remote and hit PAUSE. The image froze on the news reporter, a twenty-something *GQ* man primped and primed for the camera.

"You're late. Should have been here on time. I can't talk to you and review this material at the same time."

Archer hit PLAY and the frozen image jerked back to life. ". . . and after six long years," the reporter said as he glanced over his shoulder at a federal penitentiary in the distant background, "in approximately fifty-eight minutes, Anthony Scarponi, the most prolific hit man in U.S. history, will walk out of this prison."

"Can we back up a second, Brian?"

Archer looked at DeSantos and frowned. He hit the POWER button on the remote and folded his arms across his chest. "Fine, let's back up."

"Mind telling me what's going on?"

"If you'd been on time—"

"Fuck it. I'm here. Brief me."

Archer shook his head, then swiveled in his chair and lifted a folder that rested near his left elbow on the conference table. "You're such an asshole sometimes, you know that?"

"According to my wife, it's most of the time."

"I don't know why Maggie puts up with you." Archer spread an accordion folder and pulled out a manila file. He opened it and swung it around to face his partner. "Hector DeSantos, meet Anthony Scarponi, international assassin." A five-by-seven, black-and-white mug shot stared back at DeSantos.

"Wasn't this guy one of us?"

"In the broad sense. Specifically, a CIA operative stationed in the Far East, first in China, then the USSR. We had a number of intelligence breaches in the eighties. One of them compromised Scarponi's cover and exposed him as an operative."

"Ames?"

"A little early, but possible."

DeSantos instantly zeroed in on the Aldrich Ames spy case of 1994, when a key CIA analyst, the head of the Soviet counterintelligence branch, was convicted of having sold sensitive national security information to the Soviets over a period of nearly ten years—including the names of CIA operatives stationed overseas. Most of the compromised spies were executed, while a handful simply disappeared.

"But they didn't kill Scarponi," DeSantos said. He pulled the file closer to him.

"No. They had better plans for him."

DeSantos looked up, his eyebrows knitted tightly together. "Better plans?"

"It appears they drugged him pretty extensively. There's nothing in our file about it, but I did some digging. I think they did some heavy mind-control shit on him."

DeSantos looked back at the paperwork. "There's nothing in the file?"

"Looks like it's been cleansed."

"But why?"

Archer shrugged. "Obviously, there's something in there no one wants anyone to know about."

"We're not just *anyone*. Besides, how the hell do they expect us to do our job when they don't give us full disclosure?"

"Knox said this one goes all the way to the secretary of defense."

DeSantos shook his head. "You'd think they'd know they could trust us after we pulled Lynch's ass out of the fire two years ago. Wasn't that enough to prove we're all on the same side?"

"Nobody's on the same side," Archer said. "That's the fucking problem." He swiveled his chair and rolled it over to the wall of computers. "Let's see what Sally tells us."

"Jesus, Brian, I don't think that's such a good idea."

Archer entered an ID and password, then hit ENTER. "I already did some exploration in the database before you got here."

"I promise not to be late next time."

Archer snorted as he continued to strike keys. "You'll be late. It's your way, you can't help yourself."

"You're beginning to sound more and more like Maggie every day."

"Being partners with you is just like being married, without the sex."

"Hey, Maggie and I have great sex."

"That's why she stays with you. I don't have that incentive. Keep that in mind," Archer said with a wry smile.

A beep followed a fingerprint scan, at which point they were granted access. Archer struck a few keys and a large blue-and-gold CIA logo filled the screen. "Welcome to the CIA ISO CSS intelligence database," Archer said. "As if we didn't have enough acronyms in government . . ."

"I thought you gave up hacking."

"Hacking implies something illegal. I'm just . . . looking around."

"Browsing."

"Exactly." Archer struck a few keys and a photograph of a much younger Anthony Scarponi appeared on the screen. "Guy's file from eighteen years ago. Started as an analyst specializing in Asia and the USSR, then was granted operative status five years later," he said, reading from the screen.

"Whose password and ID are you using?"

"I don't know. Knox supplied it. Someone he said we can trust. They tied my fingerprints in with the pass codes."

DeSantos shook his head. "I still think this could come back to bite us in the ass if we're not careful."

"Then we'll watch our back," Archer said slowly as he scanned the text on the screen.

"You were right," DeSantos said, pointing to the screen.

"About what?"

"The drugging." DeSantos's finger moved across the text. "Scarponi's whereabouts were unaccounted for sometime after 1982, but he was located by a small group of Delta Force ops that went in to find our missing people. He was sighted on a Chinese research compound in 1984. The Mao Institute. Our ops were unable to approach him." DeSantos looked over at Archer. "Knox was in charge of the inquiry on that mission."

"That's interesting."

"Isn't it."

"Mao Institute," Archer said. "That's the one that's doing biological weapons research?"

"Among other things."

"Wonder where that leads," Archer said.

"Right to the secretary of defense, I believe is what you were told."

Archer gave DeSantos a sideways glance, then turned back to the monitor.

"Maybe this is our answer," DeSantos said, reading from the screen. "Knox headed up a covert international task force that was assembled to identify and locate the assassin known as the Viper. In 1991, Knox's task force identified the Viper as being ex-operative Anthony Scarponi. He assigned a former SeAL, FBI agent Harper Payne—"

Just then, the blue NSA eagle crest filled the screen, followed by large red letters: "INFOSEC password has expired." The monitor flashed, and the CIA logo reappeared.

"Shit. What happened?"

Archer struck a few keys and logged off the system. "Sally got a little tired on us."

DeSantos's jaw was clenched. "You think someone was monitoring us?"

"It's the CIA, Hector. Someone's monitoring everything."

"We should have printed the file."

Archer nodded. "Next time I will."

"If we can get into the database next time, and if the file hasn't been purged by then."

They both sat there for a moment staring at the blank monitors.

Finally, Archer leaned back in his chair, pulled a piece of Juicy Fruit from his pocket, and popped it in his mouth. "So what does all this mean?"

"It means that we don't know shit about our assignment." DeSantos slammed the manila folder closed. "It means that we're purposely being kept in the dark. By the same people who gave us this file."

"Knox gave it to us."

DeSantos reclined in his chair and rocked it gently back and forth on its spring. Finally he said, "Then I think we need to get more information from Knox before we put our asses on the line."

"I've got a bad feeling about this," Archer said, lifting the telephone handset.

DeSantos pushed the folder aside and shook his head. "I can see it now. This assignment is gonna be totally FUBAR." Fucked up beyond all recognition.

SIXTEEN

Michael Chambers sat down at the edge of the cold pavement and tried to catch his breath. Every muscle ached, his heart was pounding, and he was beyond hungry. He felt as if he'd just finished a triathlon.

He had awoken at sunrise, as the one-hour nap he had planned to take had become a twelve-hour slumber. He decided it was best to continue on without the stolen Tracker, so he removed the license plates, shoved them in the glove box, then sent the empty SUV careening over the embankment.

He popped another two Excedrins—realizing that he needed more sustenance than just pain pills—and started hiking along the sharply sloped road. After an hour's walk, he sat down to allow his body a short rest. Amidst the tall pine trees on both sides of the roadway—the hill extended above the road as well as below it—he saw a car struggling up the steep incline.

Chambers stood up and raised his arms above his head, waving rapidly. But as the car approached, he could tell it was a dark sedan, much like the ones he had seen pass him last night on the way to the gas station. He turned and looked up the roadway in the opposite direction, hoping to see another car, another way out. But there was none.

As four men in suits got out of the car, Chambers backed away from them, wishing he could disappear into thin air. But there was nothing he could do.

There was nowhere left to run.

Michael Chambers sat in the backseat of a dark blue Crown Victoria sandwiched between the two men who had corralled him on the roadway. In the front of the car, another two men in navy suits sat ramrod straight, facing the front windshield.

All four were clean-cut, Chambers noticed, and they were all in their late thirties or forties, graying slightly at the temples. He had sat there for fifteen minutes, waiting for one of them to talk. But as the ride wore on and they remained silent, he began to realize that something was not right.

"Look," Chambers said, "am I under arrest?" None of the men answered him. "You've got the credit card back. It was an honest mistake." He looked at the two human bookends on either side of him. "If you guys aren't mall security, then who are you?"

Finally, a reaction—the driver's eyes found the rearview mirror, glanced at the man to Chambers's right, and squinted, as if he was confused about something. Chambers felt like verbally echoing that sentiment when suddenly the driver spoke.

"You don't have to keep up the front with us. We know who you are, and I can assure you we've taken steps to look after your safety."

"My safety—" Chambers said as the car pulled up to a guard booth outside a building somewhere in the metropolitan area of Washington, D.C. The guard, whose uniform said FBI POLICE, took a piece of paper and a small leather wallet from the driver. They exchanged a few words, and a moment later the large red blockade marked with the word STOP began to lower into the roadway. They drove over it and proceeded down the ramp into the underground parking garage.

Chambers was taken up two different elevators, down an impressively paneled corridor, and into a room that overlooked the Potomac. It was a spectacular view, one that captured his attention as he gazed out over the immaculate white limestone and granite buildings that sat like Monopoly pieces on a playing board. Only in this case the game was politics—and power, not real estate, was the coveted commodity.

Standing there lost in the beauty of the city, Chambers suddenly noticed how quiet it was in the room. The men had left him alone. He glanced to his right, where a large, sleek black metal desk stood, behind which official-looking certificates with government seals were mounted. He read "Department of Justice, Federal Bureau of Investigation" on one—

"Agent Payne." A trim, tanned man with a full head of immaculately combed gray hair stood in the doorway, his face as hard and cold as the metal desk that stood across the room.

Chambers hesitated. "Excuse me?"

"You were a very difficult person to find." The man held out his hand. "Welcome back."

Chambers hesitantly took the man's hand and shook. "Welcome back? Have I been here before?"

His host looked confused. As he studied Chambers's face, the door opened again, and two men dressed in dark suits stepped in. "I don't think these men need an introduction, do they?"

Chambers looked at them and slowly extended his hand. "How do you do?"

One of the men took Chambers's hand and shook. "You can drop the cover now, Harper."

Chambers glanced at the other man, who was looking him over with a discerning eye.

"How've you been?" the first man asked.

"Do I know you?"

The suited men looked over at the gray-haired man, who shrugged one of his shoulders.

"Obviously," Chambers said, "I know you people. But I had a car accident and it's kind of . . . clouded my mind. Not only don't I recognize you, but I don't even know who I am myself. You said my name was Harper? Is that my first or last name?"

The two men shared an uneasy glance.

"Your name is Harper Payne," the tall man with black, slicked-back hair said. "I'm Special Agent Jonathan Waller, and this is Special Agent Scott Haviland." With a nod of his head, Waller indicated his shorter, thicker-built colleague. "We're with the FBI."

"And I'm FBI director Knox," the gray-haired man said as he settled into his chair behind the large desk. He looked at Waller. "Why don't you take Agent Payne to Admin One."

"Maybe we should get him over to the naval hospital, get him looked at."

"Debrief first," Knox said, holding up an index finger. "Assess the situation. Then you can set him up for a full physical."

"I'll get the Scarponi file, meet you there," Haviland said.

Waller nodded and led Chambers out of the room.

• • •

Administration One did not have a view of the Potomac. In fact, it did not have a view of anything: this ultramodern, utilitarian room had recessed lighting, state-of-the-art computerized projection equipment, and blue, high-backed ergonomic chairs lined up around an oval, polished wood conference table.

Upon entering the room, Waller motioned for Payne to sit. As he settled into the deep chair, the pain in his thigh caught him off guard. He pulled out the bottle of Excedrin and popped another tablet in his mouth. "Since you know who I am, maybe you can tell me how I ended up with a bullet in my leg."

"Actually, I can. Two of our agents intercepted you at Denver International Airport. You were intent on maintaining your cover, and by the time they got you to National, you were adamant about not wanting to cooperate. Their orders were to bring you in—and mission failure was not an acceptable result—so they pursued you. Airport security joined in, and you apparently made a movement they thought looked like you were drawing a gun. So one of the less experienced security officers took a shot at you."

"Obviously, I ended up giving them the slip."

"Obviously."

Payne looked around, taking in the impressive conference room for the first time.

"I take it you don't remember this building," Waller said.

"I don't remember much of anything."

Waller sighed. "Well, let's start with the basics. Your name's Harper Ellis Payne. Born January seventh, 1959, Pittsfield, Massachusetts. Graduated from MIT and joined the army, where you did some time in covert ops before applying to the Academy in 1985. You graduated top of your class and had a very impressive career."

"You're talking like I'm not an agent anymore," Payne said.

"You left the Bureau six years ago."

"Did I do something wrong?"

Waller rubbed at the back of his neck. "No, you did something right."

"I left the Bureau because I did something right?"

"You were given a deep undercover assignment, to infiltrate the operation of the assassin known as the Viper."

"Deep undercover?"

"No contact with family or friends. Reports to the Bureau were made very infrequently, and only when it was safe to do so. You had to live and breathe your undercover identity twenty-four hours a day. Sometimes it meant doing things that you felt were contrary to who you were as a person."

"Like what?"

Waller hesitated, studied Payne's face for a moment. He looked genuinely interested. There was no way the amnesia was an act, Waller concluded. "Why don't we just leave it at that for now."

"Did I kill someone, is that it?"

Waller nodded. "We all knew going in that there was a chance you'd have to prove your worth. Your allegiance. You were in a tough spot. It was an extremely difficult assignment." Waller waited for a reaction, but there was none. Payne was merely staring down at the table. "Look, I know this is a lot to absorb. You have to keep what I'm telling you in perspective—"

"How long was I undercover?"

Waller took the seat next to Payne. "As far as covert ops goes, it was an eternity. Almost two years."

"Did it have anything to do with me leaving the Bureau?"

"That assassin I mentioned before, the Viper, aka Hung Jin. Real name Anthony Scarponi. You testified against him."

"Mafia?"

"Actually, he was a federal agent." Waller chuckled. "I should emphasize *was*. You gave us an inside look at his operation like nothing we'd ever had. From what you told us, we were able to build cases against some of the people who put out the contracts on world leaders, business executives, wealthy individuals, foreign politicos, you name it. Before you went in, we didn't have an ounce of evidence against these people."

"So I worked with this guy?"

"He took you under his wing. He was very cautious of you initially, but over time you proved your worth to him. Once you gained his confidence, he put you in charge of staking out the target, providing all the background work he needed to make the hit a success."

"But how does someone go from being a federal agent to a ruthless assassin?"

"I'm not sure how to answer that. Scarponi was a CIA operative stationed overseas. He did time in China and the Soviet bloc. We had a security breach in the eighties and the Agency lost a shitload of operatives. Most of them were killed. Some are still unaccounted for."

"And Scarponi was one of them," Payne said.

"Yes. We've never been able to find out what happened to him over there, but we finally located him operating out of China, and that's when you were sent in. With your Special Forces training and covert ops experience, you were the best choice to go in. Even still, it wasn't until he came to the U.S. to put a hit on someone that we were able to move on him. You were the key."

"How so?"

"You were with him when Scarponi killed Vincent Foster, the deputy White House counsel who supposedly committed suicide by eating his gun. It was the only hit you witnessed. Scarponi was very careful to make sure you weren't privy to any hard evidence that could implicate him in any of the hits. The people who hired him didn't know who he was, and the information he gave you would've been circumstantial at best: you'd be able to testify he told you a person was a target, that he paid you to surveil them, but that's it—you didn't witness the actual hit. But as soon as the CIA fingered Scarponi as the Viper, the president got pressure from foreign leaders all over the world to bring him to trial. The Foster murder was the evidence we needed to put him away."

Payne shifted uncomfortably in his seat. "And that's where I came in."

"You took the stand in pretty damning closed-court testimony. Scarponi was easily convicted and you went underground."

"I don't get it. If he was put away, why did I have to go into hiding?"

"Because he had an army of people just like you on his payroll. Highly skilled, fiercely loyal. We knew it'd only be a matter of time before he'd get word to them to take you out. Not that they needed an invitation.

Rather than wait for some bad shit to go down, it was safer for you to take a new identity and disappear."

The door opened and Haviland entered. He handed a file to Waller and leaned against the wall to Payne's left. "How's it going?" Haviland asked.

Waller's eyes moved from Payne to his partner. "We're getting there." Waller looked back at Payne. "A week after Scarponi was found guilty, word was that a half-a-million-dollar contract had been placed on your head."

"Normally, when an agent's life is at risk," Haviland said, "their identities are changed and they're transferred to a field office in another part of the country. We were in the process of getting the transfer paperwork together when a death threat came into the office where you were headed. You weren't even there yet and Scarponi's people already knew where you were going to be." Haviland shook his head. "We figured we had a mole inside the Bureau."

"It'd take years to figure out who it was," Waller said, "if we could at all. But you still didn't want any part of it. Because of your Special Forces training, you thought you could take care of yourself. While we were trying to convince you it was a losing battle, a car bomb nearly took you out. At that point, both the CIA and FBI directors agreed that you had to enter the Federal Witness Protection Program, whether you liked it or not. Otherwise, you'd be endangering the lives of everyone in your vicinity at all times."

"You went underground with a new identity furnished by the U.S. marshal," Haviland added. "You had some plastic surgery and we never saw you again."

"About a year later you apparently decided to leave the program, and the marshal lost contact with you."

"How do you just 'leave the program'?"

Waller shrugged. "You go underground, take on a new identity. It's not as hard as you'd think. There's a black market specializing in forged documents and fraudulent identities, you just have to know where to look. Once you've got new ID, you create a background for yourself. Schools that no longer exist, scattered around the country. Jobs with defunct companies. Things, dates, places, that can't be verified. On paper it all looks perfectly legit. Last step is a move to another community, maybe even a new country. To those who knew you, you've basically just vanished."

"For the marshal," Haviland added, "it's one less check they have to cut. One more file they can archive and forget about. A very high percentage of people end up leaving the program."

"But if I already had a new identity, why would I abandon the program?"

"Could be that you thought your cover had become contaminated," Waller said. "I don't know. Once the marshal lost contact with you, they had no reason to look into it further. Until recently."

"A situation's come up and we need your help," Haviland said. "Five months ago Scarponi's attorney introduced newly discovered evidence and a witness to back it up. They're saying that Scarponi was out of the country at the time of Foster's death, and they have independent proof that it was a suicide. We know it's all bullshit, but so far, the U.S. Attorney can't refute it without you, without your testimony. Scarponi won a hearing before a federal judge and he was released from prison."

"So you need me to testify."

"The U.S. Attorney's going to ask for a new trial, but it's contingent upon our ability to secure you as a witness. If we can't, Scarponi's temporary get-out-of-jail-free card becomes permanent."

Payne sat there, trying to make some sense of what he had just been told.

"What's the matter, Harper?" Waller asked.

Payne shook his head. "How can I testify against this guy if I can't even remember who I am?"

Waller looked at Haviland. "We don't have a choice. We'll work with you, make sure you're thoroughly briefed—"

"Jon." Haviland was shaking his head ever so slightly. "Are you sure?"

"You have a better idea? We shoot holes in the new evidence or Scarponi walks. He *walks.*" Waller turned to Payne. "Already the president has been getting serious heat. They don't want some bullshit legal snafu to set this guy free in their countries. Given what you were able to do with infiltrating his network, I doubt we'll ever be in such a strong position again." Waller leaned back in his chair. "We've gotta give this a shot."

Payne turned his gaze down to the floor, rubbed the back of his neck, and then shrugged. "I just don't see how I can pull this off."

Waller slammed a hand down on the conference table. "You're missing the point, Harper: we don't have a choice."

"Look at it this way," Haviland said softly. "You've come out of witness protection. Right now, you're extremely vulnerable. Scarponi knows you're the only person in the universe who can get him thrown back in the slammer for life. Given what he does for a living, what do you think is the first thing he's gonna do?"

"But he's been out for five months, you said. And I'm still here."

"It took us that long to find you," Haviland said. "I'm sure he had the same problem. A lot of his contacts are overseas, it probably took him time to get set up."

Waller rose from his chair and leaned on the conference table with both hands, looking down at Payne. "Bottom line. You help us, you help yourself. Once we're done, we'll put you back in witness protection. Get you some more plastic surgery, this time something a little more radical"—Waller looked him over—"and you'll live a long and healthy life."

Payne sat there, mentally and physically spent. He nearly jumped when Waller tossed a file on the table in front of him.

"What's this?"

"Your personnel file," Waller said. "Open it up, thumb through it. Maybe something will jar your memory."

Haviland motioned to his partner, then moved toward the door.

"Excuse us a moment," Waller said.

As the two men stood in the hallway outside the conference room, Waller interlocked his hands behind his neck. Haviland spoke first.

"Jon, this isn't going to work—"

"What do you want to do, Scott, wave the white towel and give up? It'd be a fucking cold day in hell before I admit I caved to Anthony Scarponi. We'd never hear the end of it."

"But you have to be realistic here. There's no way we're going to be able to give Harper enough informa-

tion that it'll come out as if it were his own memories.
We're talking about cross-examination. You saw what
Friedkin did to him the first time around—"

"Tried to do to him. Harper came through okay."

"The old Harper did. But he's had a severe head
injury. Did you see the size of that bruise? I mean,
shit, he doesn't even recognize us."

"Look, Scott. Scarponi's been out for five months.
The director's on our fucking ass. We've got coverage
on his family, but how long do you think we can keep
that up before one of 'em fucks up? Let's be realistic.
If Scarponi wants to, he will get to the director's family. It's a question of when, not if."

Haviland massaged his temples. "Maybe once
Harper gets into the file, it'll all come back to him."

"Or maybe the doctors can give him something to
jar his memory."

Finally Haviland sighed. "We've got to run this by
Knox."

"He'll give us the go-ahead. He's got no choice."

Payne pulled open the manila folder and came across
his original application to the Academy. It was just as
Waller had said: he was born in Massachusetts, did a
stint with the army's Special Forces division, and
finally became a field agent with several commenda-
tions and decorations.

He looked at the photo from sixteen years ago. His
face had a more youthful look to it, that much was for
sure. But after what he'd been through—let alone the
plastic surgery they'd mentioned . . . he turned the
page and read the former director's letter to him thank-
ing him for the exceptional duty he had performed for
the safety of the people of the United States.

Payne shook his head. He wished he could remember these things. How can one lose the memories of a lifetime?

The door opened and Haviland walked in. As Payne looked up from the file, a thought occurred to him. "Was I married? Did I have any kids?"

Haviland took the chair to Payne's right. "Your wife's name was Beth. You have a little girl. Randi. I think she was four or five at the time."

Their eyes met, Payne's expression asking the question that didn't need to be verbalized.

Haviland sighed. "I don't know what happened to them or where they are. They were relocated as well. At first you thought you could keep your family intact. You thought you could protect them. But after the car bomb you realized it would never work out. It tore you up inside."

Payne sat there, pondering the thought of a wife and child. "I'd like to talk to the marshal, find out where they are."

"Impossible. If they're to be safe, you can't have any contact. None. I'm sorry."

The door swung open and Waller stepped in. "Knox gave it the go-ahead," he said to Haviland. "We ready to start?"

Payne turned to Waller with a long face. "How are you going to brief me on an entire career, almost two years' worth of details in an undercover assignment?"

Waller leaned forward. "We'll coach you, hold your hand every step of the way. We'll tell you what you need to say. We'll make it work. We have to."

Payne sighed and looked at Haviland, who nodded. Finally, Payne sat back in his chair and threw up his hands in frustration. "Tell me what you want me to do."

SEVENTEEN

At four-thirty, Lauren returned to the Neighborhood Watch Center and spent half an hour with Carla Mae going over the various messages that had come in since she had left.

"The calls have slowed down, which for now I suppose is good," Carla said. "None of them made much sense, I'm sorry to say. Some people called to offer their condolences, some wanted to bring food over. Then there were the usual pranks. Bottom line, nothing that would help."

"And these?" Lauren asked, picking up a stack of several message slips.

"Those I would give to Nick, let him do some legwork on them. They were the more promising ones."

Lauren placed them in her purse and thanked Carla again for her assistance. She then headed out, stopping at a fast-food drive-through to pick up dinner. When she arrived home, Bradley was sitting by the back door, cell phone in hand.

Lauren glanced at her watch. "I thought you were going to meet me at six."

"I finished what I needed to get done, put out a bunch of calls. Most of the other people I needed to talk with knock off at five, so I left and came here. I figured if I was sitting outside your house, it may deter your friend from coming in and doing the laundry or something."

"That's not funny."

"I guess not. Sorry." He took the bag of food from her as she fumbled for her house keys. "The fraternities threw a fit, as I expected. I've got a call in to Vork for help. But unless we can narrow it down a bit, it could take a week or two just to call all the names on every frat roster. That's if we have help and get lucky by hitting on the right people sooner rather than later."

"We don't have a week or two."

"It's just one of many things I've got in the fire. I'm sure something else will turn up."

Lauren pulled out the slips of paper Carla had given her and handed them to Bradley. "Here are some messages Carla took today. Maybe there'll be some leads in there."

"I'll get right on them."

Lauren inserted her key and unlocked the back door. She greeted Tucker with a pat to the head as Bradley placed the bag of food on the kitchen table.

"What about all these other 'things' you've got in the fire?" she asked.

"I'm trying to pinpoint places in Colorado Michael could've gone cross-country skiing."

"And?"

"And you can ski in practically any rural area where there's snow. That leaves a lot of territory to cover."

Instead of responding, Lauren began unwrapping the food.

"It's not going to be easy," Bradley said. "There are so many angles to take on this and no simple way to narrow it down. He could be in Colorado, or he could be in California somewhere. Or anywhere in the other forty-eight states for that matter."

Lauren removed a couple of plates from the cupboard and placed them on the table. She pressed her fingertips to her lips, hoping to hold back an outburst of tears.

"We're not giving up, Lauren. I told you, I've got stuff in the works. It's just not going to be easy, that's all."

Lauren nodded. "I bought you a cheeseburger and fries."

Bradley studied her face for a moment, then took a seat. "Thanks. My favorite."

They sat and ate their food in relative silence. Tucker sat calmly by Lauren's side, devouring the occasional french fry she slipped him. When they had finished, Lauren took out her handheld PC and set it down on the kitchen table. As it dialed through its sequence and logged on, Bradley cleared the table.

"You know, it would be a good idea to send out a message to everyone on your E-mail list, just in case any of them have heard from him." Lauren started to protest, but Bradley held up a hand. "I know, it's a huge long shot, but sometimes playing the long shots pays off."

Lauren frowned and shrugged a despondent shoulder. "Guess it wouldn't hurt." She touch-screened through Internet Explorer to get to the Hotmail Web site. She clicked on COMPOSE, and began to write her E-mail message. Once she was satisfied with the wording and tone of the message, she touched SEND and waited as the little PC transmitted the appeal through the phone lines to her eleven contacts.

"Done?" Bradley asked.

"Done."

She clicked OK on the screen that informed her that her messages had been sent, then began scrolling through the six new E-mails she had received. Two had been sent to her from professional organizations she belonged to, another was a joke forwarded from a friend in Los Angeles, and the fourth one was probably spam, or junk mail—from someone or some company called "lost_in_virginia."

She skipped the messages from the psychological groups and thought about just deleting the forwarded joke, but figured the humor might do her some good. She was wrong. It was stupid and she immediately zapped it from her in-box.

As she did so, the next message, the one from lost_in_virginia, popped up on her screen. The first line caught her attention immediately. "Oh my God—" She cupped her mouth with her right hand.

"What?" Bradley asked, swiveling around to grab a view of the tiny color screen.

"He's alive, Nick, and he's in Virginia!"

Bradley quickly scanned the message, then reached for the telephone. He booked two seats on a flight out of Sacramento to Reagan National, due to leave at nine forty-five in the morning. After hanging up the phone, he turned to Lauren, who had tears rolling down her cheeks.

He took her in his arms and let her cry on his shoulder.

EIGHTEEN

Hector DeSantos and Brian Archer walked the circular path across from the inscribed black granite walls of the Vietnam Veterans Memorial. Between them was Director Knox, a brimmed hat deflecting the drizzle that fell from threatening skies.

"I'm glad we were able to come to an agreement on this," Knox was saying. "Let me reiterate that there never was an attempt to keep you men in the dark."

"We understand, sir," DeSantos said. "Communication is our specialty, and when we felt we'd only received half the message, we were . . . concerned."

Knox stopped and faced DeSantos. "I know you, Hector. You felt betrayed."

"Yes, sir," DeSantos said.

"And you, Brian, you were trying to put the pieces of the puzzle together. Well, you'll have your pieces. *As we get them,* not days later this time. Agreed?"

Archer and DeSantos nodded.

"There's something else." Knox hesitated a moment before continuing. "I've been thinking this may be the end of my . . . *involvement* with OPSIG."

"Any particular reason?" DeSantos asked.

"Nothing I care to discuss." Knox glanced over his shoulder at the security-detail agents leaning against a sedan. "Let's just say it's a personal decision."

"Then it's going to be a sad day, sir, when this assignment is over," Archer said.

"I just thought you two should know."

"What about the others?"

"They'll all be told, in time."

The three of them stood there for a long moment looking at each other, the rain whipping against their coats, the cold air snaking around their exposed necks. It was an awkward moment, one where there should have been more emotion evident. But they were professionals, and their silence said enough.

Finally, DeSantos broke in. "Thanks for the heads-up."

They shook Knox's hand and the man was off into the wind, which was blowing rain straight at him. He disappeared under the watchful eye of his security detail into his black sedan.

DeSantos looked at Archer. "Well?"

Archer's jaw moved furiously as he chomped on his piece of Juicy Fruit and considered DeSantos's question. "I think it's really sad. I mean, it's like losing a brother. Knox has been with us since—"

"I mean about Scarponi."

"Oh." Archer sighed. "I think the guy's out of his mind if he thinks he can threaten the director and not have serious heat come down on him."

"Maybe he doesn't care. Maybe he is out of his mind."

Archer shook his head. "Knox is still keeping something from us. I'm not sure what though. You?"

DeSantos nodded. "Yeah. It's not all adding up." He stuck his hand into his pocket and felt a piece of paper Knox had palmed him when they shook. "With these INFOSEC pass codes he gave us, we've got access to just about any U.S. intelligence network we could want. I say we get started."

Archer turned and they began to walk back to their car. "I think we have to look at it one of two ways. Either there's nothing to be found, or he's purposely making us work for our information."

"I think you're right. Something else is going on. For whatever reason, Knox is not making it easy."

Just then, Archer's pager vibrated. "Man, I hate these things. Scare the shit out of me every time." He pulled the beeper off his belt and checked the number.

"Maggie loves mine. She clips it to the front of her pants and then pages herself."

"You guys are the kinkiest couple I've ever known," Archer said.

DeSantos pulled down on the bill of his baseball hat to prevent the increasing rain from blowing in his face, then nodded at the pager. "What's up?"

"Trish was having some cramping this morning. She wants me to meet her at the OB's office. That was my reminder."

"When you're married, that pager becomes a ball and chain, man."

Archer smiled. "For you, that must mean a hell of a good time in bed."

NINETEEN

Lauren was singing James Taylor, moving with a twirl or a skip from drawer to drawer while gathering her clothing: "all you've got to do is call, and I'll be there, yeah, yeah, yeah . . ." She tossed a pair of jeans into her suitcase as if she were slam-dunking a basketball.

Lauren kept checking the time. Three and a half hours till we leave. Then, three hours and twenty-five minutes. Three hours twenty minutes. She couldn't help watching the clock—she was finally going to see Michael again. She could feel it.

Her carry-on almost completely packed, she set it near the door. Bradley had gone out to get them some breakfast at McDonald's while Lauren finished gathering her things. The item she really wanted to carry on with her was her daddy's handgun, but Bradley had told her it would have to be locked in a gun box and checked through.

She had just zipped her flight bag when she heard the knock on her back door. "Just a minute, Nick," she called out. She bounded into the kitchen and grabbed the handles on her bag.

"All you got to do is call, and I'll be there, oh yes I will," Lauren sang as she made her way to the door. But her throat tightened the second she opened it and saw a man with panty hose stretched across his face. The scream was there, but it was caught somewhere in her constricted throat and never made it out of her mouth. She reached for the gold-plated key around her neck and backed away, wishing her gun were within reach. *Daddy. Intruders.* She was frozen, consumed by the memory, as the man grabbed her by the arms.

"I hope you liked the flowered sheets," he said in a deep, cold voice.

Lauren bolted upright. She was still dream-drunk, her heart pounding from the horrible nightmare. The noise she had heard was a thump, nothing loud, more like a muted thud, as if someone had dropped a sack of potatoes on the carpet. She sighed relief that it was only a dream, thankful something had awoken her. The LED clock on Michael's night table across the bed glowed 2:47 A.M.

Lauren reached for the small switch on the lamp and gave the dial a flick with her finger. But the room remained dark.

A foul-smelling cloth was suddenly shoved up against her nose and mouth. Lauren windmilled her arms, grabbing on to something or someone—an arm or a leg. She felt a painful pinprick in her thigh, then her strength began melting away.

"Nick," she struggled to shout. But as she lost consciousness, she wasn't sure if she had actually yelled it aloud, or if it had been a benign utterance in her mind.

Everything was black.

Now, as she was slowly gaining some form of groggy consciousness, she tried to gain her bearings.

A minute passed before she became somewhat aware of her surroundings. She appeared to be lying in a car, blindfolded, her shoes removed. Hands and ankles bound. Goose bumps had risen all over her body and she was shaking. It was freezing, and she had a pounding headache.

As Lauren lay there, the blackness of her world descended on her. Amid a stale humidity inside the vehicle, a clamping pressure tightened her chest. Her throat was closing down on her and her heart rate was increasing.

Lauren forced herself to relax. She knew she mustn't succumb to the fear, to the negative thinking that could plunge her into a panic attack so severe that it would render her completely helpless.

She felt the vehicle rocking from side to side due to rough terrain, movement she recognized from the time she and Michael had taken their neighbor's four-by-four to the back roads in Tahoe. It was part of her therapy at the time, an attempt to take her out of her "safe places"—home and work—and help her confront her fears: unknown, open spaces. She remembered that weekend well; it was the first time she had been out of Placerville since she had stopped her antidepressants.

As the car jolted hard to one side, she used the momentum to help push herself up with her elbow into an erect posture. It didn't help much other than to give her some sense of control over her body. But sitting there, she became aware of the feel of the seat, the way her knees were bent and the bounce of the ride. It felt as if she was inside some kind of pickup or sport utility vehicle.

Suddenly, the truck lurched to a stop. The gearshift

slid into PARK and the engine cut off. The front door slammed, and the rear door to her left—no, the right—opened as she felt a rush of cold air snake around her bare feet.

"Let's go." The voice was male, deep and matter-of-fact.

"Who are you?" Lauren's speech was still somewhat slurred from the drugs she had been injected with. "What do you want from me?"

Her abductor did not answer. Instead, he yanked her out of the rear seat with rough, calloused hands. She fell from the vehicle, a distance that confirmed her impression that it was a four-wheel-drive of some kind. But the fresh air felt good. No walls, no confining spaces.

The man pulled her up and fastened what felt like a collar around her neck. He pulled her along, leading her like a dog, across freezing, crunching ground cover. *Snow*.

The duct tape binding her ankles made it impossible for her to walk. She had to hop awkwardly, her bare feet slipping on the sharp, icy snow. Several times she went down—and each time she fell, he yanked on the collar until she righted herself, only to stumble and fall again.

"It's hard to breathe," she gasped, her voice as raspy as sandpaper. "You're choking me."

After traversing what seemed like thirty or forty feet, she was pushed up onto what felt like steps and into a cold, damp enclosure. When her feet thumped against the dry wooden flooring of the interior, she realized how wet and numb they were.

Lauren heard the strike of a match and smelled the sulfur as it wafted past her nose.

"Down!" he said, sticking his foot in front of her ankles and throwing her to the ground. She went down hard, unable to break her fall because of her bound arms. Her face slammed against the floor.

"Please, don't—"

Her captor shoved his knee into the small of her back, then grabbed the leg of her flannel pajamas. She heard a metallic ping behind her.

"Since you can't see, let me narrate for you. I've got a knife in my hand. A big, sharp knife." He pulled up on her pant leg and in a swift, almost practiced fashion, cut away the lower portion of the material, about midcalf. First the left, then the right.

He pressed the knife up against the back of her neck. With a quick slice, he cut away the nylon collar, then removed his knee from her back and stood, grabbing her by the arm and lifting up her entire body in one motion, like a rag doll.

He threw her down onto a hard, wooden chair. He grabbed an end of the duct tape encircling her legs and gave a quick, hard yank, unwinding the bindings with one hand while keeping a firm grip on her ankle with the other. "Move, and I'll hurt you. Very badly."

"Why are you doing this to me?" she asked. "Please tell me—"

Her captor grabbed her wrists, ripped off the tape, then stretched her hands back behind the seat. As he held her forearms behind her, he wound coarse, thick rope around her wrists. He circled each set of limbs several times, buttressing and knotting the bindings in an unusual manner. Her throat tightened again and she whimpered.

The man now turned his attention to her ankles. She heard the sound of the switchblade being unfurled again. He pressed the cold metal knife blade against her skin. "A reminder. If you don't move, I won't cut you."

Lauren kept her body still—not that she could move anything other than her legs. A swift kick, she thought, and she might be able to disable him long enough to escape. But with the blindfold on, she could miss him entirely, in which case he could become enraged. With a knife in his hands, she didn't want to take the risk. But what was the alternative? This might be her only chance. Before she finished thinking it out, her abductor began winding the coarse rope around her ankles, fastening each one to a leg of the chair. He pulled and tightened the binding in the same manner in which he had tied her wrists together. Just then, he paused—and she felt a quick, sharp slice across her right ankle. She screamed, and her captor laughed.

"I didn't move, I didn't move!" she cried.

"No. No, you didn't."

"You said you wouldn't cut me if I didn't move."

Another laugh. "Guess you can't trust me after all." After a pause, he added, "Remember that."

Lauren felt the warm blood trickle down the cold skin of her foot. She bit her lip and tried to remain in control. But her mind was racing. Was he some deranged rapist? A serial killer? Was he the one who had been stalking her?

He tightened the ropes around her ankles and strapped a similar binding around her chest and arms, both above and below her breasts. Lastly, he fastened a ligature around her neck, but this binding he left loose. That he had put it there disturbed her; everything he did seemed to have a purpose.

"What's this?" he asked, grabbing her gold necklace.

"It's something my father gave me when I was a child." Her voice was tight and uneven.

He yanked hard and the chain popped off her neck.

"Please, don't take it. Please . . ."

He did not answer her. Again, she attempted to block thoughts of panic, instead trying to find something to focus on. His breathing grabbed her attention: a steady, though rapid and shallow wheezing—it reminded her of a patient she had once treated.

"There," he finally said. "A masterpiece. I take a great deal of pride in my work, you know." His voice had a deep resonant quality to it, with a slight hoarseness. The more he talked to her, the better. She realized that the only weapon she had was her mind . . . her expertise in dealing with all sorts of psychopathologies. She was a therapist, and in front of her was a person in need of help. *A patient.* She told herself that this was the only way out, the only way she could simultaneously keep herself from losing control—and perhaps defeat her captor. Her only means of escape.

He stood behind her now, his breathing still rapid and shallow. He pulled down on something behind her head—the blindfold—and removed it.

The room was dimly lit. A broad, stout candle perhaps six inches in height sat on a small metal stand in the far corner of the room, flickering wildly from the draft that wormed its way through the slats of what appeared to be a large shed or cabin of some sort. It was no more than twenty-five feet long and fifteen feet wide, and cobwebs clung everywhere.

Lauren tried to focus her eyes, but because she'd

been blindfolded for so long, her vision was blurred. Where was he? Still behind her? What was he doing? Get him to talk.

"Thank you for taking that off. Lovely place you have here." She decided to try humor, to gauge the man's response.

"Isn't it? A friend of mine . . . found it. He said the owner didn't want to stick around for the winter." He laughed, a haunting, malignant outburst.

A shiver jolted her body.

"The ropes hurt. Would you mind loosening them, please?" Again, an attempt to communicate. The more he spoke to her, the greater the likelihood of developing some type of psychological profile of him; it wasn't a gun or a knife, but it might give her a weapon of a different sort.

The man stepped around the chair and stood in front of her. With the dim lighting and the candle behind him, she was unable to see his face. From what she could tell, he had a fairly long beard and a knit cap on. "You don't get it, do you?" he asked.

Lauren looked at the man, her heart beginning to pound against her chest.

Her vision began to sharpen; his vacant eyes were now barely visible to her. From what she could see, they were large, as if on fire. He moved slowly to his right, to the left of the chair. Lauren's gaze followed him as the flickering candlelight began to ease across his face.

"You were at the Neighborhood Watch meeting, you were staring at me in the back. You—you were the one in my house, weren't you?"

"The light begins to shine, I see. But not brightly enough. Here, let me give you a little more help. Let's see if the sun will rise. If not, I'll be terribly, terribly disappointed."

He reached up and grabbed the long hair of his beard and pulled it away from his skin. He removed the knit cap and slipped on a pair of large, rectangular-rimmed, rose-tinted glasses.

"Just how much does the rope hurt, *Gina?*" he whispered.

Lauren's voice was a mere squeak as tears poured from her eyes. "Oh, my God."

"I see you recognize me, Dr. Chambers. Very good. Very good. I have to say that your hypnosis skills are exceptional." He tilted his head slightly, as if he were studying her. "I tape-recorded the whole session. And, just for the record, my torture fantasies are real, Doctor." He paused. "Of course, my name isn't Steven. But you know that by now, don't you?"

He smiled, then jumped forward and shoved his grimy face into hers. "You," he whispered in her ear, "you are my fantasy tonight, Dr. Chambers."

TWENTY

The wall of ventilation fans roared loudly as Jonathan Waller pressed a button to the left of shooting booth number 13 at the FBI Academy's indoor range. Harper Payne—now operating under the cover of Special Agent Richard Thompson until the start of the Scarponi trial—pressed the magazine-release button on his Glock, then watched as the cardboard bottle target rolled toward them.

"Nice shooting," Waller said as he unhooked the target. "Nearly every shot in the kill zone. Only two strays outside the bottle."

"I thought I nailed every shot."

"You shot fifty rounds and missed two, Harp. That's a ninety-six. You only need eighty to qualify. Combined with what you did this morning on the pistol qualification course, you're shooting for top-of-the-class honors."

"Mind if I shoot another few magazines?"

Waller smiled. "Get this through your thick head: you did great. A whole lot better than I expected. It's not like riding a bicycle. I mean, you never forget the skills, but unless you shoot regularly, you get rusty, lose your edge. But you're as sharp as you were six years ago. It doesn't look like you missed a beat."

They proceeded into the firearms cleaning room,

which was lined with wall posters displaying exploded schematics of guns in the FBI arsenal. Squeeze bottles with solvents and lightweight lubricating oil sat on metal tables beside stacks of gauze pads, wire brushes, and cotton swabs. After the instructor reviewed the Glock's cleaning protocol with them, Payne checked his weapon in the gun vault across the hall.

"What's on the agenda now, coach?"

"Now," Waller said, "we take a walk into town."

"Town?"

They walked outside and followed Hogan's Alley Street, a paved walkway that cut through the densely wooded Academy grounds. Up a hill was a blue phosphorescent posting that read HOGAN'S ALLEY, RESTRICTED AREA. They continued walking and passed another series of signs that were nailed into one of the trees on the left side of the path. They read SUCK IT IN!, HURT, AGONY, PAIN, LOVE IT, ATTITUDE, INTEGRITY.

"Part of the physical training course for new agents," Waller explained.

They followed the winding path until it widened into a roadway at the edge of "town," where a large wooden gazebo stood surrounded by flowers and shrubs.

"Hogan's Alley," Waller said as they headed toward one of the buildings. "A five-million-dollar mock-up town where new agents train in a role-playing type environment. You never know what's going to happen when you get the call to report here. Anything goes."

Ahead of them were buildings with facades that read DOGWOOD INN RESTAURANT, BANK OF HOGAN, and ALL-MED DRUGSTORE. As they walked up behind a blue Ford that was parked at the curb with its front doors open, they noticed an agent crouched behind the hood of the vehicle, shotgun trained ahead on some unseen danger emanating from the bank.

"If I hadn't told them we were coming, it would automatically be assumed we were part of the exercise," Waller explained. The agent with the rifle glanced at them, recognized Waller, and turned his attention back to the developing drama.

"So this is like a movie set?"

"No, these buildings are real. Even though the facades are fake, the bureau maintains offices inside each of the buildings. Our photo and graphics labs are in the real estate office, the video lab is in the movie theater, and so on."

"I'd like to get in on a few of these training exercises."

"Already on the agenda for next week. Meantime, tomorrow morning we're scheduled to review HRT procedures—"

"HRT?"

"Hostage Rescue Team."

Payne nodded. "Shouldn't that agent wait for backup before going in?" Payne asked as he observed the man leave the cover of his unit and begin making his way toward the bank.

"Yup. He'll get clipped in a minute."

"Bad decision."

Waller nodded to the agent-in-charge, and they turned left on North Broad Street to head back toward Jefferson Hall, the main Academy building, which included a portion of the dorms. After walking for a moment in silence, Waller turned to Payne. "You okay with all this so far?"

"Seems like second nature."

"That's the point," Waller said with a smile. "It is."

TWENTY-ONE

You can't escape me by shutting your eyes, Doctor. But if you'd like, I can put the blindfold back on."

Lauren opened her eyes and turned so she was nose to nose with Steven. The evil of the man chilled her soul. "Leave it off," she said forcefully.

"A little sensitive, are we?" He stood up and moved away from her, which instantly made Lauren feel better. "Truth is, I wasn't going to put it back on even if you begged me. But please do. Beg me. It would make the fantasy so much better."

"You're not really into sadism, Steven. It's an act."

"My name is not Steven, Doctor. It's Hung Jin."

"You don't look Asian."

"Chinese. And I don't care what you think." He walked away from her and leaned against the wall of the cabin. "It's time to get down to business. We can play later." A wicked smile curled the left side of his mouth.

Just then, it hit her—the patient she had flashed on earlier, the one from her private practice. It was a middle-aged man with a goatee—Chipper Ford—who had a type of dissociative disorder known as MPD . . . multiple personality disorder. He had the same pattern of breathing as Hung Jin. Lauren remembered studying Ford's respirations when he lapsed into an agitated personality state, and flashing on the idea that if there was a correlation between MPD and respiratory patterns, it could be a new diagnostic aid . . . and the topic of a research paper. Ford's demeanor, the way he held his head when he looked at her, was similar as well. Of course, it didn't mean that Hung Jin suffered from the same disorder. But still . . .

He dragged a wooden chair across the rough, dirt-covered floor and sat down in front of her. "Business first, pleasure second." He leaned forward, resting his forearms on his knees. "Question number one. Where is Harper Payne?"

"Who?"

Hung Jin stood quickly and swung his arm in a short, underhanded arc. The blow to the stomach caught her completely off guard. Her breath was gone, whatever liquid in her stomach about to jump through her throat. And the pain was just beginning to set in. As Hung Jin leaned over her, he pulled up on a portion of the coarse rope that surrounded her torso, tightening its clench and preventing her from getting a full breath.

"Please," she begged. The pain was intense and increased each time she tried to force air into her lungs. "I'll tell you what I know. But I don't know . . . that name."

Hung Jin sat back down and studied her for a moment.

"Business first, pleasure second," he said in a whining, almost singsong manner. He craned his head toward the ceiling and raised both arms up, as if beckoning toward the heavens. "This is too easy!" he shouted.

Lauren gritted her teeth and pulled on her wrists in a futile attempt to loosen the ropes.

"Yes! Do you feel it? I used special knots that my Chinese master taught me. They tighten when you try to free yourself. They're quite effective. But don't take my word for it. Go ahead and pull!"

Lauren instinctively turned away. She knew this man was unstable. That much was evident during their hypnosis session. Could MPD be the cause—or the symptom? It was a guess at best. MPD affected abused individuals who developed an alternate personality as an escape mechanism. Hung Jin certainly fit the profile. But she needed more of a psychiatric basis to support such a diagnosis. Yet she felt that was what she was dealing with here. Although it was based on something unscientific—intuition—she did not have much to lose by playing what seemed to be her only hand.

The question of how to deal with him, assuming she was right, was difficult. These were far from ideal circumstances. But Lauren was used to thinking out of the box when confronted with a difficult or even impossible case. She relaxed her body and closed her eyes, taking herself back to the warm yellow tones of her office . . . the comfortable leather chair in front of her desk, the slight scent of rose floating on the air. Hoping there was something from her initial session with him that could help her.

"I'll make it easy on you," Hung Jin said.

She opened her eyes slowly, keeping her mind back in her office. She was the doctor now, Hung Jin the patient.

"The sooner you tell me what I want to know, the faster I'll be gone." He sat down again.

"What did you do before you went to China?" Lauren was fishing, looking for something that would trigger a specific response: a switch in personalities, one that might bring out a more docile, or even harmless, alternate personality, or *alter*.

"I don't think you understand how this arrangement works," Hung Jin said, his fingers curling into a fist. Lauren tightened her body, bracing for another punch. "I ask the questions, you answer them. You refuse to cooperate, I hurt you." He smiled, then took a step toward her. "Now, your husband. Tell me where he is."

Lauren's eyes began to tear.

"All you have to do is tell me where he is and I will stop this, right here. Then I'll let you go."

"I thought you said I couldn't trust you."

Hung Jin's head jerked left twice in rapid succession. His face turned crimson, the veins in his forehead bulging. "Don't use my words against me!"

Lauren flinched. "Michael was supposed to be home a few days ago," she stammered. "On the twelfth. But he hasn't called. I don't know what happened to him. You heard me say that at the Neighborhood Watch meeting—"

Hung Jin brought his fist back again and unleashed a straight-on jab that landed on Lauren's left cheek and tipped the chair back off its front legs. She cried out as the blow landed. Instantly, a numbing deafness muffled her surroundings. She felt groggy and distant and her vision was blurred.

"I know what you said at the meeting. But it's all bullshit, part of Payne's plan to get away from me. The distressed wife looking for her husband, turning to the small-town folk to help her find him. It was a nice show, Doctor. But I know the truth. You know more than you're telling me."

She shook her head to fight the dizziness, to prevent herself from losing consciousness. As her senses slowly returned, tears began rolling down her cheeks. "I don't know what you want from me," she said weakly. "I don't know any more than what I said at the meeting. This is all just a mistake. Michael didn't do anything to hurt you. I don't understand why you're trying to hurt him."

"You're right, it *was* a mistake. And because of that mistake, he caused me far more pain than I could ever cause you, Doctor. Now I'd love to debate the nature of pain and the methods of measuring whose pain is worse, but I need to find your husband. *Now!*"

"I don't know who Harper Payne is," Lauren blurted, lowering her head and turning it slightly to the side, bracing for another impact. "My husband is Michael Chambers."

Hung Jin sat down and regarded her. "I know you're not stupid, Doctor. You probably think you're protecting him. But why you'd want to protect a murderer is beyond me."

Lauren swung her head around and locked eyes with him. "What?"

"Yes, your husband is a murderer. He worked for me, carrying out contract hits."

"Michael isn't capable of killing." Lauren defiantly looked away, convinced that what she was hearing was a lie.

"Of course you don't believe me. But that's okay, Doctor, because I don't need to prove anything to you. One way or another you're going to tell me what I want to know. Willingly or unwillingly."

"Michael's not a murderer."

Hung Jin leaned back in his chair and folded his

arms across his chest. "This is admirable in a way, how you're protecting him. But I saw that flicker of concern in your eyes when I told you he was a killer. So I'll let you in on a little secret: seven years ago your loving husband was on my payroll, researching the target's daily activities, scouting out the location, planning the hit." He rose and pointed at her. "There it is again—it's in your eyes. *The windows to your soul.* You shrinks aren't the only ones who've studied the mind, you know. Right now you're doing a quick calculation in your head. *Oh my God,* you're thinking!" He craned his neck toward the ceiling. "She's finally getting it!" He looked down at Lauren. "Yes, Doctor, this happened before you met your husband. You're thinking now that maybe what I told you is true. It *is* true." He sat down again. "Ask yourself this: Of all the people you've treated, of all the mental illness you've dealt with, of all the ugliness you've seen, isn't it possible that your husband is a killer?"

"No—"

"That he did things that you would've never believed possible?"

"No!"

"Isn't it possible he's kept things from you, that our companions, our lovers, keep secrets from us they'd never reveal about themselves?"

Lauren's pulse was pounding in her ears. It was possible; she had seen it countless times. Patients telling her things they would never tell their loved ones. But was it possible with Michael?

"I guess it's understandable you'd protect your husband. I'd do the same in your position. The only thing is, I'm not in your position." The same haunting laugh burst from his mouth. "Your attitude will change shortly, when you're starving, freezing, and bleeding profusely."

If Lauren could only find a subject, an emotion, a song or scent that inspired a memory his alter could latch onto, she could make contact with it—if there was an alter. If her intuition was correct. She looked him in the eye, prepared to monitor his reaction to what she was about to say. "I bet you wouldn't treat your mother like this."

There was a slight purse of his lips, a movement her trained eye picked up. "I never had a mother."

"She died?"

"I never had a mother."

Normally, when a psychotherapist worked with a patient who had MPD, making contact with the person's alter was fairly easy. But these conditions were anything but normal. For all she knew, a more dangerous and irrational alter could emerge—if her diagnosis was even correct in the first place.

But she had to try. And that meant she had to find a way of breaking through. The finance manager she had counseled last year who had moved West from New York suddenly appeared in her mind. The way he said *mother*, dropping the *er* and replacing it with an *a*, was similar to Hung Jin's pronunciation. She decided to go fishing again. "We all have mothers. Yours was from New York. Do you remember your house in New York?"

Hung Jin sat in the chair staring at her, not answering. He seemed to be thinking about something. This was good, Lauren thought. She would keep her eyes focused on her patient, hoping to discern the slightest sign that an alter was emerging.

"Your mother, did she ever take you on trips, or to parks or on rides, like at Coney Island?" Hung Jin did not move, did not speak; he stared straight ahead, transfixed on a point beyond Lauren's head.

"Your mother loved you a lot. Try and picture her," Lauren said softly. "It'll help to shut your eyes. Go ahead and relax, let your eyes close and focus on my voice. It'll help you see your mom."

Still, Hung Jin did not respond. A few seconds later, he blinked twice; his eyes closed, then opened, and closed again. Lauren's heart rate increased. She was getting through! She already knew he was susceptible to hypnosis, and susceptibility was important to success in contacting an alter.

"I want you to remain calm and sit as comfortably as possible in the chair," Lauren told him. "I'd like you to think about your mom. Let that part of your mind that remembers her best come forward and talk with me. While that other part of your mind is talking, you will be asleep, relaxing and comfortable. When you're ready, when the other part of your mind has taken control, I want you to open your eyes."

She watched as Hung Jin's head fell backward, rolled to the left, and then moved back to center. That was it! A visual cue. She was correct in her diagnosis. Just then, her patient opened his eyes. To Lauren, his face took on a softer tone; the skin was smoother, the eyes wider, the forehead relaxed.

Her patient sighed. "I'm so tired." The voice was slightly higher and less hoarse.

"You'll get a chance to rest in a little while. Right now, I'd like to ask you your name so I can talk with you as a friend."

"My name's Anthony."

"Okay, Anthony. Mine's Lauren. It's nice to meet you."

Just then, her patient stood up and kicked the chair behind him. It flew backward across the room. He looked down at Lauren, his eyes red with fire, his face hard and his teeth clenched. His head twice jerked hard to the left.

"Anthony, please, calm—"

"You think you can outsmart me, Doctor? You can't!" He swung at her, a backhand that slammed against her right cheek and brought her chair crashing to the floor. He hovered over her body, grabbed the chair, and let loose a primal scream as he lifted her into the air and slammed her down to the ground. The force of the impact of chair against floor sent a jolt of pain up her spine. As if that were not punishment enough, he tightened the ropes around her chest.

"Please don't . . . hurt me," she gasped. "I'm just . . . trying to . . . help you. I'm just . . . trying to . . . help you."

"If you wanted to help me, you'd answer the one simple question I asked you."

Tears streaming down her face, her stomach muscles cramping from the pain, she tried to slow her respiration and lessen the painfully restricted heavings of her chest. She finally looked up at Hung Jin. "But I did. I don't know . . . where my . . . husband is."

"That remains to be seen, Doctor." He grabbed the rope around her neck and pulled. "That remains to be seen."

Lauren felt the pressure build up in her head as the

blood flow to her brain began to decrease. Her heart, trying to compensate, began pounding. She looked at him, her eyes silently pleading for him to stop.

He leaned into her face again, his nose an inch from hers. "Where's Harper Payne?"

TWENTY-TWO

With Hung Jin's face up against hers, the cabin door suddenly swung open, bringing with it a forceful draft of freezing air. The candle flickered several times before finally going out. Almost completely in the dark now, with only a splash of moonlight projecting through the open doorway of the cabin, Lauren began to sweat—while still shivering from the frigid wind that ripped through her thin flannel pajamas.

Hung Jin reluctantly turned and kicked the door closed. He reached into his pocket and rooted out a red Bic lighter, then relit the candle. He turned to Lauren and paused. "Now, where was I? Oh! That's right!"

Lauren looked at her captor and attempted to assess what this man was all about. But with her brain still deprived of oxygen, she felt she was on the verge of losing consciousness. She blinked and shook her head. *Stay awake. Focus.*

Hung Jin walked behind her and pulled on the rope. It tightened down on her chest again, a cobra coiling around her, attempting to squeeze the life out of her.

Lauren's mind went blank. Everything that she had been concentrating on so hard was gone. All she could think about was trying to get a breath.

With a sudden thrust, he yanked on her wrist bindings until they clamped down so tight her hands began to tingle. Tears rolled across her cheeks. And as quickly as her mind had gone blank, a thought jumped into her head.

Lauren struggled for a breath. "When I was . . . a teenager . . . I had a boyfriend . . . who would hand-cuff me . . . to the headboard. Tommy. He was tall and . . . very muscular, and when he . . . grabbed my arms . . . it would hurt. He'd throw me . . . onto the bed, a brass bed, and I'd be naked." She paused. "I can't . . . breathe. Loosen ropes." She waited a moment, then felt him loosen the bindings around her chest. As she suspected, he wanted to hear more. Good. "Tommy would tighten the cuffs so the metal would be digging into my skin. It hurt, but felt good. It felt so good I told him to make it tighter, and tighter, until I couldn't take it anymore."

He moved around in front of her, rested his hands on her thighs, and looked into her eyes. "Do you want me to make the ropes tighter?"

Lauren forced a smile as she tried to recall what Steven had told her while under hypnosis. What were the words he had used? "Hit me. Make me bleed."

Hung Jin matched her smile, a blissful grin that broadened his narrow face. "Yes, ma'am!" He brought his right hand across to the left side of his torso and unleashed a vicious backhand across Lauren's face. Blood oozed from her nostrils and bled down into her lips. "I want more," she said. "Do you feel it, too? Are you enjoying this?"

He began to breathe faster, his chest rising and falling quickly. But then the smile disappeared and he threw his left hand up to his temple. "Owww!" he screamed, recoiling backward, struggling to maintain his balance. He gripped his skull with both hands and thrust his head backward. "Ahh!"

Lauren watched as he moaned and dropped to his knees in agony. "I told you to keep some Excedrin nearby, you son of a bitch."

"No!" He struggled to get to his feet and leaned his left shoulder against the cabin wall.

"Untie me!" she yelled.

Hung Jin grabbed two handfuls of his hair and moaned.

"Anthony, are you there? Please, help me."

"I won't let you beat me!" he shouted. And then he did something Lauren had never seen a patient do before—not that any of this was something she'd ever experienced—but he began slamming his head against the wall until he finally crumpled to the floor, where he lay in a heap. He had knocked himself out to avoid leaving his mind susceptible to someone else's control. Amazing . . . but not very helpful. Or was it?

He lay there for what seemed to be five minutes, finally stirring and getting to his feet. He stumbled forward and stopped directly in front of her.

Lauren looked down and braced herself. She didn't know what form of retribution he would choose for what she had just done to him, but whatever it was, it would most certainly involve pain.

He leaned menacingly over her, his jaw locked and his eyes narrow. "Where is your husband?"

Lauren wearily lifted her head and made eye contact. His gaze was sterile, devoid of humanity. "I don't know," she stammered.

"Then perhaps you need some more convincing in order to properly consider your position." He grabbed the ligature and tightened it again.

Seconds later, everything went black.

TWENTY-THREE

Lauren's face was being slapped in rapid succession, weak, open-handed smacks designed to bring her back to consciousness. She lifted her head, the pounding headache threatening to get worse with each degree of inclination of her chin.

"This is it, Doctor, time for truth—or consequences."

The air was chilled and Lauren's body was shivering. She looked up at Hung Jin and groaned. In the relative darkness, she could barely make out a large, dark bruise over his left forehead.

"I'm in a bitchin' mood today, Doctor. You know why?" He bent down and rested his palms on his thighs, bringing his eyes level with Lauren's. "Because today you're going to tell me where your husband is. And if you don't, you're going to die."

"I want to . . . talk to Anthony."

"Well, he doesn't want to talk to you."

"I think he does."

"I'm sure you do. But we're not going there now. He's safe, tucked away, cowering somewhere in a corner of my mind, no doubt."

Lauren knew that what he said was actually true. Unless she could locate an efficient trigger that allowed her to touch Anthony's essence, she would not be communicating with him again. If Hung Jin was aware of her making another attempt—of challenging his authority, his power over her—she was sure he would kill her.

He grabbed a wooden chair, dragged it in front of Lauren, and turned it around backward. He sat facing her, his arms resting casually over the seatback. "There comes a time in an interrogation where you have to realize you've gotten all you're going to get and you have to just cut your losses." He pulled out his knife, popped it open, and looked at the shiny silver blade. "And I do mean *cut your losses*." That insane laugh again. "That's funny, Doctor! Don't tell me you've lost your sense of humor!"

Lauren sat there, realizing she had to tell him something, anything, to prove her value to him. But there was no guarantee that even if she did tell him where Michael was, he would let her live. At that point, she would be useless to him. "My hands . . . are numb. Loosen . . . the ropes."

With a few twists of his hands, he loosened the rope around her chest just enough to allow her to talk. She sucked in a breath and closed her eyes. Thank God. She never thought she would crave a simple lungful of air.

"You know what I'm going to ask you, so why make me repeat myself? Let me just cut to the chase. Where is your husband?"

Every muscle in Lauren's body ached. Her arms and shoulders were so sore from being pinned back that she didn't know if she would be able to move them even if he did free her. Her stomach hurt with every breath, and her ribs hurt from being bound. She hadn't been able to take a decent breath since he had tightened the ropes last night. As she sat there, she pleaded to God to make her captor release her.

Not having received an answer to his question, Hung Jin reached into his coat pocket and removed a revolver.

The blood drained from Lauren's face.

"I see from your reaction that you recognize this. It's your *daddy's* gun, isn't it? A Colt six-shooter, manufactured some forty years ago."

Lauren stared down at the barrel of the gun, the one that had saved her life two decades ago. *This can't be how it ends.*

"I'm not going to shoot you, at least not right now. We're going to play a game first. Here, let me demonstrate." He flicked the cylinder open with his thumb and turned it over, the rounds clunking to the wooden floor. He bent over and picked up one of the brass bullets and fit it into a chamber, then slapped the housing closed. "First, I give the cylinder a spin. Then, I point the weapon at my target and squeeze the trigger." He aimed the gun at the roof above Lauren's head. "And this is how we play. I ask you a question, and you refuse to answer. I press the trigger." The gun clicked: an empty chamber. "Then I ask you another question. You refuse to answer, so I press the trigger again."

Hung Jin squeezed and the gun exploded, firing a round through the roof. A fine trail of dirt fell from the hole onto Lauren's head. "You see, in this particular game you'd only have had two chances to give me the correct answer." He opened the cylinder, inserted another round, and pointed the gun at Lauren's head. "This time, you might have four or five chances. Or you might only have one."

"I can't tell you what I don't know."

"If that's the case, I won't have anything to lose by killing you, will I?" He extended his elbow and pressed the barrel of the Colt against her forehead. "Once again, where's Harper Payne?"

Lauren began to sweat profusely. She bit her lip and started to cry, realizing she had to think up a story, something convincing and something quick. If he thought she was lying, he would kill her instantly.

"If you kill me, you'll never find him."

His eyes narrowed. "Oh, I assure you I most certainly will. You were just the easiest way, and I always try the easiest way first. But I'm a hunter, a survivor. I will find him, however long it takes. Revenge shouldn't be rushed. It should be savored, like the time we've had here. Haven't you enjoyed it?"

She had played her hand and lost. Now she needed a story.

"Time's up!" Hung Jin squeezed the trigger and a blank chamber clicked. "Only five more to go. I'll give you till three to tell me what I want to know, and then we'll try again. One. Two. Three—"

"Okay!" she screamed. "I'll tell you. Just take the gun away from my head!"

A smile broke across Hung Jin's unshaven cheeks. "Very good." He nodded slightly. "But I make the rules here, Doctor. This isn't your office, remember?" His smile faded as he moved his face down even with hers, keeping the weapon against her head. "Now, you were going to give me some information."

"He's in Colorado, cross-country skiing somewhere near Vail. He went with a few of his fraternity buddies. One of them had an E-mail address that spelled out 'targard.' I swear, that's all I know."

Hung Jin squinted again, considering her reply. "I've had people in Colorado at the big resorts for the past couple of days. As of yesterday, no one had seen or heard of him."

"They were out on their own, it's a new company his friend was setting up—"

"Name of the company?"

"I don't know. I don't know, I'm telling you the truth!" She was staring right at him, holding his cold, gray eyes in her grasp.

Finally he nodded. "I'm going to verify this information, Doctor, and if I find out you've sent me on a wild-goose chase, I will kill you. And it won't be pleasant, I promise you that." He rose from his chair. "In this particular instance, you can trust what I'm telling you as fact."

He walked to the door and opened it. The high, overcast sky was bright, and it temporarily blinded her as the glare caught her across the face.

"Cody," Hung Jin called. "Get in here!"

A moment later, a stocky man with a shuffling gate entered the cabin carrying a covered plastic pail in his right hand and a spray bottle and brown bag in his left. He had a gold front tooth and his nose was so badly bent from fractures that it didn't know which way it should point.

"I got the stuff." He handed the brown bag to Hung Jin.

Hung Jin inserted his hand and pulled out a wriggling rat. "This is Simon. Simon says he's hungry. Cody, do we have something for Simon?"

Cody dug into his pocket and fished out a Ziploc containing a slice of bread, which he removed from the bag and placed on Lauren's lap.

Lauren's eyes were fixed on the rodent, which was hanging by its tail, writhing helplessly in the air.

Hung Jin slid back his sleeve and consulted his watch. "While I'm checking out your story, Cody will be in charge of keeping you alive." He turned to Cody and held up an index finger. "Water only. No food. I want her weak. Weak prisoners put up less of a fight." Hung Jin looked again at Lauren. "If you're lying, I will keep my promise. If you're telling the truth . . ." His voice trailed off. "I guess you'll have to chew on that one for a while."

He winked at her, then nodded at Cody, who began spritzing Lauren's neck, shoulders, ankles, and chest with the spray bottle. The odor of the yellow liquid was rank and stung her nose.

"What is that? What are you spraying on me?"

Hung Jin placed the rodent on her left shoulder. Lauren tensed, the muscles in her neck bulging with fear. The rat sniffed at her hair, ran across to her other shoulder, then scuttled down the front of her blouse, using the ropes as steps. It stopped on her lap, next to the bread. Extending its paws, it grabbed the booty with its sharp claws and began to nibble.

"It's urine, Doctor. The rat's own bodily fluids. We needed an incentive for them to stay around you."

"Them?" Her gaze moved from the rat to her captor's gray eyes.

Hung Jin turned and walked toward the door, followed by Cody. Hung Jin stopped in the doorway, hung the Colt from his right index finger, and looked at Lauren. "I'll leave this here as a . . . reminder of times past." He flipped open the chamber, removed the unspent round, and tossed the bullet into the far corner of the room. He winked at her, then laid the handgun on the floor, adjacent to the wall. Lauren knew exactly what he was doing: more mind games, more torture.

Cody handed him the pail he had been holding. Hung Jin removed the plastic lid and a bucketful of rats poured out, scurrying in a dozen different directions. "They're attracted to their urine. And warm, dark places." He smiled, then slammed the door behind him.

Rats were everywhere. Some scurried into the corners, some ran onto Lauren's lap, her shoulders, her head. She couldn't take it, couldn't hold her emotions in check anymore. She screamed a loud, shrill, desperate scream and couldn't stop herself, and she screamed again. And again.

And then one of the rats found a dark, warm hole and ran in.

It had climbed up the bottom of her pant leg.

TWENTY-FOUR

Agent Haviland was escorted through Mahogany Row to Director Knox's office suite. He sat down in a chair and let his mind drift off as he stared out the large window to his left.

Just then, Knox entered and moved behind his desk, followed by Liz Evanston. "Fine, tell them to make up the plaque and I'll present it in a short ceremony." Knox looked up and appeared to suddenly become aware of Haviland sitting there. "Please give us some time alone," Knox said to Liz. Then, turning to Haviland, he said, "Report."

"Agent Waller's been working with Payne. He's got his days divided into morning and evening sessions. He begins with tactical and skill-building reviews, such as target shooting, HRT situational exercises at Hogan's, and policy and procedure briefings. So far Payne's doing extremely well. Although his memory is still stunted, his instincts are intact, which is good. That would take a great deal longer to teach or relearn."

"My chief concern is his memory," Knox said tersely.

Haviland nodded. He had just received the doctor's report indicating that all the diagnostic tests had come back normal, despite the evidence of significant blunt trauma to the back of Payne's head. Haviland knew that Knox would focus on the doctor's prognosis for memory recovery. The report concluded, excising out all the medical technobabble, that all they could do was wait and see.

"I reviewed the doc's report," Haviland said. "It seems to me, when you get right down to it, that by labeling it postconcussion syndrome with atypical amnesia, or some such wording, the doctor didn't really know what the hell was going on."

Knox rose from his chair and walked to the window. "I've already arranged for another opinion. I'll make sure you're fully briefed on the results." He threw his arms behind his back and began to pace. "What kind of progress are you making with him on the Scarponi file?"

"The evening sessions are consumed by a substantive and comprehensive review of all the reports Payne generated while undercover, as well as his follow-up notes. Every morning he's up by five A.M. and at a terminal in the computer lab reviewing trial transcripts. If this plan fails, it won't be because of a lack of effort on his part."

"I don't intend for this plan to fail, Agent Haviland."

"Of course not, sir."

"But I am concerned about the time."

Haviland knew Knox was referring to the seven-day deadline in the threat letter he had received. "We can go public tomorrow with news of his return and get a trial date set. Technically, he doesn't have to be fully prepared until the day before trial."

Knox continued to pace. "I want him ready as soon as possible. I want to know for sure whether or not he's going to be able to pull this off. If not, we'll have to take a different tack. It would be a PR disaster if Payne's amnesia leaks to the press. The media would have my ass." He shook his head. "I need to know which way we're going to go before we make anything public." Knox stopped pacing and turned to face the window. "Thanks for your time, Agent."

"Understood, sir," Haviland said to his director's back. He knew that was his cue to leave.

TWENTY-FIVE

Lauren fought to keep herself alert. As Hung Jin had predicted, she was growing weak from lack of food. She had difficulty keeping her mind focused, and very few body parts did not hurt.

When Hung Jin had left, the rats had swarmed her, triggering a surge of adrenaline, an injection of pure liquid stress. Fear seeped from her pores. Sweat dripped from her skin. And her impassioned screams seemed to trigger the rats' own fear mechanisms, sending them scurrying away from her into the dark corners of the cabin.

The dark cabin. Though slits of light tore through cracks and gashes in the wall panels, she hadn't seen sunlight in two days. As a psychologist, she was well aware of the depressive effects of darkness and its disorienting disruption of her body's internal clock, or circadian rhythms. With no sense of time or place, and with her body strapped down like a suitcase to the roof of a car, the urge to panic was substantial.

But she knew she had to focus. She had a formidable enemy in Hung Jin; she did not need to make her own failings and anxieties his accomplice. She closed her eyes, calmed herself with a quick muscular relaxation exercise, then began brainstorming ways of escaping.

If she pulled on the ropes, they would tighten. If she yelled for help, no one but Cody would hear her. She had screamed earlier and no one had come to her aid. It hadn't even fazed Hung Jin, so she knew she must be in a secluded location. The scent of pine and the muffling quiet of snow gave her the impression she was in the mountains somewhere. Wherever it was, she had been driven there. It was likely within a few hours of Placerville.

No matter what course of action she took, she first had to stimulate the circulation in her numb feet and toes, hands and fingers. Slowly, she moved her ankles up and down as much as she could, hoping the minimal amount of movement would pump enough blood to have an effect. A moment later, she began feeling the fruits of her labor: not only was sensation returning, but, along with it, pain: she had apparently been abrading her scabbing ankle wound against the wooden leg of the chair.

And then an idea began to form: by rubbing her wound repeatedly against the chair, she could make it bleed freely. She tightened her jaw and worked the cut. A couple of minutes later, her ankle was slippery and gliding in its duct tape sleeve.

As she rubbed, she heard the creaking of the old, dry wood of the chair. Perhaps it was not as solid as Hung Jin had thought. With great pain, she sucked in as much breath as she could. She grunted and jerked her body to the left, attempting to tip the chair over. But the only thing she accomplished was tightening the rope around her torso. "Shit!" she gasped. She began to cry, the pressure against her chest permitting no more than a whimper from her cracked lips.

But she could not give up.

She craned her head left looking for something that could help her. From what she could make out in the dim light, there was nothing of use. She then twisted her head as far right as she could, spying the outline of what appeared to be an old, cast-iron pot-belly stove. A long flue rose from its rotund furnace, heading up toward the roof. She could make out a small crack of skylight around the seam where the flue collar penetrated the ceiling.

Mustering all her remaining strength, she pushed down on the balls of her feet and rocked the chair slightly. Although it was only a small movement, it was a victory of sorts for her. It was a sign that she had control over something in this seemingly hopeless situation. She pushed and pulled her body backward, tilting the chair a couple of inches onto its hind legs before it leaned forward again, slapping back down to the ground.

If she could only push it back hard enough to create a fulcrum with the back legs, she could smash it against the stove. She lifted the chair again with the balls of her feet and threw her torso back as hard as she could. The chair tilted and she felt the center of gravity shift.

With the air just about gone from her lungs, she was heading backward, bracing as best she could for the impact.

TWENTY-SIX

Hung Jin walked into the Cybercafé wearing medium-size, metal-rimmed glasses, a short black beard, and a nondescript navy blue Nike ball cap. He sat down at one of the computer terminals, ordered a double espresso, and logged on to the Internet.

When he had first received word that Harper Payne was in Colorado, all efforts were diverted to the grand snow-covered state. Now, as his anxious fingers played across the keyboard, he hoped to find messages of success from his colleagues. He entered the private chat room he had set up months ago as a means of secure communication and read through the posted messages. He gulped a mouthful of steaming liquid and resisted the overwhelming urge to smash the monitor in front of him.

His men had thus far turned up nothing.

It was now their appointed time to make contact and talk live amongst themselves—in code, of course. After identifying himself using predetermined phrases and receiving the proper counterresponses, Hung Jin relayed the information Lauren Chambers had provided a short time ago. His comrades' replies took time to decode, further testing his patience.

But encrypted messages or not, their conclusion was clear: Lauren Chambers's story was not valid.

Excluding the possibility that Harper Payne had been buried by an avalanche—and there were no reports over the past several days of one having occurred—they insisted they had covered the most likely areas anyone could go cross-country skiing. No one they had visited had seen a male matching the photo they had shown around. None of the resorts or lodges had any record of him having checked in. There was no evidence of a male matching Payne's description in any of the local hospitals. No cars had been rented in the name of Michael Chambers. And, perhaps the most telling fact of all, Harper Payne had never been a member of a fraternity while attending MIT.

Regardless of what Lauren Chambers had told her captor under duress, Hung Jin's men could not confirm that any of the information she had given him was true. He directed them to continue their search for Payne. He would provide further instructions shortly.

In Hung Jin's court of law—which was governed by his own warped sense of justice—the sentence for lying or withholding key information was death. Lauren Chambers was doing just that. Either one, it didn't matter. As soon as he returned to the cabin, he would extract the truth from her. If Payne did not go to Colorado to go skiing, then he went there to hide. If Lauren Chambers knew where he was, she would've been smart to give it up sooner, rather than later. It would have been less painful for her that way.

Hung Jin swallowed the remainder of the hot espresso in two gulps, then crushed the cardboard cup in his hand. He logged off and left an average tip for the waitress. Above all else, he did not want to stand out in any manner. On the slight chance law enforcement came snooping, he had covered his fingertips with an invisible polyurethane coating. He wanted no record, either physical or otherwise, that he was ever there.

He left the café and marched through the snow toward his Lincoln Navigator, thinking of Lauren Chambers, tied up in the cabin, weak and out of her mind with fear.

He couldn't wait to see her again.

TWENTY-SEVEN

In Lauren's mind, the chair was moving backward with all the acceleration of a tortoise leaving the starting line. In reality, it tipped over quite rapidly. With a thud, everything seemed to impact with the potbelly stove simultaneously: her head smashed against the flue and the seatback struck the main compartment.

The chair's spindly wooden slats split with a loud snap.

In a heap, Lauren fell to the ground on her left side, momentarily stunned from the blow to her head. Aware of the noise her fall must have made, she immediately tried to free her hands, which were still securely fastened to the chair's individual slats. Finding this more difficult than she had anticipated, Lauren refocused her efforts on the ropes binding her legs.

She grimaced in pain as she slid her bloody right ankle along the shaft of the chair leg until it slipped off the end. She dropped her head back to the floor for a second, savoring the rare moment of triumph while she rested and gathered her strength. But she knew she did not have much time. She went back to work, quickly freeing her left ankle with her right foot.

With both feet free, she rolled onto her knees and tried to lift her torso. But the center of gravity was all wrong, and with her hands still bound behind her, she was unable to gain the necessary leverage to pull her body up off the ground.

Just then, the unmistakable thump of a car door slamming pounded against her ears.

"Shit!"

Still struggling to lift her body, she remembered the stories she had heard as a teenager of the frantic woman who had lifted a car to save her child trapped beneath the wreck. Lauren needed to summon such strength within herself. Lying on her left side, she pressed her head into the sand-covered wood floor and pulled with all her might. "Ahhh!" she yelled, a deep, guttural groan that helped focus her mind. She pried and yanked until suddenly her right arm popped free of the chair's splintered back. Although her wrist was still fastened to one of the broken slats, she was able to use her hand to push against the floor as she pivoted on her head.

She lifted her torso and sat upright, then brought her left hand to the front of her body. Using both hands, she finally maneuvered the wrist bindings off the slats, completely freeing herself of the encumbrance of the wood chair.

She jumped to her feet—and almost ended up flat on her back. Her low blood pressure, combined with the lack of food, sent her head spinning. She threw her arms out to balance herself. As the dizziness cleared, she heard crunching in the snow outside the cabin. She darted toward the front door, where Hung Jin had left her Colt. She grabbed the weapon and brought the gun up, only to remember it was empty. But Hung Jin had only used one of the rounds; the rest he had dumped onto the ground. She scampered across the floor, her numb fingertips frantically running over the rough wood, searching for just one bullet.

And then she found one. Kneeling on the floor, she flipped open the Colt's cylinder. The crunching footsteps were getting louder. A whimper escaped her throat as she clumsily fumbled with the round before finally shoving it into the chamber. As she snapped the cylinder closed, the cabin door swung open.

The bright gray glare was blinding. Still on her knees, she threw the gun up in front of her chest and yelled.

Hung Jin swerved to catch the corner of the snow-covered side street that came upon him suddenly. The Navigator skidded and slid along the thick ice, but he regained control just short of the embankment. He continued on at a fast clip, faster than he should have been traveling on this road under such conditions. But at the moment all he could think about was the feel of Lauren's supple neck writhing in his hands. In his mind, her eyes were bulging as he squeezed the life out of her.

As usual, he did not expect law enforcement to be a problem. He knew how to stage the crime scene to make it appear as if something else had occurred. A suicide, a kinky sex session, a robbery gone bad. If the local authorities had enough brains to figure out what had really happened, they would probably still not think of reporting it to the feds. And without the feds's involvement, the locals would never make the connection to him.

He knew another thing, too: he had to temper his anger so he could make one last attempt at extracting the information he needed from Lauren Chambers.

Sometimes it was a delicate balance. Sometimes you needed to bring the subject to the brink of death before he fully realized his life was on the line. Sometimes you went too far, and if you couldn't revive him in time, you lost out on a good opportunity. That's why such an interrogation was more an art than it was a science. That's why he was so good at what he did.

He did not usually make mistakes.

Cody's jaw dropped as he took in the broken remnants of the chair, the blood on the floor, the scurrying rats as they searched for darkness and warmth. Just as quickly, the man's lips curled into a smile as he started to reach behind his back with his right hand.

"Stop," Lauren yelled. "Keep your hands where I can see them!"

"Or what?" Cody said, continuing to move his right hand to the back of his jeans. "You gonna shoot me? Bitches like you don't have the guts to kill."

Lauren pulled the trigger—and an empty chamber clicked.

He laughed hard, a smoker's raspy crackle gurgling in his throat. "Guess you proved me wrong, huh, darlin'?" He brought his Smith & Wesson nine-millimeter handgun forward and waved it at Lauren. "Too bad you ain't got no fucking bullets." He laughed again. "My boss would rather I didn't kill you, least not yet." He unzipped his pants and gyrated his hips. "But he didn't say nothing about having a little fun while he's gone."

He took a step toward her and Lauren began squeezing the trigger in rapid succession, the empty chambers firing in her mind like the hollow click of footsteps in an empty warehouse. "Stay back!" she said, still gripping her weapon.

The metallic click-clunk of Cody chambering a round took her breath away as she squeezed one last time. Finally, the bullet exploded from the Colt and hit her assailant between the eyes. His body hung there for a second, the dumbfounded look of a deer in headlights settling across his face as he dropped to his knees and then fell forward, his head and torso landing in a bloody heap by her feet.

Lauren sat there, panting hard. A chill blew in through the open cabin door and made her body convulse in a prolonged shiver. She threw her leg out and kicked at Cody's dead hulk, then stood up and booted his gun into the far corner of the cabin.

"This bitch has the guts, asshole. My daddy taught me to shoot to kill."

Another gust of wind blew against her face like a wake-up call, and she suddenly became aware of the dangers now facing her: Had anyone heard the gunshot? Did Hung Jin have any other accomplices? Was Hung Jin nearby? She needed to get out of there, and fast.

Clothes.

Keys.

Car.

Lauren bent down and yanked off Cody's sneakers and socks. Attempting to forget for the moment where the clothing had come from, she slid the sweaty tube socks over her cold feet. The tennis shoes were a couple of inches too large, but she had little choice. Lauren tugged on the sleeves of Cody's navy pea coat and pulled the jacket off his body. There was some blood spatter across the shoulders, but she didn't care. What mattered now was survival.

Her hands still shaking, she frantically searched Cody's pockets for car keys. But there were none. *Damn*. She shoved the spent Colt into her coat pocket, picked up Cody's loaded Smith & Wesson, and ran out of the cabin across the snow to her right, toward a blue, two-door sedan. It looked like the beatup 1970s Plymouth Barracuda a friend of her mother's had owned. This one appeared to be in similar condition.

She tried the driver's door, which creaked loudly as it opened. But no key was inside. She slammed her hands down on the steering wheel, then noticed the small, two-story home off to her right. As she approached the door, she stopped short and realized that more of Hung Jin's men could be inside. But she was out of options.

Hung Jin could return any minute—or, if Cody missed some predetermined check-in time, others could be on their way to scout out the scene. Lauren did not plan on being here when or if that occurred.

That she had gotten this far was more than she could reasonably have expected. But this was the beginning, not the ending. Holding the gun out in front of her, she opened the front door to the house and waited. Listened.

Slowly, she edged inward, eyes combing the living room chairs, sofa . . . the small bedroom to her left . . . and the kitchen. She stopped and listened again. There were no noises other than her rapid breathing. Reasoning that anyone else in the cabin would already have responded to the gunshots, she let her guard down long enough to begin searching through the kitchen for the keys. She scanned the countertops, pulled open cabinets, and yanked open drawers.

Just then, her eyes caught a glimmer of gold across the room on the round kitchen table. Lying there partially obscured by a splayed-open copy of *Guns & Ammo* was her necklace, the small key still attached. She pushed aside the magazine, scooped up her keepsake—and saw a ring of keys. She snatched them up, then grabbed a bag of pretzels and a can of Barq's root beer that were sitting on the counter.

She knotted her broken necklace and put it back on, where it belonged.

Hung Jin's heart was pounding something fierce. He was light-headed and jittery. Years ago, during his first couple of contract hits, he'd had this same sensation. Too much adrenaline. He had been taught that the hormone sharpens the senses, makes one more aware of his surroundings. But he had once made the mistake of being so focused that he lost the ability to see peripheral issues crucial to the success of his mission—and it had almost gotten him killed. Like an animal that survives in the wild, he had adapted and learned how to control his aggression.

But that was before he spent six years in prison. Before it got personal.

He turned right onto Summit Ridge and accelerated.

Five minutes to the cabin.

Lauren ran to the car, cranked the engine, and drove past the open cabin door, where Cody's body lay sprawled across the floor in an unmistakable death pose. She followed the sloping ice-covered dirt road until it widened a bit, hoping it would lead to a main artery. Out in the mountains, on an overcast day, she had no way of getting her bearings. Was she headed north or west? For that matter, was she in California? Arizona or Nevada? The disorientation was overwhelming. She grabbed for the radio and turned it up loud.

She continued driving for another half mile, at which point the road forked. She skidded to a stop and swiveled her head in both directions. To the left was a narrow roadway named Summit Ridge. To the right was Auburn Hills Pass. She rested her forehead against the steering wheel and closed her eyes. Which way? The wrong road could take her in circles or send her deeper into the middle of nowhere. As the seconds passed, she realized that putting distance between herself and the cabin—and Hung Jin—was most important. Her instinct told her to go right. She turned the wheel and accelerated.

Ten minutes later, after nearly sliding into the embankment several times because of the icy conditions, Lauren finally found signs of civilization: a two-lane road labeled Highway 88. She continued on for a couple of miles before seeing a large grouping of a dozen motorcycles parked outside an aged white building on the corner of Centerville Lane.

She parked the Barracuda and walked into the Valley Bar. Loud music was blaring from a jukebox in the corner, where a gathering of locals was laughing and hooting. The bartender looked up and caught sight of Lauren, then put down her sink rag and moved out from behind the counter.

"You okay?" she asked, appraising the bruises and cuts on Lauren's face.

"I'm fine. I had . . . an accident. I just need to make a call."

"Come on over here." The woman led Lauren to the bar and showed her the telephone. "Can I get you something?"

"No, I don't have much time. I've got to get going."

"I can wrap it to go."

"I lost my wallet in the accident. I don't have any money."

"Not a problem. I'll put something together. Meantime, go ahead and make your call."

"One thing." Lauren hesitated a second, then asked, "Where am I?"

"I know, there aren't any signs around here. You're in Gardnerville. Blink twice and you've missed us."

"No, I mean what state?"

The woman eyed her cautiously. "Nevada."

Lauren thanked her and lifted the telephone. When the woman stepped away, Lauren called Nick Bradley collect. She told him her location and gave him a brief rundown of what had happened to her. Not until she mentioned the name Hung Jin did he interrupt her story.

"Lauren, I want you to call the sheriff and wait there till they get to you. I'll make some calls myself—"

"No, Nick, no sheriff." A burst of raucous laughing in the background made it difficult for her to hear. She plugged her other ear and tried to make out what he was saying.

"Lauren, this is not something to fool around with."

"We'll call Deputy Vork from the airplane. That

way he won't be able to detain me to take a statement."

"Detain you—for what?"

"That's assuming he wouldn't arrest me first and ask questions later."

"Arrest you? Lauren—"

"Right now, I need to get to Michael, and nothing is going to stop me from doing that."

She promised to give him a full accounting of what had happened to her, then asked him to book another flight for them to Virginia. As she hung up the phone, she turned to see the bartender standing beside her with a can of Coke and a cellophane-wrapped sandwich.

"Hope you like turkey."

"Oh, I can't—"

"Sure you can. You look like you could use some help. Anything else I can get you?"

Lauren took the food and shook her head. "You've been great, thanks so much."

She got back in the car and headed down Service Route 88, which, according to the bartender, would lead her to U.S. 50 and take her all the way to Placerville. She reached for the radio, turned it up loud, then sighed deeply.

Michael, what have you gotten me into?

TWENTY-EIGHT

Hung Jin brought the Navigator to a stop ten feet from the cabin. His heart was banging so hard that he felt as if it would rise up through his throat. But as he slammed his car door shut and approached the cabin, he realized that something was wrong. Blood spatter in the snow, stretching a few feet across the threshold . . .

He stepped closer and saw Cody's body. The dumbstruck look on his face, the bare feet. The broken chair.

The empty cabin.

His howl rattled the woods. Though muffled slightly by the snow-covered mountains, the shrill noise numbed his ears. He stepped into the cabin, howled again, then threw himself down and pounded his fists into the floor until pain shot up to his elbows. He was on all fours, his knees beside his fallen colleague's bare feet. He grabbed a broken chair slat off the floor and began beating Cody's torso, the dead thumping sound drowned out by his fury.

"No!" he screamed. "No, no, no!" It was a plaintive wail of great pain. Deep emotional pain. Not because his colleague was dead, but because he had been looking forward to the challenge, to the intense satisfaction Lauren Chambers's death was going to bring him.

His hunger raged; he felt cheated. Again.

He jumped to his feet, grabbed the door, and tore it off its hinges. Then he strode to his car and set off in search of his prey.

TWENTY-NINE

Lauren brought the Barracuda to a stop in the driveway leading to the carport behind her house, where a late-eighties, brown Ford Tempo was parked. She strained to see the car's interior, but no one was inside. At least, no one she could see. Her hand immediately closed around Cody's Smith & Wesson.

She thought of driving to the sheriff's department and telling them a strange car was parked in her driveway. But dressed in torn pajamas and looking as if she'd just spent a couple of days being worked over in a cabin would invite questions, questions she could not answer just yet. Particularly with Cody's blood spattered all over her clothing.

Her other option, going to the nearest phone booth and calling Nick Bradley, made the most sense. Yet she found herself moving across the carport, weapon steadied in front of her, ready to fire . . . prepared to take down the man who had caused her so much pain. Truth was, if it was Hung Jin, she did not know what impulse would drive her at the moment their eyes met.

She crunched along the gravel, making more noise than she would have liked, her movements clumsy because of the oversize shoes. Just then, she heard Tucker barking—and footsteps coming from the far side of her house. Whoever it was did not seem to be in too much of a hurry. In the gravel, the steps sounded slow, deliberate. She held the gun out, lined up the sights—and saw Nick Bradley turn the corner.

Bradley's eyes first found the gun, then Lauren's pained expression. He moved toward her, arms outstretched. "Lauren!"

She met him halfway, near the back door. "Oh, Nick . . ." Fighting back tears, she crumpled into his arms.

"I didn't mean to scare you. But I thought it'd be better if I came early, before you got here, just to make sure no one paid you a visit." Bradley held her tight for a moment, then gently moved her back to scrutinize the bruises that covered her face. "Christ, it looks like you were worked over."

"And over and over."

"Hung Jin."

Lauren nodded, then dislodged herself from Bradley's grip and moved into the house. She sat down heavily at the kitchen table. He took the seat beside her and again examined her face. "I really think we should have you looked at. You could have some broken—"

"I'm fine." She stood up and moved over to the refrigerator.

"I'm serious, Lauren. No offense, but you look awful."

She pulled an apple from the produce drawer and closed the refrigerator. "Thanks for the assessment. And your concern. But right now, all I care about is finding Michael. Did you book us flights?"

"Like you asked. We leave Sacramento in about three hours."

"Then we'd better get going. I'm gonna grab a quick shower, change into some real clothes, and pack a suitcase. We can be out the door in twenty minutes."

Lauren headed into her bedroom and saw the container of Xanax on the night table. She picked up the bottle, placed it on the bed to take with her when she packed, then stopped. "No," she said, tossing the pills into the drawer. She walked into the bathroom and started the shower.

After throwing on a pair of jeans and a sweater top, she packed her suitcase and gave Bradley a condensed version of what had transpired at the cabin, then suggested the plan of action she had devised during her two-hour drive home. With Bradley's assistance, they would drop Tucker at Carla Mae's house, then leave the Barracuda in the parking lot of the sheriff's department. Once airborne, Bradley would call Deputy Vork and recount the details of the kidnapping, escape, and self-defense shooting of the man she knew only as Cody.

Although there would be a furor over her departure from the state until she could be questioned and cleared of all wrongdoing, Lauren felt it would be best to take care of business first and not take a chance on a lengthy detention by the sheriff. Although he had reservations, Bradley reluctantly agreed with her assessment. Due to the secluded location of the house and cabin where she had been held, it could take days before anyone found the dead body. By then, hopefully, she would be back in town.

Once they were on U.S. 50 and headed for the airport, Bradley directed Lauren to his glove compartment. "Pull out the fax. Take a good, hard look at the photo."

Lauren unfolded the paper and looked at the dark, grainy picture in the late-afternoon light. "Who is this?"

"You mean who *was* it. Special Agent Harper Payne."

Eyebrows furrowed, she turned to Bradley. "My God, he does look like Michael."

"Your husband is a hero of sorts in FBI circles. He made headlines all over the country. Hell, all over the world. Seven years ago Payne went undercover to gather evidence against Anthony Scarponi—or Hung Jin, as he called himself. Scarponi was one of the most violent and dangerous assassins in history. And one of the most successful. After testifying against him, Payne had to go into witness protection."

Lauren felt the blood drain from her face. "He was telling the truth."

"Who was?"

"Hung Jin, he said Michael was a killer, that he worked for him." She turned to Bradley. "Is this true, Nick? Was Michael a—a hit man?"

Bradley glanced at Lauren, then turned his attention back to the road. "After you called me I checked in with a buddy of mine over at the FBI. The trial transcript is sealed, as is the case file. But he did tell me that Michael got some plastic surgery and went into hiding after the trial."

"But I'd know, wouldn't I? I mean, I'd know if he was in witness protection."

Bradley shrugged. "Maybe. Probably. Unless he didn't stay in the program."

Lauren was silent, trying to think it all through. She looked down at the picture, then shook her head. The faxed photo was of poor quality, but the resemblance was obvious.

"You said his name was Anthony Scarponi."

Bradley nodded. "Hung Jin is the name he used when he was captured. He claimed to be of Asian lineage. They all thought it was an attempt at an insanity defense."

"That wouldn't be too far from the truth." She sighed and rested her head against the window. She felt fatigued, and the strain of the car ride drained her further. The confirmation that her husband may have killed people—whether while undercover or not—made her feel even worse. "So how does all this work into Michael's disappearance?"

"The government wanted Michael to testify again in a new trial against Scarponi. I'm guessing Scarponi figured that his way out of this mess was to eliminate Michael, prevent him from testifying. Michael must have discovered that Scarponi was close to finding him, and he fled . . . the cross-country ski trip was a cover, a fabrication so he could get away. If that's the case, he did it to protect you."

"Michael would've told me. He wouldn't have just left me."

"If he thought your life was in danger? I think he would have. Look at it this way. If you knew the truth and he told you he was leaving, you'd either try to stop him, or you'd want to go with him."

Lauren closed her eyes. Although she did not want it to be true, she could not argue with Bradley's reasoning. In fact, she knew he was correct on all counts. If so, the only thing that might have saved her from never seeing Michael again was a chance car accident that left him without his memory. Ironically, his amnesia may have served to bring them back together. With that thought, exhaustion took over, and she drifted off to sleep.

• • •

Lauren awoke groggy and tired exactly an hour later, as Bradley was parking the car in the long-term lot at Sacramento International. Even though she was still in a partial daze and moving slowly, they managed to check the Colt through and make it onto the plane with twenty minutes to spare.

After fastening her seat belt, Lauren rested her head back and sighed deeply. As she lay there, she remembered what Bradley had told her about Michael's association with Scarponi. How could he have killed? Even if it was part of his job to infiltrate Scarponi's organization . . . how could he have done that? Michael was such a gentle man, such a good soul. Or so she thought. That he was not the man she thought she had fallen in love with weighed heavily on her. Though the physical pain of Scarponi's torture sessions was now past her, an end to the emotional pain seemed out of reach.

The prospect of finding Michael, of once again lying in his arms, was what she had been longing for. It was what had kept her alive when others might have given up. Now, she was unsure if that was what she really wanted. After all she had just learned, she did not know what to do, what to feel . . . even what to say when she did finally find him.

As their plane roared into the air, daylight was giving way to dusk under intense cloud cover. Fifteen minutes later, the Boeing 737 had leveled off. Lauren pulled out a Walkman to help get her through the flight. "Agoraphobia," she said to Bradley. "Loud music helps."

"Anything I can do?"

"It's a lot better than it used to be. Most of the time I can manage. But the last couple of days have been quite a test for me." A smile broke out across her lips. "In more ways than one." She reclined her seat back as far as it would go, then let out a pained groan.

"You okay?"

"Everything hurts."

"You want some aspirin? I'm sure they've got something on board."

Lauren nodded and Bradley touched the flight attendant call button. A few minutes later, a man was handing her a cup of water and two Motrin. She downed the pills and laid her head back.

"I'm not one to give in to pain," she said, turning her head and watching as the fading orange sun spread its expansive reach across the horizon and hung there. On the opposite side of the plane, the sky had already turned a sapphire blue.

"I believe that."

"My daddy used to swing me in our hammock behind the house on nights like this," Lauren said, staring off at the dark sky.

"A father and his daughter share a very special relationship."

"Do you have any children?"

Bradley was looking off at the night sky as the swoosh of the plane's skin brushing through the wind currents hissed in the background. "I lost the only child I had."

"I'm sorry."

Bradley closed his eyes. "It's a part of my life I try to forget about." There was silence for a moment and then he added, "Having a little girl was the best thing that ever happened to me."

Lauren smiled. "According to my mother, that's what my father said about me."

"Is he still alive?"

Lauren looked down. "No, he died when I was fifteen." She recounted her story of the intruder and the Colt, then told him, "My father was a very proud man. He didn't handle being confined to a wheelchair very well. I don't remember him being happy much after that happened, just bitter." She closed her eyes and for a moment was lost in memories of her father. "A few years after getting shot a blood clot from his leg caused an embolism and he died. We thought we'd beaten that burglar that night. But in the end, we only bought my dad another five years. A miserable five years."

Bradley reached over and brought Lauren close. With the armrest in the way, it was somewhat awkward, but it was exactly what she needed at the moment.

"Lauren," he said, brushing her hair off her face, "I don't think you realize how much your father cherished those years he had with you. He may never have told you how much they meant to him, but I can tell you if he had it to do all over again, he wouldn't have traded those five years in a wheelchair for anything if it would've meant you weren't there to spend them with him."

Lauren was silent, her head buried against Bradley's left arm and chest. "He died in my arms, Nick. All of a sudden his body convulsed and then he went limp. I didn't know what was happening. My mother was at the market, and I didn't know what to do. I called for an ambulance and then looked at him on the floor, wearing only underwear. I guess when he died, he lost his bladder. I smelled it, the urine . . . I quickly dressed him and tried to drag him into his bed so he'd have some sense of dignity when the ambulance arrived." She went quiet again, but it was only because she was fighting the urge to cry. She lost the battle suddenly as tears dripped freely and she began to weep. "All the life had drained from his body . . . he was limp, there was just nothing there, nothing I could do. I couldn't get him onto the bed." She kept her face buried in his arm, hoping no one around her was aware she was crying. Finally, she wiped the tears away, took a deep breath to calm herself, and said, "You'd make a damned good shrink, you know that? I'd forgotten all about that night. It was very painful."

Bradley gently brushed away the few remaining tears on her bruised face. Lauren knew he was trying to comfort her—and, she had to admit, it was working. He had actually brought out repressed memories of her father that she had buried so deep no counselor had been able to reach them. Perhaps Michael's disappearance and her ordeal in the cabin had opened her mind enough that it would now be able to heal. She composed herself and pushed away, sitting upright in her seat. "I'm sorry, that was very intense."

"Please don't be," Bradley said softly, realizing her discomfort. "We all keep more than we'd like to admit bottled up inside. I think of all people, you'd agree with that."

Lauren nodded, then turned away and looked out the windows on the opposite side of the plane.

Bradley placed a hand on her forearm and gave it a reassuring squeeze. "I want you to know that I'll never let anything happen to you. Consider me your guardian angel." He smiled. "Not that you need me. Maybe I should hire you to watch over *me*."

Lauren smiled and rested her head against Bradley's solid shoulder, staring out at the night sky as the whoosh of the wind lulled her eyes closed. As he stroked her hair, she fell asleep again, memories of swinging on the hammock in her daddy's arms drifting silently through her mind.

THIRTY

Melissa Knox shut her spiral notebook, gathered her papers together, and chatted for a moment with her friend Holly, who was inviting her to a party this weekend.

"I'll see if I can make it, I have to check with my father," she said as they walked into the hallway. She turned and looked back at the area around the classroom, where Agent Stanfield was supposed to be waiting for her. He had been her personal bodyguard the last few days, a security measure her father had insisted on. As annoying as it had been, she suddenly felt naked in his absence.

"Missy, you okay?" Holly asked.

"Yeah, I just—that agent who was assigned to me isn't here."

"The good-looking guy with the tight ass?"

Melissa laughed. "That's the one. But don't get your hopes up. He's married."

"Too old for me anyway. Besides, he's too stiff. He hardly smiles."

"Aw, he's okay. Just doing his job. I talked to him a little bit on the way to school." They entered the stairwell and began descending the steps.

"So where is he? I thought he's supposed to be your

shadow," Holly said, enunciating the word *shadow* with a spooky intonation.

Melissa shook her head. "I don't know. Probably out front, waiting for me to come out of class. He knows I've got eco next, so it's not like a secret where I'm headed."

"I'll see you after class in the union," Holly said, pushing through the doors leading to the second floor.

Melissa was descending the steps of the science building when she noticed a middle-aged man dressed in a sweater and jeans approaching her.

"Miss Knox!" he called out with an arm raised, as if he were waving to her.

She stopped walking and clutched her schoolbooks in front of her chest. "Yes . . ."

"I'm Special Agent Luger," the man said as he displayed his credentials. "I need you to come with me, please."

Melissa hesitated. "Where's Agent Stanfield?"

"He was just called away to the Washington Field Office, a problem with one of his cases. Our special agent-in-charge sent me to relieve him. But on the way here I was informed that a security issue has arisen and he wants me to take you to a secure location immediately."

"What kind of security issue?"

"It has to do with the letter Director Knox—your father—received. He did tell you about the letter, didn't he?"

Melissa's eyes darted around the campus in front of her. "Yeah, he told me about the letter. But that's why Agent Stanfield—"

"Miss Knox, I don't mean to argue with you, but

it's extremely important we get off this campus immediately. I'll explain in more detail once we get in the car, where it's safer." Luger rubbernecked his head around the quad, then took her by an arm and led her off toward the street. "Car's this way."

THIRTY-ONE

Jonathan Waller stifled a big yawn as he pulled into the parking garage at headquarters. He had just received a call in which he was ordered to report immediately to Director Knox's office.

"I'm already on my way. I'll be there in less than five minutes," he said. He could tell by the strained tone of Liz Evanston's voice that something was wrong.

When he walked into the director's suite, Scott Haviland was on the phone, Knox was pacing in front of the window, and Special Agent-in-Charge Lindsey was scribbling notes on a pad.

"No, let's divert Calahan to this as well. I need some answers."

Waller's stomach rumbled, but he could tell by the tension on everyone's face that he was not going to be eating anytime soon.

"Took you long enough," Lindsey said to Waller. "We've got some bad shit going down."

"I brought Agent Payne to the doctor for a follow-up exam. I left him there—"

"Stanfield hasn't reported in," Knox said. "I haven't heard from Melissa, and according to her instructor, she didn't show up for her economics class. And my daughter does not cut classes."

The room suddenly seemed blazing hot, the air thin. Waller had broken out into a cold sweat as he sat down hard in the chair next to Haviland. "What about Stanfield's car?"

"I've got campus police scouring the lot, but it's a huge lot. A dozen agents are on their way over now."

"Make that fourteen," Haviland said, cupping the phone. He turned to face Lindsey. "Another dozen are on their way, but they're being diverted and it'll take time—"

"Call in HRT," Knox said. "Have them mobilize immediately. Plainclothes. I want them scouring that campus. Shut down the damn university if you have to. This is my daughter!"

Harper Payne was driven back to the Academy by a senior level assistant Waller had called on his way to the meeting with Knox. His thigh was healing well, the doctor informed him, and adjustments were made in his pain and vertigo medications. As for his memory problems, it would require additional workup before any kind of prognosis could be rendered. For now, he was told, the operative word was patience.

"Patience," Payne growled as he walked toward his dorm room. In contrast with the Academy's glass-walled hallways that connected all of the separate buildings on the campus, the West Dormitory's corridor was institutional modern: acoustic-tile ceilings, stark white walls, and industrial carpet.

He walked into his room, sat down on the edge of the twin bed, and looked out the large window at the lush greenery that surrounded the building. It might not be home, but it was certainly a pleasant environment. Then again, he couldn't remember *what* home was like. He stood up and began to pace. "Patience," he grumbled again. "Easy for him to say."

A knock at the door interrupted his peevish complaining. He pushed himself off the bed and grabbed for the knob. Waller was standing there, holding an overstuffed three-ring binder.

"It's hard to be patient when you can't even remember who your own mother is, Jon."

Waller arched his eyebrows. "I don't see the connection, but I'm not going to argue with you."

"Do you know who my mother was, Jon?"

Waller walked into the small dorm room and sat down on the bed. "I think she passed away about ten years ago. Some kind of car accident. Your dad went a couple of years after that."

Payne nodded. "Was I on good terms with them?"

Waller shrugged. "I think so. I don't remember you complaining about them." He set the large binder on the bed beside him. "How did your appointment go with the doc?"

"Peachy. Thigh's better, brain's not."

"If it makes you feel any better, Knox is arranging an exam with a neurologist."

Payne grunted. "Doctors know how to prescribe drugs, but other than that, they don't know shit."

"I know this has been tough on you, Harp, but you'll come through it. We're here to help."

"Then you think you can get me access to the Internet for a few minutes?"

"The Academy is its own self-contained network. We're linked to every field office and resident agency, but we're not connected to anything outside the Bureau. Security issue, to prevent hacking. The Internet's not secure."

"I sent out an E-mail to someone I think I used to know. I'm hoping she'll be able to jog my memory."

"I'll talk to my SAC, see what I can do. Maybe I can get clearance to bring in my laptop from home. Just keep it under wraps." Waller checked his watch, then stifled a yawn. "Meantime, we've got to get down to business. What do you want to start with, Policy and Procedure or Foreign Counterintelligence?"

Payne regarded Waller for a moment. "Sure you're up to it? You look beat."

"Knox's daughter and one of the agents assigned to her are missing. We think Scarponi's behind it."

"So Knox cranks the heat on you, and you in turn have to make sure I perform."

"Something like that."

"I can do this, Jon. I'm feeling more comfortable with this stuff every day. I'm beginning to understand why I became an agent in the first place."

"You were one of the great ones."

"And will be again. I'd like to stay on with the Bureau."

Waller chuckled. "C'mon, Harp, you know that's not possible. It's not safe. Look what this asshole is doing to the director. He doesn't think anyone can touch him. That makes for a very dangerous adversary."

"It just means he'll be careless and make mistakes. That's when we close in on his operation. We won't need me to make the old charges stick, because we'll have a shitload of new ones."

"A guy like this doesn't make mistakes."

"He did when he took me under his wing."

"We got lucky. Trust me, it won't happen again."

"So give me a new identity and make my face over

again. I'll gain some weight, dye my hair, grow a beard, and wear colored contacts. Assign me abroad. But don't shut me out."

Waller sighed. "I know you mean well, but I just don't think Knox will go for it." He opened the binder he had brought with him. "Meantime, we've got a job to do. Let's start with Counterintelligence."

"I'm serious about this, Jon."

"One day at a time, buddy. First we get through this trial. If we're successful, I'll talk with Knox, see what I can do."

THIRTY-TWO

Douglas Knox spent the night at home pacing his study, an array of telephones lined up along the credenza: the white one provided a direct link to the White House; the yellow was a secure line to the Pentagon; the blue, a secure line to the CIA; and the red phone rang through directly to headquarters. A Lucent Technologies corded phone, now rigged with electronic devices sprouting wires, served as his standard residential line. Although the number was unlisted, the Bureau had connected recording and listening devices to it in the event a ransom call came through.

But Knox knew better. The abductor did not want money. As he saw it, this was about power and leverage, and there were two scenarios. In the first, Melissa would be returned unharmed, with her successful abduction serving as a strong message as to what would happen if Knox chose not to cooperate: if she could be taken once, she could be taken again. But Knox knew she would not be returned alive the second time.

The other scenario was one Knox did not want to consider. For if she did not return alive, an unofficial all-out war would be declared on the responsible party. He knew it was Anthony Scarponi. But lacking proof Scarponi was behind the abduction made such an aggressive stance dicey. If the press grabbed hold of it, the FBI would be taken to task for heavy-handed tactics, the failed lessons of Ruby Ridge and Waco dredged up all over again. One thing the Bureau did not need was another bruise to its reputation.

However, for the past few hours Knox had not been concerned with public perception. At the moment, he was both an ordinary citizen whose daughter had been kidnapped as well as director of the most powerful law enforcement entity in the world.

Sylvia Knox's eyes were dark and bloodshot. She sat in a corner chair, dabbing at her tears and staring vacantly at the wall in front of her, occasionally glancing over at her husband, whose rigid face and demeanor only partially conveyed his concern. Once, he had walked over to her, placed a reassuring hand on her shoulder, and then walked away to resume pacing.

In addition to Knox's security detail, three Hostage Rescue Team agents were in the room, taking turns sitting, standing, reading magazines, and taking short breaks to smoke cigarettes on the porch.

Just as Knox had sat down to rest his legs after a continuous hour of pacing, a call came over the radio clipped to the HRT squad leader's uniform.

"Repeat? Over."

"We have Melissa Knox. She'll be at the front door in fifteen seconds, sir."

Sylvia's whimper of delight pierced the sudden silence of the room.

The squad leader looked to Knox, whose eyebrows had arched downward toward his nose. "Give me that," Knox said as he grabbed the radio. "Was anyone with her? Over."

"No, sir. She said she was dropped off a few blocks away and ran home. Over."

"Shit," Knox said, handing the man back his radio. "If she saw any of them, I want an identification tech with a laptop here within the hour."

Melissa was embraced and kissed by her mother and father, ate a container of yogurt, and then agreed to be debriefed by the HRT agents.

"And you only saw one of them," Knox said.

Melissa nodded. "Just that one agent—I mean, man. He told me to lie down on the backseat so no one would see me. I asked him what was wrong, and he said he couldn't discuss it, that it was very sensitive. Then after a while he got a call and he said he was taking me to a safe house. He gave me a blindfold to put on and said I wasn't allowed to know where we were going because the CIA uses it, too."

"How long did it take to get to the safe house?" one of the HRT agents asked.

Melissa shrugged. "I don't know, we drove around for like an hour or two. After he got that call, it was like, maybe twenty minutes before we got there."

"Did you hear any unusual noises? Bells, horns, jackhammers, trucks—"

"Maybe some trucks, big ones, you know, like tractor trailers."

"Anything else?"

"It didn't really seem like I was in a house. It smelled more like a cheap motel."

Knox exchanged glances with the agent. "What makes you think it was a cheap motel?"

"It smelled like Lysol. And immediately after walking in, there was a really soft bed. I think I smelled cigarette smoke, you know, kind of like in the drapes or something. It was gross."

"Then what happened?" Knox asked.

"He got another call."

"Did you hear him mention any names? Did he talk about anything in particular?"

Melissa thought for a moment, then shook her head. "Not that I can remember."

"What happened after he got that call?" the agent asked.

"That's when we left. He said it was time to go, that everything was secure."

"How long was the ride back home?"

"I don't know."

"What do you mean, you've got to give us some kind of an idea," Knox blurted, his frustration evident. "Ten minutes, an hour, two hours—"

"I said I don't know, Dad," Melissa said just as firmly. "I fell asleep. When I woke up, he was telling me that he'd just spoken to you. He stopped the car and said I was a few blocks from home and that I should run. I thought he was kidding."

There was a knock at the door, and one of the HRT agents walked out of the room to answer it. A few seconds later, an identification technician walked into the kitchen, followed by a handful of relief agents for the security detail and by the head of the HRT. Agents Waller and Haviland brought up the rear, shirts creased, ties removed, and collars splayed open.

"Take ten minutes to get up to speed," Knox said to the HRT assistant special agent-in-charge. "Then I want you to assemble a fresh team. I want some of them on my house, some with my wife and daughter should either leave the house tomorrow."

"Yes, sir," the man said, turning toward the door.

"Waller, Haviland, come into my study for a moment." They followed Knox in and watched as he closed both doors. "We've got us a situation here, one that requires you two to be privy to highly sensitive information." Knox looked at each of the men, reading their faces. After a brief pause, he continued, "How much background did Lindsey give you on Scarponi's release?"

Waller shrugged. "Just that he was granted a new hearing based on some bogus witness that came forward. The judge bought it and that's why we had to find Payne."

"He was under electronic surveillance," Knox said, "using a new type of microchip the Bureau developed. It was embedded deep in the buttock and was supposed to locate the offender at all times to within a ten-foot radius using the GPS system. The device was supposed to be foolproof." Knox sat down heavily in his desk chair. "A month after Scarponi was released, we received some odd readings, like he was moving almost in a drug-induced manner. A couple of agents were put on him and they finally found out why he'd been running in circles. He'd somehow removed the chip and placed it in a rat. Obviously, we lost track of him."

Waller shook his head. "Jesus Christ."

"Suffice it to say that for the past four months, he's eluded our search efforts. This threat letter we received was the first indication that he might still be in the country."

"He stayed to finish the job," Waller said. "Payne's the only one who can hurt him. He gets rid of Payne, his problem's solved."

Knox nodded. "The surveillance chip was a covert operation. He didn't know it had been implanted, at least, we don't think he knew. No one—no one gets wind of any of this, am I making myself extremely clear?" Knox looked hard at both agents. "There can be no misunderstanding about this, or I'll have your careers."

"What about Harper—"

"No one. No . . . one," Knox said, emphasizing each word separately.

The agents exchanged an uneasy look, then turned back to Knox.

"Yes, sir," Haviland said as the door to the study opened.

"Dad?" Melissa walked in holding her purse in one hand and a small electronic device in the other. "Did one of you put this in my bag?"

Just then, the device began to beep. Haviland jumped out of his seat and advanced on Melissa. "Give it to me real gently," he said, holding his hand out. "Jon, call the EOD unit and alert ATF. I think we've got us a small incendiary device."

"A what?" Melissa asked.

"A goddamned bomb," Waller said as he grabbed the red telephone.

"All right, everyone out of the house!" Knox yelled.

"Hold it," Haviland said, still cradling the suspect device in the palms of his hands. "Are we sure the area's secure? They could be using this as a way to flush everyone out into the street. Car bomb, sniper, even a drive-by—any of which could take us all out before we knew what hit us."

Knox looked at the small device, which was about half the size of a television remote.

The lead HRT agent walked in, saw the unit in Haviland's hands, and cursed under his breath. "Don't make any sudden movements." He stuck his head through the study door. "Vasquez, take three men with you and secure the area. We need a clear path to the HRT truck. You've got one minute."

"Hold it," Waller said. "One minute? In the dark—"

"One minute," Knox said as the device continued to beep. "Then we all come out and take our chances."

EOD, Metro Police's bomb-disposal unit, was at the Knox home in less than nine minutes. Fifteen minutes would have been an acceptable response time, but that it was the director's residence forced a quicker, more immediate reaction.

After having done their best to secure the vicinity, the agents began evacuating the neighbors in the surrounding two-block radius and blocked off both entrances to the street. Brief examination and X-ray analysis of the small device revealed it was safe enough to move by robotic transport to the bomb detonation truck.

The Knoxes' house was searched with bomb-sniffing dogs and was declared clear within ten minutes. The family was then moved, under cover, back into their home from the tactical room in the rear of the HRT vehicle. It took the bomb disposal technicians forty-five tense minutes of quarantine in their mobile lab to properly analyze the explosive device. When they finally emerged to brief the director on the unit and its capabilities, HRT agents were stationed at various points along the street and around the Knoxes' house.

The director sat down wearily behind his desk and ran two hands through his damp hair. Melissa and Sylvia had gone to bed, and with the exception of half a dozen security-detail agents, only Haviland and Waller remained inside the house.

"It was a bomb all right," the explosives expert said. "Very sophisticated, capable of taking down this house and a couple of the neighboring ones with it. But the two detonation-fuse leads weren't attached."

"Weren't attached," Haviland said. "You mean they came apart?"

"No, they were never together. They were purposely mounted a half inch apart."

"Another message," Knox said. His usually well-coiffed hair was disheveled and he had a sagging darkness about his eyes. "That he can do whatever he wants and there's nothing we can do to protect ourselves." He shook his head. "I'm tired of running, of being on the defensive." Knox slammed a fist down on the table. "Damn it, I've had enough. Tomorrow, the war begins."

Knox went over a few details with Waller and Haviland, then with a wave of a hand bid them good-night. "Go catch whatever sleep you can before the sun's up," he told them.

"And can you two give me a few minutes alone?" he asked his security-detail agents.

"We'll be right outside if you need us," one of them said.

"I'm sure we've had all the excitement we're going to have for a while," Knox said.

As soon as the door to his study clicked shut, he grabbed for the yellow phone. He punched a few numbers, leaned back in his chair, and rubbed at his eyes with the fingers of his right hand.

"It's me," he said after the phone was answered. "Are you really innocent until proven guilty?"

"That depends. Are we secure?" Hector DeSantos asked.

"Not at the moment. But we're going to be."

THIRTY-THREE

Lauren and Nick Bradley arrived at Ronald Reagan National Airport at six in the morning. They were both exhausted, since neither had slept well during the flight. Lauren's dream of her father had degenerated into a nightmare, and after that she was unable to fall back to sleep.

They rented a Chevy Malibu and drove to the small Best Western hotel rooms Bradley had reserved for them. The day they arrived, Bradley checked in with some of his contacts, a handful of private investigators and law enforcement people he had come to know over the years. Meanwhile, Lauren visited the mall where Michael had been when he sent her his message. Only a year ago, a simple visit to a mall would have been a devastating experience. Now, however, although her situational anxiety was still present, it was largely manageable.

Lauren had touched the panel of the AT&T kiosk and imagined her husband sitting there, his fingers playing across the keyboard, typing out the message that had given her hope and perhaps the will to survive while being held captive.

Lauren then spoke with merchants in each store, small and large, in an attempt to uncover some morsel of information she could add to the puzzle.

Due to the number of sales staff and the many shifts and days off, however, she knew her efforts were going to be inefficient and incomplete.

After five hours, her most promising lead was a woman in Dillard's department store who remembered a man who had stolen a customer's credit card. When she provided a description that sounded like Michael, Lauren showed her his photo—and received a big nod from the employee. "That's him, that's the guy. I have to notify security. They never did catch him."

Sensing more trouble than it was worth, Lauren stopped the woman as she was reaching for the phone. "I'll just go to security and tell them myself. I'm sure they'll have a lot of questions for me."

The woman directed her to the security office on the lower level. Lauren headed toward the elevator, then abruptly turned and walked out of the store. She called a cab and went back to the hotel, where she waited for Bradley to return.

The following morning, Lauren and Bradley pored over a map and set a course of action for canvassing the surrounding area.

"Isn't this a long shot?" Lauren asked.

Bradley smiled. "Welcome to the world of private investigation. It's not easy work, but at least we've got a really solid lead. We know he's here somewhere. If we stick to our plan, we should have some answers in a few days. I've put the word out on the street that we're looking for him, and you'll be camping out at the mall. Unless he can get on the Internet somewhere else, he'll have to go back there to see if 'Just Rose at Hotmail' wrote him back."

Lauren agreed that they were at least being proactive, even though she was becoming aware that finding Michael in Washington or Virginia was akin to looking for a needle in a haystack.

The only encouraging thought was that this particular needle wanted to be found.

THIRTY-FOUR

P ayne closed the binder full of condensed notes he and Jonathan Waller had assembled on the Scarponi trial and got ready to head out to the Academy's dining hall for breakfast.

Although he could not recall what his life had been like before the accident, his life since then had been filled with indecision, victimization, and defensive actions. This morning, for the first time, he awoke feeling he had control over things. Instead of reacting to events, he could anticipate them, plan responses. And he had a place where he fit in and was respected. Above everything else, he felt wanted, needed.

He felt at home.

A knock at the half-open door shifted Payne's attention. It was Waller, a black nylon bag slung over his shoulder.

"I thought we weren't getting together till nine-thirty," Payne said.

Waller made his way over to the desk. "I brought my laptop. Thought you might want to check for that message before we got started."

"A man of his word. Thanks."

Waller set the computer down, plugged it in, and attached the telephone cord. "You remember how to use Windows?"

Payne hesitated. "Start, programs. Yeah, I remember that." A broad smile creased his face. "I'm not completely helpless."

"I didn't know if that stuff had been wiped from your mind along with all your other memories."

"The doctor said there are different kinds of memory, and things done by rote are handled by a part of the brain that wasn't affected by the accident. Something like that. That's why I can remember how to brush my teeth, chew my food, fire my weapon."

"And operate Windows."

"Apparently so." Payne sat down at the desk, found the power switch, and turned on the computer.

Waller yawned. "Oh, man. Long night. I was up till three with Knox."

"What's the latest?"

"His daughter was kidnapped and returned several hours later. She's fine. Stanfield's still missing. It's almost a lock Scarponi's involved."

"I'm feeling better about my testimony, if that helps at all."

Waller managed a smile from the left corner of his mouth. "It helps a lot." He stood up and walked to the door. "I'll leave you to fool around with that thing. Meantime, I'm gonna go grab some breakfast. Meet me there when you're done."

"Will do, boss."

As the door closed, the laptop completed its bootup sequence. Payne clicked on Internet Explorer, dialed into the Web, and navigated to the Hotmail Website. Two messages were in his in-box: a welcome message from Hotmail and a reply from "just_rose@hotmail.com." His heart began pounding as he clicked on Rose's message:

Dear lost_in_virginia,

I'm so glad you wrote to me. Yes, I know who you are. Your name is Michael Chambers, and you live in Placerville, California—a small, rural town east of Sacramento. You're my husband, and we've been married for four years. My name is Lauren Rose Chambers (Rose is my maiden name) and we live in a quaint two-story house up on a hill. You're a network account manager for a small communications company nearby.

I've been very worried about you. You probably don't remember, but you went on a ski trip with some of your frat buddies and didn't come home. I've been unable to find you, and ended up filing a missing person's report with the sheriff.

Since you told me you were at a mall near Virginia Presbyterian, I've booked a flight for Wednesday morning. I'm coming to find you. Please tell me where I can locate you, and when. I'll take you home and get you over to a doctor. Don't worry, we'll be together again soon.

Write me back at the same e-mail address, or leave me a message at 530 555-9283.

I love you,
Lauren

Payne lifted the phone from the receiver, but then realized that today was Thursday. *She must be here,* he thought, *somewhere nearby.* He looked at the name again. Lauren Chambers. Michael Chambers.

He rested his elbows on the desk and buried his head in his hands. As he tried to sort through what he was feeling, he realized he was torn. He had a wife and lived in a small, rural town? Must be where he went after leaving the program. And what in the world was a network account manager? Again, his life was suddenly thrown into disarray. He couldn't let that happen.

Payne walked over to the door and lifted the shoulder harness from the hook. He strapped it to his body and turned to look at himself in the mirror. Starched white shirt, gun holster, badge. He knew who he was. Harper Payne, FBI agent. Harper Payne, the man the director was counting on to put one of the most dangerous assassins back behind bars where he belonged.

He looked at the message from Lauren Chambers, severed his connection to the Internet, and shut down the computer.

Agent Waller was waiting for him.

THIRTY-FIVE

Hector DeSantos sat down beside Brian Archer, who was jawing on his chewing gum and tapping away at the computer keyboard. Archer had worked his way through a myriad of computer networks using the new set of passwords and protocols Knox had provided. It had taken him three days to navigate the databases of the National Security Agency, CIA, Defense Intelligence Agency, and Department of Defense. But despite his diligence, he had nothing to show for it.

"Maybe this is all just a fucking waste of time," DeSantos said.

"I doubt Knox—"

Just then, a beep sounded on a laptop Archer had set up across the room on the conference room table.

"What the hell is that?" DeSantos asked.

Archer quickly moved over to the computer and opened it up. He pressed a few keys, studied the screen, and smiled. "Beautiful."

"What are you doing?"

"While you were off on that Krackhaeur surveillance, I brought my laptop in from home, the one I play around with—"

"What is it you call it, the hacker-cracker?"

"The one and only." Archer had written a program that was capable of breaking into certain securely encrypted sites. Though he only did it as a hobby, he had hacked into some sensitive corporate servers over the past two years. As a testament to his ingenuity, he had never been caught—which was a good thing considering the discomfort it would have created as he tried to dance around the issue of exactly what his position was in the intelligence community. He figured he would let his boss fight it out with law enforcement, and when the dust settled, they would all laugh about it. After all, he had to stay sharp, and the best exercise for his hacking and cracking muscles was active combat testing. In this case, the war was security, and the battlefield was encrypted networks.

"So what have we got going here?" DeSantos asked.

"I ran my worm program."

"Is that earthworm or wiggleworm?"

Archer sat back from the keyboard. "I would've thought that after listening to me all these years, you would have picked up some of this stuff by now."

"You're assuming I was listening. What you took for nodding my head in agreement while you were talking to the screen was really the bob of my head while I was napping."

Archer made a face. "Are you listening to me now?"

"If I nod off, just kick me."

"I'll do more than that." He swiveled his chair to face DeSantos. "Worm programs are like viruses, except that they don't attach themselves to files. They're used by hackers who are trying to get into someone's computer network to destroy data. A good worm, like mine, moves quickly from server to server undetected, searching for information that matches the parameters you set for it."

"You're destroying government data?"

"Good, a semi-intelligent question. At least you're listening. No, I'm not destroying anything. I've modified the program. I'm using it to look for specific information on those mainframes, kind of like a search engine does on the Internet. In this case, I'm looking for anything having to do with Anthony Scarponi. When it gets a match, it compiles a list and sends it back to me."

DeSantos tilted his chin back and looked at Archer through discerning eyes. "You're a lot smarter than I thought you were."

"Thanks." Archer leaned forward and struck a few keys, then pulled a printer cable from a receptacle in the adjacent tech wall and attached it to the back of his computer. He pressed another key and sat back. "We'll have an answer in a minute."

"I'm glad I have you around, you know?"

"How glad?" Archer asked. "Very glad or just somewhat glad?"

"Right now? Very, very glad."

Archer moved over to the far wall and lifted a few pieces of paper from the printer. "I'm never gonna let you forget you said that."

"Hey, we're a team, you know? We each do our thing. That's all I'm saying."

Archer was flipping through the pages, scanning

the printout. "And what 'things' do you do as a member of our 'team,' Hector?"

"I'm the breadwinner, my man. You play the keyboard, I play the politicos. Without me, you wouldn't have all this computer shit to do all your . . . shit on."

"We complete each other, is that what you mean?"

DeSantos held up a hand. *"Complete each other?* Now you sound like Maggie. Don't be getting philosophical on me, Brian. Get enough of that crap at home."

Archer picked up the other pages that had emerged from the printer. He rifled through them, then pointed to one of the entries. "Hmm. Looks like we've gotten some interesting hits here." He moved back to the laptop, entered an entry code, and navigated through a series of security screens. "NSA and DoD documents. Shall we call them up and read them?"

"Yes," DeSantos said in a formal British accent, "we shall."

A moment later, the screen was filled with a memo that corresponded to the documents they were looking for.

"Hit the print button. Let's get a hard copy of this stuff before we're kicked off the system again."

"It's all in code," Archer said.

DeSantos turned to his partner. "Does that surprise you? It's the fucking NSA. They live in code. I bet they talk to each other in code." He looked back at the screen. "Except I don't know how they'd pronounce these words . . ."

Archer ignored him and moved over to the printer again. He removed the new document, took it to his scanner, and placed it facedown on the glass. "I don't know how long this will take. Could be hours."

DeSantos put his feet up on the conference table, closed his eyes, and folded his hands across his stomach. "In the meantime, I guess I'd better earn my salary."

THIRTY-SIX

Payne was seated in the back row of the small, sloping stadium-style classroom at the Academy, stifling a yawn. Sleep had not been coming easy the past few days, and it was now reaching the point where he considered asking the doctor if he could get a prescription for some sleeping pills.

He blinked a few times and looked around the room, taking in the mix of new agents around him. Many were in their late twenties, while a couple were in their midthirties, barely getting in under the Bureau's cap of thirty-seven.

The instructor was discussing proper forensic crime-scene procedures, a topic Payne found fascinating. But as soon as the overhead graphic depicting mathematical formulas consisting of sines and cosines of angles was displayed, his mind began drifting off.

Suddenly, an image of a house on a hill popped into his mind. And a car, a late-model Chrysler. Forest green, high polish. It was the same one he had seen in his dreams. He sat there, trying to trace the memory, when suddenly the instructor stopped talking. The entire class had turned and was facing Payne, apparently expecting a response from him.

"Agent Thompson," the instructor said, "I'll take

that as a no, that you don't have anything additional to offer."

Payne felt his face turning crimson. "Uh, no, sir. Nothing to offer."

"Very well," the man said as the heads swiveled back to the instructor. Even though he was the only field agent taking the class, he felt that he might as well have been one of the rookies, longing for the day when he was to be presented with his credentials and job assignment. Of course, no one in the class, including the instructors, knew his true identity. With the mole still unidentified, the fewer people who knew he was at the Academy, the better.

At 5:10, class ended and the students left their assigned seats for the dining hall, where dinner awaited them. Waller was waiting in the hallway as Payne walked out of the room.

"Director Knox wants you in on the briefing of the kidnap situation," he said.

"When's that?"

"Forty-five minutes. We've got to leave now."

They were in the car a few minutes later, heading down the winding two-lane road toward the main gate at Quantico.

"Were you ever able to retrieve your E-mail?" Waller asked.

Payne turned away and looked out the side window. He had told Waller over breakfast that he was having difficulty getting through to the Hotmail Website.

"Yeah, it worked," he said, realizing that he needed to talk with someone about the message he had received. He had originally decided to keep knowledge of his wife's E-mail to himself, feeling that the internal conflict he was suddenly facing—the realization that he had made a mistake in giving up his former life—was best handled without meddling interference. But as the day wore on, guilt welled up inside him. As any man should, he felt a responsibility to the woman he had evidently married. He knew instinctively that he could not run away from such a commitment. At the same time, acknowledging that he needed an outlet, someone he could bounce his concerns off, he turned to Waller.

"I got a message," Payne said with a chuckle. "From my *wife*."

"Your wife—"

"Yeah, can you believe that? I live in a small town, some place called Placerville, and I work as a network account manager."

"Far cry from life as an agent," Waller said.

"Yeah, sounds about as interesting as watching lettuce grow."

Waller sighed. "What it is and what it sounds like could be very different, Harp. I find it hard to believe that you'd go from the kind of career you had to living a boring lifestyle."

"I guess. Maybe I needed the change after what I'd been through."

"You've got to believe in yourself, buddy. No one has as much vested in yourself as you do. No one. I'm sure you did what you thought was best at the time. But things have changed. You've been through a lot in the past several days. I say we first get you through this trial, then you can regroup, make some decisions."

Payne nodded, but looked away.

"If there's anything I can do to help, just let me know, okay? And I'm not just talking about Bureau stuff. Anything."

Payne thanked him, then fell silent, nearly drifting off to sleep several times while staring out the window as they made the forty-minute drive along I-95, up Pennsylvania Avenue, and into the parking garage at headquarters.

They took the elevator up to the lobby, where they were greeted by Chuck Seamen, the FBI policeman who had been assigned the lobby's four-to-twelve shift for the past nineteen years. Graying at the temples with an expanding waistline, he had come to enjoy the second most relaxed schedule at headquarters. Seamen engaged them in some playful banter as Waller logged them in and headed to the elevator.

After receiving clearance from Liz Evanston, Waller led the way into the vacant office. A moment later, the director entered and took his seat behind the desk.

"Good evening, gentlemen," Knox said, nodding for them to sit. "Agent Haviland should be joining us in a moment." While fiddling with some papers on his desk, Knox glanced up at Payne. "I asked you to be here because I felt it's time to begin integrating you into the current Scarponi situation, to bring you up to speed."

Payne nodded. "Yes, sir."

"As I'm sure Agent Waller has informed you, my daughter was taken by Scarponi's men yesterday morning. She was returned unharmed last night."

Haviland walked in and sat down next to Waller. "Sorry I'm late, but I was waiting on verbals from the ME and the lab."

Knox motioned him on with the wave of a hand. "Your report."

"Agent Stanfield's body was discovered this after-

noon a half mile from Georgetown's main campus,"
Haviland said. "Single gunshot wounds to the chest
and cranium. Preliminary findings indicate he was
shot in the chest first, at extremely close range with a
forty-caliber semiautomatic, most likely a Glock. The
head wound was inflicted a short time later, while he
was lying down. Body was found in his trunk, where
he apparently bled out. But he wouldn't have recovered even if immediate medical attention was rendered."

Knox sighed. "Assessment."

"As I see it, someone approached Stanfield either
in the guise of a fellow agent, campus security, or
Georgetown PD. We suspect he engaged Stanfield
somewhere in the quad and drilled him in the chest
with a suppressed round. Stanfield was then taken to
a waiting car nearby where he was driven to his own
parked vehicle, half a mile away. They stuffed him in
the trunk and popped him in the head. His credentials case was missing, so whoever took it probably
used it to lure Melissa into a false sense of security."

Knox was nodding. "Okay. Anything else?"

"Just questions, sir," Payne said.

Knox looked at him. "Go ahead."

"Was that Glock a Bureau-issued weapon?"

"Ballistics is checking it out," Haviland said.
"They're running the slugs against the database of
every handgun issued at the Academy."

"Stanfield was with HRT, right?" An affirmative
nod from Knox told Payne to continue. "So I'm wondering how a trained, seasoned agent like that would
allow anyone he didn't know to get so close to him."

"Like I said, he could've been dressed as campus
security, a fellow agent—"

"I don't buy it," Payne said. "I say he knew the guy. Maybe he's one of ours."

"I agree," Waller said. "I think it needs to be looked into."

Knox was nodding. "Excellent. That's the way you should be thinking, Agent Payne. Agent Haviland, I'd like you to follow up on that. Get me that report from ballistics ASAP." Knox pulled a computer-generated drawing from his desk and handed color copies to each of the people in the room. "Meantime, we're attacking this on another front. Melissa's given our ID tech a description, and he's produced this computer-generated likeness. It's being circulated to all the regional SACs, ADICs, and ASACs, including the ones Stanfield served under when he was stationed in Kansas City. So far, none of them have identified this suspect as an agent under their direction, past or present. It's possible he could've altered his appearance, so we have to realize this may not be of any use to us." Knox looked at the three agents. "Anything else?"

With no further questions, Knox rose. "Okay then. Agent Payne, would you give us a moment?"

Payne nodded and turned to Waller. "I'll meet you in the lobby."

Knox waited for the door to close, then looked at Waller and Haviland. "How's he doing?"

"He's not only soaked everything up we've given him, but his confidence is coming around, too," Haviland said. "He feels real comfortable in the role."

"Excellent. Then you don't foresee any problems?"

Waller threw a sideways glance at Haviland. "Not exactly a problem, sir, but maybe a distraction."

Knox folded his arms across his chest. "Explain."

"He received an E-mail from his wife this afternoon. It seems to have shaken him up a bit."

"E-mail?" Knox's forehead was deeply creased, his eyebrows arched downward. "Where in the hell would he get access to a PC? The Bureau's systems aren't connected—"

"I'm afraid that's my fault, sir. I brought him my laptop. I didn't see it as being a problem, and SAC Lindsey said—"

"I don't give a rat's ass about what Lindsey said. This investigation is being run through my office, do you understand, Agent Waller?"

Waller sighed. "Understood, sir. It's just that Harper felt like a connection with the outside might help him regain his memory faster. I thought that was our goal."

"Agent Waller, this is a highly sensitive investigation. More than just the Scarponi case is at stake. The president has taken substantial heat over his release, and he's been on my ass to make sure we put him away for good. What's never been made public is that there were some very delicate negotiations with the other countries when Scarponi was taken into custody. Even though we had jurisdiction over the Foster murder, the other countries all claimed they had first crack at him. In order to avoid a big pissing contest, which would've jeopardized our case against Scarponi, the president moved quickly. He had to virtually guarantee them that Scarponi would pay for what he'd done." Knox sat down heavily. "You can imagine what hit the fan when Judge Noonan released him on bail. If it gets out that Scarponi's on the loose and that we don't even know where he is, it would almost certainly screw up the arms pact negotiations the president has worked so hard to get them to agree to. The timing couldn't be worse."

"But it could backfire. If they find out the president knew he'd escaped and didn't alert them, wouldn't that be worse?"

Knox broke a crooked smile. "That's the point, Agent Waller. The president can't tell them what he doesn't know. If he doesn't know about it in the first place, he can't be accused of lying to them."

"You're insulating him."

"Yes."

"Which means you take the heat if we don't find him."

Knox shifted uncomfortably in his seat. "We *will* find him, Agent Waller. And Agent Payne's testimony will put him away. On the other hand, his failure to testify will have the opposite effect. It all depends on what actions we take or don't take in the next few weeks. That's an enormous burden on all of us, but I've chosen to put a lot of the heat on you two because I thought you could handle it. Now I see you make a rookie mistake with this E-mail—"

"Sir," Waller said, sitting ramrod straight, "I can assure you that it won't happen again."

"You better believe it won't or I'll pull you off the case and transfer you to the resident agency in Fairbanks, Alaska." Knox stood up and began to pace in front of the darkened window. "I found out about his wife just before we brought Payne in. When our Sacramento field office called and told me they had a lead on a guy fitting Payne's description in the Placerville area, we put a few agents on him. But we were too late. Turns out he'd left on some kind of ski vacation in Colorado. They did a search of the airlines' databases for flights leaving Colorado and immediately went there to intercept him."

"Why didn't we just tell him about his wife?" Haviland asked.

"I don't owe you an explanation, Agent." Knox stared the man down, then shook his head. According to protocol, he did not, of course, need to say any more. However, he knew it would be best if he could provide them with a reasonable rationalization, if nothing else, in case they had to give Payne some kind of justification for their actions to maintain his trust. "If we bring his wife into this, we'd be placing her in harm's way. We'd have to worry about Scarponi getting to her and using her to get to him. Not to mention the fact that she'd probably be a huge distraction for him. We need Payne totally focused on this trial."

"But if the Bureau found Payne and his wife, shouldn't we have assumed that Scarponi would, too?"

Knox sighed. "We made a tactical error."

There was an uneasy silence, finally broken by Haviland. "So what's the plan? Do we just tell him—"

"Nothing. Tell him nothing. This is not his decision, Agent Haviland. I want to be very clear on this. He is not to communicate with his wife. At all costs, I want that line of communication severed."

"And if he insists?"

"Then handle the situation. You understand the forces at play."

"He's got my laptop," Waller said. "He may've already put out a response to her message."

"Where's the computer?"

"In his room, at the Academy."

"Room number?"

"Two thirty-two West."

Knox picked up his phone and dialed the Academy. Waller and Haviland listened while their boss directed a nameless acquaintance to enter the room and disable the modem. "Make it seem like it's a software glitch or something. I don't want him to think it was deliberate." Knox hung up and looked at Waller. "No more favors for him. You know what's at stake. We need him focused. On Scarponi, not his wife."

THIRTY-SEVEN

When the door slammed, Lauren bolted upright in her bed. The room was dark. She was dressed in her clothes—that much she could tell. But where was she?

She was so disoriented. She rubbed at her eyes, but that just made them burn more. She swung her legs off the bed and realized her shoes were still on her feet. Although she had been sleeping, she was still exhausted.

She felt around the room and found a wall-mounted lamp. The sudden burst of light made her eyes ache, but she could at least see she was in a motel room.

Think, Lauren, think. Michael—cabin—gun—Bradley—plane. Okay.

Just then, there was a hard knocking at the door.

"Lauren, you in there? Lauren!"

"Coming," she said, stumbling forward.

She peered through the peephole, then turned the knob.

Bradley's head was tilted in curiosity. "I tried knocking before, but you didn't answer. I figured you weren't back yet, so I waited."

"I was asleep. I heard a door slam and it woke me." She found her way to a nearby chair. "I'm still a little out of it. What time is it?"

"Seven."

"I remember getting back from the mall around five-thirty. I lay down and that was it, I must've fallen asleep." She sat down heavily in the chair.

"I take it Michael didn't show."

Lauren rubbed her eyes. "It was one of the more boring days in my life. Sitting in a mall, watching the people come and go, isn't the most intellectually stimulating activity in the world." She rose from the chair and walked into the bathroom to splash her face with water. "If there's one good thing in all of this, it's been a hell of an effective treatment plan for my agoraphobia. The ultimate in cognitive therapy."

"I wish I could say my day was better than yours, but so far, my guys haven't turned anything up. I hit some well-known places, even the Metro Police. Nobody knows anything, let alone seen him."

She dabbed at her face with a white towel. "So now what? Back to the mall tomorrow?"

"Tomorrow we call doctors' offices and hospitals."

"I feel so damned helpless. We're in the same town and he's one person amongst millions. Unless we hear from him, how are we going to find him?"

"We'll check your credit cards again. Maybe we'll get lucky. If he's charged something, we can interview the vendor, see if Michael mentioned anything about where he's staying. It's a long shot, but the idea is to assume nothing and investigate everything."

"If he had his credit cards, he'd know his name."

Bradley nodded. "Okay, scratch that. No, try it anyway. It can't hurt. I'd also call your home machine, see if he's left a message. Then check your

E-mail. At the moment, our best lead will come from Michael himself. While you're doing that, I'm going to go get us a couple of Cokes over by the office."

Bradley left and Lauren went to work. With her heart tapping out a fast rhythm, she picked up the phone and called home. But there were no messages. She pulled out her handheld PC and dialed in. There was an E-mail from Amber at Cablecast, but nothing from Michael.

She sighed disappointment, clicked on Amber's message, and began to read.

Dear Lauren,
Got your message about a security consultant named Nick Bradley. I never heard Michael mention him, so I checked with human resources. They said no one by that name ever worked for Cablecast . . .

Paralyzed. Her hands, feet, face, her mind . . . she couldn't move or think.

Just then, Bradley walked in carrying two cans of Coke. He put them on the table in front of her and turned to close the door. "It's getting cold out there, wouldn't be surprised if we got some snow. . . . Lauren? You okay?"

She saw him reach out, his hand about to touch her shoulder, when suddenly she pushed back in the chair. "Stay away, Nick! Just stay away from me!"

"Lauren." He held out a hand like a crossing guard stopping traffic. "Just get ahold of yourself. What's wrong?"

She reached over to the table and pressed the button on the small PC. His eyes, wide and concerned, followed her actions. But he didn't move.

"Mind telling me what's going on?"

"Everything's fine. I just don't think I need your help anymore." Her voice was laced with anger. If she had a brick, she would've thrown it at him. "You can leave, go back home. Send me a bill for your time if you want."

"This is insane. I don't understand."

"Please, just leave," she stammered, backing away from him.

"No, I'm not going to leave," Bradley said, his voice rising to meet the pitch of hers. "Not without an explanation. What's gotten into you? Are you having one of your . . . panic attacks?"

"Yeah, that's it. It's all in her head. I've heard that before. I thought I could trust you. Get out!"

Bradley looked down at the PC, then turned back to Lauren. "Is it a message? Did you get a message?" She did not answer. Bradley reached over and pressed the POWER button and the LCD display instantly appeared, the E-mail from Amber still on the screen.

"That's none of your business!" she yelled.

"Jesus Christ," he said, reading Amber's letter. "No wonder you're all worked up."

"You lied to me, Nick. If that's even your real name. It all makes sense. You didn't have any business cards at the Neighborhood Watch meeting. You're not really a private investigator and your name's not Nick Bradley—"

"Lauren, calm down! Just relax for a second. This

is ridiculous." He held both hands out in front of him, palms to the floor. "First of all, I didn't have any cards because I was out of them. I told you that. Second of all, remember how you got my number when you called me from that bar in Nevada?"

Lauren looked at him. Her heart was still pounding in her ears. "I dialed the operator."

"That's right. And you asked for Nick Bradley, and they connected you."

"You lied to me. You told me you knew Michael, that you worked for him."

"That's right, I did know him. And I did work for him. But my name didn't show up on the payroll because he paid me out of a discretionary fund. He didn't know who in the company was in on the security breach. By keeping me off the payroll, I could do my thing without anyone knowing. Do you hear what I'm saying? So no one would know," Bradley said slowly.

She stood there looking at him for a moment, trying to sort it out. It made sense. What he was saying *did* make sense. But could she trust him? That's the part that gave her the most difficulty.

"I swear, Lauren, I'm here to help you. I want you to find Michael just as much as you do. You've got to believe me."

"What if you're an accomplice of Hung Jin or Anthony Scarponi or whatever the hell his name is?"

"Then I would've killed you already. You obviously wouldn't be of any use—you don't know where Michael is either."

She sat down heavily in a chair and covered her eyes.

"Lauren," he said as he carefully approached her.

She held out her hand to ward him off. "Please, I just need some time alone."

Lauren kept her head down. A few seconds later, Bradley left, the door clicking shut behind him. She grabbed the nearest object—her purse—and flung it across the room.

THIRTY-EIGHT

The early-morning sun was fighting through the slits in the narrow-slat venetian blinds of one of Bethesda Naval Hospital's second-floor windows. Harper Payne sat in a blue-and-white gown on an examination table, the thin butcher paper wrinkling and crinkling beneath him as he shifted positions.

He had been waiting for thirty-five minutes and was beginning to get restless. Although he had gotten through nearly three-quarters of the Bureau training material he needed to learn, there were still hundreds of pages of reports and trial transcripts to review. The last thing he wanted to be doing was sitting in a doctor's office wasting time. Still, he had been looking forward to the neurologist's exam because he wanted a more definitive explanation as to what had happened to him, why he had difficulty remembering things, and when his memory would return to normal. He had had yet another sleepless night, and the vivid images were becoming more frequent and defined.

As he was about to slide off the examination table to look for a nurse, the door opened and a scowling man walked in. He was in his late fifties and the only hair left on his head consisted of tufts of gray above his ears.

"Morning. I'm Dr. Noble." He took a seat on the stool in front of the counter and started to jot some notes.

Great bedside manner, Payne thought.

"Dr. Assad gave me a report of his two visits with you, and I just received your medical records from your prior doctor's office, Manfred his name is. Or was." Noble hmmphed a few times while reading the chart. "Director Knox wanted me to take a real thorough look at you today." He flipped to the back of the file, looked at a lab test. "Other than Dr. Assad, have you had an exam in the past six years?"

"Wish I could tell you, Doc, but I honestly don't remember."

"Hmm, so I'm told." Noble continued to leaf through the chart. "How's your memory been the past few days?"

"I can't remember," Payne said with a smile.

Noble sat there staring at him, his face a piece of rough-hewn stone.

Payne cleared his throat. The man obviously didn't have a sense of humor. "I've been getting some very vivid images. They seem to be from my more recent life. Nothing but fragments. A woman, a house, what I think is my car, and . . . well, some emotions, too. It's hard to describe, but I sort of feel a sense of yearning for the woman I keep seeing in my mind. I think she's my wife, but I don't really remember much about her. I just feel drawn to her for some reason."

"Uh-huh."

"I got an E-mail from her, so now I know a little bit about my life after I left the Bureau. But I'm torn, because I want to talk to her, have her fill in the blanks. At the same time, I *don't* want to know more about my recent past because it'd mean having to choose between my Bureau life and my life back home in some small town called Placerville. I made a mistake leaving the Bureau. Regardless of the risk, I shouldn't have run from it."

Noble looked at him, his face a blank. "Do you need something from me?"

"Need?"

"Counseling. I don't practice that area of medicine, but I can call in a colleague." Noble reached for the telephone on the wall.

"I was just making some observations. I didn't say there was anything wrong. I just thought . . . no, everything's fine." Payne felt like a fool. This man obviously did not care about what he was going through; all Noble was concerned about was the clinical examination. What's on paper, and what's in the body. The black and white. Diagnosis and treatment. Refer him to someone else to deal with the esoteric, emotional baggage. It's not my job.

"Let me check that thigh of yours," Noble said, having Payne lie on his left side. After slipping on a pair of latex gloves, Noble prodded the wound, nodded, and then sat down to make some notes. "It's not my specialty, but it looks good, healing nicely. If you don't get too gung ho with all that macho FBI stuff you people do, it'll heal fine, with no residuals."

Payne sat up. "No macho FBI stuff, got it."

"Anything else bothering you?"

"Sleep. I can't remember the last good night's sleep I had. And I don't mean that as a joke. I think it's probably related to the dreams, or fragments of memories,

I'm having. I toss around until I finally wake up, and then I spend the next few hours lying there trying to make sense of what they mean."

Noble pulled his prescription pad from a pocket and scribbled a few lines of chicken scratch. "Valium, ten milligrams. One before bed. Should knock you out pretty good." He handed Payne the slip and clicked his pen shut. "Any other problems?"

Payne shook his head. "I think that's enough."

For the next twenty minutes, Noble performed a comprehensive neurologic examination. Payne stood and hopped on one foot, smelled coffee grounds and cinnamon, smiled and frowned, and had his face poked with a needle. After that pleasant experience, he was taken through a mental-status examination. He counted by threes and fives, forward and backward, answered questions of general knowledge having to do with time and place, and ended with his recollection of the first thing that Noble had asked him during the examination.

Finally, Noble had Payne lie back so he could perform a general physical exam. All the while, he was questioning his patient on a variety of topics with health-related implications: Any problems moving your bowels? Any unexplained night pain? Does the room ever spin? And so on.

Noble jotted some notes in the chart, then placed an ice-cold stethoscope on Payne's chest. He listened, moved it around, and listened some more. "Hmm," he said, crinkling his brow and then thumbing through his patient's chart, beginning in the front with the earliest entry.

"Anything wrong? Did you find something?"

The doctor shook his head. "No, nothing's wrong,"

he said in a voice devoid of inflection as he continued to read. A few moments later, he returned to the exam table and listened again to Payne's chest for what seemed like several minutes. Payne was instructed to stand up, sit down, hold his breath, lie down, and jump on one leg.

Noble made a few more notes, rose from his stool, then pressed a button on the wall. "Please send Jan in with a cart." He released the intercom and turned to Payne. "Okay, I'm going to have a nurse draw some blood and take an ECG tracing of your heart. Radiology will then take you downstairs for an MRI of your brain, and after that you'll be free to go."

Payne sat up. "Wait a minute—you found something. Something's wrong."

"Did I say that?"

"No, but—"

"Then everything's fine, Agent Payne. Don't worry."

Payne looked hard at Noble, who broke eye contact. He doubted the doctor was telling him the truth. "At least tell me what you think of this amnesia, how long I might have it."

Noble clasped the file in front of his chest and folded his arms. "All right, I'll tell you what I think. I've never heard of the type of memory loss you're claiming to have. I've never seen such a case either in practice or in the journals. When someone has a head injury like what you're describing, if it's substantial enough to cause such considerable memory loss, it usually causes other neurological disturbances."

"In English, Doc."

"You'd probably be brain-dead or damn near a mental vegetable."

"*Probably?*"

"I can only tell you what I know, Agent Payne. But, I can also tell you that it seems like every day I see something I haven't seen before. There was a case I heard about on TV, of all places, that dealt with a man who would disappear for weeks at a time. Whenever he returned home to his wife and children, he'd claim that he didn't even know he'd been gone. This went on for years. This neuropsychiatrist from Stanford they interviewed went on about episodic memory and procedural memory, and how you can retain one and lose the other. I'd never heard of that. I called him up, we chatted, and he quoted a dozen references for the condition. So, Agent Payne, just because I haven't come across something in the journals I read doesn't mean it wasn't written up in one of the dozens of others I don't read."

Payne sat there, staring at the doctor, his eyebrows bunched together.

"Medicine isn't as much of a science as we'd like to think," Noble continued. "Sometimes we're just guessing, is all. Follow me?"

Payne nodded. "Then the answer to my question is, you don't know."

The door opened and a heavyset, middle-aged nurse stepped in, pushing a stainless steel cart that was supporting an electrocardiograph. "That's right, son. I don't." With that, Noble walked out of the room.

"Go on and lie back," the nurse said with all the enthusiasm of a patient about to receive a tetanus shot.

Arthur Noble sat down in his private office and poked out a phone number with his index finger. He leaned back in his leather chair and rubbed at his eyes with his left hand while the call connected.

"Douglas, this is Arthur. I've taken a look at that package you sent over." He slipped his reading glasses on, leaned forward, and opened Payne's medical file. "We need to talk."

THIRTY-NINE

The chill was still in the morning air when Lauren walked outside her motel room to take a breath and clear her mind.

Bradley was standing out there, too, sucking a See's chocolate lollipop. "A little raw, but a beautiful morning."

Lauren had a sweater on, but still felt the need to wrap her hands across her chest. "Sitting in a cabin in the Sierra wearing pajamas is raw. This is refreshing."

Bradley pulled the pop out of his mouth. "Guess it's all a matter of perspective."

Lauren had spent the night trying to decide whether she could continue to trust him. She told herself she had not had any reason to distrust him until the message from Cablecast had upended his credibility. But he did have a reasonable explanation for the discrepancy. And Carla Mae, who had known him for almost two years, more than personally vouched for him—she damn near raved about the man.

Lauren had hoped that with a good night's rest would come a fresh perspective. After lying in bed for an hour and a half, she had finally fallen asleep. Her thoughts had quickly turned to her father, and in a dream she recalled a long-forgotten conversation she had once had with him.

The roses were in full bloom, and their garden was awash with a full bouquet of sweet scents. Her father sat in his wheelchair at the edge of the concrete path that wound through the garden. He watched over Lauren's shoulder as she carefully troweled the dirt around the plants.

"Every living thing needs someone to care for it," he said.

Lauren continued to work with the dirt, gently patting it around the base of a rosebush, seemingly oblivious to what her father was saying.

"It doesn't matter if it's a bush or a tree or a dog or a person," he said. "We all need someone to care about us."

Lauren looked over at her father, the dirt-encrusted tool in her hand. "I know, Dad. You've got me and Mom."

He leaned forward, trying to let the seriousness of what he was telling her penetrate her gaze. "When you get older, and I'm no longer around, you'll have to choose who cares for you. It's important you make a good choice."

She turned back to her garden and moved to the next row of plants. "Do you think these need watering? The soil looks a little dry."

"I think a little water would be good." He wheeled a few feet forward as Lauren moved to her right. "Do you know how to choose? A companion has to be someone you can always trust to do the right thing for you. Someone who'd help you no matter what, even if it meant doing something that could hurt him." He stopped, looked at her, and waited for an indication she was paying attention. "Lauren Rose, are you listening to me?"

"I always listen to you, Daddy." She dug the trowel into the hard ground. "Definitely needs water. This spot is even worse."

Her father sighed and wheeled backward to grab the nozzle end of the garden hose. "I just want to make sure you're taken care of, that's all."

She let the water run into the irrigation canal she had made between the aisles of roses. She patted down the moistened dirt around each bush, her head tilted in thought. Finally, while still fiddling with the soil, she said, "You'll take care of me, like you always do."

Her father shook his head. "I may not always be around, pumpkin. But you'll learn to trust your heart. That's how I'll be there for you. I'll be there in your heart."

When Lauren had awoken, she remembered the dream instantly. Her mind had fallen back on what it trusted—her father's wisdom—for a solution to her current predicament.

In the morning, as she had pulled on her sweater, she realized that, in view of the cold send-off she had given Bradley the night before, he might already have returned to Sacramento. But now, when she walked out of the room, he was standing there sucking on his See's lollipop as if nothing had happened. And, she had to admit, seeing him standing there made her feel secure, comfortable in that she was not alone. Her father's advice echoed in her head: *you'll learn to trust your heart.*

She decided to listen to her father . . . to go with her instincts and let last night's incident pass without further discussion.

"I wonder how far away he is," Lauren said. She swallowed a lungful of cool air and thought of Michael. This was the longest she had been away from him since he took the job at Cablecast. She tried to think of it as his having gone on vacation, but she could not get past its being nothing like that. When someone goes on vacation, they are expected back on a certain date. Though Michael could physically be somewhere nearby, she had to acknowledge the reality of the situation: he was actually further away from her now than he had ever been since they had first met.

"So are we all right?"

Bradley's voice yanked her from her thoughts. She kept her gaze straight ahead and shrugged. "I guess so."

"Good, because we've got some work to do."

Lauren took one last look at the brightening sky, then walked back into the motel room. Bradley followed her in, picked up the phone, and dialed a number.

He turned to Lauren and cupped the phone. "They have some coffee and Danish in the lobby for breakfast if you want. Coffee's like mud, but—" He quickly removed his hand and brought the handset to his mouth. "Yes, you sure can. Can you connect me to your emergency-room administrator, please?"

While Bradley waited on hold, Lauren sat down on the edge of the bed, removed Michael's photo from her wallet, and stared at it for a few moments. *Where are you? . . . Who are you? . . . I'm trying to find you.* She touched his lips with her fingertips. "I'm trying," she said aloud.

"Trying what?" Bradley asked, hanging up the phone.

"Nothing. What did you find out?"

"We have an appointment with the Virginia Presbyterian ER administrator in half an hour. She was out sick till yesterday. I convinced her we needed to see her this morning."

"Then what?"

"I figured you'd return to the mall and I'd continue to beat a path around town, showing Michael's photo, talking to law enforcement. Someone's bound to have seen him."

Lauren shoved the snapshot of Michael back into her purse and nodded. "I guess." She rose from the bed and slung her purse over a shoulder. "I walk around malls and you ask strangers if they've seen my husband."

"Exactly."

"Well," she said, heading for the door, "we've got to do something. Let's go."

FORTY

Harper Payne slammed his fist down on the desk. "Damn it." He stared at the screen, which defiantly displayed an error message: "Internet Explorer cannot find the modem. Check your Dial-Up Networking settings and try logging on again. If unsuccessful, try restarting your computer."

He clicked START–SHUT DOWN–RESTART and waited while the laptop cycled through its boot-up sequence and restarted Windows. A moment later, he tried resending his message to Lauren. Again he received an error message: "Internet Explorer cannot find the modem. Check your Dial-Up Networking settings . . ."

He clicked on CONTROL PANEL, went into the MODEMS folder, and selected the DIAGNOSTICS tab. It indicated there were no modems installed. He ground his teeth. No modems installed? Payne sat there looking at the screen. It did not make sense—there had been a modem there yesterday. He tilted the laptop on its side and checked the phone jack connection, which was secure. He pushed a small button and a credit-card-size modem slid out. He shoved it back in and rebooted the computer. As he waited, he tapped his fingers on the desk until the desktop appeared.

He again tried to connect. The error message's shrill tone was like nails on a chalkboard. *Internet Explorer cannot find the modem.*

After having decided to send a return message to Lauren, he was anxious to establish communication with her. He scrolled through the in-box to find the E-mail she had sent him. At the very least, he could call the phone number she had given him and leave a message. He reached the end of the list and went back through it again, but the message was not there. The deleted folder was empty as well. Had someone deleted her E-mail to him—and tampered with the laptop so he would be unable to communicate with her?

What was going on?

He thought about who would have access to his room. The list could be long, from maintenance and cleaning personnel to Waller and Haviland. But no one would have a motive to prevent him from contacting his wife.

Or would they?

Waller had brought him the computer in the first place; he seemed to want to help. Haviland would not have any more reason to move against him than Waller would. If not them, then someone else.

He suddenly noticed the time and rose from the chair. He had missed his last class and wanted to get to the lunchroom before Waller did. Forty-five minutes ago he had been handed a message that they were to meet there at noon. He shut down the computer and headed out the door.

The dining hall was an upscale, high-ceilinged cafeteria-style eatery that was brimming with movement.

New agents milled about in their blue polo shirts and khaki pants, leather belt holsters fastened to their sides holding mock rubber guns, and laminated ID tags hanging from their necks. A cacophony of noise—voices, silverware, dishes—echoed off the tile flooring and wood paneling and hung in the air as a low roar, with no means of escape.

Payne walked in, nodded to the cashier—Waller had arranged for him to receive his meals free of charge—and grabbed a tray. As usual, there was an abundance of food—from hot sandwiches to meat and potatoes, pastas, salads, several types of breads and muffins, orange, grapefruit, and apple juices. For dessert, there was fresh fruit, coffee, cake, and ice cream. If an agent was not careful, it would be easy to gain a whole lot of weight here in a short time.

He helped himself to a plate of pasta, a large salad, and a glass of juice. Finding a seat at a table that was occupied by a group of DEA agents, Payne set his tray down. He started to move the newspaper that some-one had left on the table, but the *Washington Post*'s headline screamed at him from the page:

Key Scarponi Witness Stricken with Amnesia

(AP) Washington—Sources close to the FBI indicated late last night that the Bureau has located former agent Harper Payne, their key witness in the original and ongoing investiga-tions of international hit man Anthony Scarponi. According to the source, who spoke on condition of anonymity, Payne is suffering from amnesia.

This development drew snickers from experts in the legal field, particularly defense attorneys, some of whom went so far as to speculate that the government's key witness was unwilling to cooperate and return for a replay of the stress and death threats that peppered Scarponi's original trial.

Ronald Friedkin, lead attorney for the Scarponi defense team, stated in a hastily called news conference in front of the federal courthouse in New York City that in view of this development he would be asking presiding judge Richard Noonan to formally dismiss the open case against his client. . . .

Payne tossed the newspaper down onto the table. How could this happen? Who would tell the *Post* that the Bureau had found him—or worse, that he had amnesia?

He sat down amidst the commotion of new agents, who were milling about the table just behind him, laughing, discussing their latest class. Dishes clinked and silverware rattled. But Payne heard none of it.

Both fists were clenched, and the veins in his temples were bulging. He felt the drubbing of his heart and an intense pressure building inside his head.

"Sorry I didn't get here sooner."

Payne looked up, his eyes glassy and bloodshot from lack of sleep. It was Jonathan Waller. "What is this?" Payne asked, grabbing the *Post* and shoving it into Waller's chest. "What the hell is this?"

Waller took the paper and placed a hand on Payne's shoulder. "Calm down. I realize this is upsetting—"

"Upsetting?" Payne's voice had risen in both pitch and volume. The DEA agents seated at his table turned and were now tuned in to the commotion. "This is my life we're talking about. I've worked my ass off to make this thing work, and this is how I'm thanked?" Payne was now unaware of what he was saying, as if he were standing a few feet away, a bystander to his own rantings.

Waller looked around at the men and women in the room, which had suddenly become eerily quiet. "It's okay, people," he said, "continue with your lunch. Everything's under control."

"Control?" Payne shouted. "What's under control?"

"Come on, this is not the place to be discussing this." Waller led Payne by the arm out of the dining hall and into the corridor, where Haviland was approaching. Waller shook his head at his partner, then looked at Payne. "This is bad, I'm not gonna lie to you. We need to do some damage control—but we have a goal and we have to remain focused on that goal."

Payne felt his heart rate decreasing, some semblance of order descending on him. "I don't understand. No one knew about me outside the Academy. Just you and Scott, and Director Knox. Nobody else knows."

"Not true," Haviland said. "We've got people in records who pulled your file and the trial transcripts. The firearms manager who assigned you your Glock and holster, and the property clerk who ordered your new credentials. Sure, your creds say Richard Thompson, but even still, all this activity is a little unusual, not to mention the timing. I mean, where did Agent Thompson suddenly come from? They know you aren't in the current new-agent class. They have to think something's going on. Maybe they talk to each other, put two and two together. No matter how you package it, or what you name it, it still adds up to four. Even though we don't want them to figure it out, they're capable people. And that's not to mention the two doctors who examined you, and every member of their staffs who came into contact with you. You understand my point? There are a lot more people involved than you think."

"But that still doesn't explain the leak," Waller said to Haviland. "With the exception of Noble, everyone else is internal to the Bureau. And Noble and his staff are thoroughly cleared because it's a naval hospital. Noble saw Harper only because Knox asked him to, as a personal favor. They're buddies dating back to his time with the Select Committee. He certainly wouldn't leak anything."

"Then who?" Payne asked.

"Knox is looking into it," Haviland said, "which means we are, too. As soon as we know something, we'll let you know."

"And in the meantime?"

Waller shrugged. "In the meantime, we just do what we need to do."

The cameras were aimed at Douglas Knox in the large press room at the Hoover Building. A blue, floor-to-ceiling curtain provided the backdrop, with a large, round, navy-and-gold "Department of Justice, Federal Bureau of Investigation" seal mounted behind the podium.

Knox placed a pair of gold wire glasses on his nose

and glanced down at his notes. "Thank you all for coming. I'll read for a few moments from a prepared statement and then I'll answer some questions." He cleared his throat. "As you're well aware, the *Washington Post* has published an article in today's edition that makes certain assertions about the Bureau's ongoing investigation of Anthony Scarponi. While I can't and won't comment on those particulars of the case that would jeopardize the nature of that investigation, I will state that the news report is factually flawed." He looked up from his paper and faced the reporters. "Now, I'm not going to go into which facts are wrong—because it would take too long."

A slight chuckle rumbled from the crowd of reporters.

"Suffice it to say that we do know the whereabouts of Agent Harper Payne and that he will be testifying against Mr. Scarponi, as he did six years ago when Mr. Scarponi was convicted. I want to assure the people of this country that this offender will again be locked up behind bars, where he will be of no danger to anyone. That's all I've got. Thank you."

A sea of hands shot up from the crowd, along with shouts of "Mr. Director!" and "Director Knox!"

Knox scanned the journalists and chose a friendly face, Marta Henninger from CNN. "Sir, is there any truth to the report that Agent Payne is suffering from amnesia? And if so, wouldn't that affect his performance on the witness stand?"

Knox let a thin smile spread across his lips. "That's a compound question, Marta, and I know better than to answer two questions at once. Let me just say that Agent Payne is in excellent health and nothing—amnesia, the Asian flu, or a bad case of food poisoning—is going to prevent him from taking the stand and testifying effectively against Anthony Scarponi."

Hands shot up again. Knox chose another ally from the past: Steve Carter from NBC News.

"Director Knox, does this mean that you're going to have the attorney general apply for a court date for Scarponi's trial?"

"As a matter of fact, I just received word that we're on the docket for March fourteenth."

"Why was Agent Payne so difficult to locate?"

The question pulled Knox's attention back to the present. "Well, in view of the circumstances at the time, Agent Payne's identity and location became a closely guarded secret following his testimony six years ago. It took a while to find him and make sure it was safe to transport him to a secured location. More than that I can't say."

"Is it true," a reporter from the *New York Times* blurted out, "that he's being held at the FBI Academy in Quantico?"

"As you can understand, I can't answer any question that would even provide a hint of his whereabouts. So, my answer will have to be *no comment.*"

Knox continued to "no comment" a number of questions in rote responses until one struck him across the face.

"Is it true, sir, that a member of the FBI leaked this story to the press?"

"No, that would not be standard Bureau procedure, as I believe you're well aware if you've got any time in journalism under your belt, son."

Shouts for more questions went up, but Knox held

up his hand, leaned close to the microphone, and said, "Thank you all for coming." He turned to his right and was escorted off the podium to the exit, with the cries for him to answer but one more inquiry continuing even as the door slammed shut.

FORTY-ONE

He was pretty pissed," Waller said.

"Great. Just great," Knox said, pacing his office. "First Scarponi, then Melissa, then Stanfield . . . and now this." He stopped to hold his temples. "I swear, I've got sledgehammers inside my head and they're working overtime."

Waller shifted in his seat. "I think he's okay now, sir. But I've never seen him so upset. He nearly lost it. I don't think he's been sleeping too well."

"Sleep deprivation, according to Noble. It can make you depressed, paranoid, even delusional. He was given Valium. You know if he's taking it?"

"We ran some training exercises at Hogan's yesterday, and he didn't say anything about it. I'd think if he was taking it I would've noticed."

Knox sighed. "AG's on my back. Trial date's set and we don't have much time. A few weeks is all. I want him well rested and properly prepared for that trial. Not to mention we're no closer to finding Scarponi."

"Understood, sir."

"I want a tighter lid kept on him. Do it in a way that doesn't arouse his suspicions." Knox released his temples and resumed his pacing. "Tell him that because of this *Post* story, his movements will have to be restricted until the trial. For his own safety, that sort of thing."

"No problem."

Knox stopped abruptly and turned. "Wrong, Agent Waller. There will be problems. Expect them. Just make sure you deal with them effectively."

FORTY-TWO

In his small dorm room, Harper Payne closed the trial transcript. His concentration had been less than keen, with thoughts of Lauren Chambers fighting for his attention. As much as he did not want to go back to a life that excluded the Bureau, he felt an attachment to this woman he hardly knew. It wasn't a tangible feeling, one he could analyze. It was more of a magnetism, as if his thoughts were physically being pulled back to her.

Pushing the trial transcript aside, he picked up the phone, dialed nine to get an outside line, then hit 411.

"Academy operator."

"I—I was dialing information."

"I can handle that for you, sir. What number would you like?"

Was it standard procedure for the Academy operator to intercept calls like this? He was sure that according to the rules and procedures Waller had gone over with him, an outside line was obtained by dialing nine.

"What number would you like?" the operator asked again.

"I'd actually like an outside line, please."

"If there's a number I can get for you, I'd be happy to—"

"Chambers. Michael or Lauren Chambers in Placerville, California."

"Hold, please." There was a click, followed by a brief silence. Then, a few seconds later, another click. "No available listing, Agent Thompson. Is there anything else I can get for you?"

Payne stood there for a second, thinking. Thompson was his alias. But he had never told her his name. A hundred new agents were housed in the dorm at any one time, yet the Academy operator instantly knew which room was his. Did she have time to look it up during the few seconds he was on hold? Or had she been told to intercept his calls?

He ground his molars together. "No, that was the only number I needed. By the way, who am I speaking with?"

"Sir?"

"I don't think we've spoken before."

"Margaret Little, sir."

"You're so efficient, Margaret. You sound like you've been doing this awhile."

"I—yes, awhile. Thank you, sir."

"At least a year, right? I always try to guess how long people have been doing their jobs. It's my theory that you can always tell when someone's new and when they've been on the job at least a year. It's kind of an arbitrary cutoff, the one-year mark, but I really think it makes a difference. So, am I right, have you been an operator at the Academy for least a year?"

"Yes, uh, a little over a year, sir. Can I get you another number?"

"No, thanks for your help—and for being so efficient." He hung up the phone, sifted through his papers, and found the Academy directory Waller had given him. He scanned the listing of nonagent personnel for Margaret Little. There was no one by that name.

He lifted his shoulder harness off the hook on the door and strapped it to his body. He threw his navy suit coat over his shoulder and left his room. He walked downstairs, crossed through the glass-enclosed hallway to the library, and picked up the white in-house phone. He hit zero and waited while it rang.

"Academy operator."

"This is . . . Agent Waller. Who am I speaking with?"

"This is Leslie Orens. What can I do for you today, sir?"

Her manner was formal, just like that of the operator he had spoken to a moment ago. "I was just on the phone with Margaret. Can you put her back on for a second?"

"Who?"

"Margaret, the other operator. Margaret Little."

"I'm sorry, Agent Waller. There's no Margaret Little here."

"Are you sure?"

"There are only three of us here, sir."

"No problem, my mistake." Payne hung up and rubbed the stubble on his chin. Why had his phone line been diverted? Why wouldn't they allow him access to an outside line?

Was he merely being paranoid?

He suddenly felt uncomfortable, his eyes panning the library to see if anyone was watching him. Two men in suits were on the balcony above him, speaking in hushed tones with one another.

Come on, Harper. Cut it out. They're whispering because

it's a library. And they're just talking about the Wizards game. Or forensic findings. Or a suspect. Or about me.

They're watching me.

He quickly turned away and walked out, headed for the gun vault to sign out his Glock. Paranoia or not, regardless of what was going on, he was going to be prepared.

"Like you said, Jon," he said aloud as he quickened his pace, "we do what we need to do."

FORTY-THREE

Watch it!" the paramedic called out as he pushed the gurney past Lauren.

She apologized, but the men and their patient were already headed down the hall, out of earshot. Lauren and Nick Bradley walked into the waiting room, where every seat was taken by patients.

"Maybe this isn't a good time," she said to Bradley.

"Time is something we don't have a lot of, Lauren. We take what we can get. Don't worry about it. We're going to be talking with an administrator, not one of the doctors or nurses."

Within ten minutes, they were being escorted to the back office, where a woman of about sixty sat, her gray hair tied up into a tight bun. Although she was plump, a well-tailored business suit gave her a much leaner appearance.

The fifteen line buttons on her telephone were lit up, and some were blinking—indicating that several people were simultaneously on hold.

Nick Bradley handed her his private investigator credentials, and the woman scrutinized them. "I really only have a few questions," he told her as she continued to stare at the card.

"I also brought a copy of the missing person's

report," Lauren said, showing her the paperwork from Ilene Mara.

The woman took the documents, scanned through them, and handed them back to Lauren. "What would you like to know?"

"We were contacted by Mr. Chambers a few days ago," Bradley explained, "and he said he was near Virginia Presbyterian and that he'd had a car accident—"

"—and that he had some problems with his memory," Lauren offered.

"So we were hoping that he was treated here for the accident."

The woman contorted her lips, turned to face her computer, and scanned the database for the date they had given her, including a few days before and after. "You don't know if he was admitted, do you?"

"Why don't we confine your search to just the ER," Bradley said.

"The ER," she repeated as she scrolled down the list. "Nope, don't see anybody by that name."

"What if he didn't have any identification with him?"

"The police and emergency personnel are pretty good about retrieving wallets and such from accident scenes. You know, to help us with identification issues."

Bradley nodded. "Understood. But what if, hypothetically, they couldn't find any ID?"

She contorted her mouth again and turned back to the screen. Just then, the phone began ringing. "Excuse me. When it back rings, I've got to— Hello, Virginia Pres ER."

Bradley looked over at Lauren, whose gaze was fixed on the computer screen. She was squinting, trying to read the names on the list.

"There," she said to Bradley, pointing at the monitor. "John Doe. Head trauma, retrograde amnesia, gunshot wound. Brought in on the thirteenth at—"

"Excuse me," the administrator was saying as she hung up the phone. "That's confidential information."

"I'm sorry," Lauren said. "But I think I've found him. If he didn't have any ID, you'd list him as John Doe, right?"

"If he's a male, yes."

"Then he's right there." Lauren pointed. "An entry for John Doe with retrograde amnesia." The woman arrowed down to the entry. She hit ENTER and it displayed the intake notes and diagnosis, as well as the patient's disposition. "Looks like he checked himself out. A bullet was removed from his thigh, and he was scheduled for an MRI but he didn't stay for it."

Lauren and Bradley shared a glance. She knew he must have been thinking the same thing: Why would he have come in with a gunshot wound?

"Who treated him?" Bradley asked.

"Doctor Farber. I'll see if he's available."

After waiting nearly an hour, a man in his early thirties approached them dressed in surgical scrubs. A mask hung from his neck and a slight smear of blood was on his shirt. He noticed the red stain and called over to an orderly. "I need a new top," he said, indicating the blood.

"I was told you were looking for me," Farber said to Bradley.

"We're looking for information on a patient of yours, a John Doe who came in a few days ago with a gunshot wound to the thigh—"

"I've already told you people everything I know."

"Oh—we're not police," Bradley said. "This is the patient's wife, and I'm a private investigator. We're trying to find him."

"You and everybody else."

"How's that?"

"He came in without identification. He'd been in a major car accident and had sustained significant head trauma. If I recall, it appeared as if he'd also had a previous, but recent, blow to the head. He was amnesiac, so he didn't remember any prior injury."

"The administrator said a bullet was removed from his thigh."

"Correct." The orderly brought over a new scrub top, and Farber slipped off the soiled shirt and shrugged on the new one in the hallway, in front of Lauren and Bradley. "Excuse me," he said.

Lauren pulled the photo of Michael from her purse. "Is this the man you treated?"

Farber took the picture and looked at it. "That's him."

Lauren sighed. "Thank God."

"You said there were others looking for him?" Bradley asked.

"Yeah." Farber handed the photo back to Lauren. "The police. When a patient presents with a gunshot wound, I'm obligated by law to report it."

"Because he could've been either the victim or instigator of a crime," Bradley said to Lauren.

"I'd scheduled him for an MRI scan, to evaluate the extent of any brain swelling. But when the techs arrived to take him to radiology, he was gone. The next thing I knew the police were questioning me. Did I know where my patient went, did he say anything to me about where he might go or where he'd come from, that sort of thing. They were really after this guy.

The place was swarming with cops. When the FBI arrived, I knew it was pretty serious."

"The FBI?" Lauren asked.

"Yeah. They closed off all the entrances and exits, except for the ER, but even then everything and everyone coming or going had to be searched. That went on for about three hours. It created a load of logistical problems for us. After we got a call about a multiple-car pileup on the interstate, we had to give them the boot out of here. By that point, I got the sense they'd accepted the fact he wasn't in the hospital." Just then, Farber's pager beeped. He looked down at the number and started to back away. "Excuse me—"

Lauren was staring off down the hall, Farber's voice suddenly off in the distance.

"Hello . . . Lauren, what's on your mind?" Bradley moved an open hand in front of her face. "You're zoning out on me."

She turned and met his eyes. "Why would the FBI get involved just because someone was brought into an emergency room with a bullet in his thigh?"

Bradley took her by the arm and led her down the corridor. "Could be he fit the description of a fugitive they were tracking."

Lauren nodded. "Or it could tie in to Michael's involvement with Scarponi."

They walked in silence for a moment, dodging the continuous flow of nurses, technicians, and gurneys streaming through the corridor.

"I'm still having a problem with that," she said. "I can't see Michael as a cold-blooded killer."

They turned a corner and headed for the exit. "If Michael's job was to infiltrate Scarponi's group, he may've needed to do things that proved he was worthy of his boss's confidence. That could've included murder, as repugnant as that may sound. I don't think anyone can understand what it means to take an assignment like that. But if the long-term goal was to put this guy away for good so no one else would be harmed . . ." Bradley's voice tapered off. "As upset as you are about it, if it's true, think about how Michael must feel. He's had to live with what he's done."

"Night before last I lay awake thinking. How well do we know someone, even your lover? You think you know him. But unless you grew up with him and know everything that's ever happened to that person, how do you know? How do you know who he really is?"

Bradley placed a hand around her shoulder and squeezed. "Sometimes all you have are your instincts. Sometimes that's all I have to go on. Life is a crapshoot. Sometimes you have to go where your heart takes you. Sometimes there aren't any concrete answers."

"Go where my heart takes me."

"Exactly."

"You sound like my father again."

"What does your heart say?"

"My heart says that Michael is still my Michael."

"Okay. Now what?" he asked, talking to her more like a teacher than a private investigator.

Lauren was silent as they stepped through the emergency room's automatic doors into the parking lot. She stopped walking and threw a hand up to her forehead to deflect the glare of the sun, which was emerging from behind gray thunderclouds. Taking a deep breath of the damp air, she said, "I think we should start with the FBI."

"Good choice." He pulled the car keys from his

pocket and glanced at Lauren. "When this is all over, maybe you'll come work for me."

Lauren forced a smile. She looked up at the cloud that had suddenly blocked the sun, casting a pall of darkness over the ground. Her heart had indeed told her which way to go. First with Bradley, and now with Michael.

But what if she was wrong?

FORTY-FOUR

Jonathan Waller slammed the phone down and cursed under his breath. He checked his watch, which read 7:05 P.M. "Why does this shit happen to me?" he spat into the still air of his office. "My one night off in a week and I get a call. Isn't fair."

He grabbed the down elevator and within five minutes was approaching Haviland in the parking garage of the Washington Field Office. He was walking fast, the rapidity of his speech matching his stride. "Just got a call from Martinson at the Academy. Aside from a morning session, *Agent Thompson* didn't make any of his classes today."

"And what did Harper have to say about it?" Haviland asked, running to keep up with his partner.

"I can't find him."

"As in . . ."

"As in no one's seen him, he's not in his room, and he signed out his Glock from the vault."

"Shit."

"Exactly."

"What about his log-on codes? Has he logged onto the mainframe at all today?"

"Good thought. If he has, it'll help us pin down his movements during the day."

"And it may give us a clue as to what's going on in his head."

A moment later, they were in their car, headed toward I-95 South and Quantico, Virginia.

It was almost 9 P.M. when Payne walked up Pennsylvania Avenue toward the main entrance to the J. Edgar Hoover Building. Orange traffic cones lined the curb encircling the entire city block, and cement planters were placed in front of the wide steps that led to each of the entrances. Although these measures were security precautions taken to combat terrorism against federal buildings, they isolated FBI headquarters from the neighboring structures and government agencies.

Payne recalled the Bureau regulations that governed admittance to headquarters: anyone entering the building without an escort had to have a top secret security clearance and a special building pass. Since he had been in and out of the building before to meet with Knox, he already had clearance. And Knox himself had provided the building pass when Payne's credentials were returned to him, in anticipation of future meetings.

As he pushed on the door to the entrance, he clipped the laminated pass to his jacket and pulled his shield from his pocket. He was immediately approached by Chuck Seamen, the FBI policeman, who recognized him from his prior trips to headquarters.

"How you doing, sir?" Seamen asked.

"Was hoping to turn in early tonight, but Director Knox wanted me to meet him here. I'm exhausted, that's how I'm doing." Payne closed his credentials case and shoved it into his jacket pocket. "How's your evening?"

"Quiet so far, which is fine with me."

"I hear you," Payne said with a smile.

"You say you're here to meet with the director?" Seamen said to Payne's back as he placed his gun, keys, and a small box on the conveyor belt.

"Yeah, he said to meet him here in an hour. I'm a little early."

Seamen thumbed through the logbook and found the next vacant line as Payne walked through the metal detector.

"What's in the box?" Seamen asked as he examined the innards of the electronic device on the X-ray monitor.

"Descrambler, for the director. That's what the meeting's about." Payne took the pen, signed in, listed the director's office as his destination, and wrote in his pass number. He swiped his ID card and passed through the electronic turnstile.

"Thanks, Chuck," he said as he headed toward the bank of elevators.

A bell clanged, indicating the car's arrival. The doors slid open and Payne stepped inside. He left the elevator on the seventh floor and headed down a back hallway toward Mahogany Row. By taking this route to the director's suite, it allowed him to bypass the security station. However, it meant he had to have a six-digit code for the keypad outside Knox's office.

The keypad, though, was the least of his problems. With the descrambler he had appropriated from the electronics lab at Hogan's Alley before leaving for headquarters, entry to the director's office would merely be a temporary annoyance.

The more significant problem was one he could not have planned for: through the small fireproof window in the door, he saw lights on in Knox's office and two bodies seated in chairs in front of the desk. Surprisingly, the director was still there, apparently in a meeting.

Payne could stay and wait around for him to leave, but the longer he remained in the building the greater the chance that he would be questioned as to his intentions.

Payne leaned against the mahogany paneling and tried to regroup. There wasn't anything specific he had hoped to find when he decided to break into Knox's office. Payne was gambling that a thorough search of the suite would tell him why he was being monitored, and why his contacts with the outside world were being controlled. He wanted a look at the bigger picture, not the pixel by pixel account he was getting.

But now his strategy would have to be altered.

He took the elevator down to the basement, where the Computer Analysis Response Team, or CART, was located. He saw the touch pad on the far wall and glanced around the corridor as he approached. It was empty. A camera was mounted on the ceiling behind him, aimed at the CART entrance. If he was good, and lucky—in that order—he could attach the descrambler and block the camera's view with his body. That was the part that demanded considerable skill. But he would have to work fast and hope that security was not watching its monitors too closely. That's where the luck part came in.

In a matter of seconds, without looking down or breaking stride, Payne removed the device from its box. He walked up to the keypad and pried off the front of the panel with his fingernail. He slapped the descrambler onto the microelectronic innards and waited while it went through its routine. He shielded the device from the camera, while moving his fingers slowly, as if he were punching in a number. If a guard glanced at his monitor, he wouldn't see anything out of the ordinary. However, if he was intently watching, he would realize that it was taking the person on his screen a ridiculously long time to enter his code.

Finally, the red LED light on his descrambler went green. With his left hand he pulled down on the door handle, and with his right he removed the device and snapped the cover back on the touch pad. He was in.

After the door clicked shut behind him, Payne felt the rush of cool air and heard the whirring hum of the large air-conditioning system. He passed through the data center and moved toward the back of the suite. He stepped through a glass door and entered a room filled with cubicles, each one sporting a computer terminal. He looked around and noticed a few people working late at their desks, poking at keys and thumbing through manuals.

Payne walked down a couple of aisles and chose a vacant terminal. After settling into the seat, he began the log-on sequence. Realizing it would likely be difficult to break into the director's files on the mainframe, and that the server administrator would immediately begin to monitor his movements should he attempt to do so, he decided to try a different approach. He logged in using his Academy pass code, the one he had been given to access portions of the Scarponi trial transcripts.

Again breaking his situation down to the barest common denominators, he came back to Knox and Scarponi. Figuring that obtaining information on

Scarponi would be comparatively easy, he logged on to Division Six's database, hoping to locate a psychological profile on the famed assassin. Although he was not entirely sure of what he was looking for, he hoped that one document might contain information that would lead him to another document, and so on.

During the next fifteen minutes, he crawled through hundreds of folders and files on the Division Six server. There were a variety of official records, some preceded by the word SECRET prominently displayed in large red letters across the top. Payne skimmed through the first paragraph of each of the reports—some of which would have been fascinating reading on another day and time: domestic terrorism-risk assessments, NSA encryption analyses, and a host of internal reports from the division. Serial-killer profiles. Criminal investigative analyses. Search warrant requests.

And a threat assessment prepared for Director Douglas Knox re Agent Harper Payne.

Payne looked around, over his shoulder and past the other terminals that sat to each side of him. He leaned in close to the screen and began to read. The cover page was splattered with the large, red-lettered words

CONFIDENTIAL
FOR DIRECTOR'S EYES ONLY

He scrolled to the body of the report, where key words and phrases caught his attention:

> High level of sophistication . . .
> Offender went to great lengths to obtain
> confidential information, specifically
> Director's home address . . .

Conclusion/Threat assessment: High risk level.
Recommendations/Options:

1—Place security detail on high alert;
2—Assign additional HRT operators to members of Director's family;
3—Initiate 24/7 surveillance on Director's home;
4—Review current security procedures at Director's residence;
5—Restrict Director's access and movements;
6—Perform frequent sweeps of HQ for weapons of mass destruction, i.e., explosive, chemical, biological devices;
7—Launch comprehensive investigation immediately, to include a warrant to secure the retrieval of all phone luds of Anthony Scarponi, visitor logs to Scarponi at Petersburg, and an interrogation of Scarponi;
8—Employ electronic surveillance methods in accordance with Bureau procedure and regulations memo G98Q;
9—Comply with offender demands per threat letter (unacceptable per Bureau procedure).

Payne paged down and found a scanned copy of the letter Knox had received at his house. One part caught and held his attention: "HARPER PAYNE. DEAD OR ALIVE, YOUR CHOICE. FAIL TO DELIVER HIM AND YOU'LL PLACE CERTAIN PEOPLE IN YOUR LIFE AT RISK." He stared at it until his eyes began to burn. Melissa Knox had been kidnapped, then returned. It was a message. A message that Knox had better cooperate or next time she would be killed.

Payne buried his face in his hands, then began massaging his forehead to ease the emerging headache. Between lack of sleep and the stress he was under, the headache was not surprising—and was certainly the least of his problems. But he did not have time for it. The pieces to what was happening to him were starting to come together . . . as was his understanding of the players, the issues, and the rules of the game.

But more needed to be done.

He logged off the terminal, walked out of the data center, and in a daze, headed down the corridor toward the elevators.

His mind was a snowstorm of thoughts, swirling furiously. With each thought grappling for immediate attention, he fought to focus. Once more he reduced the situation to its fundamental roots: faced with choosing between the safety of his family or a former agent with a damaged mind, Knox would toss aside his Bureau hat and his fathering instincts would control his actions. FBI director or not, he was, above all else, a human being, a husband and father.

To what extent would he go to find other alternatives . . . such as focusing Bureau resources on taking Scarponi down to render the threat inconsequential? Knox would definitely go to great lengths to try. If nothing else, to give the appearance of a convincing effort. But even if he really pushed, how successful would he be against one of the most prolific and successful contract assassins in history—one who had escaped capture for years, even with the vast resources of the international law enforcement community trained on him?

And what did Payne know about Knox? Had his life been devoted to government service? Was he the kind of man who wouldn't compromise his morals and duties to protect his family? Payne kept coming back to that question. Even if Knox did not plan on having Payne killed—or the equivalent, arranging for him to be unknowingly placed into Scarponi's sights—there were other ways for Knox to meet the gist of the hit man's demands.

He could discredit me. Leak the amnesia story to the press, deny it publicly, and put me on the witness stand to fend for myself. By withholding key information about the undercover operation, he'd make me look bad under cross-examination. It would just about guarantee a not-guilty verdict for Scarponi—who could never be tried again for the same charges. Case closed. Harper Payne, a discredited and useless former agent left to fend for himself. That's why Knox pushed for an expedited trial date: to lessen the chance I'd get my memory back in time to testify.

I'm a pawn.

How deeply are Waller and Haviland involved?

Payne was massaging his temples again, fighting to contain his anger, when the elevator doors slid open. He walked past Chuck Seamen without seeing or acknowledging him.

"I thought you had a meeting with the director."

The voice came from behind him. He turned, his mind still a blizzard of thoughts. It was Waller, standing with Haviland near the bank of elevators.

"What are you doing here?" Payne asked, his brow arched downward and his hands clenched at his side.

"We were going to ask you the same thing," Haviland said.

"I had a meeting with—"

"Yeah, we heard," Waller said, a penetrating stare locked on Payne's eyes. "Director's in a meeting. He asked us to bring you to his home, he'll be along in a little while." Waller motioned toward the elevators. "Car's in the garage."

"I've got my own," Payne said, turning toward the door.

"No, you've got Agent Ginsberg's," Waller said, forcing a smile. "You were obviously paying attention during the class on vehicular theft."

"We have to talk, Harper," Haviland said.

Payne sensed the firmness in Haviland's voice. Payne stepped forward and joined them as they strode into the elevator. Not until the doors clamped shut did he realize he was losing the control over his life he had fought so hard to regain. With uneasiness beginning to well up inside his chest, he took a few deep breaths to try to make it go away. But as hard as he fought the emotion, a recurring thought was flooding his mind.

Bad things were about to happen.

FORTY-FIVE

Hector DeSantos entered the situation room, his Pierre Cardin leather attaché in hand. Brian Archer was sitting at the conference table, papers scattered beside his laptop. His hair was a disheveled mess and he was huddled over a document, tracing a portion of it with a pencil and an index finger.

"Brian," DeSantos said, "I'm sorry—"

"You're sorry you're late again," Archer said without lifting his eyes from the page. "I know, Maggie kept pulling you back into bed for another go-round and you couldn't break away." He looked up at DeSantos. "Or is it that you slept late because the alarm didn't go off? Or did you drop your keys down the sewer—"

"All right, all right. Point taken."

"At least you're not bullshitting me by saying it won't happen again."

DeSantos took a seat next to Archer and handed him a piece of Juicy Fruit.

"What is this, a peace offering?" Archer took the gum, folded it into his mouth, and nodded at the paper-strewn table. "The computer finished decrypting the first NSA document."

"No shit?"

"No shit." Archer selected a paper from amongst

the maelstrom of pages on the table and handed it to DeSantos.

He took the document and read from it: "'CARD Report. Memogen Project confirmed with SCP. Subject Scarponi is an ideal blank blank. Blank blank blank excellent proposal. Cooperation with blank blank blank blank is required. Approval blank assistance blank blank blank. Blank blank secret.'" DeSantos looked up from the document, his brow knitted with consternation. "Three days of word crunching and that's all it came up with?"

"It's a little incomplete."

DeSantos tossed the page onto the table. "A *little* incomplete?"

"Our decryption software isn't that swift."

"You mean it sucks."

"It needs work," Archer corrected. "But that's why we have the NSA."

"Yeah, but in this case we can't give it to NSA because that's where we got it from in the first place. They'll know their own code."

Archer leaned back in his chair. "I know a guy there, we've hacked together before."

"You live in a weird world, you know that? Us normal people, we hang out together, throw back a beer or catch a movie. You hang out and hack."

Archer ignored his partner. "He'll take a look at it without a problem, Hector. And, he'll keep quiet about it if I ask him to. He owes me."

DeSantos was shaking his head. "I don't care how much shit you've done for this geek. You're not seeing the big picture, Brian. What if he's the one who developed this code for this—this Memogen Project, whatever that is? We'll have breached his system. I don't think he'll take that lightly. Faster than you can say 'we're cooked,' we'll be filleted, fried, and served up in federal court. That's after they start asking questions—like, 'Why were you hacking into our secure network? Where did you get the pass codes? Why did you do it?' The fact we're government employees won't count for shit. Heat will come from all over the fucking place."

"Knox will clear it up—"

"Knox won't do shit. He'll put a fucking football field between us and himself. And if you don't think he'll do that, you've had your head buried in computer code too long."

"Knox is the one who gave us the entry codes to begin with. His handwriting is all over this. Who else would have access to what he gave us?"

"Knox doesn't know what we did."

"Don't be so sure."

DeSantos laughed. "He sure as hell didn't intend for us to use some *earthworm* program to hunt around the NSA and DoD databases."

Archer held his hands out, palms up, professing his innocence. "He didn't say not to. Maybe he wanted us to find this stuff."

"Yeah, and maybe he didn't."

"Why wouldn't he? What's in here we're not supposed to know about?"

DeSantos was silent for a moment, then shook his head. "I don't know. But none of that matters, Brian. We don't know what we stumbled onto here. We could've just put our feet in some fucked-up shit that we have no business being in. Without knowing what we're up against, we can't be making calls to anyone even remotely connected to NSA, especially a techie analyst who works there. For now, we keep this between us. We don't even tell Knox. No one. No exceptions."

Archer rubbed at the strained creases in his forehead. "None of that matters if we can't figure out what the rest of the memo says."

"Don't you know anyone else who can crack this code?"

"There's always the yellow pages. They've got to have a listing for encryption cracking specialists," Archer said facetiously.

"Wait a minute, I know someone. He may not the best source, but it's worth a shot."

"Who does he work for?"

"The state of New York."

"Too risky."

"I don't think so." DeSantos stood and opened his attaché. "He doesn't exactly *work* for the state." He pulled out a small black book. "He's in Attica."

"The prison?"

"Like I said, he might not be the best source. But if we're desperate . . ."

"You're out of your mind."

DeSantos thumbed through his book. "Think about it. He's got no connections to feds. He can't hurt us."

"Forget about hurting us. Why would he help us?"

"He helps us out, we help him out a little with his parole."

"What's he in for?

DeSantos smiled. "He broke into the state's abandoned-items database and started assigning some of the assets to himself. White-collar crime."

"And he ended up in Attica?"

DeSantos shrugged. "He pissed off the prosecutor, the judge, and the jury. He can be a little obnoxious."

Archer eyed DeSantos suspiciously. "I don't know about this."

"'Subject Scarponi is an ideal blank blank for this project,'" DeSantos repeated. "Aren't you the least bit curious how Scarponi is tied in to all this?"

"Even if we jump through all the hoops and get this thing deciphered, I doubt we'll have all the answers."

"Probably not. But shit, my curiosity is piqued."

"Curiosity killed the cat."

"So I'll have to be a little smarter than that dead feline."

"I don't like this." Archer looked up at his partner with dark eyes. "You mark my words: this is going to be trouble."

FORTY-SIX

Scott Haviland was driving his Bureau-issued blue Chevrolet Caprice along Pennsylvania Avenue headed toward Interstate 395. Waller, sitting in the backseat with Payne, was leaning against the door facing his passenger. None of them had spoken since leaving the lobby of headquarters. Payne was not interested in making small talk; he wanted answers, but he had to be careful. He did not know to what extent Waller and Haviland were involved, if at all. Regardless, he was not about to tip his hand and tell them what he knew unless it was to his advantage.

Finally, realizing it was to his benefit to initiate the conversation, he turned to Waller. "So what did you want to talk about?"

"You missed your day of classes today."

"Something was wrong with the laptop. Modem wouldn't work."

"Where were you all day?"

"Trying to figure out what was wrong with the computer."

Waller looked away for a moment, staring out the front windshield. "Something's up, Harp. We want to know what it is."

Payne grunted. "You want to know what's up."

Waller turned back to him. "That's right."

"I'm conducting an investigation."

"On what?"

"It's ongoing, I can't discuss it just yet. You'll know when I'm done."

"Not good enough. You know standard Bureau procedure."

"Yeah, I do. And no one seems to be following it." Payne looked hard at Waller, locking eyes with him. He needed to show strength without giving any indication that he knew what was going on. Of course, in reality, he only had theories and assumptions. He had no facts.

"Knox is concerned."

Payne nodded. "I can understand that. I'm very important to him."

Waller turned his attention back to the front windshield. "You're going to have to be more specific with the director. He won't tolerate evasive answers."

"Or what, what's he going to do? He needs me. I'm his case. Without me, Scarponi goes free." *Which might be exactly what he wants,* Payne felt like saying.

Waller sighed, then extended his hand. "I need your firearm, Harp."

Payne looked at him. "My firearm?"

"You're behaving irrationally, and given the opportunity to explain, you've failed to provide support for your actions. I don't know if it's all part of that blow to the head or what, but if you give Knox a good explanation, it'll be returned."

Payne casually reached into his jacket, removed his Glock from its holster, and pointed the barrel at Waller's head. "Sorry, partner. Can't go that route, not yet." Glancing over at Haviland, Payne said, "Keep both hands on the wheel where I can see them, Scott."

He turned back to Waller and held out his left hand. "Give me your wallet."

"Harper, this isn't the way to go."

"My life, my concern. Hand it over, now."

Waller's gaze seemed to focus on the gun, which was two inches away from his eyes. Payne knew that Waller had assessed the situation, and given a choice between being severely reprimanded by Knox for allowing this to happen—or facing the prospect of a bullet ripping through his brain—he would take the lesser of the two risks.

"Come on, Jon," Payne said. "Remember what you said to me a few days back? If I ever needed anything?"

"The offer still stands. But I can't help you break the law."

Payne grunted. "Exactly what law am I breaking, Jon?"

"Fidelity, Bravery, Integrity. It's how we swore to conduct ourselves, Harper. It's not just a catchy phrase on the Bureau seal."

"I think I'm being pretty damned brave holding a gun to your head. As for fidelity and integrity, first you have to prove yours to me before I commit to them myself." Payne wiggled the fingers of his free hand. "Your wallet."

Waller clenched his jaw, then reached beneath his jacket.

"Slowly, Jon. Keep it clean."

He produced the wallet and handed it to Payne, who shoved it into his pocket.

"Now slowly remove your weapon with two finger-tips and hand it to me."

Waller complied, and Payne took it with his left hand. Pointing the Glock in his right hand at the back of Haviland's head, he now had both of them at gunpoint. "Same thing, Scott. Two fingers, remove your weapon."

With his right hand, Haviland complied.

"Now point the gun toward the windshield and release the magazine onto the floor."

Haviland held the firearm out and pressed the small release. The metal clip of fifteen bullets dropped and clunked to the floor.

"Good. Now toss the gun down."

The gun thumped somewhere on the passenger side.

Payne pressed the release on Waller's Glock and placed the magazine in his pocket. He unchambered the remaining round still inside the gun and tossed the weapon to the floor in the front of the car.

"Okay, gentlemen, this is good-bye for now. When I've completed my investigation, maybe we'll enjoy a beer and laugh about this."

"Don't count on it," Waller said.

"No, I guess not." Payne turned to Haviland. "Stop the car, Scott."

Haviland stayed silent, his eyes focused on the road.

"I said, *stop the car.*"

"He's not going to let you off, Harper. You can shoot us if you want, but I don't think that's what you're about."

"That's part of the problem, Jon. I don't remember what the fuck I'm about. Now stop the goddamned car!"

"You can go ahead and shoot us," Haviland said, "but I'm not stopping this car."

The sudden acceleration was obvious. Payne glanced at the speedometer and saw the needle gliding past forty-five miles per hour. As he looked down to grab for the door handle, Haviland suddenly slammed on the brakes.

Payne's head and left shoulder smashed into the front seat. He felt a hand on his arm as Haviland floored the accelerator. He fell backward, fighting to maintain a grip on his handgun with his right hand while trying to find the door handle with his left. The door popped open—and the frigid wind hit him in the face, momentarily taking his breath away.

He closed his eyes and—despite Waller's hand gripping his suit jacket from behind—he leaned forward.

And leaped from the moving vehicle.

FORTY-SEVEN

The initial impact was absorbed by his shoulder. But as Payne tumbled and rolled along the pavement, the only thoughts spinning through his mind related to protecting his head. Another concussion was something he definitely did not need.

A few more rolls amidst the blaring of an approaching horn and he was scrambling to his feet. He dodged an oncoming van and zigzagged across the avenue. As he landed on the curb with his left leg in full stride, he felt a ripping sensation in his thigh. He knew the stitches had torn open, at least partially. But the adrenaline was pumping, and if there was any pain, he was not feeling it.

He half-hobbled and half-ran down the street, in the opposite direction Haviland had been driving, looking for a restaurant, somewhere he could hide. But this was Washington, and this part of the city had no night life to speak of. It consisted mostly of government buildings that had long since closed. He needed a side street, a bar or hotel, somewhere to get off the main drag.

Twenty yards away, he saw something better.

Haviland slammed on the brakes, the tires screeching to a halt. "You see him?"

"Where's my fucking gun?" Waller was on the floor in the backseat, his hands skimming the carpet, fingers getting nicked by the sharp edges of the seat track. "Turn the goddamned light on!"

Haviland hit the switch on the overhead dome light and located the two guns.

"He took my clip," Waller said. "Give me the one from the glove box."

"What are you going to do, shoot him?"

"Whatever I have to do to stop him. Take out his other leg if I have to. Son of a bitch."

Haviland handed him the spare magazine and grabbed the radio handset.

"What are you doing?"

"Backup—"

"You fucking out of your mind? Knox will have our badges if we broadcast Payne's escape across the radio."

"And if we don't find him?"

"We will," Waller said, slapping the clip into the handle of his Glock. "He's a gimp, he won't get very far."

"So we go it alone?"

"Alone."

Leaving the car in the middle of Pennsylvania Avenue, Waller opened the door and dodged a couple of oncoming cars as his eyes suddenly locked on a moving figure a couple of blocks away.

Haviland was running alongside Waller, nine-millimeter in hand. "There, by Seventh—"

"I see him."

"He's headed for the Mall."

"Then we've got him."

• • •

Payne was winded. His lungs were burning from the cold air, and he was now beginning to feel pain in his leg. But going back to the Academy and continuing on as Knox's puppet—or worse—did not appeal to him. He needed to find out what the bigger picture was . . . and despite his suspicions, he needed facts.

And then there was Lauren.

He turned right off Pennsylvania Avenue and crossed through a wooded planter, which provided dense cover from the silhouetting headlights of the oncoming traffic. He emerged in a cobblestone plaza, which was part of the side entrance to the National Gallery of Art's West Building. He shuffled alongside the structure, moving parallel to Fourth Street. Forty feet ahead was the Mall, the 146-acre elm-tree-lined park that stretched from the Capitol at the east end to the Lincoln Memorial at the far west end.

Payne turned right, following the footprint of the Gallery, now moving parallel to the Mall. Unfortunately, because the art museum was such an exceptionally long building—more than two blocks in length—it left him exposed, unable to escape should Waller or Haviland locate him.

He glanced to his left, and in the shadows of the dim streetlight, he noticed a man walking toward him. He threw his back against the darkness of the building's cold marble facing. Payne squinted, trying to make out the gait and size of the man. Could it be Haviland or Waller? As he stared, he could see the silhouetted form of a leashed dog at the man's side.

He gulped down a few bitingly cold breaths of air before rolling off the building's side and continuing on, scampering along the base of the steps of the entrance, in the direction of the west end of the Mall. Built in Washington's time-honored multicolumned-facade-and-canted-roof motif, the entrance was designed to be grand—and the illumination, with bright orange mercury spotlights, certainly helped accomplish this goal.

But the foot of the steps was comparatively dark. After making his way across the stairs, he stayed close to the bushes that lined the entire front of the building. If he could make it to the edge of the Gallery before Waller or Haviland saw him, he would greatly increase his chances of success. He hoped that they were off searching another part of the District by now, since he figured that from their perspective he could literally be anywhere. If a cab had been passing as he was fleeing Haviland's car, he could be on the other side of the Potomac by now, headed for the airport. Or back the other way, headed toward Union Station and a rail system that could take him anywhere in the District, or, for that matter, anywhere in the country.

He realized the ability to be instantly somewhere far away from here was not only appealing, but his best hope for a successful escape while he regrouped and tried to determine his next course of action. But he had a bad feeling that Waller and Haviland were not far off—and if he was not careful, he would end up running right into them.

He tried to picture the map of the District he had studied late one night at the Academy. If he recalled correctly, about three blocks away his closest means of escape awaited him . . . the entrance to Washington's subway, the metro.

• • •

"I saw him, over by the Gallery. West Building," Waller said in between breaths.

"I don't . . . see anything," Haviland puffed. After having recently recovered from a broken ankle, he was still out of shape—and the chase had left him deeply winded, his throat burning with each gulp of air.

"He was there."

"Where's he . . . headed?"

Waller pondered the question as they continued their pursuit at a slow jog. "If I were him, there's only one place I'd go."

"Don't keep it . . . a secret, Jon. Where?"

"Metro."

"Which station? . . . Archives or Smithsonian?"

"My bet, Archives. Closer."

"Let's cut him off," Haviland said, heaving large clouds of vapor into the air in front of him.

"And if we're wrong?"

Haviland nodded. "So we split up. You go Metro . . . I'll go Mall."

"This is insane," Waller said. "Should've called for backup."

Haviland stopped and leaned over, resting his hands on his knees as Waller continued on. "You know, Jon," he said, calling after his partner, "sometimes . . . you're such an asshole."

Payne shuffled alongside the building, approaching the west end of the National Gallery of Art.

But out of the corner of his eye he caught the shadow of a figure advancing on him. Although it was too dark to make out the man's face, the tall build and stealthy, catlike movement told him it was Waller.

Payne cut right on Seventh Street and glanced back over his shoulder, but was unable to locate the form he had just seen. In the darkness and the cover of so many trees, he couldn't be sure that Waller wasn't only a few feet behind him. Although the thigh wound was still painful, it was tolerable and permitted him to move fairly well as long as he was not running at full stride.

He jogged across Constitution Avenue and headed toward Pennsylvania, a short block away. To his left was the stately National Archives building, to his right the more staid Federal Trade Commission. He didn't dare look over his shoulder, as he was in a rhythm now, moving quickly toward his goal: the brightly lit metro entrance that was now partially visible up ahead of him.

As he approached, he could make out the vertical sign with the large *M* at the top, which read ARCHIVES–NAVY MEMORIAL STA

Payne crossed S
vator, headed for
three escalators de
of the subway ent
with a woman, gi
head down, steppe
took his first look i
where he had just
ment.

Once he hit the
past the automated
and approached the
glanced at the stat
which was empty
directions—and he

torso across the flat surface of the low-lying turn-stile. He pulled himself over it and landed on his right leg. He continued on, down the stairs and toward the tracks.

As he moved, he caught sight of security cameras, mounted high on the ceiling, beaming his image into the empty station manager's booth—and who knew where else. He hoped it would be a moot point: by the time anyone recognized the person on the screen as him, he would be long gone.

In the subway tube, the distant pinpoint of light told him a train was a couple hundred feet away, approaching the station. The muted, greenish, recessed lighting accentuated the cement, honeycomb walls, which arched high above him. Yet the beauty of the architecture failed to elicit a memory of having been here before.

Wait. What was that? Hard footsteps, dress shoes. Running toward him from above.

"Harper!"

is Glock and aimed it up at the voice, y became associated with a silhouet- above him, on the main floor of the

," Payne called out. The handful of atform scattered, moving for any nd: a bench, a trash can, the side of

own the track, the train's two dis- arging as they approached.

d was extended out in front of him. own and we can talk."

Payne asked, turning around and check all possible routes of entry he station.

"Put the gun down, Harper. I don't want anyone getting hurt."

"Everyone's taken cover, Jon. People do that—they see guns, they tend to hide. But keep talking, it's your job. You know, buddy up to me, get me to drop the gun so you can take me in without incident." Payne glanced at the tracks again. The building, rumbling echo in the tunnel indicated the train would be here in a matter of seconds—a fact he knew Waller was aware of as well. "I can't go with you, Jon, at least not now."

"Don't do this. We can still work something out."

The train pulled to a stop and the doors whooshed open.

Payne glanced at the train, then back up at Waller, who had just stepped onto the escalator.

"That wasn't smart, Jon," Payne yelled.

"You're not gonna shoot me. You'd lose everything—your career, your life. You'd never see Lauren again."

Just then, a tone sounded and the metro's doors began sliding closed. Payne stepped into the train. As the doors clunked shut, he turned to check on Waller—but he was gone.

"Shit." Payne quickly moved toward the back of the car. A few people, a man in a business suit and a couple of teenagers in jeans, eyed him with fear as he hobbled along, the gun still clutched in his hand. Payne noticed their gazes, slid his firearm into its holster, and removed his credentials. "FBI," he said in explanation, holding up the open case as he shuffled through the car. Once again, he craned his neck to see through the windows, trying to locate Waller. But there wasn't any sign of him.

Payne walked through the two doors and into the next car just as the train lurched forward. No one else was in the car. He sat down heavily and buried his tired head in his hands.

Waller was on the train. He could feel it.

"What the hell's wrong with you?"

Payne opened his eyes and focused on Waller's frowning face. "Jon. Have a seat."

Waller's body was rigid, as if prepared to pounce. When Payne made no effort to flee, Waller seemed to relax a bit. He glanced around, appearing to look for some trap, some reason why his fugitive was not attempting to escape. Apparently satisfied it was safe to sit, he settled into the seat next to Payne. "I don't get it, Harper. What's gotten into you?"

Payne looked at him with heavy eyes. "You want to know what's gotten into me." He chuckled. "Fair question, I guess." He let his head fall backward and he stared at the ceiling as the train lurched slightly from side to side. "You won't understand . . . you don't know what I know. Then again, maybe you do."

Waller shook his head. "I don't know what you're talking about. Maybe you're just on overload. We were working at an extremely aggressive pace. Maybe I was pushing you too hard." He extended his hand. "I need your weapon."

"Why?"

"Why? Because you disobeyed orders, Harp, because you held fellow agents at gunpoint and stole my fucking wallet, because you're acting irrationally. You leaped from a moving vehicle, for Christ's sake. Those good enough reasons?"

"No, they're not. Not for me, at least."

"Direct order from Knox, okay? He wants you to see a shrink, find out what's gotten under your skin. If everything checks out and he gives you a clean bill, you get it back. Right now, it's just a precaution."

Payne looked at Waller's open hand. "Knox has to protect his star witness."

Waller nodded. "Can you blame him?"

Payne sighed. "No, I guess not. But I'll want it back." He reached inside his suit jacket.

"Two fingers! Take it out with two fingers—"

"If I was going to shoot you, Jon, you wouldn't have gotten out of Scott's car alive." Payne pulled out his weapon, pressed it down into Waller's palm—then wrapped his fingers around the back of Waller's hand.

"What the fuck—"

In a lightning fast move, Payne slapped a handcuff on his partner's left wrist. Waller pulled back—but not before Payne had flicked the other end of the restraint around the metal pole that ran the length of the seat in front of them.

Waller reached for his gun with his free right hand—but Payne's left was already on the weapon and yanking it out of the holster.

Payne backed away and slipped the nine-millimeter into his own shoulder harness.

"You're out of your fucking mind—"

"Am I? Do you really think I've lost my mind, Jon?"

"I don't know what to think—"

"Well, I do. Now, give me your set of cuffs. And the key."

"No."

Payne chambered a bullet and held his Glock out in front of him.

Waller looked at the barrel of the gun and swallowed hard. "You're not going to use that on me, you just said so yourself."

"Truth is, Jon, I don't know how I'm gonna react. I'm so damned confused . . . the stress is unbearable. I got hit in the head so hard I don't even remember my wife. When you're confused and stressed-out, and your back's up against a wall, you get paranoid, you do things. Things you may regret later. Do you really wanna push me?"

Waller hesitated, his gaze shifting between Payne's hollow, intense eyes and the barrel of the gun. He dug into his pocket, produced a small ring of keys, and tossed them at Payne, who removed the long, thin, black key. He dropped the rest to the floor and kicked them beneath Waller's seat.

Payne motioned him on with the gun. "Now the bracelets."

Waller reached behind him and produced the handcuffs.

"Attach one end to that pole in front of you." Payne approached cautiously, keeping the weapon as far away from Waller's reach as possible. He took the free end of the cuffs and fastened them to his partner's right wrist. He reached into Waller's inside suit pocket, removed his cell phone, and turned it off.

"Why are you doing this to me, Harper? I've been trying to help you."

"Because I've got a whole bunch of questions and no answers. I need those answers to get on with my life. You've helped me, yes. You've done your job. You've shown me who I *was*. But now I need to find out who I am. Lauren Chambers has the answers I need, and for some reason, you're keeping me from communicating with her. What are you afraid of?"

Waller sighed, shook his head. "I shouldn't be telling you this, but Knox was concerned that if you spoke with this woman who claimed to be your wife, we'd be placing her in danger, and you'd lose your focus on the trial. He wanted you to be totally free of any extraneous thoughts or complications. It was just going to be for a few more weeks."

"That *complication* is my wife, Jon. I need to know how I fit into her life now."

"A little while ago, you wanted to stay on the job, remember?"

"What's that got to do with anything? I'm glad I'm back, I told you that. Believe me, that's not the problem—"

"Then don't fuck it up, Harper. Do your thing, take the stand and testify. Then your life's your own. Stay or go. Your choice."

"She thinks I'm missing. I need to at least tell her I'm okay."

"I'll see about getting word to her. We'll make things right by you, I promise. But you've gotta help us out." Waller nodded toward the cuffs. "You can start by getting these things off me."

The train pulled to a stop at the Foggy Bottom station. Payne backed toward the door, then stopped.

"I need to do some thinking. Figure some things out."

"Harper—don't leave me here."

"I need some space, some time."

The tone sounded and the doors began to close. Payne jumped through them and stood there, watching Waller through the window. Waller's face was a deep crimson, and he was yelling, using language Payne would've taken offense to if this had been some other time.

But this wasn't some other time.

Payne turned away and headed toward the escalator. "Like you said, Jon . . . we do what we have to do."

FORTY-EIGHT

Scott Haviland stood at the bright opening to the metro's Archives–Navy Memorial Station. He stared down at the wallet in his left hand and saw Jonathan Waller's smiling face looking up at him from the Virginia driver's license. Not surprisingly, the wallet was nearly empty; photos of Waller's two brothers were still inside, but the cash and credit cards were gone.

Haviland tucked the wallet inside his suit jacket and walked the length of the platform before descending a level and searching for a sign of either his partner or Harper Payne.

But he really did not expect to find them. He surmised that Payne had jumped on a train and that Waller had followed him aboard.

Haviland sat down on the bench and spread his arms across the seatback. The station manager had thought he recalled seeing two men matching their description entering the station a few minutes apart, but he could not be sure. Haviland turned his head first to the left, then to the right, taking in the expansive, high-ceilinged terminal. Not one person was in the entire station, it seemed. No one to question, no one who might have seen which train they had taken.

Haviland again tried reaching Waller's cell phone,

but was forwarded to his voice mail . . . which meant that either he had turned it off so it would not ring and give away his position, or he was for some reason unable to answer it. The uncertainty gnawed at Haviland.

He called his wife and told her not to wait up for him. He then slipped the phone back in his jacket pocket and began tapping out a rhythm on the cement floor with his foot.

He thought about calling Knox and informing him of their status. But he did not want to take the chance of someone intercepting the call, let alone that, if his partner was successful in apprehending Payne, he would not want the director to know they had lost him in the first place. No, he would hold off a little longer before hitting the panic button.

For the time being, he could do nothing but wait until Waller called him back.

At a few minutes past one in the morning, Haviland and Waller stood at Douglas Knox's front door. They had called him a few moments ago to wake him and let him know it was urgent they meet with him immediately.

They sat down heavily in the chairs arranged in front of his desk and briefed their boss on the events of the past few hours.

The director wore a burgundy robe and leather moccasins, his gray hair tousled and his complexion ruddy and disturbed. "What am I supposed to do, huh? What the hell am I supposed to do?" he bellowed.

Waller kept his eyes on the desk in front of him. "I'm sorry, sir."

"Sorry?"

Waller knew it was the wrong thing to say—but he genuinely meant it. He felt responsible for allowing a key witness in one of the most important FBI cases in decades to escape. No matter how he wrote up his report, there was no way to avoid disciplinary action. But how it would affect his career wasn't his biggest concern. It was saving face in front of the director. "He's one of us, I thought I could trust him."

"And the CIA thought it could trust Aldrich Ames," Knox spat.

Waller cringed at the comparison to one of the most damaging spy cases ever to hit the U.S. intelligence community. He knew the two situations were vastly different, but he kept the thought to himself. "Yes, sir. I blew it, nothing I say can excuse what I did."

"I shoulder some of the responsibility as well, sir," Haviland said.

"Fine, you're a fuckup, too." Knox stood up, shoved his hands into the robe's pockets, and began pacing. "How could you let this happen? Do you realize what's on the line? We've got a court date four weeks away. With Payne, I've got control over what happens. Without him . . ."

Waller glanced at Haviland, who was staring straight ahead at the bookcase. Waller felt like reminding the director that they did not have Scarponi either—and without the defendant, the trial would be of limited value. But he decided to keep his thoughts to himself.

"Have you got any idea of where he might be? Any way of tracking him?" Knox finally asked.

"Aside from putting out an alert," Haviland said, "there are no means of tracing him unless he uses one of Jon's credit cards."

"We can't put out an alert," Waller said. "We still don't know who leaked the information about Harper's amnesia. If it gets out that we lost our witness, every TV station would drag us through the stables until we had horseshit coming out of every orifice."

"Let alone what Scarponi's attorney will do with it," Haviland added.

Knox stopped pacing. "He's not going to use a credit card. It'd give us an immediate electronic trace on his location. He knows that. We're not dealing with some dumb fugitive here." There was silence for a moment while Knox stared at his meticulously neat desk. "Okay. Contact Metro PD. Tell them we've got a be-on-the-lookout for one of our own, Special Agent Richard Thompson. Tell them we suspect mental instability, and to use extreme caution. We don't want him harmed. Then have Lindsey put out the same BOLO." Knox shook his head. "Best we can hope for. Above all else, we need to find him."

"Since we don't know who the leak is," Waller said, "I don't know how long we can keep a lid on things."

"I don't either. But you two have left me no choice. That is, unless you find him fast."

"We'll do our best."

"Make sure that's good enough. I'm giving you forty-eight hours. If we don't have him by then, you two are suspended indefinitely without pay."

Waller and Haviland rose from their chairs and turned to leave.

"Forty-eight hours," Knox called after them as they made their way to the door.

FORTY-NINE

Payne was sitting in a cab, his head resting against the cold window. After leaving Waller cuffed to the subway car, he had boarded another train headed in the opposite direction. He then switched to the Red Line, took it into Maryland, and called a taxi service. He directed the driver to drop him at a small independent motel near Bethesda he had located in the yellow pages.

As the cab glided along the George Washington Memorial Parkway, he closed his eyes for a moment— and saw the face of a woman in her midthirties, large brown eyes, and brunet hair. Full lips. "Lauren," he said, opening his eyes. "That's Lauren."

The driver glanced at him in the rearview mirror. "You talking to me?"

Payne sat up straight. "No, no. I just . . . I just remembered something." He tried to lock on the memory and suddenly saw himself surrounded by snow-covered mountains with a group of men. They were wearing backpacks and skis . . . and then the image was gone. The harder he tried to concentrate, the more distant the memory became.

After leaving the interstate, the cab hung a few turns and pulled into a pothole-infested parking lot. The driver called out over his shoulder, "Hey, buddy, this is it. Presidential Motor Lodge." He paused a moment, taking in the state of the motel. "You sure you don't want something a little nicer? There's a Best Western a couple miles up the road—"

Payne craned his neck and squinted out the dirty front windshield at the run-down structure. "No, this is perfect, thanks." He pulled a roll of bills from his pocket and paid the man, courtesy of Jonathan Waller. "Remember, I want a cab here at eight o'clock tomorrow morning."

"Boss already knows. Someone'll be here."

After the cab drove away, Payne waited outside the office door, pressing a buzzer and peering at the front desk through the cracked window. It was a small room, perhaps ten by twelve, crammed with tourist brochures and guides, a well-worn brown Formica counter, and a small black-and-white television propped in the corner, its antenna a twisted wire coat hanger.

An unshaven man with a torn white undershirt stretched across his large belly appeared from behind the counter. He stepped as close as he could get to the door. "Yeah?"

"I called forty-five minutes ago, about a room for tonight."

The man nodded, then waddled over toward the counter and pressed a button connected to a buzzer. Payne pushed on the door and entered the office.

"Payment due up front," the man said as he slapped a clipboard and registration form on the counter.

Payne filled in the blanks with completely false information. He produced his credentials and flashed them, hoping the man wouldn't take the time to read the name. "I'm a federal agent," he said, closing the case and shoving it back in his suit jacket pocket. "I'll give you my credit card number, but I don't want you putting it through till I'm ready to check out, is that clear?"

The man nodded.

"I'm doing surveillance on a suspect who's staying in your motel. But he's very clever and has an electronic linkup to the credit card companies. If you put this through, they'll alert him within seconds that I'm here."

The man nodded again. "It's that guy in eighteen, isn't it?"

Payne looked around. "I can't divulge that information, sir. But you seem like a pretty sharp guy."

The man nodded, a half smile breaking through his unshaven face. "So I guess you want either seventeen or nineteen."

Payne reasoned that in a dive like this, both rooms were probably open. "I'd prefer nineteen. Better angle." The more detailed the lie, the more believable it was.

"I got ya." The night manager turned to a board with keys dangling from bent nails. He chose a set and handed it to Payne. "Charge won't go through till mornin'."

Payne thanked the man and walked around to room 19. As the door swung open, the strong odor of mildew flared his nostrils. "Great," he said, flicking on a light. He hung his torn suit on the lone wire hanger in the closet, cleaned his oozing thigh wound, washed his abraded hands and face, and sank down into the soft mattress.

Within minutes he was asleep, again dreaming of the brunet woman he knew only as Lauren Chambers.

FIFTY

Achilling drizzle misted the air along the path that rimmed the Tidal Basin, but Hector DeSantos did not mind it. The way he saw it, the thick air made it more difficult for someone to electronically eavesdrop on his conversation. Sometimes all it took to defeat high technology was good old-fashioned Mother Nature.

DeSantos's legs had a spring to them this morning, giving him the impression he could run twenty miles if he wanted to. He sucked in a mouthful of moist air and blew it out, enjoying the solitude of the moment. As it currently stood, life wasn't too bad for him.

He increased his pace and streaked past the Jefferson Memorial, where another runner joined in stride beside him. It was Brian Archer, dressed in gray sweats and a Redskins ball cap pulled down low over his brow.

"So what's the urgency?" Archer asked. "And why here?"

"Thought we'd go for a run, spend some quality time together. We haven't done this in months."

"I could've slept another hour, Hector. This better be good."

"Good isn't the word, bro."

Archer waited a few strides, then said, "Well, you gonna share the news or did you invite me out here to play games?"

"You're uptight this a.m., my man! Loosen up!"

"You're in too good a mood, Hector. You had some bizarre session with Maggie this morning, didn't you?" Archer puffed. "I can tell."

"I got some answers on that document."

Archer kept his gaze straight ahead. "Oh yeah? That con came through?"

DeSantos's eyes quickly danced over at his partner. "This is amazing shit, Brian. Kind of stuff we're usually smack in the middle of, not shut out of."

"You're enjoying this, aren't you?" Archer looked over at DeSantos, whose long, lean legs had slipped into a rhythmic stride with gazellelike grace.

"Hell yeah," DeSantos said, then paused to gulp some air. "This is the shit I live for."

Archer moved to the right to allow another runner to slip past them. "Then maybe we should handle this at my place. Somewhere secure."

"We're here," DeSantos said, "let's at least get the run in first."

They jogged for another fifteen minutes, passing many of the three thousand winter-barren Japanese cherry trees. After circling back, they drove into nearby Georgetown, where the Archers owned a modest two-story brick house trimmed with steel-blue-and-oyster shutters, and accented by an ornate wreath that hung from a brass hook on the front door.

Small security cameras mounted high above on the eaves recorded their arrival. DeSantos good-naturedly waved to the one above his head, then wiped his running shoes on the bristly welcome mat. He followed his partner into the hallway and glanced at the decor. "Love what you've done with the place."

Archer followed his partner's gaze, which took in

the rustic country motif: distressed oak furniture, frilly white curtains with denim trim, braided rugs, old pottery tastefully placed around the kitchen. DeSantos flashed on the last time he was invited over for dinner three months ago. He had tracked in soil on the bottom of his shoes and scratched the entryway's twenty-five-year-old wood flooring. The Archers had just dropped $2,000 refinishing the floor, and DeSantos had spent the next few days feeling guilty and begging for forgiveness.

"Remember the re-fi?" Archer asked. "We pulled ten grand out and this is what it got me. Lots of furniture and . . . all this fancy country stuff." He walked into the kitchen and grabbed a couple of glasses from the cupboard. "I was fine with my La-Z-Boy and the old Hide-A-Bed."

DeSantos filled his glass with water. "The shit didn't match, Brian."

Archer shrugged. "It's better to take on more debt?"

"Hey, you're married, bro. Debt comes with the territory. Speaking of which, where's Trish?"

"In the nursery, sewing some curtains. She's really getting into this baby stuff."

"Her first kid. Must be like playing with dolls."

Archer placed his glass in the sink, then regarded his partner. "That's very intuitive, Hector. Where the hell did that come from? What do you know about mothers and babies?"

DeSantos shrugged, left his glass on the counter, and moved down the hall toward the basement door. "I'm a very intuitive person, especially when it comes to women. You know that."

Archer slapped him across the back of the head. "You're so full of it."

DeSantos flipped on the stairwell light and headed down into the damp basement. Archer followed him and watched as his partner pulled a tiny electronic device out of his front pocket.

"What are you doing?"

DeSantos placed an index finger over his lips. "When was the last time you swept?" He pressed a button on the device and began moving it around the room.

"There are no bugs down here," Archer said, hands on his hips.

DeSantos winked. "Allergic to spiders, can't take a chance. Those spindly little creatures have a way of putting up their webs in the worst places." He continued to move the unit around for another moment, then switched it off. "Okay, we're clear."

"I already told you that." Archer pulled a chain, and a fluorescent fixture flickered on, suffusing the basement with harsh white light. Beside him was a barbell resting on a stand adjacent to a weight bench, where a stack of iron plates sat neatly arranged in size order.

DeSantos lifted an eighty-pound plate and placed it on the Olympic barbell. He began tightening the end bracket while Archer repeated the procedure on the other end.

"You first," DeSantos said as he removed his jacket.

Archer lay down on the bench, shifted his torso a bit, then lifted the bar off the stand and completed a press.

"About the document," DeSantos said.

"First, I have something to ask you," Archer gasped, completing the next rep. "A favor."

"I don't like the sound of this. The last time you

asked me for a favor it was something really important, something that required the R-word."

Archer groaned as he hoisted the heavy weight. "Responsibility . . . is not . . . a dirty word." He motioned for DeSantos to take the barbell from him. As his partner laid the weights in the stand, Archer swung his legs off the bench and sat up. His chest was pimpled with sweat and he was breathing hard. "Too much weight. Haven't worked out in two weeks."

DeSantos pulled a padded bench over from the far wall and sat down. "So you're serious. You need something," he said, leaning forward.

"It's really not that big a deal. I mean, it is, but it's not something you have to dread. It's a good thing."

"You need money? Whatever you need, bro, you know, you got it."

"Hello!" called a voice from the stairwell. "Honey? That you?"

"We're down here," Archer shouted. "Hector's here, we're talking shop."

Trish Archer carefully descended the stairs, her baby-engorged abdomen arriving a couple of steps before the rest of her. She brushed a wisp of short, straw-blond hair behind her ear and smiled at DeSantos, who had walked over to the bottom of the landing. "Hector," she said, throwing her arms around him.

"Brian keeps me apprised of your . . . progress," he said, looking down at her stomach. "He's right, you do look like a whale."

Trish's mouth dropped open as she looked at her husband. "You said what?"

"You're going to get me in trouble," Archer warned.

DeSantos laughed. "You look positively radiant, even in fluorescent lighting."

Trish planted a kiss on his cheek, then stuck her tongue out at her husband.

"Honestly, honey, I didn't call you a whale."

Trish's hand went to her abdomen. "Oh, just got a kick. Want to feel?" she said to DeSantos.

"Nah, I'll pass if you don't mind."

"Oh, come on." She took his hand and placed it where hers was, in the lower right portion of her abdomen. "Did you feel it?"

"What is that?"

"That's her foot pushing against your hand. Go ahead, push back against it, gently."

DeSantos applied some pressure and the foot retracted. "That's cool. Do you do this?" he asked Archer.

"When she lets me."

DeSantos stepped back and regarded her abdomen the way a painter studies a blank canvas. "Aren't you, like, close to bursting?"

"Could burst any moment," Archer said. "That's why God invented pagers, isn't it? So husbands could be at their wives' beck and call twenty-four hours a day?"

"Speaking of which," Trish said, "did you ask him yet?"

DeSantos looked at Archer. "Ask me what?"

Archer sat down on the bench again. "Trish and I want you to be Presley Jane's godfather."

DeSantos stood there looking at Archer, expressionless. "You mean, like Don Corleone, like, 'He made me an offer I can't refuse'?" he asked in a hoarse voice.

"No," Archer said, "the other kind of godfather."

DeSantos felt like bursting out in laughter, but realized his partner was serious. "I don't know what to say."

"Say yes."

DeSantos sat down on the bench. "Godfather?" he asked, his eyes downcast. He brought his gaze up to meet Archer's. "You said it yourself, Brian. What the hell do I know about kids? I can't be someone's godfather. I'm lucky to still be married. I'm a playboy, you know? Maggie puts up with all sorts of shit." He stood up and rested his hands on his hips. "Why me?"

"Because I've got no family, Trish's parents are dead, and the kid needs someone we trust." Archer paused for a moment. "Really, it's not that big a thing."

"You'd make a great godfather," Trish said.

DeSantos was off in thought, staring at the wall. He had lived his life avoiding responsibility. He had to be damn near threatened at gunpoint to marry Maggie. He chuckled at the thought, for it had turned out to be the best "decision" he had ever made. He looked at the Archers and smiled. "Sure, what the hell. It'll be good for me."

Trish smiled. "See?" she said to her husband. "We didn't even need to threaten him with a shotgun."

"You told her about that?" DeSantos boomed. "You promised, that was a secret!"

"Speaking of secrets, we need to get back to business." Archer looked over at Trish, who took the hint.

"I'm leaving. You boys with your hush-hush spy stuff, when are you ever going to grow up and get real jobs?" She moved over to the stairs and slowly ascended them. "Join us for dinner next Saturday, okay?"

"I'll check with Maggie."

"From macho commando to whipped husband. The transformation has been quite amazing," Archer said.

"Fuck you."

"So tell me what was in that document," Archer said as he heard Trish close the upstairs door.

"We got most of the memo," DeSantos said in a low voice. "This con was good, but some of it was just too jumbled to make out. Seems the Intelligence Support Agency is engaged in some sort of research project with the CIA and DoD. Knox was mentioned but it's not clear what his role is."

"What kind of research project? And what does Scarponi have to do with it?"

DeSantos shook his head. "About the only thing we definitely get from it is that Scarponi is a target. Even though it's in code, they were still stingy about what they were putting down on paper. Basically, it seems as if Scarponi's going to be their guinea pig."

"Guinea pig? For what?"

"You want my theory on all this?"

"If you've got one."

"I gave it some thought during my run before you got there, put my paranoid psychosis to work. It suddenly all came together." DeSantos moved the bench closer to Archer. "What if the CIA-ISA-DoD group is planning to do some kind of experimental medical research on Scarponi without his consent?"

"The government involved in clandestine research on unsuspecting citizens? Gee, that'd be a first," Archer said sarcastically.

"Let's accept for a moment that for whatever reason, Scarponi has whatever it is they need for this study. Except that in Petersburg, being such a high-profile inmate, he's watched over by prison rights groups and there's no way they can move on him. And let's assume that Knox is an important piece to this puzzle. As chief counsel on the Select Committee, he had access and contacts and ties to all sorts of people. And being director of the FBI, he has big-time resources there, too."

"So Knox lucks out," Archer said. "When this new evidence comes out, he goes along with it and does some magic behind the scenes to make it easier for Scarponi to get released."

"Meantime, the U.S. Attorney joins in and tells the Bureau it needs Harper Payne to take the stand again to impeach this new evidence Scarponi's attorney has come up with."

"But," Archer said, "the marshal's office tells the Bureau that Payne's left witness protection and is freelancing it. DOJ throws a fit, and Knox jumps because the boss roared. So he kicks everyone's butt and the Bureau goes ass-wild trying to find Payne."

"Right. Now here's where my paranoia kicks in. What if this 'new evidence' is bullshit. What if Knox arranges it, fakes it, manufactures it. He sets up this whole scenario so Scarponi is released under the cover of an official court ruling. Behind the scenes, he uses the Bureau's latest electronic surveillance technology to place a device in Scarponi so he can be tracked at all times within a few feet of wherever he is."

"And Knox plans for it to appear as if Scarponi escapes. Knox's group would then secretly recapture him and hand him over to the researchers running the study. As far as everyone is concerned, Scarponi has slipped underground and disappeared the way anyone would expect a world-renowned hit man to do."

"But Knox's plan backfires when Scarponi finds a way out of the device," DeSantos said. "And he really does escape."

Archer nodded slowly. "And now the heat is on Knox. His alliance is pissed because he's let Scarponi slip through their fingers. The DOJ wants him back because if the president finds out about his escape, the shit will hit the fan. The DOJ will look like incompetent idiots and give 'the system' a huge black eye. If we can't keep a killer like Scarponi in prison, other countries won't trust us with extradition of future criminals. It brings all sorts of international political pressure to bear."

"And to top it all off, Knox gets this threat letter from Scarponi. His daughter's kidnapped to send a strong message. His family's in danger."

"So what does a guy like Knox do?" Archer asked.

DeSantos looked at Archer. "You're the guy with a kid on the way, Brian. You tell me. Who does he put first?"

"His family," Archer said without hesitation.

"So now all sorts of shit is going on. Everything and everyone is coming down on Knox. Does he arrange for Scarponi to get a clear shot at Payne so the threat is removed?"

"Or does he intend to protect Payne and instead use him as a pawn to lure Scarponi?"

The two men were quiet for a moment as they processed what they had just discussed.

Finally, Archer broke the silence. "Are we getting a little too far out here? I mean, Knox, an appeals court justice, the CIA, ISA, DoD . . . it's a hell of a conspiracy theory, Hector."

DeSantos chewed on his lip for a moment. "I know it reeks of paranoia, but we've seen shit like this before. Hell, look at OPSIG. *We've been part of stuff like this*. It's just that in the past, it's run a whole lot smoother and on a much smaller scale. They were sloppy. When Scarponi got away, everything got all fucked up."

"So what do we do with this?"

"I guess we try to find out if we're on the right track."

"Here's another piece of paranoia for you. Did Knox intend for us to figure this stuff out? I mean, he gave us those codes and let us hack away."

DeSantos chewed on his lip some more. "Better yet, is he relying on us to figure it out, to save his ass?" He ran both hands through his hair. "What a fucking mess."

"I thought you said you lived for this stuff."

"That was before I was a godfather. Now I've got to be more responsible. Shit like this is just too dangerous. Have you thought of that, Brian?"

Archer smiled. "Looks like godparenthood has had a positive effect on you already."

FIFTY-ONE

Harper Payne's eyes popped open. He stared at the water-stained ceiling in the dim light, wondering for a moment where he was. He propped himself up on an elbow, then switched on the bedside lamp and looked around. The motel. Bethesda.

He showered and redressed in his partially torn suit, stripped off the bedsheet, and tossed it in the Dumpster in the parking lot. Although he couldn't hide that he had stayed there, he did not want to make Waller and Haviland's job too easy for them. They would be stuck trying to run down the night manager to show him an identifying photo before they would know for sure that this is where he had spent the night.

Even if they picked up the electronic trace on Waller's Visa, they would have to confirm that it was in fact Payne who had used the card and not someone else he had sold it to. Of course, by the time they had verification it was him, he'd be long gone. But that Payne was still in the area would give them a trail and a place to start—infinitely more than what they had at the moment.

Payne thought about paying with cash, but his supply was limited and he didn't know where he would end up or what he would need it for. He was sure, however, that the Bureau would not turn off the spigot on the credit card. It was their proverbial bread trail, and as long as Payne was willing to lay down crumbs, they would be content to gobble them up.

At 7:55 A.M. he took a walk in the parking lot, waiting for the cab to arrive. He stood in front of a pickup with tinted windows and looked at his reflection in the glass.

"Who are you?" he asked the mirrored image. Ever since he had received the E-mail from Lauren Chambers, the question had been bouncing around in his head, without resolution. A small-town computer geek or a decorated FBI agent who got the short end of the career stick?

Who are you? If he returned to Placerville, he couldn't be sure he would ever regain the memories of the times he and Lauren Chambers had spent together. Could he be in a relationship with someone he didn't even know, when she knew everything about him? And was he the same person as he was before—would he have the same likes, desires, attractions? Could he learn to love her again?

If he chose instead to return to the FBI . . . would he be taken back without conditions? If this was, indeed, the course he wanted to pursue, then he was making a gross mistake in continuing to run. He needed to turn himself in and, assuming his colleagues found Scarponi, take the stand and testify on information he could now recite in his sleep. Cooperate and be free; it was that simple.

Or was it? What if Knox was trying to discredit him so that his testimony would be rendered ineffective? If that was the case, his chances of being reinstated to the Bureau were nil. As he had been taught to do during his Academy refresher courses, it was best to reduce a problem to its most basic components—and then find solutions to those remaining parts. The way he saw it, until he could be more certain of Knox's intentions, he could not consider returning to the FBI. Which left him with the dilemma of how to resume his life with Lauren Chambers.

Just then, tires crunched against the gravel-dotted asphalt behind him, where the taxi was pulling into the motel's parking lot. A minute later he was on his way up the interstate. He leaned his head against the seat and thought about the choices he had to make. Regardless of which path he chose, one thing was now certain.

There was no turning back.

FIFTY-TWO

The fork was dangling aimlessly from Lauren's right hand, haphazardly swiping at the scrambled eggs and moving them around the plate. Her chin was resting in her left hand, her eyes fixed somewhere on the table.

"A dime?"

Lauren looked at Nick Bradley. "A dime? For what?"

"Your thoughts."

She dropped her gaze back to the plate. "You ever realize how deceptive eggs are?"

Bradley's brow crumpled. "That's what you were thinking?"

"They start off as a gelatinous liquid, and we mix them briskly with a fork and scramble them up and they become this rubbery yellow stuff. They transform so easily from one form to another."

Bradley cleared his throat. "Uh, Lauren, if that's what you're really thinking, we need to find one of your colleagues and set up a session. Fast."

She put her fork down and sat back in her seat. "How long till our meeting?"

Bradley consulted his watch. "An hour."

Lauren nodded. Ever since he had told her yesterday afternoon that, after nearly a dozen calls, he had secured an appointment with a low-level assistant at the FBI, her mind had been unable to focus. She figured she was on overload, her body still fatigued from her night in the cabin. Not to mention the torment of knowing she was so close to—yet so far from—finding Michael. She felt helpless. "The situations where you have the least amount of control cause the most amount of stress." Her gaze met his eyes, which appeared to be filled with concern. "Did you know that?"

"Look, in an hour we'll be sitting down with someone who's in a position to give us the most useful information we've had since you got that message from Michael. You should be very encouraged."

She forced a smile. "Yeah, that's good, I'm encouraged."

"You want anything else to eat?"

Lauren looked around the Denny's dining area and studied the faces on the patrons seated around her. "How many of these people are saddled with depression? How many are happy with their lives?"

"Probably many and few, in that order." He smiled, trying to lighten her mood. Just then, his cell phone began to ring. They looked at each other, her thoughts screaming for it to be Michael. *Please, let it be. Please . . .*

He flipped open the phone and answered the call. When he shook his head, her shoulders slumped forward again. He stood up and walked away from the table.

Lauren sat there, wondering if she was chasing a shadow. What if she never found Michael? She realized she could go on looking for another week, two weeks, or more and not be any closer to him than she was now. Was this whole thing just a waste of time?

As her mind wandered, as the doubts mounted, she saw Bradley approaching.

The involuntary downward pull on the corners of his mouth made his face resemble that of a bulldog. Lauren instantly took it to mean one thing: bad news.

Bradley sat down heavily and placed his phone on the table.

"Let me guess that it wasn't the police telling you they've found Michael," she said, her voice matching her spirits.

"The FBI canceled our appointment. Guy said they've got nothing on a Michael Chambers and that if we had any questions, he could handle them over the phone."

"What about the scene they made at the hospital?"

"They were tracking a suspect in a bank heist who fit Michael's description. When the call came in, they went hog wild thinking it was their guy. Turns out they caught the perp the next day at the Maryland border."

Lauren slammed a hand on the table. "Damn it, Nick, we know the FBI is trying to find him so he can testify. Shouldn't we just go down there and meet with them, someone high up? I mean, I am his wife. They have to tell us what they know."

Bradley frowned. "They don't have to tell us anything. In fact, I've been trying to get us in to see someone who's in a position to give us some information. But no one admits to knowing anything. That's why I was hoping to do an end run with that hospital incident, catch a rookie who didn't know about the tight clamp the Bureau has on this case. But I've hit a brick wall."

"So the FBI's a dead end."

"Unless something changes." Bradley placed a hand over hers. "I'm sorry."

Lauren sat there, staring straight ahead, blind to everything around her . . . as if she had just peered into the searingly bright white of a blizzard. "Then we're done," she finally said. She picked up her purse and rooted through it, pulling out her wallet. She yanked out a ten, slapped it atop the check, and stood up. "It's over."

"What do you mean?"

"I mean that's it. I'm done. We're never going to find him. This is a ridiculous exercise, Nick. The police are looking for him. I mean, goddamnit, they're the experts. They can cover a hundred times the area we can. I'll call Deputy Vork and tell them Michael was here and let them do their thing. I can't take this anymore."

She turned and stormed out of the restaurant.

FIFTY-THREE

An hour later, the cabdriver dropped Harper Payne off at Union Station. Taken in by the perfect melding of modernity with Old World architecture, he stood for a moment and marveled at the workmanship. The marble floor tiles, the low-level lighting, the ornate iron railings.

While he stood there, people scurried about the station, some with shopping bags hanging from their hands, others with newspapers tucked neatly beneath an elbow as they rushed to catch their trains. None of them, however, looked as if they had the weight of the world on their shoulders, as he did.

But no one leads the perfect existence, he reminded himself. Everyone has his or her own issues, those things that make us wish we are someone or somewhere else. Only in his case, he didn't really know what he wished for. Right now, most of all, he sought peace and stability in his life.

But first he needed confusion and deception to be his ally.

He stopped into Anne Ricardo on the concourse and bought a Totes rain hat on clearance, a cheap pair of sunglasses, and a red and green plaid scarf. He took the items—which cost him a grand total of $24—into the rest room for evaluation. Bundled up, he would be more difficult to identify.

However, the ripped suit coat certainly drew unwanted attention. After spending another three dollars on a travel sewing kit at a luggage store, he sat in a toilet stall and quickly repaired the torn shoulder seam and knee area with black thread. While he was at best a neophyte seamstress, he did a decent job and figured it would only be visible at fairly close range.

His next stop was a Clipper Mike's salon, where he purchased a home hair-coloring kit. Heading toward the east end of the station, he located another well-appointed men's room and sat down in a stall. He read the instructions on the box and twenty minutes later was rinsing his hair in front of the sink. He lifted his head, looked in the mirror, and regarded his blond hair. It was certainly a different look. It seemed to make him look a few years younger, which was good. He rubbed some of the dye into his eyebrows, rinsed them off, and held his head under the wall-mounted hand dryer. A few minutes later, he was headed off in search of food.

He bought a croissant sandwich in a café and ate it while walking out of the terminal and across the street to Union Station Plaza, a small park adjacent to Columbus Circle. During the walk, he again began to think about the visions he had been having of a woman whose name he knew but whose face he could not fully picture. A woman he had warm memories about, memories that were isolated and without context.

As he entered the park, he spotted an empty bench in the sun where he could sit and think, make some decisions. The day was perfect for this time of year, with billows of cumulus clouds scattered against a deep blue sky. It looked as if someone had blown a handful of cotton balls into the air.

The sun was warm and felt good against the brisk air. He took a deep breath and exhaled. As he sucked in another lungful, the image of hiking along a path through a narrow pass with snow-covered mountains on both sides flashed in his mind like a still photograph. Waterfalls . . . Yosemite. It was spring, and he was holding Lauren's hand—*Lauren*. Our anniversary—

"*Oy, gevalt!*" An elderly woman, with a deeply etched face, large Coke-bottle glasses, and honey-tinted silver hair, had plopped down onto the bench next to Payne. "These legs just don't want to carry me like they used to. Such a shame. When you have the time to go and see places, you're too old to enjoy them. God help me."

Payne looked over at the woman and nodded, then turned his attention back to the image of Lauren and their trip to Yosemite. He had insisted they spend their third anniversary amongst the beauty of nature rather than trapped in the house, as they had done the two previous years.

They had pitched a tent in a clearing away from most of the other visitors that traditionally flocked to the park every spring and summer. They hiked along El Capitan, picnicked at the base of a waterfall, and then continued on before returning to their campsite in the afternoon. After shedding their gear and pulling off their shoes and socks, they lay down in the tent for a nap and instead spent the next hour making love . . . the air outside the freshest he had ever smelled, the air inside fogged with humidity and the sweet smell of coconut-scented sunblock. The slickness of his wet skin rubbing against hers, the peaceful quiet afterward as they fell asleep in each other's arms . . .

He remembered all that, as if it had happened yesterday.

"Maury, I don't care what you say, I don't want to move to Florida. The condo's too small, and I don't want to be around a bunch of old people."

Payne looked at the woman. Other than himself, there was no one nearby. He shook his head and turned away from her. Focus, he told himself. Yosemite, Lauren. He clamped his eyes shut and tried to get the image back—

"I don't care if the Silvermans are moving. I still love our house."

He opened his eyes and studied the old woman for a moment, suddenly feeling a rush of sympathy. Here was someone who had, in a sense, lost her mind, just as he had. Although his faculties were intact, he knew what it was like when thoughts and memories went awry.

"I'm Harper Payne."

She turned to look at him. "What kind of a name is that, Harper Payne. Not Jewish, that's for sure."

Payne smiled. In reality, he didn't know what religion he was.

"Well, mine's Ethel Rothstein. I came from Poland, Bialystok. Nice place, that bakery we had. Not much, but it was our place. All my relatives, three sisters, four brothers. That was before the war. When I was twenty-seven, I went to live in Auschwitz. Maybe you've heard of it?" she asked dryly.

Before Payne could respond, the woman continued.

"My entire family perished. Fievel, Ida, Eli, Sholom, all gassed in the chambers. And my children, Joseph and David, God rest their little, innocent souls." She looked up at the cottony sky, her eyes clouded with tears. "I'm the only one who survived."

"I'm sorry." As bad as his situation was, Payne realized others had experienced far worse.

She looked up at him, leaning her torso back and craning her neck to get a good view of his face through the thick lenses of her glasses. "My Maury here says you look like a nice man." Her voice rose and fell as if she were singing the words. "Tell me, are you married?"

"Yes, ma'am, I am."

"Call me Ethel, for God sakes. So you have children, yes?"

"No, not yet. But we're planning to start trying in a few months." How did he know that? He was remembering! Lauren, their house on the hill. Yosemite. His memory was coming back.

"What, you don't want to talk now? I asked you a question, *Mr. Harper.*"

"Huh? I'm sorry, I was thinking about my wife."

"You have a picture?"

Payne hesitated as he tried to recall the incomplete image of Lauren's face. Was she tall? Short? Thin—

"Again, he's not talking to me, Maury."

"I'm sorry, Mrs.—Ethel. I've—we've been separated."

"You young people these days don't understand the concept of commitment. You think—"

"No, no," Payne said, holding his hands up. "We're not separated like in divorce. We're . . . it's a long story. Let's just say I had an accident and I've got some memory problems. I'm trying to find her and she's trying to find me."

"What do you think this is, the 1800s? We have phone books now, the police will know how to find her. Come, I'll help you." She grasped his right arm with a surprisingly strong grip.

"No, wait. Ethel, I can't go to the police. It's very complicated, and I can't go into it now. But I appreciate your concern."

"What, you did something wrong, is that it?"

He looked away, trying to think of a way of ending the conversation. She was a lovely old lady, but he needed to concentrate again, map out a plan. "Look, Ethel, I don't mean to be rude, but I've got to run. I've got some thinking to do."

She looked at him with heavy eyes, in a manner that made him think he had hurt her feelings.

"You know, Mr. Harper, back in the old country we used to have a saying: no matter what God throws your way, it's always a test. He's testing us constantly, to see what we're made of. He tested us at Auschwitz, he tested us after the war. Maury said He's been testing us for almost six thousand years. But it all comes down to how badly you want something. The more you want it, the harder you'll have to work to get it. In your case, finding your wife is what you have to work for. The question is, how much do you want to find her?"

The question caught him off guard. He looked into the old, sagging eyes of Ethel Rothstein and saw something he was not expecting to see. Deep inner strength. Something he had found himself lacking these past couple of weeks. Then he realized what it was that he was missing: not just some memories, but his soul.

She turned away from him. "If you have to think about it that long . . ."

"Very much. I want to find her very much."

Her eyes locked with his again. "Then you must not give up," she said slowly. "Never."

There was something special about her, this woman who had sat down beside him on a park bench in the middle of Washington. In the midst of a place known for its cold, hard wheeling and dealing, he had found a warm soul who had given him direction. "Thank you," he finally said.

"For what, some old advice? My Maury, he could've given you something better. He was a rabbi, God rest his soul."

"You realize that he's passed on?"

She smiled. "Of course I know. He's been dead ten years now. Talking to him keeps my memory of him sharp. I imagine his voice in my head. We were married forty-five years, you know. After that many years, you know how each other thinks." She paused, looked at Payne. "What, did you think I was crazy or something, talking to somebody's who's not there?"

"If there's one thing I was thinking, Ethel, it wasn't that you were crazy."

"Sure you were. But that's okay, Mr. Harper. We all get a little *fermished* once in a while."

Payne smiled. "I think I'm getting over a bout myself." He gave her a peck on the cheek and stood up. "Take care of yourself, Ethel."

"That's Maury's job. He keeps watch over me, just like he did when he was alive." She reached out with wrinkled hands and took his right hand firmly in hers. "In fact, Mr. Harper, Maury tells me you're going to find your wife, very soon."

"From your mouth to God's ears."

Ethel Rothstein smiled. "Those conversations I leave to Maury."

FIFTY-FOUR

H arper Payne returned to Union Station, his brain clear, his objectives suddenly apparent, his soul renewed. With the image of Lauren standing in front of El Capitan and Ethel's words of wisdom firmly ensconced in the back of his mind helping him to focus, he scouted out the AT&T Internet kiosk on the ground floor of the main concourse.

He knew that once he swiped Waller's credit card, he would have only a matter of minutes before a massive Bureau alert would be issued. There would be little margin for error.

He found a pay phone and called for a cab. They were due to meet him at the west entrance in fifteen minutes, which he figured would give him enough time to send Lauren a message and get up the escalator to street level.

Payne was ready. He sat down at the kiosk and held the Visa card in his hand. His heart was a jackhammer inside his chest. He looked at the clock on the terminal's east wall. Noon, straight up. He swiped the card through the magnetic reader and waited while the account received authorization.

He took a deep breath, trying to calm himself. *You've got plenty of time, Harper. Just get the message sent.*

He tapped his fingers on the counter, watching the little hourglass and the flashing word "Processing."

Something's wrong. The Bureau must have rigged it so it would appear as if authorization were being granted, while in reality all it was doing was stalling, keeping him there while they descended on his position. *Do we have the technology to do that?* Come on, Harper—think!

Just then, the AT&T WorldNet screen appeared. He let a breath of air escape his lips as he logged on to Hotmail. He typed in just_rose@hotmail.com and tapped out the message he had prepared in his head.

Lauren,

Don't have much time. I'm a federal fugitive, so I've got to keep moving. Meet me in historic Fredericksburg, at the Princess Anne Building on Princess Anne between William and George Sts. at 5:30 PM tomorrow. I might not be able to log back on, so if you send me a message I may not get it. Send it anyway in case. I'll be there, bleached blond and crew cut. Maybe wearing a hat. If you don't get this in time, I'll return every three hours if it's safe.

This may sound strange given my condition, but I can't wait to see you.

He logged off, not bothering to take the time to reread what he had written. He checked his watch: 12:05. *So far, so good.* He stood up and let his eyes roam the busy station as he headed toward the escalators.

Before he had walked ten steps he saw four men in dark suits approaching, twenty feet away. Their faces, dress, and demeanor said "FBI." Their pace was quick, their strides firm and determined. How could they be looking for him already?

Although he had the fleeting thought of putting his head down and walking right past them—he had changed his physical appearance significantly—he did not want to chance it. In a pinch with no other options, he would risk it and feel good about his ability to succeed. But at the moment, he had safer alternatives. He stopped by a garbage pail, pretended to throw something in it, and then reversed direction, walking toward the west end of the station. He caught sight of a security guard heading toward him, prompting him to turn right toward the tracks.

His watch read 12:09. *Shit.* He wasn't going to make it, not if the cab was going to be prompt and leave if he was not there. If it did strand him, he could always take the metro. But that was fraught with potential delays, and it made it easier for the Bureau to track him once they located him. It would be as simple as sending out an immediate alert to the station managers at each stop along the line so that the moment his train arrived, undercover transit officers would be ready and waiting for him.

At the moment, however, he had no choice. He pulled a couple of dollar bills from his pocket and fed them into the fare kiosk. A small card emerged from the machine and he headed toward the train tracks.

As he boarded a waiting metro subway car, he noticed a couple of empty seats toward the rear. He sat down and picked up the newspaper that was lying across the chair.

A moment later, a man in a gray suit rose from his

seat and looked out. "Something's gotta be wrong. Why are we just sitting here?"

The man's friend bent forward to look out the darkened window. "Not a good day for this," he said, pushing back his shirtsleeve to check his watch. "I've got a meeting . . ."

Payne's pulse began galloping again. Had the Bureau put out an alert to search all trains before departure? Perhaps that passenger was right—something was wrong. Maybe it was time to panic.

He craned his neck around and saw two men in dark suits approaching the car. He rose from his seat and headed for the doors, hoping to reach them before the agents did. But even if he was able to get out before they arrived, they would surely stop him to check his ID. As he passed the window to his right, he saw another grouping of agents dispersing, preparing to check the trains on the adjacent tracks. There was now no doubt as to what was going down.

They were looking for him.

With few options and no time to implement them, he decided to confront the agents head-on. He pulled out his credentials, left the subway car, and walked toward the approaching men. Payne looked the lead agent directly in the eye, held his case low, and used his middle finger to partially obscure the last name on his Bureau identification. "Special Agent Thomas," he said, reasoning they might have been alerted to his cover name of Thompson. "He's not in this car. I'm going to head on up to street level, start with the shops."

The other agent nodded. "We've got all exits to the station blocked. It may take a while, but we'll find him." The man squeezed past Payne and boarded the

subway car parked on the opposite side of the platform, to his left.

As Payne turned and headed away, he heard the
man speaking to the passengers: "We're federal
agents. Please remain calm. We've got orders to
inspect everyone's identification, so please have photo
ID available . . ."

Payne walked away from them at a fast clip, passing
the fare machines on his way out. As he approached
the brown steel doors that led to the main part of the
depot, he began to run. He hit the door with his right
shoulder and blasted through it. Ahead of him was an
escalator that stretched up to the lower concourse—
but it was a down escalator and it was full of people
intent on reaching their trains.

He thought about turning around and heading back
into the metro, but just then, he heard shouting from
behind him. He whipped his head around and saw several agents running in his direction.

"Freeze! FBI!"

Payne was paralyzed with a sudden flush of adrena-
line-charged fear. The air suddenly turned murky; his
head became light and he felt dizzy. He continued to
push forward, but he was caught, caught in a night-
marish haze that made him feel as if he were moving
in slow motion.

The agents' guns came out of their holsters and a
collective scream erupted from the commuters, whose
concern, only a moment ago, was whether they would
make their trains on time. Like a trail of ants whose sin-
gle-file line had just been disturbed by a falling pebble,
the people scattered in every possible direction.

Payne turned his head and began pushing his way
forward, swimming through the sea of cowering

humanity. He burst through a crowd and nearly fell forward, but got bumped and driven upright. He pushed forward again, climbing over the backs of the crouching commuters, attempting to make his way up the down escalator. "FBI, let me through!" he shouted as he shoved and wormed his way around and between them, finally disappearing into the confused mass of terrified travelers.

"Thompson—give it up!" he heard as he made it onto the lower concourse. The agents' voices were muffled, but frantic. "We've got agents on every level!"

He began to run again, passing an upscale pharmacy and the Metro Market food court, nearly knocking several people down as he went. Ahead of him was another bank of escalators—these traveling in the correct direction—and he hit the moving steps in stride.

A few seconds later, he emerged on street level beside a B. Dalton bookstore. He turned right and walked quickly past the shops, trying to blend in with the swirling mass of activity.

He glanced behind him—he didn't see the agents or security guards—and headed toward the First Street metro exit. He caught the time on the large clockface near the revolving doors: 12:25. Would the cab still be waiting for him?

Payne emerged outside beneath an arch-covered patio and noticed a couple of agents eyeing the exit, two-way radios up to their ears. He ducked into a crowd and moved along First Street toward the front of the station, where the taxi stand was located. To his left, a lone cab was parked at the curb. Was it his? He didn't care if it wasn't—he was taking it.

Payne jumped inside and slammed the door shut.

"Fredericksburg," he said, panting out of fear as much as from his sprint out of the station.

"I'm waiting on a fare," the heavyset man said.

"I'm the guy you're waiting for. Barry Simon. Sorry I'm late."

"Another minute and you'd have been stranded," the cabbie said, yanking the gearshift into drive. "Wait policy's ten minutes, then I'm free to take any fare that comes my way."

Payne tuned out the driver and craned his neck to look out the back window as the taxi pulled away.

"Fredericksburg, you said?"

"Yeah." Payne ducked down behind the rear seat as the agents that had been pursuing him came running out into the street. They were rotating their bodies and rubbernecking their heads, turning round and round.

Lost sheep without their dog.

Payne leaned back and closed his eyes as the driver turned the corner and accelerated.

FIFTY-FIVE

It was noon when Lauren returned to her motel room. She grabbed her suitcase and began gathering her clothing, fighting back tears and struggling to keep her composure. She stopped, a pair of jeans in her hand, and looked down at the garbage can near her foot. She kicked it and sent it careening across the room into a wall. The jeans went flying after it, and as if that weren't enough, she shoved everything off the desktop with the swipe of her hand.

"Are you done yet?" Bradley asked, standing safely a few feet behind her.

She grabbed the phone and heaved it at the door. It ripped from the wall and smashed to the floor.

"I understand you're upset, frustrated. Angry."

She suddenly stopped, turned, and faced Bradley. "Upset? You think I'm upset?" she screamed.

"Lauren, please, calm down." He took both her hands in his, but she twisted away from him.

"I don't want to calm down!" She grabbed the end of the suitcase and yanked it off the bed, then seized a glass off the nightstand. As she brought her arm back to throw it, he reached out and stopped her.

"Enough!"

She wrestled her arm away and swung at him. He ducked and the follow-through spun her around. He threw his arms around her torso, capturing her arms and pinning them against her body. She continued to writhe and jump, pushing them both backward onto the bed.

They landed faceup, Lauren atop him, still squirming. He tightened his grip, then rolled them both over, burying her face into the covers. They remained prone for a moment, her body finally relaxing into submission.

But he felt her chest heaving and realized she was sobbing. He pulled his arms out from beneath her and sat up. "I'm glad you got that out of your system," he said gently. He waited for her to respond, but she did not move. "Lauren, think about what you've been through this past week. Your husband's missing, you've been followed, kidnapped, tortured . . . and as if that's not enough, you killed someone in self-defense. If a patient came to you with that recent history, you'd probably admit him to the hospital for round-the-clock counseling."

A few seconds passed before she pushed up onto her elbows and wiped some fingers across her moist eyes. "I don't know how to deal with this. I'm a damn Ph.D. and I don't, I mean, I can't . . . I don't know what to do to help myself."

"Doctors make the worst patients. My brother was a doctor, and he always got sicker than he needed to because he was so stubborn. If he'd treated himself the way he treated his patients, he would've been a lot better off."

"You talk like he's dead."

"Might as well be. Haven't talked to him in years." Bradley sat there staring down at the bed for a moment, then stood up. "Point is, Lauren, you've been through a hell of a lot and I think you've done an incredible job of handling whatever's been thrown at you."

"Speaking of throwing," she said, sitting up on the edge of the bed, "sorry about the mess."

Bradley waved a hand and bent over to lift the suitcase off the floor. "I hope you're not still thinking of leaving."

Lauren knelt beside him to help clean up. "I don't know what to think, Nick. We've been here four days and we've got nothing to show for it. We're no closer to finding Michael than we were before we got on the plane. How long should we stay here running into dead ends? A week, two weeks? Three weeks?"

"If that's what it takes, yes. He's here, in this town, Lauren. Do you really want to fly three thousand miles away from him?"

She looked away. "No. Of course not."

"Then let's do something constructive." Bradley picked up the handheld PC from the nightstand and handed it to her. "You've got a direct link to Michael. Let's use it."

Lauren started the PC and dialed into the Internet. After the familiar hisses and tones, the connection was established. She selected RETRIEVE AND READ MAIL and began tapping her fingers on the table while waiting for her little computer to download any messages she had received. Although she knew she should hope there would be one from Michael, her emotions were spent. She was numb. To her, it was a clear sign that, deep down, she had given up. She walked over to the window, leaned against the wall, and stared out at the parking lot.

Bradley sat down on the bed and hunched over the tiny computer screen. "Don't you want to read your messages?"

Lauren kept her gaze on the landscape. "Please, Nick, I'm not in the mood for jokes."

"I'm not kidding."

Her head whipped over in his direction. "What?"

He nodded at the small device. "Come look."

Lauren hurried over to the desk and saw the YOU HAVE 1 NEW MESSAGE prompt. She touched OK with the stylus and saw the "lost_in_virginia" moniker in her in-box. "Michael! We've got something from Michael!"

With Bradley leaning over her shoulder, she opened the message and began reading. "Thank God," she said under her breath. Tears glazing her eyes, she glanced up at Bradley. "I don't understand. The FBI was looking for him, right? So he could testify against Scarponi. They need him. Why would he be a fugitive?"

"I don't know. Maybe he didn't want to cooperate."

"That doesn't make any sense. Wouldn't he want to testify and put this guy back in jail?"

Bradley turned away and did not answer her.

Lauren sat there for a second, then shook her head. "Something's very wrong." She found the small gold key around her neck and squeezed it in her hand, then sank down onto the edge of the bed.

Bradley sat down next to her and put his arm around her shoulders, drew her body close to his. "I wish I could tell you this all makes sense. But I can't, because it doesn't. Right now, I think we need to keep focused on meeting up with him tomorrow. We can't worry about what other people are doing. Let's take things a day at a time. Hell, even an hour at a time. Okay?"

She sat there for a long moment before speaking. "You've become such a great friend, Nick. I don't know what I'd do without you."

He handed her a tissue and gently rubbed her back.

"I'm here for you, for as long as you need me to be. I promise."

"You're more than a friend, Nick. You're kind of like the big brother I never had. I can tell you anything, whatever's on my mind. I've never had that feeling about anyone ever, not even my therapist. Just Michael . . . and you."

Bradley creased a corner of his mouth into a smile. "I'm honored."

She could feel the tension leaving her muscles. "I'm sorry I doubted you."

"Not a problem. But I'm worried about your health. With all you've been through, with all the stress you've been under, I think it's important for you to get some sleep."

"Now you're acting like my doctor."

Bradley laughed. "I've learned that in my line of work you've got to be a little of everything. Least of all what people expect you to be." He brushed the hair back off her face, then stood up. "Get some rest."

"But it's the middle of the day, I can't just go to sleep—"

"You can and you will. Meantime, I'll snoop around and see if I can find out what Michael did to land himself on the FBI's fugitive list. It might affect the way we handle your meeting with him tomorrow."

She closed her eyes and he covered her with the blanket. "Think good thoughts about seeing Michael again. Before you know it, it'll be five-thirty and you'll be in his arms."

"This whole thing will be over, right?"

"It sure will," Bradley said with a smile. "It'll all finally be over."

FIFTY-SIX

The wind had picked up and was blasting everything and everyone in its path, slamming against the fifty U.S. flags flapping in the bright floodlights at the granite base of the Washington Monument.

DeSantos stood in darkness outside the ring of flags, surveying the general area. After the latest tour bus had pulled out of the parking lot five minutes ago, he had nodded to the park ranger, whose four-to-midnight shift was over.

A moment later, Archer completed his walk around the perimeter and nodded. "Clear."

"Good, then all we're missing is our host."

Another blast of wind hit them head-on, and they turned their backs to shield their faces. "I wish he'd get here already. It's fucking cold out here," DeSantos said. "I don't know why we couldn't just meet in a car, or at my house or something." He rubbed his gloved hands together.

"It's Knox. You never know what the guy's thinking. And we're in his good graces. Imagine everyone else."

"My toes are starting to go numb." DeSantos stomped his feet. "Must be twenty-five below with the wind. I'm leaving in ten minutes if I can still walk."

"Want some gum?" Archer asked, chomping away on his Juicy Fruit.

"No, I don't want some gum. Gum ain't gonna make my body warm."

"The cold is all in your head, Hector. Just ignore it."

"This isn't more of that mind-body bullshit, is it?"

"As a matter of fact, it is. You can bring blood to your extremities—"

"I know how to get blood to one of my extremities. Does that count?"

Archer shook his head. "I can't believe we asked you to be Presley's godfather."

"Hey, I warned you, bro. I y'am what I y'am." DeSantos began to jump up and down. "So much for mind-body bullshit. I'm still freaking cold."

"Then take your mind off it. Guess how many people visit the monument each year."

"I don't want to guess."

"Just go with me on this, will you?"

DeSantos rubbernecked his head into the darkness, then checked his watch. "Fine. Eight hundred thousand."

Archer looked at him, his eyebrows bunched together. "You're so damn lucky, you know that?"

"What I don't understand is why so many people are fascinated by a big stone dick sticking up from the ground."

Archer glanced sideways at his partner, then shivered as another blast of air wormed around his pants.

"Don't tell me you're cold, too. It's all in your head, Brian. Remember?"

Archer started moving his legs, dancing without music, and said, "Trish and I took a tour about four years ago. You wouldn't believe how many granite blocks—"

"Gentlemen."

Archer and DeSantos spun, their hands instinctively moving to their weapons.

Douglas Knox was standing in a black wool overcoat, his collar turned up above the level of his ears. "This is how my elite intelligence masters protect themselves?"

"Brian's fault," DeSantos said. "He was complaining about how cold he was. I was trying to distract him, take his mind off it."

Archer threw DeSantos a nasty look, then turned to Knox. "You said it was urgent."

The director nodded, then shoved his hands into the pockets of his coat. "Payne is going to be in Fredericksburg tomorrow night, five-thirty, Princess Anne Building. He's set up a rendezvous with his wife."

DeSantos was itching to ask how Knox had gotten hold of that information, but in the intelligence community, such details were unimportant. When a job was bearing down on you, what mattered was the here and now, and what lay ahead. The past was old news. If you knew and trusted your sources, how certain data came across your desk was of little importance.

"Does Payne know we're going to be there?" Archer asked.

"As far as he's concerned, he's going there to meet his wife. We're not part of the equation. If he senses we're there, he'll take off. We're not his favorite people right now."

"Obviously you don't need us to be chaperones," DeSantos said wryly.

"Scarponi is going to be there, too."

A shrill gust kicked up a swirl of loose soil and slapped it against their coats. Archer shrugged it off and took a step closer to Knox, who was rubbing some grains of dirt from his eyes. "Are you sure?"

"The news leak on Payne's amnesia," Knox said. "I had it back-traced and found its source. Not the person, but the pathway. I planted a dummy message and sent it back along the same channels. I'm betting our mole forwards it on to Scarponi."

"This the same mole who was feeding Scarponi six years ago, after his trial?"

"I'm sure of it," Knox said.

"A bit risky, isn't it?" Archer asked.

Knox squinted angrily, then hung his head and began to pace. After moving a handful of steps in each direction, he zeroed in on Archer's face. DeSantos moved closer as well, and the three of them now formed a tight triad. If nothing else, their proximity generated heat.

"I intend to recapture Scarponi," Knox said firmly. "I won't—I can't—tell the president he's escaped. And I sure as hell can't tell him that Payne also took leave of our company either, now, can I? The buck stops on my desk, gentlemen. So if I have a chance to capture both of them in one operation, I'm going to take that stone and kill the two birds." He paused for a long second, then said, "To make this happen, I need your help."

DeSantos looked over at Archer and instantly knew what his partner was thinking: How much of what Knox was saying was the truth, and how much was bullshit, laid out for the purpose of using them to get Scarponi back for his group? In the split second that this all bounced around in his mind, he decided not to broach the topic, and he hoped that Archer would feel the same way. With all they had seen so far, he did not feel they could fully trust Knox. At least, not yet.

"I need one of you to hover on the perimeter, the other on the inside. Grab Scarponi and take him safely into custody." Knox said it matter-of-factly, as if he were asking them to go shopping for groceries. "Once you have him in your vehicle, you will proceed to the safe house on Mission. And I don't have to tell you to exercise extreme caution with him at all times."

"What kind of backup will we have?" DeSantos asked, already knowing the answer.

"None. No one can know we're expecting Scarponi to be there. All other available agents will be focused on identifying and safely securing Payne." Knox pulled a folded piece of paper from his pocket and handed it to Archer, who opened it. "A map of historic Fredericksburg. The X's show where all my agents will be. You two are the Y's. We can only guess where Scarponi will be, but I've denoted his possible locations with Z's."

"This is gonna be one hell of a fucked-up operation," DeSantos said, shaking his head. The logistics of it all were fraught with problems, a fact he was sure Knox was aware of.

The director's face hardened suddenly, and with barren trees swaying in the wind against the park's streetlights, shadows cut angrily across his features. "No, this will not be a fucked-up operation, Hector. If it is, we lose Scarponi, maybe for good. No matter how much he wants Payne, at some point he may decide it's not worth it. In which case we'll never see his sorry ass again." Knox pulled a cigarette lighter from his pocket and ignited the corner of the map Archer was holding. The paper began to burn, the flames flickering in the wind, reducing the map to carbon.

As the ashes floated away on the breeze, a blast of

wind caught DeSantos's wool coat and ruffled the bottom, sending tendrils of cold air up his back. They skipped across the gooseflesh that was covering his arms and legs, causing him to shiver.

DeSantos thought about what Knox was proposing and was uneasy. He had studied Scarponi's file in depth. Like a dog trained to sniff ordnance, he felt he understood his adversary well. And he knew that Scarponi would never give up. Not until his target had successfully been neutralized. No, either Harper Payne or Anthony Scarponi was going to end up dead in Fredericksburg.

And it was becoming increasingly clear that if Knox had his way, the one carted away in the meat wagon was going to be Harper Payne.

FIFTY-SEVEN

When Harper Payne awoke in the small, cheap Fredericksburg motel room, he rubbed his eyes, wondering if the dreams he'd had last night were authentic memories of times with Lauren or fabrications of what he imagined their lives to have been like. *They were so real . . . they had to be real.* He sat on the edge of the mattress, grinding his teeth, angry at himself for having lost his memory, at having lost his connection to a life that he was beginning to think must have been enormously satisfying and fulfilling.

He thought of Lauren, of what he remembered—or imagined—her to be like. More memories began to crackle in his mind like the flash of lightning against a clouded night sky . . .

The time they got lost in Tahoe while hiking in the mountains, spending the evening wrapped in each other's arms.

The white splash of stars across the night sky, the sound of coyotes howling in the distance. What had begun as an intensely frightening experience became a fiercely romantic one . . .

Feelings, emotions, isolated images. They had to be real.

Sitting there on the bed, he thought of what it

would be like seeing her face again, smelling her hair, holding her.

He could feel her now! Her soft skin, the shape of her toned arms, the sloping curve of her back as it swooped down into her waist. How wonderful it felt to be able to see her again, to be able to remember. It was like being liberated from solitary confinement. In some ways, it was worse . . . unlike a jailed felon, he had done nothing wrong—he was a victim of a mind trapped within itself, unable to find a way out.

With his memories coming back to him, he felt energized. Stronger, more determined. He stood up and walked into the bathroom to shower. Five hours until he would see her again.

Only this time, it would not be a dream.

It was four-thirty in the afternoon and the sun had begun its orange burn as it headed for cover behind the backs of buildings and ultimately the horizon.

Payne had chosen to reunite with Lauren in historic Fredericksburg, a small colonial Virginia town. There were period museums, such as the one devoted to former president James Monroe, as well as the Mary Washington House and the old-time Hugh Mercer Apothecary, where the sick were treated with bloodletting, anesthetic-less limb amputations, and crude, homemade pharmaceutical remedies.

The rest of the town had an Old World charm to it, with shops still occupying buildings dating to the 1700s and 1800s. There were several banks and a handful of ornate churches. At the moment, Payne was sitting in the bell tower of St. George's Episcopal, a recently renovated structure originally constructed in 1849 of nondescript masonry. With its forward-set, four-story steeple, it had the look of what could be considered "classic" church architecture for its time.

Inside, however, its two-story sanctuary was adorned with tall, intricately leaded stained-glass windows, polished wood benches, and large brass chandeliers. Payne was surprised to find such beauty inside a building whose exterior was so prosaic and uninspiring.

After having fully explored the church's interior, he climbed into the cramped fourth story of the tower, peering through the fixed, downward-angled wood slats of the window casing. The air was so stale and dusty on his tongue that he felt as if he had just chewed a piece of chalk. Between the large brass bell that hung behind him and the thick decorative window slats in front of him, there was little circulation of fresh air.

From his perch, he had a view of nearly a third of the block across the street and to his right. Ahead of him, he could see clear up George Street, while to his left the next half-block continuation of Princess Anne was visible. It was not an ideal location, but it was the only one he had seen in which he could sit at such a height off the ground without being out in the open, and without being subject to anyone questioning him about his intentions. The church, while still operational, was for the most part abandoned during the week, except for child-care classes in the basement.

At 5:10 P.M., with all the details taken care of, his thoughts once again turned to Lauren. He leaned back against the cold metal of the bell and resumed his watch. She would be here soon.

Lauren was sitting in the front passenger seat of the rental car, but she knew that from Nick Bradley's perspective, the seat might just as well have been empty. She was deep in thought, thinking of Michael, envisioning the moment when he would wrap his arms around her and kiss her gently up and down the neck, as he always did . . . when she would hear the slight raspiness of his voice, a sexy hoarseness that only she seemed able to detect.

"Hey, you alive over there?"

She blinked and was suddenly aware Bradley had said something. "What?"

"Just wanted to make sure you hadn't slipped into a coma."

"How much longer?"

"I'd guess about five minutes."

The mere mention of the words *five minutes* sent her heart into a frenzy. It immediately quickened its pace, as if it had a mind of its own. Despite her attempts to slow it, to calm herself, the muscle galloped on.

They drove up Amelia Street and pulled over to the curb a few feet from its intersection with Princess Anne.

"It's five-fifteen, we're a little early," Bradley said. "According to the map, we're only about a block and a half away from your meeting place."

She did not answer him. Instead, she pulled up on the handle and popped open her door.

"Lauren," he said, placing a hand on her wrist, "I know you're anxious to see him, but let's show some caution. Michael said he's a fugitive. Remember, I was hounding the FBI, trying to get information out of them. That landed us smack in the middle of their radar screen. I'm not entirely sure what their motives are, so I have no idea what to expect from them, how aggressive they'll be. On the other hand, they don't quite know what to expect from us, either. I took special care to make sure we weren't followed. I did my best, but no guarantees."

"Are you saying we could've led them here?"

"I'm not saying we did, but they could've been watching us or tracking our movements with an electronic bug they planted somewhere on the car. Back home, I've got things that can scan for that kind of techy stuff, but out here, we're kind of winging it."

She fell silent, withdrawing into herself. Was she possibly hurting Michael by coming here to meet him? Should they just leave now and find some other way of connecting with him?

"He'll be here in a few minutes, if he's not here already," Bradley continued. "Go on. But if you see anything strange, walk away, go down the street, and I'll get the message. I'll swing by and pick you up, then we'll regroup, okay?" He gave her hand a gentle squeeze. "Please, don't take any chances."

She nodded, then stepped out of the car.

Jonathan Waller accelerated as they turned off I-95 and curved around the ramp for exit 130A, headed toward Fredericksburg.

"Take it easy, Jon," Scott Haviland said over the loud squeal of the tires. "We don't want to attract attention."

"And we don't want to lose Harper again either."

"We've got backup set up all over the damn town. He's not gonna slip away this time."

Waller shook his head. "And if he knows we're gonna be here?"

"No way. There's no way he knows we intercepted his E-mail."

"Unless he knew that his wife's E-mail was deleted by somebody at the Academy. If that's the case, he would've figured that we've got her E-mail address and could tap into the mail server."

"That's a lot to assume. Besides, his brain's scrambled and he's confused. I don't think he has a clue."

"And if he did figure it out, this could all be a waste of time," Waller said, braking hard to stop at a red light. As he waited for a car to pass, his eyes darted around the intersection. It was clear, and he accelerated through.

Haviland shook his head. "If he did send that E-mail as a ruse, then he wouldn't have had us searching Union Station all day. He planted that info with the motel clerk so we'd do exactly what we ended up doing: wasting our time."

"Yeah, and like I said, it was bullshit."

"Then again, as far as he's concerned," Haviland said, "we're an hour away from here looking for someone who isn't going to show."

Waller turned hard onto Route 3, the momentum again pressing his partner against the passenger door. "I wouldn't be so sure. He may've lost his memory and he may be confused about things, but his instincts are razor sharp. The biggest mistake a perp could make was underestimating him."

"But we're not a stupid perp and we're not underestimating him. We're almost there and we've got ample backup."

"Backup's a double-edged sword. If he sees one of our vehicles—"

"If he's in a position to see one of us, Jon, one of us will be in a position to see him." Haviland looked away. "Besides, Knox seemed pretty upbeat about the whole operation."

"Oh, he was plenty nervous, trust me. He didn't stop pacing the whole time we were in his office."

"This will all come to a head in fifteen minutes. We'll have Payne and we'll be back on track again toward nabbing Scarponi. You'll see."

Waller depressed the accelerator again and the engine roared. "For our sake, I hope you're right."

FIFTY-EIGHT

Perspiration was rolling down his forehead and stinging his eyes. The stale, humid air inside the bell tower was something Payne had not anticipated when he chose the location, but it was too late now to make a change. Things were set.

He leaned against the small window and flapped his jacket lapels. He wanted to remove his suit coat, but his shirt was bright white and the navy blue jacket made it that much more difficult to see him in the dark enclosure.

He pressed his face against the slatted window and breathed in a few mouthfuls of forty-degree air. Remaining in a crouch, he looked out over the street, keeping watch not only for Lauren, but also for any sign of law enforcement personnel. The worst thing he could imagine was being minutes from reuniting with his wife, only to have it stripped away at the last moment by a local cop who may have been briefed on an FBI be-on-the-lookout bulletin.

The last charge he had made on Waller's Visa was in the outskirts of Fredericksburg, just before leaving the motel. He knew Waller and Haviland would pay a visit there, questioning the clerk who had put the card through. But Payne had purposely asked about Union Station—how often Amtrak runs; if he left at five in the evening, what time would he arrive in New York City's Penn Station; where you buy the tickets; how much they cost. Even though the clerk did not have a clue to most of the answers, it did not matter—the purpose was to plant the information with him so that when Waller and Haviland went fishing, they'd hook a big one. Regardless of whether they thought it was a ruse, he knew they would have to check it out. The extra detail of reserving a seat on an Amtrak Metroliner for five-thirty this evening was a nice touch, he thought—but again, meaningless if they were wise to his motives.

As a safeguard, he had sold Waller's Visa card to a shady-looking character twenty miles up the freeway at a rest stop. Hopefully, the perp would have a ball and charge up a houseful of items, essentially driving Waller and Haviland out of their minds as they tried to figure out what he was up to.

Payne wiped the beads of perspiration from his forehead and focused on the dark Crown Victoria that was passing by on Princess Anne and turning left in front of him onto George Street.

The navy Crown Victoria cruised down William Street, a couple of blocks from George. As it passed Hector DeSantos's Mustang, DeSantos checked his mirror and nodded. "Looks like everyone's in position."

"I never understood why the Bureau always buys the same cars for their undercover fleet," Archer said. "Perps aren't as stupid as we always want them to be."

"Especially in this case, when the perps are a pro and an ex-agent."

"We don't make the decisions."

"No, we just do what we're told to do and collect our paychecks."

"Since when do you 'do what you're told to do'?"

DeSantos shrugged. "Guess that means I just collect my paycheck." He turned right at the next street, his eyes roaming for signs of Payne or Scarponi. "Anything?"

"Nothing. But at least we've confirmed where everyone else is and made a pass of the area. It's been a few years since I've been here." Archer glanced at his watch, then subconsciously patted his shoulder harness, making sure his Browning nine-millimeter was there. "Circle around and drop me off near Princess Anne. It's almost time."

Lauren walked up the street, passing a Merrill Lynch investment office and an alley that opened into a parking lot. Another few seconds and she arrived at the columned, four-story Princess Anne Building, the location Michael had chosen for their meeting. She climbed the eight steps and stood on the semicircular veranda in front of the main entrance to the building, four white columns surrounding her like centurions standing guard.

Lauren looked down the street to her left, then removed her right glove for a moment before replacing it. It was a signal to Nick Bradley, who was sitting two blocks away in their rental, that all was okay.

Her left hand found its way down to her black, ballistic nylon fanny pack, which she had purchased at a gun shop on her way back to the motel two days ago. From the exterior, it looked like the typical run-of-the-mill pouch that strapped to one's waist. In reality, it was a gun holster for the new millennium: it had a Velcro strip that ran the entire length of the pouch, providing her with instant access to the firearm with a single flick of her wrist. Feeling the Colt inside, she leaned against one of the columns, secure in the thought that she could defend herself if something went wrong.

As the sun set, she looked out over the street, folded her arms across her chest, and waited.

FIFTY-NINE

Waller turned right onto Princess Anne and stopped the car two blocks from the rendezvous point. They continued on foot, looking a lot like the locals, wearing jeans and winter coats, knit caps with the Washington Redskins logo embroidered across the front, and tennis shoes.

As an added precaution, Waller also sported a mustache and black-rimmed glasses. Haviland, fitted with a thick beard, used a slow, shuffling gait to complete his disguise. With Payne supposedly in the vicinity, Waller wanted to make sure they were not easily identified.

A moment later, they stopped walking. Haviland surveyed the street in front of them while Waller glanced off in the opposite direction. "I see her," he said, elbowing his partner. Haviland indicated Lauren Chambers with a nod of his head.

Waller adjusted his earpiece and spoke into his lapel microphone. "Located Target A."

"Roger that," came the response. "We're stable and holding our position. No sighting of Target B."

Haviland turned to Waller. "Why don't you head toward that pottery shop across the street. I'll stay back at this end of the block, keep a wide-angle view of things." It was a minor alteration of their plan, but after having seen the layout of the buildings in the flesh instead of on a map, the change made sense.

Waller nodded, received confirmation of the squad's approval, and pulled the front of his cap down as he trudged up the street in a leisurely manner. He threw occasional glances into the storefronts in an effort to appear like an ordinary citizen browsing the numerous antiques and fashion shops for bargains.

Each step brought him closer to Lauren Chambers. And, he hoped, to Harper Payne.

"There she is, the wife." DeSantos nodded at Lauren Chambers standing a block and a half away. He parked the car at the curb and his eyes combed the street. "And no sign of Scarponi or Payne with show time approaching."

"That's Jonathan Waller, isn't it?" Archer asked, indicating a spot twenty feet away.

"Hard to tell. According to the photos and stuff you pulled up on everyone in the operation, I'd say maybe."

"Sure looks like him. But he's out of position."

DeSantos shook his head. "Like I said last night, bro, this is going to get all fucked up."

"We make do with what we've got. No guarantees in this biz."

"I can't believe Knox left us so fucking bare. We're probably being watched right now. And nobody's got any idea who we are."

"Nobody ever knows who we are. That's what makes us so effective."

DeSantos nodded, but felt uneasy about the entire mission. He knew they had to improvise and think on the fly—he had no problems with that. It was the way this thing had been thrown together, with little preparation and even less intelligence. He couldn't escape the feeling in his bones that something bad was going to happen. It wasn't something he could articulate, even to Archer. Whatever it was, though, his intuitions were usually accurate.

"I'll get as close to the wife as I can," Archer said, pulling a newspaper from his briefcase. "Now that I see where she's at, I'll take a seat on that brick wall and read. Whoever sees Scarponi first will signal the other." He moved his mouth down toward his jacket collar and spoke into it. "Testing, testing. Do you copy?"

DeSantos touched his earpiece. "Yeah, I copy. Look, how about we both go. Instead of splitting up, we huddle together, play it like we're standing and talking—"

"Now's not the time to change our plans, Hector. We go with what we have, it's a decent setup. I'll be near Chambers and you'll be on the roof of the bank, letting me know if something bad is going down."

"Before it happens."

"Preferably, yes."

"Doesn't this remind you of Zebra Fifty-nine?" DeSantos was referring to the disastrous operation of nearly eight years ago when he'd taken a bullet from a Russian mobster who was attempting to establish ties with a syndicate operating out of the D.C. area. Their mission ops plan was much like the one for their current assignment—more than one federal agency engaged in clandestine maneuvers, with none of them briefed on what the other was doing, or going to be doing. The result was confusion . . . and a trip to the ICU for DeSantos. Afterward, Archer went on a private manhunt, eventually catching the Mafia member and instituting a little outlaw justice of his own with the help of a few Special Ops buddies. The mobster, while marginally recognizable after they were done with him, just didn't have the head for intelligence anymore.

"Honestly," Archer said, "no. Zebra Fifty-nine was a different time, different place."

"But there are parallels, you do see that."

Archer nodded. "I see it. But there's no time to change our plans."

DeSantos knew his partner was right. It was go forward now or don't go at all. "Besides, with all the plainclothes around, someone's bound to see him," Archer said as he pulled a stick of Juicy Fruit from his pocket. "I would think they've all been briefed on the possibility Scarponi will show up here."

"No one else knows about the planted message Knox sent. As far as they're concerned, it's the remotest of possibilities. For that matter, we can't even be sure Scarponi got it."

"Then this should be a cakewalk." Archer winked and folded the gum into his mouth.

DeSantos patted his partner's arm and said, "May the force be with you."

Archer smiled and started to reach for his door handle when suddenly he grabbed his groin. "Ah!"

"What!" DeSantos shouted, moving for his gun.

"Pager," Archer said, moving his coat out of the way to check the display. "Shit, it's Trish. She's in labor."

"You sure?"

Archer showed him the readout. "Nine, nine, nine, five. It's our code. Her water broke and contractions are five minutes apart."

"Hate to be rude, bro, but tell me quick—what do you want to do?"

Archer clipped the pager back to his belt. "We've got a neighbor, we're covered."

DeSantos's eye caught the clock on the dashboard. "Then let's do it."

"Scarponi better surrender," Archer said, then popped open his door. "I'll never forgive him if he makes me miss the birth of my daughter."

DeSantos tried to smile, but the sense of foreboding kept his face stiff. "I'll be sure to tell him that. Right after I yell 'Freeze.'"

Their doors clicked shut and they headed off in opposite directions.

From a distance, Lauren watched as a man resembling her husband first passed a pottery store and then walked by a man wearing a Redskins knit cap. Her heart began racing again—*Michael was only thirty feet away now.*

Waller glanced up from his newspaper and watched as a forest green Dodge Neon pulled over to the curb in front of the Princess Anne Building. He tucked his chin down toward his lapel mike and spoke.

"I've got a green Dodge stopping in front of Target A. Four men are getting out. I'm on it."

Nick Bradley peered through the small binoculars he had trained on Lauren's face. The sun had set and dusk was descending on the town. A couple of small antique streetlamps provided a muted, yellow hue. Despite the dim illumination, he was able to make out a smile spread across Lauren's lips; she had obviously just caught sight of her husband. But just then, her face hardened.

She was talking to Michael, so what could be wrong?

Suddenly, a man wearing a leather bomber jacket and holding a newspaper stood up, obscuring his vision. *Who the hell is that?* Bradley dropped the binoculars down from his eyes and tried to orient himself. Four other men in dark coats were moving in on Lauren, encircling her and Michael. The man in the bomber jacket was moving in as well.

"No!"

Bradley was unsure if he had actually screamed the warning or if he had merely thought it. But before he could get completely out of the car, a barrage of suppressed gunshots spit forth—and amidst a forest of legs, he saw Michael crumple to the pavement.

Lauren was screaming and
someone was trying to get a hand across her mouth and
Brian Archer was bringing his gun up, trying to make out the
faces, so many faces, he wasn't prepared for this and
a gun was shoved into his chest against his Kevlar vest and
multiple rounds exploded
into him.
Cough cough cough
the suppressor thumped thumped in his ears and
it was then,
it was then that he realized he'd been hit
and it was then that Zebra 59 flashed in his mind
and it was then that he realized he was falling to the ground.
And it was then
that he thought of
Trish.

• • •

Bradley's fingers tightened around the nine-millimeter SIG in his pocket. Where was Lauren? His eyes scanned the street, trying to sift through the crowd of leather jackets. He tried to track the escaping men as they approached the corner of Princess Anne and George Streets.

More gunfire exploded as bodies fell. One of the men attempted to get up, but stumbled—then righted himself and ran off. He'd been hit all right—but by whom?

"Converge, converge!" Waller shouted into his lapel mike. Haviland was already in full stride and passing him, turning left onto George as a black Chrysler peeled away from the curb. Waller also turned left, hoping to catch a glimpse of the injured man who had run off, disappearing somewhere amongst the stores and shops.

Haviland called off the license plate and location of the vehicle into his two-way and turned back to confer with Waller, who had yielded the task of canvassing the area on foot to the cops of the town of Fredericksburg. As Haviland waited for an affirmative response over his radio, he ran toward Waller, who was examining one of the two bodies that were sprawled across the pavement in front of the Princess Anne Building, thirty feet apart.

"Please tell me that's not Harper lying there dead—"

Waller shook his head. "It's not, thank God."

"Then who is it?"

Waller removed the wallet and consulted the driver's license. "Sean McCracken."

Haviland shook his head. "Who the hell is Sean McCracken?"

Waller stood up and scanned the street. "How the hell should I know?" He pulled the mike on his collar toward his mouth. "Anything?"

He pressed the receiving plug deeper into his ear. "Stand by. We're in pursuit," came the response. Waller stood and moved toward the other body lying faceup in the street. "This one's alive—call an ambulance!" As he knelt down beside him, a man came rounding the corner, gun in hand. Waller did a shoulder roll and brought his weapon to bear. "Hold it! FBI!"

The man stopped immediately, but he appeared not even to see Waller. His attention was focused on the downed man. "No . . . ," he said in a low moan.

"Who are you?"

DeSantos heard the voice somewhere off in the distance, tinny and muffled. After all, this was just a dream, wasn't it?

"Who are you!" the voice demanded again.

DeSantos suddenly became aware of the man kneeling on the ground a few feet from Archer's fallen body, the barrel of his weapon aimed squarely at his chest.

"I'm a federal agent," DeSantos answered in a low, breathless voice.

"ID!" the man shouted back.

DeSantos reached into his back pocket.

"Slowly!" the man with the gun cautioned. "Toss it over here."

"That's my partner. I need to help—"

"Ambulance is on its way," the man said as he flipped open the credentials case. "Department of Defense? What the hell? We weren't briefed—"

"I don't give a flying fuck what you were briefed on," DeSantos said as he knelt beside Archer. He lifted his partner's jacket and unhooked the protective vest. The rounds had penetrated the Kevlar. "Holy fuck."

"That . . . bad." Archer's voice was weak, and his eyes were still closed.

"Stay with me, bro. Just . . . stay with me. Hang in there. Ambulance is on its way."

But try as he did to make his voice strong and convincing, DeSantos knew in his heart Brian Archer was not going to survive. DeSantos had seen the wound. He'd seen *many* wounds over the years, and this was just not the kind you recovered from. "Think of Trish—of Presley. They need you, Brian. *They need you.*" It was a plea to God as much as it was to his friend. His eyes began to water and he brushed against them with his forearm, trying to keep his vision clear. He grabbed his partner's hand and squeezed. "Stay with me."

"Take . . . care. Of . . . my girls . . ."

"I will, man, I will. I promise."

"Zebra . . ." Before he could finish his thought, Archer's hand went limp. But his partner understood the reference.

"No!" DeSantos screamed at the top of his lungs, a deep, agonizing scream that seemed to echo into infinity.

"No!"

"No!"

"No!"

Jonathan Waller watched the DoD man whose credentials identified him as Enrique Ramirez. Waller had once seen a partner of his die, many years ago. The memories were still fresh. The way he'd cradled his friend's body, how lifeless it was. Waller had sobbed right then and there, in front of the whole homicide division, the first time he had cried in nearly a decade. It was his first assignment in the unit, one that he would never be able to forget. He later decided that his partner had died because Waller had followed the rules, and the rules said stay—when his instincts told him he should have gone. That was the last time Waller would do what the rulebook said unless in his heart it was what he felt should be done.

He knelt beside DeSantos and placed a hand on his shoulder. "I'm Waller, FBI."

"I know who you are."

"Sorry about your partner. If there's anything I can do—"

"I'm going to fucking kill him," DeSantos said, shrugging off Waller's hand and rising to his feet.

"Who?"

"Anthony Scarponi. Which way was he headed?"

"Scarponi?" Waller looked confused. "We were here for Payne."

"There were four perps in leather jackets."

"I hit one of them, but he got away."

"Was it Scarponi?"

"I don't think so, I didn't get a good look—"

"Which way did the other three go?"

"Look, I don't think that's a good idea. You're all worked up—"

DeSantos grabbed Waller by the collar of his jacket and pulled him close. "I don't care what you think! Which way?"

Waller nodded in the direction of George Street. DeSantos released his grip, then ran off, leaving his dead partner behind.

"He's a fool," Haviland said, coming up behind Waller.

Waller shook his head, still watching as DeSantos's body disappeared into the darkness. "It's exactly what I would do."

"No word yet from Fredericksburg PD on our wounded foot soldier," Haviland said, bringing his partner's attention back to the matter at hand.

Waller grasped his lapel mike and held it in front of his lips. "This is Waller. I hit one of the perps; there's some blood on the sidewalk. My guess is he's pretty mobile."

"Copy that, already passed on to FPD," the voice replied.

Waller ground his teeth and looked at his partner. He felt strangely agitated and didn't know how to deal with it. *Focus,* he told himself. *Focus. Get back on track.* He spun around, his eyes first taking in the carnage, then roaming the street and surrounding buildings.

Haviland kicked at a rock. "All that and we didn't even get Harper."

Waller turned to face his partner, his features suddenly relaxing. "Yes, we did," he said matter-of-factly, exuding the confidence of someone in complete control. "He's in the bell tower of the church to your left, across the street."

SIXTY

Nick Bradley made a quick survey of the area, then walked briskly down the street as three law enforcement personnel—by the looks of them, FBI agents—were hovering over the fallen men. With the shooting having ceased, people were slowly emerging from their shops, attempting to get a glimpse of what all the commotion had been about.

As he walked, Bradley kept his right hand on the SIG beneath his coat, just in case it was needed. *When plans get broken, when promises aren't kept, anything can happen.*

"I can't believe this," Bradley muttered, his eyes roaming the area, trying to catch a glimpse of Lauren. He continued on down the street, circled back, and made another pass.

Damn. Where the hell is she?

He stood there on the street corner, rubbing the knuckles of his left hand against the stubble on his cheek. Nothing was simple anymore, it seemed. As the days had passed, Bradley had found that he'd committed the ultimate sin: he had grown attached to Lauren. His goals were still the same, but the methods by which he had to go about accomplishing them had changed. He knew firsthand that relationships introduced unwanted and unnecessary complications. He cursed himself for becoming involved with her. For allowing himself to care.

He took a few moments to prioritize his needs, then headed for the antiques shop down the street.

Harper Payne was frozen. Not so much by the cold, but by what he had just witnessed. Moments ago, he had watched Lauren as she walked down the street, headed for their meeting place. His heart had seemed to rise in his chest, and he found it difficult to breathe. He knew her walk, the blue jacket she was wearing. He remembered.

Now, he looked down at Waller and Haviland, who were standing over the body of the man he had paid $25—with the promise of 25 more—to meet with Lauren and give her a message, a message designed to have her get back in her car and drive another few blocks to a different meeting area. It was an extra step, a security measure to make sure she wasn't being followed by one of Knox's men.

His decoy, dressed in a baseball hat and blue windbreaker, had waited in the doorway of a music store down the block. Payne had caught the man's gaze and waved a white handkerchief in front of the window. His contact then nodded, acknowledging the signal, and headed off toward Lauren. The rest ended in disaster.

As Payne's gaze remained transfixed on the street below, he thought of Lauren. He had come so close, and yet he had nothing to show for it. He had watched, helplessly, as the three men had quickly made their way down George Street. The glimpse of a blue jacket bobbing up and down amongst them could have been his imagination—it was getting dark and it was difficult to see, let alone make out colors—but it could also have been Lauren. Now, he could only hope that she was somewhere safe.

At the moment, however, if he was to hold out any hope of helping her—and himself—he had to deal with two much more pressing issues. And they were standing thirty feet below him.

"Ideas?" Haviland asked.

Waller glanced up and down the street. The small crowd of people—tourists, locals, shop owners—were inching closer, drawn by the sight of two men lying in puddles of blood. "Whatever we do, it's gotta be fast. If we let Payne give us the slip again, Knox will have our asses."

"Agreed."

"We've got two problems," Waller said in a low voice. "First one is the armed skel who's prowling the streets. That DoD guy, Ramirez, said he and his partner were expecting Scarponi to be here. If that's the case, whoever took out Sean McCracken and Ramirez's partner is one of Scarponi's men. Given what just went down here, my bet is he's looking for Harper. They probably saw this guy approaching Lauren Chambers, assumed it was Harper, and took him out."

"So we get to Harper before he does."

"That's problem number two. Bagging Harper is going to be up to us," Waller said. "Backup units are off in pursuit of the three perps. Hopefully, Harper's still up in that church tower. But if we both leave the body and he's watching us, he'll know something's up and he'll take off. If there's a back entrance, we'll never get to him in time."

"So I'll go in and flush him out," Haviland said.

"I should go, I know how he thinks. You stay here and make sure he doesn't come out as I go in. You can join me when I have visual."

"After all that's happened, you sure this isn't personal? Between you and Harper, I mean—"

"And what if it is?" Waller asked, locking eyes with his partner.

Haviland shook his head. "I hope you know what you're doing, Jon."

That makes two of us. Waller backed off and headed across the street toward the cemetery to the left of the church, just in case Payne was still watching.

Once out of sight from the church's tower, Waller ran toward the building and threw his back up against the eggshell-colored brick facade. He inched along its exterior and eased the left entrance door open.

With his back against the wall, he rolled inside, gun out in front of him. He quietly pulled the door shut behind him and stood there, frozen in place, waiting for his eyes to adjust to the relative darkness.

Seconds passed. Waller used the time to listen to his surroundings. He could hear voices in the distance. Children's voices. Not a good sign, not when there were guns around.

Damn you, Harper. Stop this game, stop it now. Before anyone else gets hurt.

As his vision improved, he quickly surveyed the layout of the floor. Across the lobby to his right, the staircase that led downstairs to the basement was barely visible. Now that he had a look at the interior, he realized he could use Haviland's help. He brought the lapel mike up to his mouth and signaled his partner. "Come in the east entrance, to the right of the building," he whispered. He informed Haviland about the children, then began ascending the spiral steps that led to the second, third, and fourth levels of the church, including the bell tower.

As he neared the second floor, he tucked his chin down toward his collar. "Scott—"

Just then, he heard a door open above him, in the east wing of the church. Waller dropped to his knees and held his breath. He was a little more than halfway up to the second landing. Suddenly, Haviland's voice began crackling in his earpiece, which, although confined to his ear, sounded to him as if it were being broadcast over a loudspeaker system. He grabbed the plug and yanked it from the receiver on his belt, immediately cutting off the transmission.

A few seconds later, he reinserted the plug and pulled the mike to his lips. "Shh," he said, hoping that Haviland would get the hint and realize that Payne was only ten to twenty feet away from Waller now.

The cries of an ambulance were approaching, getting louder with each passing second . . . no doubt on its way to tend to the two downed bodies. Suddenly, the wails reached a climax, then stopped abruptly. Two doors slammed shut, followed by the arrival of two additional police cars charged with cordoning off the crime scene the paramedics were about to trample through.

Beyond all the extraneous noise, Payne's ears picked up the sound of someone in the stairwell. He descended the steps to the second floor and waited for a few seconds, the high-impact-plastic handle of the Glock suddenly feeling warm and reassuring in the palm of his hand. He moved through the doorway into the horseshoe-shaped balcony that overlooked the rows of pews and ornate altar below. Loud creaking in the worn, century-old wooden floorboards was like a loudspeaker announcing his location. He grimaced with each step, realizing that he had to get out of there as quickly as possible.

As he attempted to climb behind a piano that was blocking the path connecting the east and west wings, he suddenly heard the metallic click of a bullet being chambered. He stopped and dropped down at the end of the piano.

"It's over, Harper. Move away from the piano and drop your weapon."

Payne stood so he could get a look at where Waller was in relation to his potential escape routes. "I'm not going with you, Jon."

"It's not up to you."

"I think it is." Payne backed to his right. He was moving toward the three-deep rows of benches that extended forty feet from the near wall of the church—the side that overlooked Princess Anne Street—to the far wall, where the altar was located.

Waller was standing in front of the first row of benches on the opposite side of the balcony from Payne, behind a white wrought-iron railing that overlooked the first floor of pews. Waller's Glock was clasped in his hands at chest level, pointed at his colleague and prisoner. For a long second the two men just stood there, staring at each other.

"You're not going to shoot me, Jon. I'm worth too much to you. Knox would have your creds in a second."

"*You* have my credentials, Harp. You took them from me, remember?"

Payne's eyes roamed the area, looking for the easiest way out. But there was none. "Now you know how I feel. I took your identity from you just like mine was taken from me." Payne heard a noise coming from the far wall. "Where's Scott?"

"I've tried to give you your identity back. You're forgetting that."

"Then why'd you try to keep me from my wife? I know what you were up to—"

Just then, Haviland appeared twenty feet to his right. "Stop right there, Scott," Payne said, twisting his head from Waller to Haviland and back to Waller. This was not good. He couldn't simultaneously watch two adversaries standing at ninety degrees to one other. "Both of you, drop your guns. Now!"

"I got ripped a new asshole for surrendering my weapon to you the last time," Waller said. "You're not getting it again."

"Why don't you just come with us," Haviland said. "We'll sit down, talk it out. Can't do that with guns pointed at each other."

Payne backed toward the door that was now fifteen feet away, the one that led down the stairs to the front of the building. But even if he made it to the doorway and down the steps, Waller would only be a few steps behind, as an identical door and staircase was on the west side of the building. And the steps spilled out into the same ground-floor lobby.

As Payne stepped back, the creaking floorboards echoed in the empty church. "I'd rather go it alone," he said as he reached the door. He turned the knob and gave it a shove.

"Harper—"

But before Haviland could finish his sentence, Payne disappeared into the dark spiral stairwell.

SIXTY-ONE

Payne heard the quick, creaking footsteps of Waller and Haviland following behind as he ran down the stairs in the dim light, the small flower-shaped windows letting in what little light was coming from the streetlamps. He hit the lobby on the run, slammed through the front door, and jumped down the steps.

And came face-to-face with Scott Haviland.

How'd he get out here so fast? But in the instant the question popped into his head, it became a moot point as Payne dropped his head and left shoulder and plowed into Haviland's abdomen with the skill of a running back. Despite his stocky build, the shocked agent was lifted off the ground and sent sprawling backward to the concrete.

Haviland let out an agonizing groan as his back hit the pavement, his Glock flying from his hand and landing a dozen feet away. Payne scooped it up on the run as if it were a fumbled football and headed down George Street, sprinting as fast as he could. His destination was not an end zone, but continued freedom— and another chance to link up with his wife.

As he ran by the National Bank of Fredericksburg, he slowed a bit, half-limping and half-running past a parking lot and a few brick houses. He cut right onto Charles and noticed the iron-gated entrance to the

Masonic Cemetery diagonally ahead of him. With the descending darkness and large-canopied maple and cedar trees blocking the light from the nearby street-lamps, the headstones would provide adequate cover from his pursuers. It was a good place to hide.

He darted out into the street—but heard footsteps approaching from behind. He spun around, the Glock still in his hand, expecting to see Waller.

But in the dark street, he could only glimpse the vague silhouette of a man, a spark issuing from his weapon. In the split second that followed, Payne became aware of a burning sensation as he gulped a mouthful of cold air. The intense, close-range explosion suddenly registered in his ears, ringing longer than the actual gunshot and continuing until he hit the pavement and lost consciousness.

SIXTY-TWO

J onathan Waller had run right by his partner, who
was writhing in pain on the sidewalk and simultaneously trying to catch his breath. Waller sprinted up
the street and heard the discharge of a handgun in
the middle of the intersection of George and Charles
Streets, twenty-five yards ahead of him. Boom, boom,
boom. Three shots.

And suddenly Waller's heart was in his throat.
There was simply no other way of describing his fear
at that instant—a pulsing, choking fullness that pre-
vented him from breathing.

As he came running around the corner onto
Charles, his eyes immediately locked on the police
officer crouched next to a body that was laid out
faceup near the Masonic Cemetery's front entrance.
The torso was on the blacktop, the head against the
curb.

In the darkness it was difficult for Waller to see. He
held out hope that the victim who was spread across
the road was the leather-jacketed man he had
wounded only a short time ago. But if it wasn't the
perp, the alternative was too painful to consider. As he
approached, he saw a Glock nine-millimeter handgun
lying in the street.

At that moment, his heart, having appeared to drop

down out of his throat, lost its rhythm for a second. A mere flutter in his chest. Despite the cold air, he instantly began to sweat and suddenly became aware of how truly exhausted he was. And as he stood now in front of the fallen man, he heard the officer calling for an ambulance over his two-way. That's when he finally gathered the nerve to look at the victim, when he saw the face of Harper Payne.

For the first time in his life, Jonathan Waller was frozen, unable to think, unsure of what to do.

"He had the gun in his hand and he turned toward me with it, it looked like he was bringing it up to fire . . ."

The cop's voice was somewhere in the background, in some far-off place, where Jonathan Waller wished he could be. Away from here. *Anywhere* but here.

Scott Haviland's ribs were aching something fierce, and every breath reminded him of the blow he had taken moments before. With his left hand strapped across his torso as if holding his chest would lessen the pain, he came limping up to Charles Street and tried to size up the scene with one quick glance at the dark roadway, which was now illuminated by a quarter moon poking through the thick cloud cover. His eyes darted from one figure to another: perp on the ground, cop barking into his two-way, partner standing over the body.

But something was wrong. Waller's posture was depressed: his shoulders were drooping and his arms were hanging limply at his sides.

"Jon?" Haviland asked.

As Waller turned toward him, Haviland's first impressions were confirmed: this was not good. It was then that Haviland saw the face of the man lying on the ground. It was then that he again heard the screams of sirens approaching in the distance.

"It's Harper," Waller managed.

"Oh, man. Is he alive?" Haviland asked, crouching down to slap a couple of fingers against Payne's neck to check for a pulse. Blood was accumulating beneath his head, pooling in a puddle against the curb.

The cop knelt next to Haviland. "I didn't know the guy was one of us, I'm really sorry."

Waller bent down and grasped Payne's hand in his own. "The man says he's sorry," Waller said wryly to no one in particular.

SIXTY-THREE

The ambulance screeched to a stop in front of Colonial General, a hospital similar in size to Virginia Presbyterian, where Harper Payne's journey had begun only ten days earlier. The nurses, the doctors, the paramedics . . . everything and everyone was moving quickly. To the untrained eye, the activity appeared to be haphazard and random. But in reality it was harmonious, the medics working off each other like the notes of a classical masterpiece.

For obvious reasons, Payne was being afforded the best medical care in the most secure environment possible. Every person in the room was a member of an elite group of specially selected personnel who had been mobilized from Bethesda Naval Hospital as soon as the call had come in from Fredericksburg. Though they wore necklaces with encoded biometric markings, to the general hospital staff with whom they usually worked they appeared to be normal practicing physicians and nurses. When a crisis involving high-ranking federal officials struck, however, they were summoned by secured communications to one of several predetermined and uniquely equipped locations.

Sworn to secrecy about everything they saw and did, their reports and operative notes were never committed to paper. They answered only to the army chief of staff and the national security adviser. Surprisingly, no checks and balances were afforded their work. Their success or failure was never questioned by non-military personnel.

Outside the bulletproof doors of the secured emergency room, two guards stood sentry. Inside, monitors and machines beeped and hissed. A nasotracheal tube was inserted, a portable X-ray unit was brought in, and a defibrillator was charged and ready. Harried movement, notes of a masterpiece.

Finally, Payne's vitals were deemed stable and he was rushed off to a private elevator down the hall, where Dr. Vance Taylor, a squat, graying man, was accosted by Waller and Douglas Knox, who had just arrived via helicopter.

"What's the story?" Knox asked, grabbing Taylor by the arm.

The surgeon attempted to pull his arm free. "I don't really have time to talk, Director."

"We'll ride with you," Knox said as he and Waller entered the elevator. The doors snapped closed and the car lifted.

"As best I can tell, he only took one bullet," Taylor said. "It passed clean through and didn't strike any vital organs. There'll be no limitation of function. Biggest risk is infection, and we've dosed him with antibiotics."

"But all that blood, and he was out cold," Waller said.

"We've looked for a second bullet, but I don't see another entry wound, and the skull X-rays were negative. I'm having him brought downstairs for a CT."

"Then where'd all the blood come from?" Knox asked.

"This is just a guess, but the force from the gunshot could've knocked him backward. If he tripped or fell and struck his head on the curb, it would explain the five-centimeter gash on his scalp and all the blood you saw. The scalp bleeds profusely and always looks like a wound much worse than it actually is."

A bell rang as the elevator neared their floor.

"So that's it, then. Just a clean bullet wound and a cut on his head?"

Taylor held up a hand. "I didn't say that. If he hit his head like I think he might have, he could have a sub-dural hematoma. If it was more of a glancing blow and merely a laceration, he'll be fine. The CT will tell us all we need to know."

The elevator stopped abruptly and the doors slid apart. "In English," Knox said.

"The blow to the head might have caused some bleeding around his brain. If that's the case, we have to relieve the pressure immediately or we could lose him. Now, if you'll excuse me, I need to get to radiology."

Taylor stepped out of the elevator, leaving Waller and Knox standing there, staring at the closing stainless steel doors. Then, Knox turned to Waller, his face contorted into a hideous Halloween mask of anger. "How the hell could you have let this happen?"

Nick Bradley walked into the bar near his motel and ordered a Scotch, straight up. He buried his head in the crook of his elbow and exhaled deeply while the bartender prepared his drink.

When the man placed the glass on the counter in front of him, Bradley lifted his head and then peeled a couple of bills off his money clip. His eye caught an image on the news playing out on the television mounted above the far end of the bar.

"Hey, can you turn that up?" Bradley asked the barkeep.

The man reached below the counter and pointed a remote at the TV. As the volume rose, Bradley could hear the news reporter setting the scene.

". . . and it appears as if the government's case against Anthony Scarponi could be in significant jeopardy, unless their key witness, former FBI agent Harper Payne, makes what would appear to be a miraculous recovery . . ."

Bradley's gaze remained locked on the TV as images of the street in Fredericksburg flashed across the screen. An officer-involved shooting team was examining and documenting the scene behind the reporter as she babbled on about the Scarponi case.

"We now switch to Ray Jamison at Colonial General

Hospital, where Agent Payne was brought a little over an hour ago."

Bradley threw another mouthful of Scotch down his throat, the burn bringing his mind back into focus. He placed the glass back on the bar and grabbed for his cell phone, which was now ringing. He answered it with his eyes still fixed on the TV.

His back straightened. "I've been trying to reach you, where the hell have you been?" He paused, waiting for the answer. He shook his head, then slid down off his stool. "Did you see the news? This wasn't supposed to happen." He listened for a second, then broke in. "No. Absolutely not." He turned and glanced around, realizing his voice had been a little too loud. "We need to meet," he said as he pushed through the bar's front door. "Right now."

SIXTY-FIVE

The birthing room was decorated with primary colors, children's hands of all shapes and sizes splashed across the walls. It was a comfortable environment, with a couch, chairs, and plenty of room to stretch out and relax with your newborn.

Presley Jane Archer, a seven-pound-five-ounce, pink bundle of joy had just been brought back into the room to see her mother after being examined, scored, and footprinted.

Hector DeSantos stood in the doorway as the baby was reunited with Trish, whose attention was so focused on the newborn that she did not even see him standing there. The nurse smiled at him on the way out, then closed the door behind her.

After Archer had gone down in the streets of Fredericksburg, DeSantos went on a hunt, sniffing out his prey in every way he knew how. But he had come up empty. Anthony Scarponi had gotten away. But DeSantos knew that sooner or later—preferably sooner—he would bring justice to the grave of Brian Archer. Zebra 59, his partner's dying words, meant that DeSantos's sole focus would be to track down and settle the score with Archer's killer.

DeSantos had walked through the hospital corridors, fresh with the knowledge that Trish had given birth to a healthy girl, trying to wipe the anger, the depression, the terror, off his face. He had stopped at a rest room and stood in front of the mirror, attempting to smile, attempting to hide what was in his heart. As he had done so many times in the past in so many dire undercover situations when he needed to, he was actor first, commando second.

Now, as he stood in the doorway, his heart pounded fiercely against his chest, not out of fear, but out of sadness because of what he was about to do. He had to take a mother's most joyful moment and turn it into a nightmare. But there was no other way. He knew that as the hours passed and Trish did not hear from her husband, she would begin to worry, then ask questions. And the one she would call would be him.

And that's the way it should be, that's the way he and Brian had always wanted it.

He forced a smile across his face and held out the modest bouquet of flowers he had picked up in the hospital gift shop on the way up. Pink and yellow roses with a smatter of baby's breath. How appropriate. Trish looked over and smiled.

Her face was haggard and her complexion pale. It had no doubt been a difficult labor. But then again, in his limited experience with pregnant women, he had never heard of an easy labor. Only ones less difficult than others.

"Where's Brian?" Trish asked.

"We were called away and were in the middle of a mission when the page came through," DeSantos said, maintaining the phony smile. "He wanted so much to be here, you know that."

Trish smiled. "Of course, he wouldn't have missed this for the world."

DeSantos felt his stomach seize up on him but he forced himself to hold it in, to choke off the emotions. "So, this is Presley?"

Trish turned the baby around to face DeSantos. "Say hi to Uncle Hector," Trish sang.

DeSantos touched the newborn's soft facial skin with the back of his forefinger and felt a surge of emotion well up in his throat. He fought back tears and summoned the strength to say, "She's beautiful."

"I see Brian in her eyes, don't you?"

DeSantos smiled. "Yup. And her mother's beautiful face."

Trish planted a kiss on the baby's cheek, then said, without looking up, "So when's Brian coming?"

DeSantos knew the question was going to come; it was just a matter of when. He was going to tell her what he had prepared himself to say in the car, that he was sorry, that Brian had died in the line of duty, that his last thoughts were of mother and daughter, that he, Hector, was to look after them. And that he was going to get the son of a bitch who had killed her husband. But he knew that as soon as he started to speak, Trish would know. It would click in her mind and that would be it. Brian was dead. That would be all that mattered to her. But to DeSantos . . . what mattered to him was making sure Anthony Scarponi paid for what he had done.

DeSantos pulled up a chair and set it next to her bedside. "Trish . . . about Brian." He looked down, but the tears started to trail down his cheek until he tasted the salt on his lips. He picked his head up, unable to hide it anymore, and saw that she knew.

She shook her head. "God, no, please. No." A tear ran down her cheek and dripped onto Presley's knit cap. Trish's pale face turned beet red and she began to sob, and the baby began to cry, and he leaned over to hug both of them.

SIXTY-SIX

The pressroom at Colonial General was crowded with tripod- and shoulder-mounted television cameras, reporters, and support personnel from the Washington media corps. A continuous white noise of chatter had poured from the journalists ever since they were herded into the room twenty minutes ago.

With the babbling growing louder and the newspeople becoming restless, the side door swung open suddenly and two men entered, followed by a contingent of suited security-detail agents. The embroidered name above the vest pocket on the knee-length, white lab coat of the first man read VANCE TAYLOR, M.D. The doctor introduced himself and alluded to the presence of FBI director Knox, then addressed the press corps.

The doctor's face was long and his shoulders were rolled, as if he had just been through a harrowing experience. He paused, placed both hands on the lectern, which was emblazoned with the hospital logo, and sighed. "As you know, Special Agent Harper Payne was involved in an accidental shooting in Fredericksburg a little over two hours ago. Unfortunately, despite our best efforts, he suffered a subdural hematoma, which resulted in uncontrolled bleeding in his brain. We attempted to relieve the pressure but were unsuccessful. Agent Payne died on the operating table thirty minutes ago, at nineteen hundred hours."

A noticeable murmur rose from the reporters.

"Director Knox has a statement and then I'll answer questions." Taylor turned to Knox, whose tie was loosened at the collar.

Knox kept his gaze on the lectern as he spoke. "As all of you know, Agent Payne was pivotal to the case we had against the well-publicized assassin Anthony Scarponi. I can only assure you that the FBI will do everything in its power to bring justice to the people of this country, in spite of tonight's events." Knox looked up at the stunned faces standing before him. He cocked his head and with a choked voice said, "As for Agent Payne, may his soul rest in peace. I can only say that his courage, fortitude, and service to this country have not and will not go unappreciated. Thank you."

Hands sprang up from nearly every reporter in the room. Knox turned away, giving them the clear sign that he had no intention of answering their questions. He stepped back and allowed Vance Taylor to take the lectern, then hurried off through the exit.

SIXTY-SEVEN

Nick Bradley sat in his darkened motel room holding his nine-millimeter in one hand and his cell phone in the other. For ten minutes he struggled to find the right words. It would be a fast call, he figured, just long enough to hook Scarponi and keep his attention. He would drop the bomb, then back away.

The television, turned down to a barely perceptible level, droned on about the death of Harper Payne. Another investigative special, more legal analysis, and higher ratings for the networks. All the interest of the O.J. trial or the Lewinsky scandal but in a condensed version. It would draw viewers for a week at most, then fade from the public's mind—but for those seven days, the story would dominate the airwaves. Because viewers brought money to the networks' bottom line, and the bottom line drove the news.

The female reporter was holding an umbrella in front of the FBI's Washington Field Office and caressing the camera with her large brown eyes. "Services for the deceased agent will be private, at an undisclosed location, the Bureau announced this afternoon. Agent Payne's former wife and daughter, both of whom he had not seen since going underground in the Witness Protection Program six years ago, are expected to attend. Attempts to locate his current wife have thus far been unsuccessful. As you can imagine, the mood was somber at the FBI field office where Agent Payne was stationed, but it was business as usual . . ."

Bradley shut the television off and stared at the phone. With his plan now completely laid out in his mind, he realized it was time. He placed the call and left a cryptic voice-mail message, designed to motivate Scarponi to call him back without delay.

For ten minutes he sat by the phone. Although he was confident Scarponi would return the call, the waiting was difficult. Finally, the phone rang. Perhaps appearing too eager, he pounced on the handset.

"You didn't wire the funds," Bradley said, starting the conversation with an aggressive stance.

"You've never called me before."

"You've never stiffed me before."

"Fair enough," Scarponi said. "Fair enough. Well, it's this way, my friend. I don't need your services anymore."

Bradley could tell from the tone of the man's voice that he had already heard the news of Payne's death. "You'll want to hear what I have to say," Bradley said, hoping that Scarponi would not disconnect him.

But several seconds passed without a response.

Bradley realized it was now or never. Scarponi, guarding against any possibility this was a setup, would not remain on the phone long enough for it to be traced. "Harper Payne is not dead."

Scarponi laughed. "This is a joke, right?'

"No joke. Payne is alive."

"What are you talking about? The news—"

"Designed just for you. Disinformation released by the Bureau to keep you from gunning for Payne while the feds forge ahead with their plans for the trial. They're confident they'll eventually find you. Every allied country is on high alert. Borders are tight. Interpol is coordinating the effort. And the CIA has made it their goal to bring you back to trial. You've made them look like fools."

"You're just trying to prove your worth, prevent the cash cow from taking his milk elsewhere."

"Have you ever had reason to doubt my sources? After everything I've given you over the years, has my intelligence ever failed you?"

"Maybe you're due. Maybe you're now working with the feds against me. Maybe they're onto you and they're using you to pass on bad information."

"If you think Payne's dead, you stop gunning for him. Don't you get it?"

Scarponi was silent again. Bradley knew the Viper understood what the feds had done. It was a good move on their part, and Scarponi no doubt respected them for it.

"Do some digging and find out for yourself," Bradley said. "Verify what I'm telling you. Then call me back. I've got some more information you might be interested in." With that, Bradley pressed END and severed the connection.

He sat there in the dark tapping his foot. Scarponi was, by design, extremely unpredictable, and not knowing how he was going to react bothered Bradley a great deal. At the least, the assassin would attempt to confirm what Bradley had told him. But there would be no way to do that, not unless other well-placed moles were on his payroll.

Bradley closed his eyes, took a deep breath, and blew it out slowly. Stressing out about it wasn't going to help him any. The best thing he could do would be to keep his mind busy with other matters.

But there were no other matters. None that had any significance. This was it.

The SIG remained in his hand, warm and at the ready, just in case it was needed. If someone burst through his door, they wouldn't get one step before having a meal made of lead.

His eyes kept following the second hand around the dial. It had circled more times than he cared to count—but fifteen minutes later, the jarring chirp of the cell phone made his heart skip. He stood up and forced himself to walk slowly across the room, where he had left his phone. He didn't want to appear too anxious to answer the call. He closed his eyes and willed himself to relax while he waited for the fourth ring.

He pressed SEND and, in a low voice, said, "Yeah."

"You said you had more information. I'm listening."

Bradley brushed a sleeve across his wet forehead, then began laying out his terms.

Nick Bradley slipped the cell phone into his pocket and realized that what he had just set in motion was irreversible. He had told Scarponi about the plans the Bureau had to move Payne to a military hospital on the outskirts of D.C., outlining the specific route the ambulance would be taking. As far as Scarponi was concerned, the information was worth far more than the $10,000 he had promised to pay.

Bradley walked into the bathroom and splashed his face with cool water, then, while toweling off, heard a car door slam outside his room. Could Scarponi have found him? Now that he had the information he needed, was Bradley merely an expendable part, worth no more to him than a disposable razor?

Bradley stood in the bathroom, his torso wet from an instant mat of perspiration. He crouched down and scampered across the room to the curtained window. If they were going to fire on him, they would aim for his chest, five feet off the ground. Keeping below their line of fire was an old trick he had learned two decades ago in the marines.

Bradley heard a room door close, then carefully parted the drapes and saw a taxi pulling away from the curb. No one was in the vicinity, though it was difficult to see in the stark lighting of the parking lot. *Could it be Lauren?*

The SIG still in his hand, crouched down low, he cracked open the door. All was clear. He moved outside, dressed only in pants and a cotton shirt. The cold night air stung his skin and induced a shiver as he stayed low, his eyes combing the parking lot.

He tried to slow his breathing, as he was blowing very visible wisps of vapor into the air. This not only drew attention to his presence, but to a sharp assassin, it was an instant tip-off that he was crouching.

With his left fist, he rapped on Lauren's door. His placed his ear against the cold metal and listened intently for any signs of movement. There was nothing. He rapped again and thought he heard something—a hard object dropping onto a carpeted floor.

He moved to his right and stood up, his right shoulder leaning against the stucco wall. He stepped back, then coiled his leg and thrust it quickly into Lauren's door. It burst open, the wood jamb splintering apart. He quickly ducked back, to the left, out of sight.

The dim light from the parking lot spilled into the

room, which was otherwise dark. He waited a second, crouched down, and swung around square with the interior, his gun out in front of him.

Before he could react, he saw Lauren standing in muted light, at the far corner, her Colt aimed at him. Her eyes were narrow slits and her mouth was tight.

"It's okay! It's me, it's Nick," he shouted. He dropped his arms and waited for a look of recognition. But her body remained rigid.

He stood up in a gradual, measured fashion, keeping his arms—and his weapon—at his side. "Lauren, honey, it's okay. Are you all right?" He moved toward her slowly, slowly, slowly, until her gun was pressed up against his body. Suddenly, she burst out crying and buried her face into his chest.

"You're safe," he said as he stroked her back. "There's nothing to worry about now."

Lauren was sitting in a chair in Bradley's room, huddled over a cup of hot tea. Her face was drawn and her eyes were still and glazed. "That man told me to go a few blocks down, that Michael would meet me there. But when he got shot, I just ran away, I kept going." She took a sip of tea. "I found this bar and I was, I guess, I was kind of in a state of shock. I was there, but I wasn't. I think I had a drink, then called a cab." Lauren looked at Nick's watch. "It's nine-thirty? Must've had a few, I was there awhile."

Bradley was sitting on the edge of the bed, forearms resting on his thighs, listening to Lauren. He eyed her for a second, then looked away. "Did they have the news on while you were in the bar?"

"Some basketball game, I think. I wasn't really paying attention. Why?"

"There was an accident," Bradley said, his eyes down-cast. "In all the confusion, Michael was shot. He's—"

"Shot—is he okay?"

"He was taken to a hospital and treated, and every-thing's going to be fine. But the news is reporting he was killed."

"Why?"

"They received a statement from the FBI saying Michael was killed. The Bureau is hoping Scarponi will hear that he's dead, so he won't continue to go after him."

"How do you know—"

"Trust me. I have my sources."

"I need to see him. I want to see my husband, Nick."

"They're transferring him to a military hospital, for safety reasons. Scarponi won't stop until Michael's dead."

"But I thought you said the FBI told the media he'd been killed so Scarponi would leave him alone."

"Scarponi's smart. He may not fall for that."

"Get me in there, Nick. I want to see him." She reached onto the adjacent desk and picked up her Colt. She stared at it for a second, then began to run her fin-gers along the barrel. "First I want to talk to Michael, see that he's okay. Then I'm going after Scarponi. I want him dead."

"Maybe we should just let the FBI handle Scarponi. The guy's a trained assassin, Lauren. You can't—"

"Don't tell me I can't, Nick. I've been telling myself 'I can't' for four years now. I need to do this."

Bradley got up from the bed and walked away from her. "Lauren, what you're talking about is . . . well, it's a suicide mission, not to mention first-degree murder if you do take him out."

"How do we find him?"

"You're not listening to me."

"And you're not answering me. How can we find him?"

Bradley sighed and leaned back against the wall. "I don't know. He's a fugitive, even the FBI hasn't been able to find him."

Lauren stood and shoved the gun into her waistband. "I've gone nose to nose with this man. I think I know what makes him tick. If I can find a way of contacting him, he'll come to me."

Bradley reached out, took her hand, and gave it a reassuring squeeze. "First things first. Let's go see Michael, then we can revisit this."

"You're placating me, Nick. You don't need to do that anymore."

"I'm only trying to help you focus. Since the day I met you, your one and only goal was to find Michael. We now know where he's going to be. Let's go see him."

"I guess my goals have changed a bit." She put her jacket on and faced Bradley. "I feel like I've awakened from a fog, Nick. Something happened to me in that cabin. I don't mean physically, that much is obvious. I'm talking emotionally. The Lauren Chambers of two weeks ago wouldn't have handled that situation very well. But I've got my head back together."

"You killed someone, Lauren. If that's not enough to change someone, I don't know what is."

"It's more than that. It's not so much a change as it is a return to *me*, to a time five years ago, before things started to go wrong. Before the depression, the panic attacks." She shook her head. "All the therapy, the medication. All it did was help me get by. But it didn't really solve anything. It took Michael's disappearance and the fear that I'd never get him back to give me the kick in the ass I needed."

"I'm glad you found what you were searching for."

She took in a deep breath through her nose and closed her eyes, as if savoring it. "This must be what it's like when an alcoholic gets off the booze and realizes she can smell things again, taste things she hasn't tasted in years." She opened her eyes. "That's what it's like for me, Nick. Yes, I started out just wanting Michael back. But now I want more. I want to put an end to all this."

Bradley nodded as if he understood, then grabbed the car keys off the dresser. "It'll all be over soon, Lauren. That much I can promise you."

Lauren pulled her arms across her chest and warded off a shiver. Bradley had said those same words to her once before, when they were preparing to head into Fredericksburg.

And that ended up being a total disaster.

SIXTY-EIGHT

I n the off chance Scarponi's henchmen would come looking for him, Bradley fabricated an excuse and moved Lauren to a different motel, the Days Inn in downtown D.C. They checked in under the assumed names of Adrienne and Chad Kendall and paid cash in advance. Bradley told the night clerk they had a child, and they were given a room with two queen beds.

From the next morning until four-thirty in the afternoon, Lauren sat in the room flipping the television channels, passing time while Bradley was out attempting to arrange a rendezvous with Michael. She was to wait in the room in the event he needed her to meet with a Bureau official. He explained it would be best if he went alone because he might need to stretch the truth, and it was easier for one person to lie than for two to coordinate their stories on the fly.

Meanwhile, Lauren remained on edge, listening to the news repeat the top story of the day—of the month, and perhaps the past few months. Even though she knew it was untrue, it bothered her to hear, over and over, what a tragic death her husband had endured. Not until one of the stations mentioned Harper Payne's former wife and child did the full impact of Michael's private, past life hit her. How she would deal with this she did not know. But for the moment, it was something she chose not to think about. First and foremost, she wanted Michael back.

A half hour ago she had ventured over to the window for the umpteenth time and gazed out at the charcoal blotches of clouds hanging against the gray sky. Although it only had been a little before four, the black clouds hovering above were bringing darkness a bit earlier.

With the Colt resting on her lap and the television volume turned low, a loud knock on the door broke the tedium and made her heart drop down to her stomach. She grabbed the handle of her weapon and slid off the bed.

"It's me," Bradley said through the door. "I'm coming in."

Lauren listened as he slipped his magnetic key card in the lock and opened the door. His face was taut, and as he stood there straddling the threshold, Lauren knew something was brewing.

"We've got to go," Bradley said. "Now."

SIXTY-NINE

Jonathan Waller was summoned to Director Knox's office at seven o'clock in the evening. Waller had just arrived home and spoken to his girlfriend, who was on her way over to have a romantic dinner with him. And she was bringing a special something for dessert. The way the Scarponi case had been going, they had not had much time together. Unable to reach her while she was en route, Waller left a note on his door containing a huge apology. He could only imagine her reaction when she got to his house expecting a long-awaited evening together, only to find a note and no *significant other*.

He pulled into the underground parking garage at headquarters at five after seven and was admitted into the director's office a few minutes later. Knox was in sweats and running shoes, his suit coat hanging in the far corner of his suite, on his bathroom door.

"You're not my favorite person right now," Knox said to Waller before he could sit. The director was leaning against the windowsill, his arms folded across his chest.

"No, sir."

"I'd like to give you a chance to make amends for the abominable work you've been passing off as a member of the Bureau, to show me you can follow orders and procedure and complete an assignment without screwing up."

Waller kept his mouth shut, something Haviland often said he should do in times like these—but rarely did.

"I've assigned you to part of the group that rides with me during Agent Payne's transport tonight to Vandenheim Air Force Base."

Waller nodded, pleased that he was being given the opportunity, but confused all the same. He had assumed he was automatically going to be included. Not wanting to stir up problems, he again held his thoughts. "Thank you, sir. I'd like that."

"I thought you might. There's a briefing that starts in ten minutes, in Strategic Planning One. I'll be there as soon as I can shower and throw my clothes on."

Waller thanked Knox again, then headed to the elevators. If Waller was to have any hopes of getting a favorable final evaluation from the director to his superior, SAC Lindsey—if he was to have any hopes of salvaging his career—then he had to make sure the role he played in Payne's transfer was significant. Without screwups. Without variance from established procedure.

He walked into the elevator and pressed 4, then smiled. Well, best he could hope for was to avoid screwups.

SEVENTY

Thunder was blasting the countryside and a light rain had begun to fall as darkness descended on the outskirts of Bristow, Virginia. The Advanced Paramedic Response ambulance was tooling along Route 28 at fifty miles per hour, its headlights beating down on the one-lane road.

In front of and behind the ambulance were unmarked FBI escort vehicles, navy blue Ford Crown Victorias. Hanging back a mile and a quarter was a black Lincoln Navigator, running with nothing but its windshield wipers on. It was closing ground on the ambulance, and Anthony Scarponi, driving the tank of a vehicle, was like a hungry animal closing in on its quarry. Before leaving the States for good, he was intent on making this hit his last big hurrah.

"Looks like the mole came through for us," Scarponi remarked. "APR ambulance with two escorts, just like he said."

In the front passenger seat was Rocko McCabe, a Vietnam War veteran, a man who had never quite recovered from his post–traumatic stress disorder. In and out of VA hospitals for twenty years, he had come under the tutelage of Scarponi during one of the assassin's trips to the United States in the late 1980s.

McCabe had long, flowing hair drawn back into a

ponytail. His face was leathery with deep-set grooves, worry lines he had acquired during his army days when he was a sniper—a legal, and lethal, assassin. If there was one thing the drugs, depression, and poverty hadn't taken away from him, it was his steady eye for a rifle scope. It was the one skill Scarponi considered essential to his colleague's employment.

The M20 three-and-a-half-inch bazooka was straddling McCabe's lap in pieces. They had three eight-pound armor-piercing rockets in the vehicle with them, though one close-range shot from McCabe's hands would be more than enough to take out an ambulance carrying Harper Payne on a one-lane road in northern Virginia.

"I've been waiting for this day for six years," Scarponi said. "I've dreamt about it more times than I can remember." His hands were pearl white from gripping the steering wheel. "There's something about revenge that's so . . . I don't know, fulfilling."

The passenger in the backseat was Griff Daniels, a buddy of McCabe's during their service days. Unlike McCabe's, Daniels's head was clean-shaven—though at the moment, he had a five-o'clock shadow poking through his scalp. It was actually Daniels who had introduced McCabe to Scarponi thirteen years ago. In Vietnam, Daniels's expertise was also in long-range sniping, and he and McCabe often challenged each other to shooting contests—where the targets were anything and everything. Cans, helmets, trees, tanks, commies. And civilians.

"What'll you give me if I take out this ambulance?" McCabe asked, a Merit dangling from his bottom lip.

"A fucking medal," Daniels said. "How's that?"

"Focus," Scarponi said sternly. "No screwups."

"Have I ever let you down, boss?"

"It's not you, it's that contraption I'm worried about." Scarponi nodded at the two-piece aluminum smoothbore tube McCabe was busy assembling. "Couldn't you get something a little more . . . low-key?"

"Lots of ways to take out a truck. But you wanted a clean hit. No doubt, you said. No doubt. This beauty will take out a tank. A fucking ambulance? There'll be nothing left, inside or out."

"I haven't seen one of them things since Korea," Daniels said. "Where the hell did you get it?"

"This old coot owed me big bucks about ten years ago," McCabe said as he snapped the front barrel hook into place. "Got him a shitload of weed for some war wound he got in Korea. Said they gave him a Purple Heart that didn't do shit for him, but the VA wouldn't give him enough painkillers to keep him sane." McCabe threw the barrel latch handle into place and examined the connection. "Anyway, after he used all the weed, he was gonna stiff me on what he owed me. I convinced him that would be a quick way to end his shitty life, and he offered me this baby as a trade," McCabe said, tapping the launcher with his right hand. "It'll do the job, boss. I know how important this is to you."

"It better," Scarponi said. "The backup plan is a whole lot messier." He depressed the accelerator and the 5.4-liter engine powered the heavy SUV up to seventy, effortlessly moving the Navigator to within 125 yards of the trailing escort vehicle. On a moonless, overcast, rainy evening, Scarponi knew that it would be difficult to see a dark vehicle following at this distance. Suddenly he felt the blood surging in his temples, the flood of adrenaline in his veins. His pupils were dilated and his focus was on the large ambulance looming in the distance ahead of him.

"Coming up on marker eighteen," McCabe said. "About three-quarters of a mile to go."

"Then it's time," Scarponi said. He dialed his cell phone and spoke with his advance scouts, who had located two other FBI undercover cars stationed in the brush alongside the road, no doubt waiting to hand off surveillance to other agents once the ambulance passed. "Take them out," Scarponi said. "Repeat, begin Operation Bleach." He received confirmation, disconnected the call, and matched speed with the Crown Victoria, holding his position at one hundred yards. "Okay, boys, line up your shots carefully. We only want to do this once."

"If I can't hit a target like that, at this distance, with this howitzer, you should put me out of my misery." McCabe snuffed out his cigarette while Daniels lifted his Heckler & Koch MP5 semiautomatic submachine gun that was fitted with a laser sight. He opened the right rear window and waited. "I'm in position," he shouted above the wind noise.

Scarponi retracted the power moon roof. After the top had rolled aside, McCabe quickly maneuvered his feet so he was standing on the center console, his back against the roof's opening. Satisfied with his footing, he reached down and hoisted the twenty-three-pound rocket launcher into a position such that it was sticking straight up, almost parallel with his body.

McCabe stood up fully, the cold, driving rain pummeling his face. He pulled down a pair of clear plastic goggles to deflect the oncoming fifty-five-mile-an-hour headwind, then maneuvered the five-foot tube through the opening and moved the bazooka's rear support onto his shoulder. The high-explosive anti-tank rocket was loaded and ready for launching. He rested the front-tube-mounted bipod on the roof of the Navigator and settled the right lens of his goggles against the weapon's reflecting sight.

"Ready," McCabe shouted.

"Ready," Scarponi echoed. He moved the Navigator to the left of the road, giving Daniels an unimpeded shot at the rear window of the Crown Victoria. The plan was to take out the driver of the escort vehicle with a precision shot to the head. The car would undoubtedly swerve off to the side. Meanwhile, McCabe would have a clear shot at the ambulance, which was several feet higher than the trailing car. To work effectively, they would shoot simultaneously. None of them would know what hit them . . . least of all Harper Payne.

McCabe took a deep breath and let it out slowly as his hand fingered the electronic firing device.

Scarponi's excitement was so high he could barely speak to give the order. The imprisonment of the last six years flashed in his mind . . . the physical and emotional torture, the blackness of solitary confinement, the putrid food, the demotion of his humanity to a piece of rotting garbage. He cleared his throat and said, "Do it!"

"Fire in the hole!" McCabe yelled.

SEVENTY-ONE

Jonathan Waller was in a Sikorsky Black Hawk helicopter, infrared binoculars in his hands. The Black Hawk was "America's helicopter," a workhorse that had over twenty years' combat experience tucked away in its twin-turbine engines. With the capability of carrying nearly two dozen soldiers deep into a war zone, the Black Hawk and its myriad incarnations were used by the army's Special Ops unit, the navy, air force, Coast Guard, FBI, and Marine Corps.

Waller's headset was muffling almost all of the cacophonous rotor noise, and with the chopper's smooth rocking movements, he was lulled to memories of the time when he had taken an air tour of the island of Maui, Hawaii. As they had flown above the ten-thousand-foot ceiling of Mount Haleakala, the synchronized classical music score had built to a crescendo. While the dark countryside of Virginia was nowhere near as dramatic as the clear turquoise waters of the Hawaiian Pacific, it was, nevertheless, hypnotizing.

Until he casually pressed the infrared binoculars to his eyes.

Until he saw the rocket launcher protruding from the top of the Navigator, until he saw the burst of flame pouring from the rear of the bazooka.

"Holy fucking shit!" Waller cried.

But it was too late.

The back-blast was enormous, the shock wave furiously slamming against the Navigator with a loud *whoomp!* Rocko McCabe was thrown backward, his head smashing against the moon roof's opening just before he crumpled onto Griff Daniels's lap in the backseat.

"Impact!" Scarponi screamed.

The rocket pierced the back of the ambulance less than a second after it was fired, penetrating the metal as if it were a sharp knife slicing through sponge cake. After a split-second delay, the ambulance's metal substructure burst upward toward the heavens, a swirling round fireball surging off the blacktop, lighting up the murky darkness brighter than a baseball stadium.

Scarponi veered hard to the right, missing the Crown Victoria that was careening left off the road. The driver's-side wheels of the Navigator left the asphalt for a second as the vehicle continued moving onto the shoulder and then into the brush. It barreled through the periphery of the burning wreckage, fire licking up its sides, blistering its finish.

Daniels was already spraying nine-millimeter rounds across the windows and tires of the leading escort vehicle. At the instant the FBI agent locked his brakes in disbelief, a bullet blew apart his skull.

"Woo-hoo!" Scarponi whooped as the inferno receded in his rearview mirror. McCabe sat up from the backseat, dazed and disoriented. He turned toward the ruinous fire on the roadway framed by the large back window and smiled. "Right on!"

• • • •

Waller had pulled the binoculars away from his eyes at just the right instant. Had he still been looking through the infrared glasses, the light flare from the explosion would have blown out his rods and cones for at least the next fifteen minutes.

"My God," was all Hector DeSantos could say.

Douglas Knox was seething. "Take us in!" he said to the pilot. "Don't let them get away—"

Waller twisted a knob on the control panel in front of him and yanked his headset microphone close to his lips. "This is Air Unit Five," he shouted, his voice cracking. "Need backup and medevac at mile marker eighteen!"

Harper Payne, sitting next to Hector DeSantos on the right side of the helicopter, could not pull his stare away from the distant blaze. "He's crazy. Scarponi, the guy's lost his mind."

"Obviously, he thought you were in that ambulance," DeSantos said.

"ETA for backup?" Knox asked.

Waller repeated the request and waited about ten seconds before he received the reply. They all heard the answer over their headsets: two of the additional units that were stationed ahead of them at mile markers twenty-five and forty were not responding. Required time to get ground vehicles to that location: *at least fifteen minutes.*

Payne looked over at Knox and saw the man's shoulders slump forward in defeat. He was clearly dismayed over the turn of events.

The chopper vibrated hard as the pilot pushed the throttle to 152 knots—175 miles an hour—and the distance to the burning plume began decreasing rapidly. Knox slammed his fist into the console. "I will not let Scarponi get away again!" he shouted into his microphone. His voice was high, his demeanor frenzied. Desperate.

As they passed above what was left of the ambulance, DeSantos shook his head. "Jesus." The carnage was devastating, almost warlike. "Talk about overkill."

Waller shook his head. "More like roadkill."

"Get us down close!" Knox said to the pilot. "Hector! You and Waller are going in."

"What about me?" Payne asked. "All this—all those HRT agents in that ambulance—they're dead because of me."

Knox swiveled in his seat to face Payne. "You're not going anywhere, mister, and that's not up for discussion. You should be in bed recuperating. I took you along as part of our deal to gain your cooperation. I said nothing about letting you jump out of a moving helicopter."

In fact, the plan as Payne knew it did not call for any of them to jump out of a moving helicopter. They had set up the entire scenario expecting Scarponi to attempt an ambush of the ambulance. That was the reason for filling the back of the vehicle with HRT agents, ready—and waiting—for the assault. But plans had a way of falling apart at the worst possible moment. In this case, their strategy had literally blown up in their faces.

Payne grabbed a pair of infrared goggles and zeroed in on the Navigator, which was moving back onto the roadway from the side brush about a mile away from them. DeSantos pulled a SIG-Sauer nine-millimeter handgun from his belt and checked the magazine: it was full, but Payne had the feeling DeSantos already knew that. DeSantos reached into a shoulder holster and removed an equally compact Beretta 92; again, he checked the magazine. Satisfied, he replaced it and withdrew a stiletto. Even in the muted green glow from the cockpit instrumentation, the blade was imposing. Whatever Hector DeSantos's background—Payne guessed the Green Berets—this man was prepared for action.

Payne patted his chest and felt his Glock securely seated in his shoulder harness. Although he had the Bureau's most technologically advanced handgun and a spare magazine, he felt oddly underpowered.

"Fifteen seconds to intercept." The pilot's voice came through their headphones and instantly sent DeSantos and Waller into action. They moved toward the back door of the right side of the aircraft and steadied themselves as the helicopter descended rapidly behind the Lincoln Navigator, tilting with its nose up, like a large bird swooping in for a landing.

Payne felt his stomach tighten. Just ahead of them now was the man who had wreaked so much havoc on his life . . . the man who destroyed his promising career, the man who was responsible for separating him from his wife and daughter . . . and again, for severing his ties with Lauren. The emotional pain was great, the desire for revenge building as they neared Scarponi's vehicle.

Knox turned to the pilot. "Bring us down faster!" He looked back at the approaching SUV. "Get ready to drop," he said into his mike; DeSantos and Waller knew Knox was talking to them.

As the Black Hawk descended to within thirty feet, DeSantos slid the door open. He removed his headset and tossed it on the seat behind him. He pulled a black woolen mask over his face, then leaned partially out of the passenger compartment.

Cold air struck his face with a vengeance, but the mask absorbed most of its wrath. DeSantos glanced over at the pilot, who was attempting to level off the chopper while keeping the speed steady at seventy miles per hour. It was now directly above the Navigator.

"Ready?" DeSantos yelled.

"Ready!" Waller said.

Scarponi felt the unmistakable vibratory thumping above and instantly knew what it meant. "Chopper!"

"Got it," McCabe said. He grabbed for the bazooka and felt around in his canvas bag for another armor-piercing rocket.

Daniels moved to the passenger's-side window and steadied his MP5 submachine gun. "I'm on it." He took aim and fired.

The nine-millimeter rounds pinged loudly off the skin of the Black Hawk as the pilot instinctively pulled up on the stick. The helicopter tilted suddenly, sending DeSantos and Waller reeling backward, into the passenger compartment. "Shit," DeSantos said as he struggled to right himself.

Payne moved toward the still-open door just as Knox was shouting at the pilot through his headset: "No! Descend—back over the car!"

"We've been hit—we have to assess damage," the pilot shouted back.

"Assess later," Knox yelled. "Get us back down there!"

The pilot dipped the craft, nose down, flying an erratic pattern as Waller, who had gotten his feet back beneath him, began firing off rounds at the phantom shooter in the Navigator. Just then, a bullet pierced the front right portion of the windshield. The pilot slumped to the side, moving the control stick, sending the helicopter veering off to the right, away from their intended target.

"Pilot's been hit," Knox shouted as he pulled the man off the stick.

"How bad?" Waller asked.

DeSantos reached over and turned the pilot's head, exposing the oozing wound in his skull.

"His flying days are over."

Waller climbed into the front and helped Knox move the pilot out of the cockpit as DeSantos settled himself into the command seat. He quickly brought the chopper back in line with the Navigator and increased the airspeed to resume their pursuit.

Seconds later, they were once again directly above the SUV. More gunfire pocked and pierced the copter's metal skin. DeSantos kept the nose up, knowing from experience that the airframe of the Black Hawk was better suited to taking on close-range gunfire than its cockpit or hydraulic pumps.

Waller squeezed off a few rounds, then held his fire as the sniper had apparently retreated back into the car's cab.

"DeSantos has to fly the bird," Waller said to Knox. "Am I going in alone?"

Knox adjusted his headset and helped DeSantos reseat his. "No, stay where you are. Hector, keep us out of range for a minute. Anyone have any useful ideas? I'll consider anything."

"If we had Hellfire missiles strapped to the side of this bird like we had in Desert Storm," DeSantos said, "I could recommend a bunch of options."

"Come up alongside," Waller said, "let me get a good look at the sniper. I may be able to take him out."

"Unacceptable. You might hit Scarponi and I want him alive." There was silence for a moment, and then Knox threw a switch on the control panel. "Hector, are you on my frequency?"

"Here, chief."

"Raise Rodman and Hodges on the SATphone. Apprise them of our status and tell them to be ready. We're going to have to deviate from our plan."

"Acknowledged."

Knox hit the switch again and was back on the general frequency that was compatible with Waller's headset.

DeSantos twisted his body and reached behind his seat to pull the satellite phone from his rucksack, then turned back and faced Knox. "Hate to say this, chief, but we've got another problem." DeSantos nodded to the rear compartment of the Black Hawk.

Knox and Waller turned around. The three of them shared a disturbed look when they saw that the cabin was empty.

Payne was gone.

SEVENTY-TWO

I'm hit," Daniels struggled to say as he pressed his right hand against a bleeding chest wound.

Scarponi cursed, then swerved to the right and left, driving erratically to prevent the agents in the helicopter from getting off any more lucky potshots at them. "How long?" he shouted at McCabe.

"Ready—open it up! All I need is one look." He tilted the smoothbore tube of the rocket launcher toward the ceiling, and Scarponi pressed the button that retracted the moon roof. Just as it began sliding open, a loud thump caught their attention. They all looked up simultaneously. Something—*someone*—was on top of the vehicle.

Payne was lying facedown on the Navigator, his fingers digging into the cold, slick metal top, reaching for the rail of the luggage rack. He lifted his head into the wind and saw, inches from his face, a stitch of light growing wider as the moon roof slid open.

"Shit," he said into the wind as he struggled to hold on with his left hand and both feet while he reached into his leather jacket for the Glock. A large tube was emerging from the opening, pointed skyward. *Jesus Christ, the launcher.* Payne yanked his handgun and took out the slack in the tensioned trigger. He shoved the weapon through the moon roof, alongside the bazooka, down into the passenger compartment. And began firing randomly.

The car swerved violently to the left, then to the right, and he knew his efforts had had an impact. He was so intently focused on struggling to hold on to the top of the vehicle that ten rounds had exploded from his gun before he realized the tube of the launcher had disappeared from the opening.

Payne suddenly became aware of the proximity of the Black Hawk above him—until more weapons fire popped in the wind—coming from the SUV's rear window—and the helicopter once again retreated back into the darkness . . . but not before turning on its brilliant spotlight, adding an eerie illumination to the Navigator, which now seemed to be traveling at greater than ninety miles an hour.

"Stay with them," Knox shouted. "Keep back a hundred feet and weave so they can't get a fix on us." He rubbed his temples and began tapping his foot, the insatiable desire to pace forcing him to find some other form of stimulation. He slipped on his infrared goggles, zeroed in on Payne, and gasped. "Holy mother of Mary. He's going to get himself killed. What the hell is he doing?"

DeSantos was busy with the controls, maintaining the desired distance while flying an unconventional, erratic pattern. "With all due respect, chief, we've become Captain Ahab. And the whale is doing his best to get away."

"The hunter and the hunted?"

DeSantos nodded.

"Then let's act like a hunter. Take us in."

• • •

His fingers were painfully numb. Payne's arm and shoulder muscles burned as he strained to maintain his grip on the rails. At the moment, he had many enemies: the driving wind, the light but slippery rain, the shifting movements of the SUV . . . and his chief foe, Anthony Scarponi, who was attempting to shake him loose.

But when the bullets started popping through the Navigator's roof to either side of him, his comfort level plunged significantly—not that it was high to begin with. It was stupid for him to have jumped from the chopper, but he was not about to let Scarponi get away. For his future with Lauren to amount to something more than just a life on the run, he needed to stop Scarponi. Here, and now.

Payne grabbed the edge of the moon roof with his left hand and returned fire. The SUV swerved abruptly and tossed Payne to the right, his hand catching the luggage rack as his legs slid over the passenger side of the vehicle. Dangling in front of the window.

He reached down with his Glock and fired blindly into the Navigator, the tempered glass shattering and crumbling to pieces. With nothing left to do but attack, he swung his legs into the front seat.

And let go of his grip on the roof.

SEVENTY-THREE

Now, some may say that coming face-to-face with a man whose sworn purpose in life is to kill you is a form of suicide. But for Harper Payne, it was his only means of staying alive.

His feet landed firmly on the front seat, but his buttocks struck the open window hard and sent a shock wave of pain up his spine. He grabbed on to the top of the doorframe—and the Glock flew from his right hand. Where it landed—inside the cab, outside on the asphalt—he didn't know. What he did know is that the person behind the wheel was Anthony Scarponi, and he was smiling. Smiling, no doubt, because the man he had struggled to find for so many years had suddenly delivered himself.

Scarponi pressed two buttons on the steering wheel and then swung at Payne, whose attention was diverted for an instant by the clearly dead bodies of two men in the backseat, their torsos punctured quite thoroughly by Payne's nine-millimeter rounds.

The punch landed squarely on Payne's jaw, sending him backward into the door. Scarponi climbed out from behind the wheel and grabbed Payne's arm—the Navigator was obviously tooling along on cruise control, as stopping meant coming under attack from the agents in the helicopter.

Payne shook his arm free and landed a jab to Scarponi's nose, driving him against the steering wheel. Scarponi bounced right back at him and was about to throw a punch when suddenly the Navigator careened off the road, crossed over the shoulder, and continued on through dense underbrush. Scarponi fell backward against the dash.

They both grabbed each other by the throat, hate seeping from their pores like perspiration. "Die, you fucking bastard!" Scarponi croaked, Payne's hands cutting into his vocal cords.

The pressure was building inside Payne's head. He could feel the veins in his temples bulging and he began feeling light-headed. He tried to kick with his feet, but one leg was pinned beneath the dashboard and the other was caught by the steering wheel.

Just then, the Black Hawk circled around to the front of the SUV, banking and sideslipping so its spotlight could burn through the windshield and illuminate the two men as if they were actors on a stage.

Although Payne was aware of the helicopter, he knew they could do nothing to help him. The stench of burning oil and a thin fog of smoke began bleeding into the car's interior, stinging his eyes. Through the haze, Scarponi's eyes were filled with fury. "I treated you like a brother!"

"I was . . . doing . . . my job."

"I've got a job to do, too," Scarponi said. As if the anger had infused him with a sudden burst of strength, he lifted Payne up by the neck and smashed his head against the door.

Pinpricks of agony exploded in Payne's mind as he fought to maintain consciousness.

"My job," Scarponi yelled, "is to kill you!"

The Navigator banged and thumped along the rough brush, each jolt forcing Scarponi's hands deeper into his adversary's neck. Payne struggled to maintain his own grip on Scarponi's throat, but he felt his grasp weakening. Thoughts screamed through his oxygen-deprived brain. *Do something now or die! Squeeze harder or pry his hands away!*

He chose the latter.

But the instant he released his grip from Scarponi's neck, he realized it was the wrong decision.

With Payne's arms no longer restraining his head, Scarponi coiled back, then rammed his skull into Payne's forehead.

SEVENTY-FOUR

DeSantos watched in horror as he saw the assassin's hands around Harper Payne's throat. But not until Waller screamed did he realize just how awful the situation really was.

"Engine's on fire!"

Flames danced from beneath the Navigator's hood as the SUV plowed through the dense underbrush.

"How fast are they going?" Knox asked.

DeSantos glanced at his airspeed, which was holding at 70 knots. "About eighty," he shouted.

Waller leaned into the front seat. "We've got to stop it and get Payne out of there before it blows."

"I'll bring us about, you take out the tires," DeSantos yelled. As the chopper maneuvered alongside the SUV, Waller leaned out the doorway and fired off several rounds, puncturing tires and sending the vehicle into a frenzy, bouncing hard as it slowed to a still-torrid fifty-five miles per hour.

"Trees!" Knox said.

DeSantos pulled on the cyclic and the helicopter immediately strained skyward. Knox's face sagged in anguish when he turned and saw the thicket up ahead of the Navigator, seconds away from impact. As they ascended above the height of the trees, DeSantos closed his eyes and waited for the sound of crunching steel, knowing there was absolutely nothing he could do.

Knox motioned toward the clearing in front of the thicket. "Get us down, get us down!"

DeSantos lowered the craft rapidly and set it amongst the brush thirty yards from the Navigator. The SUV was a crumpled mass of metal, its engine compartment wrapped around a large-trunked spruce. Smoke billowed up into the soupy night air as flames engulfed the entire front end and seared the lower branches of the neighboring trees.

Knox remained in the helicopter and radioed their position as DeSantos and Waller ran toward the flaming wreckage, guns in hand, anticipating . . . just about anything.

Waller knew there wasn't time to follow established procedure, and judging by the look on DeSantos's face, he was not alone in that thought. They hurdled a fallen fir tree and were immediately hit by a plume of thick black smoke. DeSantos fell to his knees in a coughing fit. Waller stumbled but continued on, approaching the wreck in a crouched position.

He grabbed the door handle and pulled it open.

SEVENTY-FIVE

Harper Payne fell out of the SUV's front seat and landed against Waller, who was knocked backward to the ground. Waller gulped a mouthful of air, filling his lungs with smoke. He rolled to his side, attempting to move out from beneath the weight of Payne's body, knowing that Scarponi could emerge from the interior at any second, firing at will. But his lungs exploded in a fit of violent hacking, and he was unable to move.

Just then, DeSantos appeared through the thick black fog and grasped Payne's body by the armpits. Freed of the weight on his chest, Waller was able to get to his feet and help pull Payne twenty yards from the wreck, where the density of the smoke was thinner. The cleaner air helped Waller, as his coughing subsided enough that he was able to catch his breath.

DeSantos groped for his comrade's wrist to check for a pulse. Satisfied that Payne was still alive, he nodded at Waller and they shifted position, each grabbing one of Payne's arms and slinging it over their shoulders. They carried him between them another ten yards, toward the helicopter.

"Medevac is on the way. ETA two minutes," Knox shouted above the noise of the rotors. "He okay?"

"Don't know—he's unconscious," Waller said. They set Payne's body on the ground, faceup.

"I'm going back in," DeSantos said, disappearing into the black fog in search of Scarponi.

"I hope he knows what he's doing," Waller said to Knox, the thump-thump-thump of the chopper's blades drowning out much of their conversation.

"I owe him the chance to prove that he does," Knox shouted back.

With a handkerchief acting as a crude—and only minimally effective—filter for his nose and mouth, DeSantos fought through the smoke, groping his way around the interior of the Navigator. His Beretta was in his right hand, ready to fire. He attempted to slow his respirations to maximize the amount of time he could remain in the toxic environment. If all went as he hoped, he would find Scarponi's dead body, then retreat to safety.

But his desires faded quickly as he found the interior of the SUV to be vacant, aside from a couple of corpses in the backseat that did not fit Scarponi's description. DeSantos began coughing, his makeshift filter no longer effective. He turned and began running, but tripped on a thick object—a fallen branch? A piece from the wreckage? *A leg?*

Waller was crouched next to Payne's body, again checking his pulse. He had completed a cursory exam—at least from what he could recall of his first aid training—and found a possible fracture of Payne's left forearm and fresh abrasions and bruises about his face. His pulse was weak and his skin clammy. Other than that, Waller could not glean much else from his limited knowledge.

He glanced at his watch, then felt the rumble of another helicopter. He looked skyward and saw the spotlight of a medevac chopper emerge from behind the canopy of the trees. As the emergency vehicle began to descend, someone came running toward them from inside the swirling plume of darkness.

Waller drew his weapon—but in that instant a deafeningly loud explosion of heat and light burst from the smoking wreck. Metal pieces blew upward and outward, fiery pieces of the SUV's interior blasting in all directions as two smaller explosions ripped through the wooded area.

The approaching helicopter retreated, quickly gaining altitude. Waller was using his body to cover Payne while Knox was somewhere to his right, hugging the ground. As the metal and rubber fragments landed, small fires began burning in a scattered pattern throughout the field. A few smoldering pieces struck the idling Black Hawk before impotently falling to the ground.

DeSantos emerged from the periphery of the explosions, his clothes torn and his face covered in black soot. He stumbled toward the Black Hawk as the medevac attempted to land forty yards to the east.

Knox got to his feet, met DeSantos at the cockpit door, and yelled, "Scarponi?"

"Not there. Two other bodies, best I could see." DeSantos climbed into the helicopter and began throwing switches. The rotors began accelerating to full speed. Out of the corner of his eye, Knox saw the medevac personnel approaching on the run from their own helicopter, a stretcher spread between them. To their left was another figure, breaking off from the paramedics and heading toward the Black Hawk.

"Where are you going?" Knox shouted to DeSantos.

"To pay off a debt."

"Hector—"

"I'm going to find the son of a bitch."

Just then, the approaching man came up alongside Knox. Knox grabbed his arm and pulled him close so he could be heard over the spinning rotor blades. "Rodman, go with Hector. I want Scarponi alive."

Troy Rodman nodded, then ran to the other side of the cockpit and climbed into the front passenger seat. He lifted a pair of infrared goggles off a knob on the control panel and fastened the visor to his head.

Knox banged on the window beside DeSantos's face. "Alive, Hector, I want him alive!"

Knox backed away and the bird lifted off. He ran toward Payne and Waller, where the paramedics had assessed Payne, started an IV line, and hooked him up to oxygen.

"I'm going with Payne in the medevac," Knox said to Waller. "You stay here. Backup should be here any minute. Fill them in on what happened." Knox trotted off toward the other helicopter, following the medics as they loaded the stretcher into the chopper. He had known when he signed on as FBI director there would be a certain amount of risk. But he had always thought the risk would be more from a stress-induced heart attack than from racing above the Virginia countryside in a helicopter chasing an escaped felon. That just wasn't part of the job description.

As the bird lifted off, he was still feeling the pump of adrenaline. What other FBI director would get himself into a situation like this? The lift from the blades brought the sensation of weightlessness, of being outside his body . . . kind of the way he felt when taking his morning runs. In response to his own question, he shook his head. The answer was obvious: no other director would do such a thing. But then again, no other FBI director had been army Special Forces in Vietnam. No other director was Douglas Knox.

SEVENTY-SIX

The medevac helicopter descended from the dark, windswept heavens and hit its mark on the helipad beside the Vandenheim Air Force Base Security Police Building, a stone's throw from the adjacent military hospital. Knox leapt from the rear door of the chopper into intense brightness, as a circle of round mercury spotlights were trained on the landing pad. Before he took a step, he was met by several FBI agents and a contingent of Security Police in crisp, well-turned-out uniforms and polished boots. Bringing up the rear were two fatigue-clad men who headed straight for the director.

"Hodges and Ventura," Knox yelled above the din of the Black Hawk's blades, "when you're done with Agent Payne's body, meet me at Hangar Three-Fourteen." The two OPSIG agents, colleagues of DeSantos, Archer, and Rodman's, nodded and proceeded into the rear compartment of the helicopter.

Surrounded by the agents and police detail, Knox was ushered into the Security Police Building and through the armory, a rectangular room that was rimmed with stalls outfitted with military garb: bulletproof vests, helmets, two-way radios, and an assortment of paraphernalia a small troop would need heading into an emergency situation.

Knox entered the large assembly room and stopped. He gave a quick look around at the mass of security personnel and nodded. "Okay. Bring our guests in here," he said to one of the security cops.

Lauren Chambers sat beside Nick Bradley on a wooden bench in a small anteroom. When they had been escorted there shortly after their arrival, they were told they had to wait, as Harper Payne was being brought via ambulance to rendezvous with them at the base. Security Police were abundant, guarding every Entry Control Point and select areas in between.

They had sat for almost two hours without receiving so much as one update from the security cops. Lauren repeatedly asked for information, but each time she was told to sit down and wait patiently—or leave. Still, she knew they would not have allowed her to come there if they hadn't intended to reunite her with Michael. Otherwise, what was the point? The government had their witness back, and whether or not Michael wanted to testify, at least he was safe. He could do his deed for the U.S. Attorney and then be free to go wherever he wished. Or so she hoped.

Suddenly, movement was everywhere. Several security cops moved into the room and two moved out. Three converged on one another near the far doorway and spoke in hushed tones, their rigid postures a sign of their training rather than the particular urgency of the situation, she figured. A moment later, one of the policemen turned to face them.

"Come with me," he said, then ushered them down a long, spotless hallway.

They entered the assembly room and were led to a tall, silver-haired man, who was pacing in front of a closed door. His face was stern and stressed. He stopped in his tracks and looked at Bradley, completely ignoring Lauren's presence. He nodded at two agents who had come up behind Bradley, then simply said, "Take him away."

"What's this about?" Bradley asked as one of the men snapped handcuffs on his wrists.

"You're under arrest."

"For what?"

"Wait a minute," Lauren said, "he's with me. There must be some kind of mistake."

Another agent took hold of her arms and pulled her backward, out of the way. "There's no mistake."

"Please, Dr. Chambers, don't interfere," the man with the silver hair said.

The agents pulled a struggling Bradley through a set of doors ten feet away as he continued to argue with them. "I didn't do anything . . ."

The metal door closed behind them and the room was suddenly quiet again.

"What's going on? Who are you?" Lauren demanded.

"FBI director Douglas Knox."

"Where's my husband, where's Michael?"

"It gets very complicated, Dr. Chambers." Knox placed a hand on the crook of her elbow and indicated he wanted her to walk with him to a bench along the far wall. "If you'll take a seat and allow me to explain—"

"I'm not interested in sitting," she said, yanking her arm away. "And I'm not interested in talking. I just want to know where my husband is, Mr. Knox. I've been waiting here for two hours. Now either tell me where Michael is or I'll go to the press and tell them what I know!" Her face felt blush red.

"And what exactly is it that you know?" Knox asked quizzically.

Lauren thought for a moment before answering. "I know that my husband isn't dead."

"Interesting. You'd tell them that, without knowing the whole story?"

"I'd tell them just about anything if it would make you tell me the truth!"

"Fine," Knox said, his brow bunched with anger. "We'll do it your way. You want to know where your husband is? He's dead, Dr. Chambers, that's where he is!"

Knox's voice echoed in the painted cinder-block room. The scores of agents and Security Police were still. No one moved, no one spoke, no one seemed to breathe.

Lauren stood there looking at Knox, unsure whether he was telling her the truth. "That was just a story for the media, so Scarponi would stop trying to kill him." Though she did not intend to project her uncertainty, there was a waver in her voice.

Knox stepped closer to her. "And who told you that?"

"Nick, Nick Bradley, the man you just arrested."

Knox's mouth curled into a disparaging frown. "That man is a mole, Dr. Chambers, a spy. We've been after him for six years. He's been using you to get to your husband. I wouldn't trust anything he told you."

Lauren's eyes darted around the room, touching each of the men surrounding her in the periphery. *Was this possible? Could Nick be a spy?* Suddenly her mind was a flurry of thoughts . . .

all the inconsistencies in Bradley's stories . . .

the fact that Michael was not just her husband, but really an FBI agent and an assassin . . .

*and now Bradley—someone she'd come to know so well,
someone she had come to trust—was actually a spy who'd
been using her?*

She looked up at the FBI director and forced certainty into her voice. "Nick Bradley is a small-time private investigator in Placerville, California."

"That's his cover. He was working with someone else here in Washington. That's all I can tell you."

"No, that can't be right. You've got it all wrong."

"Look, Dr. Chambers. I know that learning your husband is dead is a terrible shock. You came here thinking you were going to see him. We had to allow the situation to play itself out so we could get Bradley here. That's why we chose this location as a rendezvous point. There isn't a place much more secure than an air force base. Once Bradley was in here, there'd be no way for him to escape. It was a perfect plan, if you ask me."

"Enough lies! Michael's not dead and Nick's not a spy."

Knox sighed, shook his head, then folded his arms across his chest. "I'm going against my better judgment in telling you this, but maybe it'll put your mind at ease that I've given you full disclosure. It's absolutely essential you don't repeat anything I'm about to tell you. Not ever. Do I have your word?"

"Of course." She would have agreed to just about anything at this point to get at the truth.

"Okay. Yes, we did release disinformation to the press describing Agent Payne's death in the shootout at Fredericksburg. Truth is, he was only superficially wounded. But this evening, while we were transferring him to this facility, he was engaged in an operation designed to assist us in apprehending a dangerous fugitive, the man you mentioned before— Anthony Scarponi. Against my direct orders, he leaped from our helicopter and attempted to subdue Scarponi, who was in a sports utility vehicle below us. Scarponi's car went out of control and your husband was severely injured. A medevac helicopter was summoned at twenty-one hundred hours and he died en route, presumably from internal injuries directly related to the impact. I'm sorry."

Lauren felt the life drain from her body. Her shoulders slumped and she was light-headed.

"I can arrange for you to get some counseling, if you would like. At the moment, I have to brief the president. Agent Haviland," Knox called to a man standing off to the side, "can you please take care of Dr. Chambers?" He turned back to Lauren. "Agent Haviland will see to your needs."

Lauren composed herself as Knox headed toward the door. She couldn't let him leave, not yet, not without having some form of confirmation that what he had told her was true. "Wait," she said, starting after him. "If Michael's dead, I want to see his body."

Knox stopped and swung his body around dubiously, as if it were a bother to have to continue dealing with her. "Fine, I'll see if it can be arranged. Maybe sometime tomorrow afternoon."

Lauren lunged forward with the alacrity of a cat, grabbing Knox's lapels with both hands. "I've had enough of your bullshit," she yelled. "I want to see my husband *now!*" Her eyes were blazing with anger, her skin clammy with fear.

Four men were upon her a split second later, instantly unlatching her grip on the director using a pressure point on her thumbs. She struggled with the agents, but was unable to break their hold.

"Let her go," Knox said calmly.

The men instantly released their grips but did not move from where they stood: at the ready, poised to immediately neutralize another outburst.

The click of a door opening behind Knox drew everyone's attention. A stocky black man walked in and nodded to the director, whose face appeared to brighten.

"Rodman," Knox said to the man, "are we ready?"

"Yes, sir."

Knox looked over at one of the agents off to his left. "Agent Haviland, escort Dr. Chambers to Hangar One-Nineteen so she can see Agent Payne's body. I'll meet up with her as soon as I'm finished with my call to the president."

"Thank you," Lauren said.

Knox turned and walked out of the room.

SEVENTY-SEVEN

Lauren was transported by Agent Haviland to Hangar 119 in a small motorized vehicle. After being admitted through the Entry Control Point by a young, efficient guard, they drove along the flight line as fast as the small cart could carry them. Twelve-foot-high fences topped off with barbed wire were visible in the diffuse lighting, while elsewhere red ropes hung at waist height clearly delineating restricted areas. A vaporous after-rain haze hung lazily around the security lights that sat like centurions atop tall metal posts, giving the base a desolate, lonely feel.

As they rode, Lauren tried hard to contain her swirling storm of thoughts. Finally, realizing this might be her last chance to extract a morsel of information that could provide some insight into the events surrounding Michael's demise, she decided she had nothing to lose. Unfortunately, Haviland stubbornly professed ignorance. "I can't tell you any more than Director Knox has, ma'am. Off the record, though, I enjoyed working with Harper. Your husband was very good at what he did. You have my condolences."

Lauren acknowledged his comments but told him she was in no mood for eulogies. "Just take me to see my husband, Agent Haviland. That's all I want."

"Yes, ma'am."

"And it's *doctor*. Enough of this *ma'am* crap." Lauren was still angry, but she was proud of herself, too. None of the fears or overwhelming urges that had crippled her for so many years had stopped her. She had defeated them. She had turned the corner.

Lauren looked up and saw that Haviland had driven them into what appeared to be a maintenance hangar of some sort, judging by all the tools and dissected engine parts lining the west wall. Above the assorted machined fittings and painted pieces was fire-fighting equipment: extinguishers, hoses, axes, alarm bells. Across the way, an eye washbasin sat beside an unmanned Maintenance Control Booth. In fact, no one was around, something that struck her as odd.

Haviland turned along the painted lines and stopped in a yellow zone, behind a parked military ambulance. He nodded at the back of the vehicle. "Someone will take you to your husband's body. Good luck, Dr. Chambers."

Lauren climbed out of the small electric cart and walked over to the rear of the ambulance. Haviland made a U-turn and drove off into the distance, heading for the exit. Lauren turned back to the vehicle, took a deep breath, and pulled the door open.

SEVENTY-EIGHT

Hangar 314 was cold and quiet. Knox completed his briefing call to the president and provided all the details at his disposal: Scarponi's fugitive standing, the plans under way to locate him, and of course, Harper Payne's status. It was a tough call to make, but the charade had gone on long enough. He knew that at this time of night the president would not want to keep him on the line debating his tactics, lamenting what had gone wrong, or chewing him out for failing to disclose Scarponi's escape months ago, when it had first occurred. Plus, Knox had the perfect excuse for not having delivered the news in person.

The director had made the call in a small, glass-enclosed office. Getting up from the wooden chair afterward was a chore. He was mentally and physically tired, he was filthy from the mixture of sweat and dirt, and his throat was raw from the soot and other small particulates that had blown off the exploding Navigator and resulting forest fire. But most of all, he was just plain tired. Tired of all the stealth, all the details and secrets he had to keep straight, and all the political maneuverings he had to make.

He trudged toward the military transport vehicle that was waiting for him against the east wall of the hangar. After he slammed the door, the driver started the engine and drove off.

Lauren climbed into the back of the ambulance and the door clicked shut behind her, leaving her in complete darkness. "Hello?"

Suddenly, the vehicle began to move, throwing her backward. She fell and landed on the floor against the padded bench that ran the length of the interior. She pulled herself up and sat down. "Is anyone here?"

Again, no one answered. She made her way in the dark toward the front of the ambulance and felt around for a window of some sort that would give her access to the driver. There was nothing. She banged on the wall. "Where are you taking me?"

The lack of a response did not surprise her. In fact, it fit in quite well with her already bizarre week. The ambulance continued on for another few minutes, at which point it seemed to leave the paved roads of the base for something that felt more like a secondary artery of some sort.

With the vehicle bouncing and swaying as it navigated the uneven terrain, Lauren held the bench with both hands, staring into the darkness. At this point, all she cared about was getting answers. Answers about Michael, about Bradley, about the rest of her life. She needed closure.

The ambulance listed left before coming to a lurching stop. The rear door opened and the stocky man she had seen a short time ago in the assembly room climbed in. He reached above his head and flipped a switch, bathing the interior in light. "Agent Troy Rodman. I was with Director Knox—"

"Where's my husband?"

Rodman looked at her a long moment, as if he were sizing her up. He then reached over to the front wall and banged on it twice with a fist. The ambulance began moving again.

"There are some things we need to discuss first, Dr. Chambers."

Lauren looked away. "I don't have anything to say to you."

"But I have some things to say to you. And I think you'll want to hear them." Rodman sat down beside her. "Approximately eight years ago, Harper Payne was an FBI agent who went deep undercover to infiltrate the organization of a prolific international hit man, Anthony Scarponi. He worked with Scarponi for two years before the Bureau pulled him out and terminated his assignment. He testified against Scarponi and a list of Scarponi's 'customers' and put them all behind bars. That was six years ago.

"After the trial, Agent Payne was placed in the Federal Witness Protection Program. He remained in it for a year or so, then dropped out of sight. A few months ago, Scarponi's attorneys came up with a new witness they said would contradict all of Payne's testimony. The judge bought their story and the Bureau knew it would have to somehow find Payne so he could testify again. But finding him wasn't easy.

"After searching for weeks, the Bureau received a tip that proved promising. Agents were dispatched to Placerville, and they began observing your husband."

"How could I not have known that Michael was once an FBI agent?"

"Things are not always what they appear to be, Dr. Chambers." Rodman inched forward on the bench and angled his body to face hers. "Think for a moment.

What did you know of Michael's life before you met him five years ago? And of what you *did* know, how much of it did he himself tell you, and how do you know what he told you is true?"

Rodman paused for a moment, and when Lauren started to answer, he held up a hand. "That was a rhetorical question, Dr. Chambers. Point is, we don't always know the person we think we know so well. This is how the CIA operates. Its operatives are everyday people. The person at the phone company, the attorney in Pocatello, Idaho. Perhaps your gynecologist. The Agency uses these people *because* they're everyday people. They can go on business trips and carry out intelligence missions and no one will ever suspect them. For security reasons—theirs as well as the Agency's—even their spouses don't know they do covert work."

Lauren folded her arms across her chest. "You're saying I didn't know my husband well enough?"

"I'm saying that things are not what they appear to be."

Just then, the ambulance turned sharply and pulled to an abrupt stop.

"Why are we stopping?"

"We're picking up a passenger," Rodman said.

The back door swung open and Nick Bradley climbed into the rear compartment. Lauren sat there, her head tilted in confusion. "I don't understand," she finally managed just before Bradley sat down opposite her. "Knox arrested you, he said you were a spy."

"That was all a show, for my protection. It had to look convincing, in case there are other moles." Bradley turned to Rodman. "I take it you haven't told her yet."

"Not yet."

"Told me what?" She looked back and forth between the two men. "Look, I've had enough! One of you better start giving me some answers. No more top secret CIA garbage. I want the truth, Nick, and I want it now."

"You're absolutely right," Bradley said. "I owe you an explanation." He looked away and said, "I owe you more than an explanation, but for the moment it'll have to do." He unzipped his leather jacket and leaned back. "When Carla Mae called me and told me about the Neighborhood Watch meeting she'd arranged for you, it didn't seem any different from all the other meetings she'd gotten together over the past two years. She told me your husband was missing and asked if I could come by early in the afternoon and help put up the fliers. When I showed up and saw Michael's photo, I suddenly realized that you had something that could help *me*."

"What do you mean? What did I have that could possibly help you?"

Bradley looked at Rodman, then at Lauren. "Your husband."

Lauren cocked her head. "Nick, what the hell are you talking about? I didn't have my husband, that was the whole problem."

"I know you didn't, but that was the beauty of it. I knew you would go looking for Michael. You had to, any person who wanted her spouse back would have. Just like I knew you'd look for him, I knew Scarponi would look for him as well."

"Scarponi? What's he got to do with this?"

"Scarponi wanted Harper Payne dead. Kill Payne, and there's no one left to testify against him. He's a free man. Right?"

Lauren nodded.

"So as soon as Scarponi is released from prison, who does he go after?" Bradley spread his hands apart, as if the answer was obvious. "He goes after Harper Payne. He's looking for him just like the feds are looking for him. Only Scarponi lets the feds do the work for him. He's got a mole planted in the Bureau, tracking their progress. When they figure out that Harper Payne is in Placerville, bang—the feds dispatch agents and Scarponi dispatches his men. But Michael's gone on his trip and the feds regroup, track him down, and snatch him up, sort of. But Scarponi doesn't know the feds have Payne. He's a smart guy, so he knows his best way to get to Payne is you. All he has to do is watch you, follow you, tease and torment you, and you'll lead him to what he's seeking."

"So that answers what Scarponi wanted with me. What about you? What did you want with him?"

"To be completely honest, I wanted Scarponi dead. I knew that if I hung out with you, he'd eventually come around looking for Michael. And even if he didn't, you'd lead me to Michael, and then I could use Michael as bait. Either way, I'd meet up with Scarponi and get my shot."

"You used me," Lauren said, her hands gripping the bench tighter. "All that stuff about being my big brother and my guardian angel, about the child of yours that you lost, all of that was bullshit."

"No, no, it wasn't, Lauren. At least, well . . . okay, in the beginning it was. I apologize for that. But as I got to know you, you became more of a person I cared about rather than just a means to an end. That's when things got a little out of hand for me, because I got personally involved. That was my biggest mistake."

"And my biggest mistake was trusting you."

Bradley held up a hand. "That's not what I meant. In law enforcement, you lose your edge, your effectiveness, when you can't think objectively. I lost my objective edge when I started caring about what happened to you."

Lauren was silent for a moment, thinking through what Bradley had told her. "Even if I can get past that, which I'm not sure I can, I still don't understand what was in it for you. What was this all about? Why did you want Scarponi so badly?"

"Can't I just say that it was important to me and leave it at that?"

"No, Nick, you can't. You owe me the truth."

"You're placing me in a tough spot, Lauren."

"The truth, Nick."

Bradley bowed his head for a moment, as if considering his options. Finally, he cleared his throat. "There's no easy way to say this." He looked up and met her tired eyes. "Lauren, I'm Harper Payne."

SEVENTY-NINE

Lauren's jaw went slack as she just sat there, staring at him. The truck hit a pothole and shook her from her daze. "You're what?"

Bradley leaned forward and rested his forearms on his knees. "I was the man the FBI was looking for when they came to Placerville. Your husband bears a striking resemblance to what I looked like before I had my second session of plastic surgery. The marshal's office supplied the Bureau with a photo that was taken after I'd seen their surgeon. Because I knew that photo existed, and because I'd learned to trust no one, I had a second operation no one knew about. Michael looks like I did before the second surgery."

"So the FBI thought that my husband was you." Lauren shook her head and tried to contain her anger. With bloodshot eyes, she glared at Bradley. "Everything you told me, Nick, everything *was* a lie."

"Not everything. You have to understand—"

"I'll tell you what I understand, Nick—or Harper, or whatever the hell it is you want to be called now. Bottom line is, you used me like a pawn. That's what I understand."

"I realize you're upset with me. You have every right to be."

"And what about you, Agent Rodman? How do you fit into all of this?"

"Some information remains classified, Dr. Chambers. Like it or not, that's the way it's got to be."

"So am I supposed to assume the FBI was in on all this?"

"The Bureau was as much in the dark as you were. After agents made contact with your husband, he was involved in an automobile accident and banged his head up pretty good. The head trauma caused a great deal of memory loss. The Bureau was in a difficult position. They needed Harper Payne to testify, but he couldn't remember anything. They did their best to reeducate him."

"But the fact remains that Michael was never in the FBI. Couldn't they see that he didn't have the skills? Wasn't there something that tipped them off that they had the wrong person?"

"Michael spent eight years with the Army National Guard's SoCom, short for Southern Command," Bradley said. "That's where the skills came from that the Bureau mistook for his prior FBI training."

"Michael was never in the National Guard," Lauren said.

Rodman raised an eyebrow. "Goes to what I was saying before, about how much we really know about our loved ones."

"It was twelve years ago," Bradley said.

"I don't understand. If you were the Agent Payne they needed to make the government's case, why didn't you just step in and take his place?"

"At first, I didn't know what was going down. I really did leave the Witness Protection Program, so I was out of touch with everything and everyone. I don't read the papers and I don't watch TV. I live in a small town and keep a low profile. But the second I saw Michael's photo on that flyer, I thought I knew what had happened. Someone, probably working for Scarponi, screwed up and mistook Michael for me."

"So if you knew that, why didn't you do something?"

"Because I was guessing, because I didn't know where Michael was. Just like you, I didn't know what had happened to him. For all I knew, Scarponi could've killed him. I had to find out."

"You could've gone to the FBI."

"I spent years trying to distance myself from the government because contact with them could put my life in danger. So it was a selfish decision. Like I said before, I thought I could use you and Michael to get at Scarponi."

"After the incident in Fredericksburg," Rodman said, "Agent Payne contacted us. One of my colleagues acted as the go-between."

"Where's my husband's body?"

Bradley consulted his watch. "Lauren, please let us finish. We don't have much time."

"Time? For what?"

Rodman took a seat next to Bradley, opposite Lauren. "Dr. Chambers, please listen. Director Knox had suspicions that your husband wasn't really Agent Payne. Something showed up on a physical exam that didn't make sense. A heart murmur that the real Agent Payne didn't have. But the director didn't have any choice. He had to go along with the charade until he could put all the pieces together, to be absolutely sure. Because of the mole, the former director had Agent Payne's fingerprint card destroyed as an added precaution. There was no way to verify Knox's suspicion about your husband. Plus, the director had other pressures on him that I'm not at liberty to discuss with you."

"I started working with an agent," Bradley said, "who brought me into the operational plan that was devised to somehow fix the whole situation. By now, everything was a mess. Somehow, they needed to recapture Scarponi, while at the same time protect you and Michael in the event they weren't successful. He's a dangerous assassin, Lauren. He's had a contract out on me for several years. His people had already decided that Michael was me. It's not like the Bureau could call up Scarponi and tell him, 'Don't gun for Michael Chambers. It's really this guy Nick Bradley you want to kill.'

"But we caught a break. There was a mole in the Bureau years ago who almost got me killed. He was feeding sensitive information about my whereabouts to Scarponi. Since technology is a great deal more advanced than it was even six years ago, the Bureau was able to backtrace some internal data paths and identified who the mole was. They pummeled him for information and got his contact information for Scarponi. Then I went to work, posing as the mole. We set Scarponi up by giving him something he couldn't pass up—the chance to kill Harper Payne."

"But all loose ends had to be tied up," Rodman said.

Just then, the ambulance came to a stop. Rodman reached above him and quickly extinguished the interior light. The ambulance's rear doors opened into the pitch-black of a one-lane country road. From what Lauren could see in the darkness, nothing was around.

A man dressed in black clothing, with black paint

on his face, extended a hand toward her. "Come with me, ma'am. Quickly."

"Who are you? Where's my husband? I want to see my husband, goddamnit!"

The man in black reached in and grabbed her arm. "Please, we don't have time. It's dangerous out here. We've got to go *now*."

She did not move. "Not until you tell me where my husband is!"

He yanked her from the back of the ambulance and pulled her, with a modicum of effort, out into the darkness.

As she fought him, her eyes caught the stare of Troy Rodman. "Am I just another loose end, you son of a bitch?" She dropped down to her knees, the way a tantruming toddler does when trying to wrest himself free from his parent. "Nick, help me, please!"

The man in black clamped a large, meaty hand across her mouth.

"I'm sorry, Lauren," Bradley called after her. "I'm sorry about everything!"

EIGHTY

P ut me down!" Lauren screamed through the man's hand. She was writhing, swinging her arms wildly. She pulled out of her jacket and nearly broke free, but he grabbed her and flung her over his right shoulder like a sack of potatoes. It was raining again, and she could feel the wet pinpricks of drops pelting her bare back.

The man carried her toward an army transport vehicle parked ten feet ahead of the ambulance. The man reached out and opened the truck's back door. It was completely black inside, what the night sky would look like without the stars and the moon and the lights from surrounding cities.

Lauren was pushed inside, the door was slammed shut—and locked.

She banged on it with the open palm of her right hand, then cursed under her breath. But she suddenly realized she was not alone. Before she could speak, a bare bulb lit the interior.

Douglas Knox was sitting on a bench, partially blocking her view of the man who was beside him. But it didn't matter. Lauren knew who it was.

She ran forward into Michael's arms and he squeezed her in an embrace she didn't want him to release.

"Lauren," he whispered in her ear, "I missed you so much."

"Michael," she said, holding him tightly.

"I'm very sorry to have put you through so much grief, Dr. Chambers," Knox said. "It was necessary, to make it believable."

"Believable—"

"Michael was knocked unconscious in that car accident I told you about earlier this evening. He was examined and airlifted by special medevac personnel to the base hospital, where he was treated by a covert trauma team."

"You're making it sound worse than it is," Michael said. "I'm fine, just a little bruised—"

"He's got a fractured left forearm and, more importantly, a mild concussion," Knox said. "Which, in his current state, needs to be closely monitored."

Michael took Lauren's hand and they sat down together on the wooden bench that ran the length of the covered cargo vehicle. The truck began to move, and they all grabbed for something to hold on to.

She reached over to stroke Michael's hair and felt the lump on the side of his head, saw the bruises on his neck from Scarponi's fingers. "They told me you were dead."

"Again," Knox said, "please accept my apologies for everything we've put you through. If it's any consolation, I just received word that Anthony Scarponi was fatally wounded in a confrontation with some of my men. I guess things have a way of working themselves out."

Lauren closed her eyes and sighed. "Thank God." She rested her head against Michael's shoulder and took his hand. "Are you sure you're okay?"

"These bumps and bruises . . . they're nothing. The break will heal in a couple of months. And my memory is a whole lot better than it was even a week ago. Every day I remember more. That new knock on the head didn't screw things up too badly." He squeezed her hand. "I'm still trying to get over the shock of learning I wasn't really an FBI agent. Another identity crisis to deal with."

She smiled. "That much I can help you with."

"Most important thing is that I have you back. I was told the real Harper Payne took good care of you."

Lauren lowered her gaze. "I grew very close to him. But it's all so infuriating. It was all an act, everything he told me was a lie."

"Agent Payne thinks the world of you," Knox said. "From what he told me, you turned out to be more than he'd bargained for. He may have filled a void for you, but you filled a void for him as well. When he went into witness protection, he left behind his wife and four-year-old daughter. Leaving them was the hardest thing he's ever had to do."

"The child he lost . . . ," she mumbled.

"What?" Michael asked.

Lauren turned to Knox. "We kind of left things in a bad way. I didn't know . . . can I see him, talk to him for a moment?"

Knox glanced at Michael. "I'm afraid you'll never cross paths with Harper Payne again. He's going back underground. But thanks to you, he'll be able to see his daughter again, even if it's only on a very limited basis. His wife's remarried, but that's something he'll have to come to terms with. At least he'll be able to have contact with the ones he loves."

Lauren stared off at the dark wall behind Knox.

"You don't have to worry about him," Knox said. "As you've seen, he's a survivor. He'll deal with it." The director picked up a leather attaché from the floor and popped open the latches. "On a happier note, you and Michael have each other. I've arranged for you two to be sequestered together."

"*Sequestered?*" Lauren asked.

Knox looked from Michael to Lauren. "Benjamin Fox, meet Amy Fox. The two of you are entering witness protection."

"But if Scarponi's men think Harper Payne's dead, then Nick—I mean Harper—and Michael are safe."

Michael shook his head. "Scarponi had a very loyal, extensive network. We don't know what kind of state it's in, but it looks like he moved quickly to reassemble it. If that's the case, it's still very dangerous."

"And they think you're Payne," Lauren said.

Michael nodded. "Exactly."

"We prefer to be somewhat conservative," Knox said. "We're not taking any chances." He reached into his attaché and removed a couple of large envelopes. "Your new lives are in here. Passports, driver's licenses, bank accounts, cash, credit cards, birth certificates, the whole nine yards. You've got jobs in the town of Bellevue, Washington. Michael will be an agent with the Bureau's resident agency there. After spending all that effort on his training, we may as well get some return on our investment," Knox said wryly.

"And you're a family mediation specialist," Michael said.

"Well, I wanted a new start in life. Guess we're both getting one."

"Ben Fox has that one-syllable ring to it," Michael

said, "don't you think? Bond. James Bond. Fox. Ben Fox."

Knox smiled. "I had something else in mind. I thought Fox was a name worthy of both of you."

They looked at Knox. "How so?" Lauren asked.

"A fox uses its cunning and ability to fight off its predators out in the wild. Both of you have those qualities."

"As a family mediation specialist, they'll come in handy," Lauren said.

Just then, the truck pulled over to the side of the road and came to an abrupt stop.

"So that's it?" Lauren asked. "New life, new identities?"

Knox nodded. "That's the way it's done. The U.S. marshal's been doing it for fifty years. They've got their shit together. One of our people there arranged all of this for you. I didn't run it through the usual channels. These identities won't show up anywhere in the marshal's database. Hector DeSantos is in charge of your case. You have a problem, speak only to him. He's one of the best. His info's all in there, along with your personal bios. Read them, memorize them, then burn them."

"But our house, our belongings," Lauren said. "My clothes, my car, photos . . . Tucker—"

"Gone. Friends, family, all gone. You can never have any further contact with anyone or it could severely endanger your lives. No letters, no phone calls. Even E-mails are risky. I'll see if I can find a way of getting your dog to you, but even that's a risk."

Lauren shared a brief look of uncertainty with Michael.

The director rose and extended a hand. "Thank you,

Agent Fox, for everything." Knox moved over to Lauren, whose head was bowed, staring off at the ground. "Best of luck to you, Amy. I hope this is the start of good things for both of you."

With that, Knox turned and left through the door in the rear of the truck. A second later, the army vehicle pulled back onto the road.

Ben reached into the manila envelope and pulled out a black wallet. He let it fall open, exposing his FBI credentials. "Fox. Ben Fox," he said with a British accent.

Amy reached out to him. Instead of taking her hand, he pulled her close. As he held her, feeling her warmth, her strength, he realized that even if he did not remember one more detail or event, it would not matter. He ran his fingers through her tousled hair as the swaying bulb played an odd pattern of dim light and shadow across the interior of the truck.

Lying there in his arms, her body finally began to relax. This is where she wanted to be. She felt safe, strangely complete. The last time she remembered feeling that way was when she'd lain in her daddy's lap as a young child. She closed her eyes for a moment and was instantly back in time, resting with her father in their hammock, the wind blowing gently through her hair, not a care in the world.

She reached into her blouse and pulled out her chain. The gold key was dangling there, swaying with the hypnotic rocking of the truck.

"I've still got the two most important things that matter to me. You, and a keepsake from my father."

"After all you've been through," Ben said, "your father would've been very proud of you."

"Yes," she said as she fingered the key, "I bet he would've been."

EIGHTY-ONE

Hector DeSantos waited in the black Volvo cabover truck, the engine idling and an incessant pounding of flesh against metal banging against his eardrums. He had done his part for God and country . . . but most of all, for his fallen friend and comrade, Brian Archer. Like a shark, he had tracked down his prey . . . and if what he thought was going to happen did, in fact, occur, then justice would be served.

A moment later, an army transport vehicle pulled up behind him and flashed its headlights three times: two long and one short. DeSantos placed his infrared goggles on and scanned the countryside in front of him, then tapped his brakes twice to signal all clear.

Douglas Knox climbed into the cab of DeSantos's truck and slammed the door behind him. "It's done."

"Good," DeSantos said, and hung a U-turn, heading back toward Washington. The banging in the back cargo hold continued. Knox did not comment or ask what it was. It was clear that he did not need to.

"I know about CARD and Memogen," DeSantos said, using buzzwords he and Archer had captured from the encrypted document. He didn't know for sure how it all fit together, but like a loose thread on a piece of clothing, he had to either yank on it or leave it alone and ignore it. He couldn't ignore it.

Knox turned away and looked out the dark side window. "It's better we don't talk about it."

"Better for who? I need to know, I need to close this chapter in Brian's life."

"You'd be closing this chapter and opening another. It's a need-to-know situation."

DeSantos looked at Knox's reflection in the black glass. "I need to know, sir."

"You know how this works, Hector. Once I tell you, you're committed. In for a penny, in for a million dollars."

DeSantos was unfazed by this challenge. He knew the score and what it meant. This was something he had to know. "What does CARD stand for?"

Knox sat silent for a moment, then, keeping his eyes on the dark road before him, said, "Covert Arms Research Division. It's an offshoot of the Boys in the Basement. It's a joint effort and has roots in the NSA and ISA, but it's run by the Defense Department. They develop and test, analyze, and gather intelligence on new weapons potential . . . both in the U.S. and abroad. They were one of the groups monitoring the Soviet Bonfire Project germ-warfare experiments during the late eighties."

The banging in the back had stopped, easing DeSantos's already tattered nerves. "But how does all this fit together with Scarponi? Is he a former CARD agent?"

"One of CARD's ongoing research projects involves mind control. There was a very significant study being done at the Mao Institute in China in the eighties and early nineties. After the Ames debacle, Scarponi was one of our operatives who was captured and sent to China. According to the ISA, he was used, basically, as

a guinea pig. How extensive it was, we don't know.
CARD felt that the Chinese techniques warranted further study. Scarponi was the key."

"But you couldn't study him while he was in
prison," DeSantos said. "You needed him at CARD's
research facility. So you created a bogus 'new witness'
who could challenge the government's original evidence against Scarponi."

"We used someone OPSIG has worked with overseas, someone who could take the stand and convinc-
ingly prove Scarponi's alibi for the Vincent Foster
murder."

"So you released Scarponi with an electronic monitoring device. But everything got all fucked up and he
got out of it."

Knox nodded. "Sounds like you had most of it figured out."

DeSantos glanced over at the thick metal wall that
separated the truck's cab from its cargo hold. "You
know, I wanted Scarponi dead. For Brian."

"I know you did. But you kept your emotions in
check. That's why I've always known I can rely on you,
Hector."

The banging in the rear compartment suddenly
resumed, this time accompanied by shouting and primal screams in what sounded like Chinese.

DeSantos thought of everything Knox had just told
him and knew he was not being given the whole story.
But in the end, it didn't really matter. He was now
involved, and like it or not, he would get all the details
in time, when he needed to know them. With covert
ops, that was just the way things were done.

He continued staring at the dark road ahead, thick-
ets of brush blowing by in the white beams of his

headlights, while the incessant banging of a hand slamming against metal echoed in his mind . . . and the benign shouts of a crazed man in an iron cage floated away into nothingness.

The hunter had become the hunted.

ACKNOWLEDGMENTS

I'm getting a reputation for having long acknowledgments, but I believe it's important to recognize those people who help me tell my stories. I would like to thank:

Supervisory Special Agent **Mark Safarik,** profiler at the FBI's National Center for the Analysis of Violent Crime, who assisted me with FBI policy and procedures, threat analysis and forensics, and who took me behind the scenes at the Academy. Every writer needs good contacts to make sure his information is technically accurate. Years ago, Mark started out as a good contact—and became a good friend. I thank him for the many hours upon hours of time he's given me over the years. I could not have written *The Hunted* with the accuracy and richness regarding the FBI without Mark's assistance.

Special Agent **Jeff Mullin** of the FBI Academy's Firearms Training Unit, for his assistance and personal instruction at the Academy's indoor shooting range. **Nester Michnyak**, at the FBI's headquarters in Washington, and Special Agent **Laura Bosley,** at the Los Angeles Field Office, for their extensive time and effort on my behalf.

Jeannine Willie at the California Department of Justice Unidentified/Missing Persons Unit, for her candor and time in educating me about the state's missing persons program. I hope that I have accurately conveyed the difficulties and issues that this courageous group of people face daily.

The El Dorado County Sheriff's Department and its staff: **Shannon Murphy,** community service officer, provided valuable information on the department's rules and procedures for handling missing persons. **Jim Applegate,** community service officer, who spent a great deal of time with me discussing the department and its history, and who took me through the paces a person filing a missing persons report would go through. These are very accommodating people who handle the interviews of bereaved people with much greater care and compassion than the characters depicted in the book. The scenes contained in *The Hunted* involving the El Dorado Sheriff's Department were of course fictional and were intended to provide drama, character development, and conflict. They were not intended to reflect on the fine people of the real sheriff's department.

Fred Ilfeld, Jr., M.D., psychiatrist, and **David Seminer,** M.D., neurologist, for their information and thoughtful discussions on the effects of head trauma and posttraumatic amnesia. Dr. Ilfeld also provided important information on agoraphobia and MPD. **A. David Lerner,** M.D., who took me on a private tour of our local hospital, including . . . the morgue. David and I are best kept apart, as we have a propensity for getting into trouble when we're together . . .

Paul Seave, the U.S. Attorney of the Eastern District of California, for his assistance on matters pertaining to federal law involving the character Anthony Scarponi's release from federal prison.

Professor **Joseph Taylor** on the legal mechanics of prosecutorial options should additional evidence come to light years after a conviction.

My brother, attorney **Jeffrey Jacobson,** and my good friend, attorney **Perry Ginsberg,** for their feedback and comments on the manuscript, and assistance with all other things "legal" in this novel. In addition, to my other draft readers, **Colin Swift** and **Randy Kerslake,** your attention to detail and probing questions helped make *The Hunted* a better read.

Sid Dunn, executive vice president of AEPi, for his background information on fraternity record-keeping methods. **Jane Davis,** for her wonderful ideas on Web site design and promotion and **Michael Connelly** for putting me in touch with her; **Steven Schneiderman** of Schneiderman & Associates LLC (www.FreeAssistanceNetwork.com), for his tremendous knowledge base and net savvy. Paramedics **Monique Becker** and **Doran McDaniel** and trainer **Jeff Rheault.**

John Lescroart and **Richard Herman,** who took me under their collective wings and helped guide me through the challenges of publishing. Fine writers and good friends, thanks for your support and wisdom. To Dick, thanks for all things air force, covert, and military. "Check six," buddy.

Paul Ortega, IBM, for assistance with computer worms, hacking, cracking, and all that techno-fun stuff. **Gerry Gaumer,** National Park Service's Washington Monument site manager, and Park Ranger **Peter Prentner. Debbie Meier,** registered veterinary technician, for her assistance with rat and mouse behavior. If you read this novel, you'll understand why. **Stephanie Bersee,** Warrenton-Fauquier

Visitor Center, for being "my eyes." **Robbie Fox; Bill Caldwell**, retired police officer, armorer, and firearms instructor, for his help with proper firearms usage and terminology. **Marc** and **Dena Benezra** for your love and support over the years.

John and **Shannon Tullius** . . . without your efforts, the Maui Writers Conference would not exist. Through the conference, you do a tremendous service to the writing community. **Thomas Shragg**, M.D., and his staff, and **Patrick Vogel**, M.D.: there aren't enough thanks.

My mother- and father-in-law, **Marion** and **Russell Weis**. No son-in-law could wish for better family.

The many readers who made *False Accusations* a best-seller, and especially to those who took the time to E-mail me about how much they enjoyed reading it. I appreciated your comments.

Stacey Kumagai, my publicist, for being a true media monster; **Bert Lee, Bill Buckmaster, Lydia Smith, Dave Marquis, Bobby Howe, Robin Rinaldi, Dana Gage, Eric Amorde, Eliot Troshinsky, Nelson Aspen, Tim Conway Jr.** and **Doug Steckler, Christopher Noxon, Chris Leary**.

Individuals who went the extra mile to ensure the success of *False Accusations*: **Drs. Leonard** and **Wayne Rudnick, Kathy Kerr, Karen Brady, Holly Smith, Terry Baker, Ed** and **Pat Thomas, Terry Foley, Kathleen Walsh, Davina** and **Barry Fankhauser, Dave Krause, Pam Poffenberger, Mickey Grundofer, DaVonna Johnson, Lita Weissman, Tom Hedke, C. J. Snow, Barry Martin, Michael Ruffino, Linda Keough, Andrew Greeley, Linda Forestal, Lyn Caglio, Rich Carter, Michael Graziano, Tony Gangi, Melanie Een, Mary Beth Quallick, Marc Delgado,**

Sheldon MacArthur, Katie Layman, Erika Cowan, and Donna Passanante. And to all the other booksellers who worked hard to help me tell my stories . . . I wouldn't be here without you.

My agent, Jillian Manus, who did an absolutely fantastic job with this manuscript . . . a manuscript that would not have been written had Jillian not had the foresight to encourage me to write it in the first place.

Kip Hakala, assistant editor at Pocket, for your insightful comments and for helping me get everything accomplished on time.

Emily Bestler, vice president and editorial director, for opening the can of worms and forcing me to do something I didn't initially think was necessary. It ended up making the manuscript a better read, one I'm truly proud to have written.

My wife, Jill, who gets the ultimate thanks. She sees things I don't see and edits my material with a sensibility I sometimes lack. And, she has the guts to tell me when she doesn't like something I've written (which, fortunately, does not happen too often . . .).

If I have left anyone out, please accept my apologies; it was not intentional. E-mail me and let me know and I'll correct the oversight. Though I have attempted to be accurate wherever possible, errors of fact, unintentional or intentional, should not reflect on the professionals noted above.

Visit
❖ Pocket Books ❖
online at

....

www.SimonSays.com

....

Keep up on the latest new
releases from your favorite
authors, as well as author
appearances, news, chats,
special offers and more.

SIMON & SCHUSTER
A VIACOM COMPANY
www.SimonSays.com

Pocket
Books

2381-01